BAD THINGS HAPPEN

Bad Things Happen

Tim Buckley

Matador
9 Priory Business Park,
Wistow Road, Kibworth Beauchamp,
Leicestershire. LE8 0RX
Tel: 0116 279 2299
Email: books@troubador.co.uk
Web: www.troubador.co.uk/matador
Twitter: @matadorbooks

ISBN 978 1848762 909

British Library Cataloguing in Publication Data.
A catalogue record for this book is available from the British Library.

Printed and bound in the UK by T International, Padstow, Cornwall

Typeset in 11pt Sabon by Troubador Publishing Ltd, Leicester, UK

Matador is an imprint of Troubador Publishing Ltd

For my angel.
And for ours.

Special thanks to Mark for the cover and for everything else. And thanks to Johny "Midnight" Reid for the crash course!

CHAPTER 1

There are days and moments that become the landmarks by which we navigate the brief histories of our lives. They are the time-stamps by reference to which every event, no matter how significant, is marked before or after. That day was to become my Pharos, the beacon whose beam would forever illuminate my memories and reminiscences. Sometimes, those days creep up on us, unexpected, unbidden. But on a bright late-summer morning, staring out over a calm sea from high on the cliff-top, I had a sense that everything was about to change. And so it would. But in all of the daydreams that I'd choreographed of that day, I could never have imagined how the scenes would play out.

I had arrived in Dublin the afternoon before. Looking down from the plane, in the clarity of mature summer, I could see all the way up the coast to the Mourne Mountains. I hadn't been back for almost five years, but the sight of the fields and the housing estates and the roads of County Dublin stirred in me a nostalgic sense of home. It was the same every time I had come back from London – the absurd niggling disappointment that amid the bustle of traffic and the chaos of school playing fields, maybe the place hadn't missed me nor even noticed I was gone.

The taxi had dropped me in Howth, a small fishing village on the coast just north of the city. The soundtrack to the twenty minute drive from the airport was the driver's dogmatic diatribe on the ills facing the country and his bitter assurances that I was better off out of it. I was glad to escape. I wandered over to the harbour wall, bag slung over my shoulder, and looked out to sea. To my left, fishing boats were preparing for a night shift trawling for whiting and pollack and mackerel. Beyond the winking lighthouse at the harbour entrance, the swarms of gulls, razorbills, gannets and guillemots swooped and screeched around the rocks on Ireland's Eye.

This was the village in which I was born and in which I spent my childhood. And yet, after nearly twenty years away, I was checking into a small hotel on the harbour front. I had thought about calling my father, telling him I was home, asking him if perhaps I could come and stay. But I hadn't really spoken to him for, I don't know, almost a year? And so I hadn't had the nerve to make the call. It had always been so, ever since I could remember. My mother had died giving birth to me, her first child. I had come early, with scant warning, and there had been no time to get her to the hospital. An awkward and harrowing birth begat an awkward and often harrowing child, and the effort had been too much for her.

She had been my father's soulmate and muse, and there was never any doubt in my young mind that, given the choice, he would have sacrificed me to save her. Not that he was ever unkind or cruel. He provided for me in a way that was the envy of my friends. But there was no bond between us, and I think that I presented him every day with a reminder of what he had lost.

My father was born to a wealthy Dublin family, and his inheritance had allowed him to pursue a life in the arts. A painter of no little ability, he was hailed as one of Ireland's greatest living artists and feted among Dublin's art cognoscenti. His obligations to and place among Dublin's social elite meant that I spent my evenings at home with nanny after nanny, each of whom in turn would be hired only to leave soon after, driven away by my father's austerity and the loneliness of life in the big

2

house with only a small boy for company. As soon as I reached the age of twelve, I was enrolled in a boarding school miles away. For both of us, I think, this was a chance to start again.

I know he blamed me for her death. Maybe he would never admit it, but he did. And all through my life I was a source of disappointment to him. Try as I might, I could never bring him pride or joy. And I tried. I painted and studied and played music and football, but nothing was worthy of more than a cursory "Good boy, well done". Nothing I did merited the bear-hug, or the whoop of pride of the other fathers. We never went to the ice cream shop after school to celebrate a passed piano exam or a gold star. We never sat over dinner recounting tales of some epic footballing victory over St Jarlath's or St Joseph's. And yet I idolised him and craved his esteem, his acceptance even. But my efforts served only to prove to him that I was as self-centred and careless of others as I had been the day I was born.

I went to bed early in the small room on the hotel's top floor, but slept only fitfully. I finally surrendered to the demon insomnia and got up as the sun rose early over the nose of Howth. I pulled on my running shoes and kit and made my way through the deserted lobby to the front door.

Running gives me time to think, to disentangle the problems that vex me. When I run, there are no distractions, no interruptions. The metre of my footfall somehow provides a rhythm for my ponderings. The curved peak of my running cap creates a tunnel that bounds my vision and focuses my thoughts. Through the dark days after Caitríona, it became a sanctuary to escape both the reality of her loss and the well-meaning but cloying sympathy of my friends. In those days, I needed clear space in which to make some sense of what had happened, to somehow make a plan for the future.

The early morning air was heavy with the smell of fish and diesel as I turned away from the pier and its winking lighthouse, and headed for the dirt track that quickly climbed to the crest of the high cliffs. To my left and below, the sea lapped at the rocks and fizzed gently with each receding wave. At the cliff edge, there was a new billboard set in an ornate wooden frame. I stopped as I came to it and paused my stopwatch. Set into the frame was a map of the coastline below showing the whereabouts of the wrecks of ships that had come to grief on its rocks. It showed some ten or fifteen wrecks, where each was bound, and a shivering estimate of the number of lives lost with each one. The Leinster, the Queen Victoria, the Prince – looking out to sea that morning, it was hard to imagine it so wrathful and violent as to claim even one ship, but below the glistening surface lay the victims of its latent power or of the German U-boats that patrolled the coastline during two world wars.

There might be, I suppose, in some parallel dimension, a chart that records the lives that have come to grief on the jagged rocks or beneath the howling gales of fortune. Our names, perhaps, appear beside the picture of the wreckage, surrounded by the flotsam of lost ambitions, the jetsam of vanished dreams. Was some traveller at that very moment perusing a billboard and shaking his head, saying to his companion "Ah, the Aengus, what a tragedy that was, what a waste..."?

I shook myself free of the place to where my mind was wandering, restarted my watch and set off again. Caitríona couldn't bear the whining of the self-proclaimed hard-done-by, and I fight to stop myself sliding into the same trap. It seems to me that those who feel most sorry for themselves are often the very ones with most for which to be thankful. It is, perhaps, their being accustomed to good fortune, spoiled by it, that makes them more vulnerable to misfortune. I never wanted to yield to that weakness lest I should fail Caitríona or, if ever we should meet, appear weak to Aoife.

The path wound its way down from the cliff-tops toward the Baily lighthouse. The morning sun was taking the faint chill out of the air. My pace had quickened in my idle musing until I had to stop, out of breath and sweating hard. I stood bent over, hands on knees. A lady taking her dog for its morning stroll was coming toward me. The little terrier ran up enthusiastically and sniffed at my ankles curiously, and the lady slowed as she tried to decide if I was in need of some help. I rubbed the little dog's head.

"I'm grand, thanks," I said to her, panting like the terrier, "thank you."

She smiled sympathetically and walked on. I sat down on the soft grass and looked again out to sea. Aoife's birthday was a little over a month away. It was twenty years since I stood in the maternity hospital as a startled eighteen year-old, wondering how I had ended up there and what the future could possibly have in store for a fool who had thrown it all away.

I had met Caitríona shortly after leaving school to start university in Dublin. She shared a house with one of my class-mates and three other lads – one of whom was her brother – all hailing as they did from the same town in County Wexford. I had met up with them in a pub in the heart of Dublin's student flatland. Surrounded by the sound of excited country accents, we talked about life in Dublin and the price of a pint, and we debated the controversial issue of the day – the provision of information on where and how to obtain an abortion, a question that deeply divided the student community at the time. A third year Law student, she was almost three years older and a lifetime more sophisticated than me. Her opposition to abortion and to the distribution of information that might encourage it and undermine the life of the unborn child was total, violent. One of our group was a Students Union representative from the Agriculture faculty, and his ill-advised assertion that the Union had not only a right but an obligation to provide such information to its members precipitated a tirade of such vitriolic incredulity that he silently finished his stout, picked up his satchel and mumbled away from the table. I was enraptured.

In the days that followed, I could think of little else. I suppose the awe in which I beheld my new-found liberty in the city and the university gave me an innocent verve and an eagerness that was in some way attractive. To my bewilderment, it appeared that Caitríona thought so, and where others in her position might, for the sake of her own credibility, have sought to hide a romance with a younger student, Caitríona almost flaunted it as a symbol of her scant regard for convention. I was caught in a whirlwind that provided an education of which Cardinal Newman might not have wholly approved, but one that accelerated my journey from boyhood to manhood. And as I grew in maturity and experience, so our relationship burgeoned and became one in which I was an equal partner. We spent our time engaged in student politics, in raucous socialising and in furious, passionate lovemaking. It was an idyll that hit a sudden and insuperable impasse sometime after Christmas.

Caitríona had been feeling unwell for a couple of weeks, a condition she dismissed as the result of some particularly heavy drinking over the Christmas break. It was only when she missed a second period that she became really worried and agreed to go to the doctor. The change that the dawning realisation cast on her was immediate and dramatic. The explosive extrovert that had so captivated me three or four months before withdrew from life and into herself. On the morning of her appointment with the local GP, she seemed to me so much smaller and younger, a meek and timid shadow of herself. In hindsight, we knew the answer long before we came out of the doctor's surgery. We walked in shell-shocked silence along the canal, and sat down on a bench. The early spring chill made sure that we were alone, and we huddled together for warmth and solace in silence. We stared into each other's eyes, searching for an answer that neither of us could find.

In the couple of months that followed, we lived in a daze. We told nobody, spent long evenings alone together trying to figure out the right thing to do. Intense though the early days of our relationship had been, we had never strayed into discussions about the future. The thought of Caitríona as a mother, or of us as parents, had seemed as far away as senility and death. Yet now that I was faced with an irrefutable reality, I was forced to confront those thoughts. And when I did, I had to admit that in this intensely ethical, wildly courageous student was the germ of a passionate, devoted mother. I started to reconcile myself with a view of the future that would have seemed as alien as a television soap opera only weeks before. I painted in my head romanticised pictures of us as happy parents, successful young professionals and tireless socialites, and somehow I reconciled these three into one achievable persona.

Caitríona plucked me violently from this naïve reverie. She had, in the weeks that followed the positive pregnancy test, regained a great degree of her hitherto feisty demeanour. She dealt with the uncertainty and the fear with a heightened abrasiveness and an even greater disdain for the views of those with whom she disagreed. Even her closest friends were beginning to avoid her. As her final end of year exams approached, she used this increasing isolation as an excuse to study even harder than usual. She was neurotically obsessed with not throwing away what she had worked so hard to achieve. Then I made an offhand remark about how we would manage no matter what happened, and the dam burst.

"What did you say?" she demanded, putting her cup of tea down on the table.

"You know," I said, putting my arm around her shoulder to draw her closer. "We can get through anything. Even if we have to put our plans on hold for a few years, we'll still be fine. Who knows, we might even make a good family!"

She stared at me as though I had suggested termination, and the coldness of her glare froze the smile on my face.

"Are you really that stupid?" she whispered slowly, almost spitting out the words. She pulled away from me, and buried her face in her hands. "Jesus, how could I have let this happen? What possessed me?"

She stood up, and stared down at me. From a whisper she moved to a menacing growl to a furious scream.

"We have nothing. No money. No qualifications. No jobs. D'ya think my parents are going to be standing beside us, shoulder to shoulder? I can just see my mother rubbing my bump, can't you? She'll be *so* excited."

She was incandescent with rage and I worried that she might make herself unwell. I stood up and reached out to sit her down. She slapped my hand away.

"Get your feckin' hands off me," she screamed. "Do you not understand what's happening here? Can't you see? Are you that blind?"

"Caitríona, calm down, please," I appealed to her, partly for her own good, partly to stem the words that were stabbing like knives. She had never spoken to me like that before, and I suddenly realised that in a few short months she had become the very point of my life. I couldn't lose her, couldn't imagine a life without her. And yet my hero was filled with contempt for me.

She relented a fraction.

"I should have realised that you just don't have a clue," she said, her hand to her forehead. "I should have seen it. Jesus Christ, do you have any idea just how screwed we are? I've ground out the last three years to try and get this degree, to try and give myself a chance. I'm no legal genius, Aengus, I've had to scrap for everything and it's been hard. But it's all I've ever wanted, you know? I want be able to stand up for people who can't fight for themselves, and if I don't get through my finals, then I'll never be able to do that."

She shook her head.

"And now even if I do get through these exams, it'll take some CV to convince a law firm to take me on. Me and a baby. Do you see yet? Everything I've dreamed of is over, before it even started."

She sat – more fell – down into the armchair.

"We can't keep this child. I just can't play Mammy."

And so the decision was made. I don't know if I agreed or disagreed, but I knew what she said was probably right and I had no alternatives to propose. We got through the rest of term, and Caitríona sat her exams with her condition less and less concealed beneath the billowing clothes she had taken to wearing. After her last exam, she was secreted away in her Wexford home, like a Provo taken to a safehouse. I was, unsurprisingly, persona non grata in her parents' house, and Caitríona was reluctant to come to my father's house. So we saw each other only infrequently during the summer. The separation was like torture.

Caitríona's pregnancy had only deepened the chasm that separated me from my father. I had taken to addressing him by his christian name during university, partly because I thought it might annoy him, partly because "Dad" seemed so at odds with the relationship we had had. I remember the evening I told him. He was sitting in his study, reading, when I came home. I knocked on the door and made my way in.

"Hi, Lochlann," I said, quietly. "How's it goin'?"

He turned his head to look at me.

"Well, thank you. And you?"

"Yeah, good."

Silence.

"Listen, I need to talk to you, it's kind of serious."

He removed his reading glasses and swivelled his chair to face me.

"It's about me and Caitríona, my girlfriend. The thing is…"

I faltered, lost my nerve. I was tempted to turn tail and flee out the door. But I couldn't escape his stare.

"The thing is… Caitríona's pregnant. She's going to have a baby. We're going to have a baby."

He said nothing for what seemed like forever, just looked at me. I tried to find some emotion in his stare – anger, pity, disappointment – but there was none.

"What are you going to do?", he asked.

"I don't know. We haven't really figured it out."

Another long pause and then, as though I was choosing a new car, he said:

"Well think about it and let me know if there is anything you need, anything I can do."

I needed a father. I needed someone who cared enough to be aghast, distressed, to shout at me, to tell me what an idiot I was and then to tell me what to do and that it would all be fine. Instead, I got a barely-interested observer and a tepid offer of assistance. I nodded and walked out of the room.

I hadn't really known what reaction to expect from Caitríona's parents. Although Caitríona would have taken that as yet further proof of my naïveté, it was simply that I had had no experience of a normal family. As it was, her parents seemed to oscillate between one day berating her for the selfishness that threatened to destroy the good name they had worked so hard to nurture and the next behaving like the model family they had apparently been in the days before her aberration, ignoring completely the event that, in a couple of months, would change her life forever.

Those days we did spend together were spent mainly in the waiting rooms of the maternity hospital in Dublin. We felt like pariahs among the beaming, glowing mothers with their wedding rings and designer maternity wear. I have never seen Caitríona, so capable and strong, look so helpless. I felt impotent and useless in a world where I had no status and no idea. We couldn't face the ignominy of the ante-natal classes, among suited fathers-to-be taking an hour out of the office on St Stephen's Green, slapping each other's backs and predicting in loud voices that junior was sure to be another 'Rock man or play football for Dublin.

In the eighth month of pregnancy, Caitríona finally became too great a threat to the good reputation of her parents, pillars as they were of the local community. So she was banished back to Dublin and I went to find us a flat. I refused to go cap in hand to Lochlann, and so between her student grant money, a student loan from the University branch of the Bank of Ireland and what I had squirreled away from a summer spent working behind the bar in a pub in Dublin, we could just about afford a one bedroom flat south of the city. It was no place for an expectant mother and yet, in that tiny flat, those last few weeks were somehow almost idyllic. Back together, we found the strength that had escaped us throughout the summer. Moving a single light bulb from room to room because we couldn't afford another, and taking napkins from the local chip shop while the owner wasn't watching because we had no toilet paper, we were happy for the first time in nine months. Perhaps it was the fact that the limbo period was almost over. The birth and its immediate aftermath terrified us, but at least it was almost here and we could only face that with which we were faced. We had both squeaked through our exams, so Caitríona had her degree and I had made it through to my second year.

Together, we made it through the interviews at the convent that would organise the adoption on behalf of the Adoption

Agency. The nun in charge was a benign old woman who had seen too much of this before to be shocked or to make obvious her disapproval. The social worker who took our case, Siobhán, was a kind young girl, who took to embracing us both while appearing on the verge of tears. It was at the convent that we met with the prospective adoptive parents. Although forewarned, I hadn't expected the emotions it would bring. Mostly, I was intimidated. An obviously successful couple in their late thirties, they reminded me of so many of the well-to-do friends of my father who had populated my childhood. Looking back, I suppose they were as scared as we were. For them, we were the people that could shatter their dream, a dream that had maybe taken years to come true and was now so close they could almost touch it. I remember now how tightly they held each other's hands as we negotiated the stilted conversation.

My abiding memory of that time should be one of despair, of pain, of fear. But it's not. When I remember those days, I remember mostly the strength I drew from Caitríona and the sense that we would get through it. And unlike nine months before, Caitríona did not treat my optimism with contempt – I think maybe she in turn drew some strength from it.

Aoife was born at three o'clock in the morning. I felt throughout her labour and delivery, as I had through all of Caitríona's pregnancy, that we were the hospital's under-class, worthy only of grudging and contemptuous attention when those more deserving were comfortable. Siobhán had arranged that we would have a room, and Aoife lay in a cot beside Caitríona's bed. We had chosen her name on the spur of the moment some weeks before. Known as the greatest woman warrior in the world, Aoife was the mother of Cúchulainn's only son, Connlach. It seemed right that we should leave her a name that might give her the strength and courage to fight for her place in the world.

Siobhán had warned us, especially Caitríona, to avoid getting too close, to avoid at all costs bonding with our baby. But Caitríona could not ignore the crying child beside her bed and would get up to whisper soothing words.

"It's ok, Mammy's here…", she crooned softly, and lifted her eyes to look at me as Aoife stopped crying. Through her eyes I thought I caught the briefest glimpse of… what? Love? Fear? Doubt maybe? Or maybe I just wanted to. Then the shutters came down again, and she smiled at me.

For months we had both prayed for this to be over, and yet in those few days after Aoife was born we existed somewhere outside reality, knotted with a fear of what was soon to come, yet somehow tranquil. The day finally came when we would have to say goodbye. We had sat on the bed in silence for what seemed like hours, staring at her as she slept in her cot, oblivious to the life-altering events that were about to unfold. There was a knock on the door and Siobhán appeared, ashen-faced. I wondered how long you would have to be in that business before you became used to those days. She came to the bed and hugged Caitríona.

"Why don't you say your goodbyes and go on outside. There's no need for you to be here when we take her," she said.

Caitríona nodded. She put her hand lightly on Aoife's chest.

"Goodbye, my little angel," she whispered, silent tears streaming down her face. "I hope you'll forgive me some day."

She hesitated the briefest of seconds, turned and walked quietly out of the room without looking back. No histrionics, no drama. In the moment of perhaps our greatest shame, I have never been so proud of her. I looked over at my sleeping baby. I could find no words, no final gestures. I pulled open the door and walked down the stairs after Caitríona.

The path had descended from the cliff-top and ran along the side of a rocky beach. A family of holiday-makers, in spite of the early hour, was setting up a breakfast picnic beside a rock-pool. Two little children were running to and from the shoreline, squealing with delight as the approaching water chased them in and then ebbed. Their parents watched with that concentrated mixture of emotions, part joy at their fascination, part worry for their safety. I watched them as I had watched a thousand families before and wondered.

Aoife's arrival into the world was going to send us down one of two roads. Either she would bring us together and make us stronger in the face of whatever life threw at us, or she would prove our undoing, forcing us apart as we sought to push her out of our lives. In the years that followed, it turned out to be the former. Once I had graduated, we decided to leave Dublin. It was a decision based partly on a desire for something new, and partly on a need to get away from the past, at least for a while. And so we moved to London. Caitríona found a job that provided a perfect outlet for her penchant for political ranting, working for a law firm that specialised in representing social and environmental activists. After three years studying art, I took a job as a graphic designer with a marketing agency. My father's disdain at this commercialisation of my gift was barely concealed. Within four or five years of Aoife's birth, we had become the kind of people we had tried so desperately to avoid at ante-natal classes. Young, professional and passably successful. My work took us on secondments to New York, Hong Kong, Dubai, Johannesburg, always housed in luxurious accommodation, always coming back to London.

Beneath the façade too, we were quietly getting on with our lives. And yet, even after we were married we hadn't yet found a way to talk about her, nor did we ever discuss having more children. Had I loved Caitríona just a little less maybe I would have questioned the path we had taken. But I loved her absolutely, and no price was too steep to see her happy.

As time went on, I began to feel a growing guilt that everything we had might have been at the expense of fulfilling our obligations to Aoife. I had refused Lochlann's offers of financial support, accepting only what I considered mine by some transparent definition of right. So I had spent three years struggling through University on student grants and a barman's tips. We had never been able to afford a nice holiday or a birthday dinner in a nice restaurant. The luxury of a car was beyond even fantasy. And suddenly we had the trappings of a comfortable life. Not that we were rich. We fretted like everyone else over buying our first house and spent endless evenings over a calculator working out what level of mortgage we could afford to borrow. But we were twenty-somethings with a house, a car and prospects. And I couldn't help but feel that we would perhaps have had none of this if we had kept Aoife. And I couldn't escape feeling guilty that, although I would never admit it even to myself, I was glad Caitríona had made the decision for me.

CHAPTER 2

Time has an irresistible momentum. Try as we might, we can't swim against its tide nor move out of its raging current. There have been times – there still are – when I've just wanted to stop, to take stock and to plan for the life I want rather than make do with the life my world has assigned to me. We lurch from one artificial point in time to the next, from corporate year-end to Christmas to the two-week summer holiday in Spain, and at each point we wonder how we ended up there. I felt like I was losing Aoife. It was as though I had pushed her over the rail on a speeding boat, and now that she was fading into the distance in our wake, I could hardly keep sight of her. We couldn't talk about her, but I couldn't leave her behind.

I know Caitríona thought about her. I would often catch her day-dreaming, her eyes in a thousand-yard stare. When she saw me watching, she would smile and make a bad joke and rush off to do something frightfully urgent. I knew her as well as I could know anybody, but still I couldn't tell what she felt – guilt or remorse, or a sense of having made an irredeemable mistake that stole away from her life forever something of great value. She would go to great lengths to avoid being seated near children on trains or aeroplanes. She turned down invitations to christenings and birthday parties. And on those few errant occasions when we unwittingly ended up in the company of our friends' children, she would recoil with horror if a proud parent proffered their issue to give her a kiss or to show Auntie Caitríona their new tooth.

Of course, it became more and more difficult as our friends went through their reproductive prime, and children began to slowly take over our collective world. Inevitably and inexorably, their lives were painstakingly constructed around preparing for, celebrating or simply learning to live with new arrivals, and our carefree crew became shackled by the constraints of babysitting, school holidays and random illness.

It was the celebration of one such arrival that brought us together at a friend's house one Friday evening in late Summer. They were two of our closest friends, and their journey to this first child had been an all-too-common modern-day tale of longing and disappointment. That the child had arrived healthy and without complication was truly a cause for celebration.

As usual, we were late – never intentionally, but always just too late to see the newborn before the first of many bed-times. As usual, Caitríona's gift of champagne or something sparkly for the newly glamorous mother steered us clear of the baby shops, and as we stood chatting before dinner in clearly defined groups of excited wives and back-slapping husbands lamenting climbing handicaps, as usual Caitríona was drawn to the group of men and joined in the innocent banter.

She seemed unusually quiet though, withdrawn almost, and I wondered what had happened at work that day to preoccupy her. She excused herself to go to the bathroom, and I watched her walk away across the room. As she passed the new mum, glowing with something close to disbelief that all of this was finally, impossibly hers, Caitríona reached out and took her hand. She said something, and they both laughed quietly.

As she moved to walk on, another of her friends took her arm and drew her back into the excited conversation. They were passing around tiny pink dresses and sun-hats that the little one had been given, and someone held out a little suit with "Mummy's Girl" scribbled in mock child script across the front. Caitríona reached out and took it, and despite the manly joking and girlish giggling that filled the room, in my mind everything went quiet for a moment. I watched in what felt like slow motion as she gently caressed it and stared at it. It was like a movie scene. The world flashed by out of focus, but we were still, yards apart but together, still and invisible. She looked over and saw me watching. There was the briefest pause, she raised her eyebrows in weak conspiratorial disdain, and smiled softly. She quickly handed back the little suit, the blur came back into focus, and the moment was gone. But never forgotten.

I thought about her too. Maybe not so much in the early years, but more and more as we got older and more settled. I found myself wondering more often where she was, what she was doing, what she looked like and, most of all, how it might have been if she was with us now. The passage of time dulled the memories of how life was before we had what we now took for granted. What I felt was never so much regret as a nagging sense of maybe something better foregone. I don't think I ever once said to myself "I wish we hadn't…", but I often wondered silently "What if…". That sense of curiosity over time became a sense that something was missing, and in time the need to fill that hole took root and grew. I never discussed it with Caitríona. As the years went by, it remained the only subject that was out of bounds. We discussed everything else, had no secrets from each other, basked in each other's company. And it did not create a barrier between us. Those were just the rules of the game and I respected them.

Fate and time conspired to create the circumstances that tested my resolve. Only months before Aoife's eighteenth birthday, the Irish Adoption Board launched the National Adoption Contact Preference Register. Since adoption became legal in Ireland in 1953, some forty thousand adoptions had been processed. And yet for over fifty years, no facility existed for either adopted children nor natural parents to seek information nor contact. Letting sleeping scandals lie was the chosen strategy of two Irish generations raised in a Catholic state, but in a world of ubiquitous information, that was about to change. Adoption had always been associated with illegitimacy, a taboo subject alluded to only by raised eyebrows and euphemism. As late as the 1960's, thousands of Irish children were sent to America for adoption because they were illegitimate and unwanted at home. With the launch of the new register, however, every household in Ireland received an information booklet through the post, along with an application form for those affected to join the register if they wished. Imagine the consternation that the morning post must have caused in thousands of Irish homes that day, as ghosts from the past once again raised their unwanted heads.

That morning, I gathered up the assorted bills, bank statements and junk mail as usual as I came downstairs to put on the first coffee of my working day. Caitríona was still sleeping, so I sat at the kitchen table to open the morning's post. I flicked through it as I did every morning, subconsciously hoping for no bad news and maybe even a bit of good fortune. A letter with an Irish stamp always caught my attention, especially one addressed in my father's hand. I opened it, and pulled out the brown Adoption Agency envelope with the Harp insignia. I stopped dead and stared at the envelope. For a moment, as I stared at it, I was certain beyond any doubt that Aoife had asked them to find us. Then I saw that it was addressed to "The Householder" and my heart sank. I tore open the envelope.

It was as though someone in high office had been casually eavesdropping on my silent reflections. Everything I had imagined in my far-away moments was there, everything I needed to find the baby I had abandoned. If I needed any further convincing, the irony of its timing was stark. All through the literature, the Agency pointed out that applications to join the register would not be entertained from anybody under eighteen years old. In a few short months, Aoife would be eligible. Maybe, somewhere in Ireland at that very moment, her adoptive parents were reading the same booklet. Maybe she had even found it herself. Was she excited? Or bitter? Or afraid of hurting those who had loved and raised her?

"Anything interesting?" Caitríona yawned and stretched past me towards the coffee-maker to pour herself a cup. "Want a top-up?"

"Er, no... no, I'm fine," I said to her back, gathering up the assorted letters, flyers and envelopes and stuffing them in my briefcase. "Nothing interesting, just the usual. I'll sort them out later in the office. I better jump in the shower, I'm going to be late."

How many others around Ireland, I wonder, had frantically hidden that letter from sight that morning? I thought about my father and imagined his reaction to the letter's arrival. In the months leading up to Aoife's birth, we had discussed her only briefly and infrequently in stilted conversations. And yet when I told him that we had decided to give her up for adoption, he had been clearly shocked. I don't know what he had expected, but I think now that he considered my giving her up as a slight on my mother's memory. She had died to give birth to me, and yet I was prepared to give away my own child lest it should interfere with my life's plan.

I knew I had to talk to Caitríona about the letter, but I needed time to prepare my case. All that week, I could think of nothing else. I studied the Adoption Agency website carefully in the quiet moments at work, toggling quickly to a random spreadsheet like some guilty workplace internet surfer if anyone looked like coming into my office. By the time I took the train home that Friday evening, I had planned every last detail of my campaign.

I could smell her perfume as I opened the door. She was coming down the stairs, and she threw her arms around my neck and kissed me.

"Hiya," she said with a broad grin. "Good day?"

She took my hand and pulled me towards the kitchen.

"I'm just in," she went on, oblivious to my silence. "Traffic was a shocker. And now I need a glass of wine. And so do you."

She went to the fridge and pulled out an open bottle of rosé. She poured us two glasses and handed me one, raising hers in a toast.

"What are we drinking to?" I asked.

"Another week without getting killed or fired. To life's small mercies." She raised her glass again and took a mouthful. Her frivolity gave way to concern when she registered my tone. "Are you ok, love? You look worried."

I pulled the envelope from the inside pocket of my jacket and handed it to her.

"This came Monday morning. Lochlann sent it on."

She put down her glass, and pulled the contents from the envelope. My legs felt suddenly weak, and I sat down. I watched her face, looking for any clue as to what she was feeling. The face I knew so well, could read so easily, became an unfamiliar mask and gave me none. She finished reading and put the sheaf of papers on the table.

"Did you ask for this, Aengus?" she asked quietly.

I shook my head.

"No. They were sent out to every household in the country, to launch the new database."

She nodded.

"So now what?" she asked.

I paused, ready to rehearse the lines I had been practising all day. But I fluffed them, and there was no prompter at stage left to help me out.

"I'd like to register. I'd like to say we are willing to make contact."

She looked at me for a moment, then came over to where I was sitting and crouched in front of me. I knew this woman so well, and yet I would never have predicted her response. A furious rejection of my stupid notion, I could have predicted. Even a nodded agreement through tear-filled eyes. Instead, she took my hands and looked at me.

"Love, we can't. Not now. She's just eighteen, her life must be all over the place. She's doing her Leaving Cert, going to University, crying over boys, fighting with her parents. The last thing she needs is us wading in, with all that emotional baggage. Not now."

"But what if she thinks we just don't care, couldn't be bothered? What if she wants to contact us, but can't find us? Don't we owe it to her to make ourselves available, to at least be there if she needs us?"

"Not yet. We owe ourselves as well. We had a rough start, but we built a life. A good life. We got through it together, and we're still here. I don't want to ever risk that. This isn't some minor distraction, is it? If we go there, we'd better be ready for everything it brings. And we don't have a spare minute in the day, our lives are full as it is. We're knackered half the time, how would we manage everything this would bring?"

She stood up and leaned over to cup my face in her hands.

"We had good reasons for doing what we did, and they haven't changed. We weren't ready to be parents then, and we're no more ready now."

I realised that she too had been rehearsing, if not for today, then for the inevitable. She retold a confused and desperate part of our lives as though we had had mature and rational discussions, and then arrived at a logical conclusion. Maybe that's the way her mind made peace with it, but it was eighteen years too late for that conversation. Eighteen years ago, mixed up and naive, I hadn't known what to do nor what I wanted. I had relied on Caitríona to do the right thing, and my complicity then made me an accessory to the crime. And besides, I knew that everything else she said was true. We had worked hard to construct a life in which we were, to all intents and purposes, happy. Crossing this minefield threatened to blow it all apart.

The breeze had picked up slightly and gently blew balmy air into my face as I ran, ruffling the feathers of the gulls as they walked along the cliff edge. The train of thoughts that accompanied me as I ran was approaching a station I didn't want to visit. I didn't want to go there, but there was no way off the train. In that September my world was, without warning, torn asunder. During a particularly mild week of that Indian summer, two policemen in shirt sleeves came to the office and asked if there was somewhere quiet we could talk. They said that her car had been hit by a truck that veered out of control on a bend in the road. They said she had been killed instantly. They asked if there was someone I wanted them to contact, a friend or relative. They said they were sorry.

In truth, there was no-one to provide comfort. We had what seemed like legions of workmates and social acquaintances, but our own relationship was such that neither of us had formed or nurtured deep friendships outside the bubble we inhabited. I felt desperately, irredeemably alone. In the days that followed, I understood for perhaps the first time the true nature of despair. It wasn't that I had no interest in anybody nor in anything, it was that nobody and nothing else existed. I inhabited a place in total and complete isolation. I didn't eat, I couldn't sleep. I hallucinated that it had all been a nightmare or a mistake or a plot or a bad joke, and came back to reality with a jolt of real physical pain. I had no sense of future, no sense of what I would do or of how I would live in the weeks and months ahead. The future was an abyss, the edge of which was just beyond now. In truth I don't know how I negotiated the weeks after I lost her, I don't know because I simply don't remember. I think I was given sedatives by a friend who was a doctor, but I don't know. It's not that I can't remember, it's that I wasn't there.

For the year that followed, I thought little of Aoife. It wasn't that I forgot about her, it was that I simply couldn't let her into my head. Partly, it was because she reminded me of the days leading up to her birth, in that dingy flat on the south side of Dublin. Those were the days when we were, I think, the closest we have ever been. And partly it was because I would have felt somehow disloyal to Caitríona to think about Aoife and, inevitably, about making contact with her. Caitríona had made clear her feelings, and I wasn't ready to question them. In that year, I spoke to Caitríona every evening. I told her how my day had been, what I had done, asked her how she was and listened intently to her response.

I found myself suddenly unable to make decisions, and I realised how much I relied on her advice and her guidance. Things that would have been minor irritations – a row at work, a problem with the car – were inflated into great dilemmas simply because they were all that there was. A year before, they would have been relegated to the second division of considerations after where to go for dinner and what to do at the weekend. I can't explain the sense of isolation I felt. Surrounded by people – nice, good people – I was constantly consumed by overwhelming loneliness, bitterness and melancholy.

The trail had turned inland away from the shore, climbed to the Summit and now descended back into the village. Townsfolk and holiday-makers, perhaps awakened by the heat of the summer sun that belied the early hour, were wandering about. An old man and his wife sat at a table outside a café, each with a frothing coffee mug. They were deep in conversation. Animated, excited gestures reinforced their every point, laughter punctuated the discourse. They touched each other all the time, a hand on the shoulder or arm or thigh. If someone had asked me just two years before how I would grow old, this was the picture I would have drawn. The two of us, just happy to be.

The most striking difference in life without Caitríona was the expanse of time to be filled. My friends had picked up wives and children and houses in need of endless repairs. I could sense their awkward embarrassment as they declined an evening in the pub, or invited me to come join them for dinner at their home instead. But seeing someone else's textbook family served only as a cruel reminder of just how totally ours had disintegrated. And so I would thank them and, with a cheery "maybe next time", hang up the phone. My desperate concoction of social events had nothing to do with trying to enjoy myself – they were designed just to fill the time. In the days before I lost her, I would have filled that time by simply being with Caitríona. Talking, laughing, reading the papers, going for a walk in the hills, having a beer in some quiet pub watching the world go by – happy just to be.

In time, I felt dislocated, disconnected from the place that had become my home. I was once again an outsider in a city I had known for more than ten years, I didn't belong. The places we used to frequent were now out of bounds, not just because of the memories they reawakened, but because I had no place there. The coffee shop on Chiswick High Road, that had been our Saturday afternoon home, was now alien to me. The river-side at Richmond, where Sunday morning strolls gently cleared Saturday night hangovers, was a place I barely recognised. I heard eastern European and Asian and African voices in shops and on trains, and I felt like a trespasser in their world. I wondered if these immigrants making a new life here ever learned to feel really at home or if, like the thousands of Irish emigrants who had made journeys to America and

Australia and England, they brought their culture with them and carefully nurtured it in foreign soil. Never really belonging.

If there is a general discontent that pervades our world today, how much is due to our increasing disconnection from it? The endless quest for wealth and adventure rips us from the communities, even the countries, in which we were born, and plants us in alien environments. Yet our sojourns are so often temporary, stopovers on life's grand journey, and it is this very transience that makes us lose sight of what we stand for. Even for our parents, self-definition used to be such a simple thing. Now, in strange cities and strange lands, we search out new tribes and new, more convenient codes. Old, established communities were built on virtues and mores that evolved over generations, yet now are locked away in storage like the abandoned belongings of many a modern-day Diaspora. Not because we discard them, but because we forget them. Once noble and dignified, community self-regulation has lost its authority. Instead we have to rely on judicial systems designed for another time and ill-equipped for the task.

I had always thought that belonging was a function of place, where we live our lives. I think now it has as much to do with the people with whom we share those lives. Maybe more.

This emerging sense that I was living outside the world I used to inhabit was catalytic. I needed to find Aoife. I couldn't decide what my motivation was. I was wary of committing the greatest treason, as Eliot would have put it, of doing the right deed for the wrong reason. I couldn't claim that I had spent the preceding eighteen years desperately trying to find my daughter. I had been busy with other things, selfishly pursuing dreams and aspirations and goals. I could not justify what felt like a betrayal of Caitríona for anything less than a whole-hearted belief that it was, firstly, the right deed done, secondly, for the purest of reasons. The decision occupied my every waking moment for weeks.

I had never really agreed that this was too fragile a period of Aoife's life to risk encroaching now, but to acknowledge that even sub-consciously felt almost like an insult to Caitríona's memory. If Aoife wanted nothing to do with me, she was under no obligation. If she did, then I owed it to her. If she wasn't sure, then she still had time to consider her reaction.

I couldn't bear to even think about Caitríona's other argument, that it risked shattering the life we had built. That life was a distant and impossibly poignant memory. It was a year since I had lost her, and I felt like she was getting away from me. Lots of people missed her. They would phone me or send me emails or approach me awkwardly to say that they still thought of her, and that she still made them smile. But I wanted her to be more than an incidental memory that sat in the sidelines of people's busy lives. I wanted her to remain always as important to someone as she was to me. I wanted to share her, so that she could never get away from me. And I wanted Aoife to know her, and to be proud of her.

At the same time, I truly worried what Aoife would think of our failure to break cover, of our failure to make any attempt to find her or at least to make ourselves available. When I thought of her, I had always pictured her young life filled with ponies and picnics and happy families. But losing Caitríona cast clouds over my imaginings, conjured possibilities and circumstances too ugly to bear. What if she needed a friend, what if she had her own traumas to overcome and felt as alone as me? What if she needed me?

Those were my reasons, and I came at last to the conclusion that joining the register was the right deed. I just hoped that Caitríona would understand.

The application form was available from the Adoption Agency website, and I was surprised at how straightforward it was. It seemed somehow inappropriate that the initiation of so momentous a process should be so simple, so uncomplicated.

I completed the administrative details required. Section four asked what level of contact I wished to have. I ticked "Willing to Meet" without hesitation. I signed the form, attached a photocopy of my passport for identification purposes and sealed the envelope. Dropping it in the post-box, I felt a kind of relief for the first time since Caitríona left me. I took it as a sign of her approval.

Thereafter, my first task every morning was to log onto my email account to check for progress. For the first couple of weeks, there were regular administrative updates, confirming my ID and Password, clarifying some personal details, confirming that I was registered and that they would be in touch if Aoife registered and agreed to some form of contact. After that first burst of activity, the trail grew cold and I was greeted every morning by an empty inbox. I remained philosophical. After so many years, it would be foolish to expect immediate results. I took comfort from the fact that even if Aoife had registered and ticked the "No Contact" box, the Agency would have notified her of my registration. Unlikely as it was, I was invigorated by the prospect.

It was maybe a month or six weeks after I had mailed my application form, and I sat in my office with a cup of coffee. As I had done every morning since registering with the Agency, I started my day by opening my personal email and checking for an update. The note from the Adoption Agency was titled simply "Your enquiry". I put down my coffee and opened the note. I read it once, and again, then again, lest I should in my desire for progress misread or misinterpret it. But it was clear.

It said that the party with whom I sought contact had registered with the database some fifteen months before. Having conducted the requisite identification checks and having completed the matching procedure, they were now pleased to confirm the nature of her registration. She had, it appeared, registered as "No Contact but willing to share information". In the event that a related party registered with the database, she had instructed the Agency to forward a letter to them. It was attached and I clicked on the icon and opened the attachment.

The attachment was an electronically scanned copy of her letter, and it took my breath away. This was my first hard evidence that she existed in a world outside my head. Here was a letter in her hand-writing – tangible, physical evidence that she communicated with other people, that they could see and hear her, that they reciprocated. Up to now, she had existed only in my realm. Now Aoife existed in the greater world.

Her letter, though ambiguous, betrayed a sense of curiosity and perhaps a need to start what might be a protracted long-distance courtship. She said she had moved with her parents to Paris as a young child, but that she had spent all of her summer holidays back in Dublin. She had won a place at a school of music to study the violin, her passion in life. In the evenings, she worked as a musician in clubs in Paris, all the while writing music and dreaming of a recording contract. She gave no surname. The words on the screen made me breathless, light-headed. I stared at them for what must have been close to an hour without moving, gruffly waving away anybody who came to my door. Her registration made clear that she was not prepared for contact, but there was not for an instant any doubt that I would go to Paris to find her. I ignored the nagging voices in my head, taunting me that she clearly felt no need of me, that I had no right to go there, that my reasons were redundant. The fact of her registration and her letter betrayed, at the very least, a curiosity. That was enough.

My work had suffered from the general apathy that consumed me since I lost Caitríona, and I think it was with a sense of concerned relief that my boss accepted my resignation. I left for Paris the following week. I didn't know where she was nor the names of the clubs in which she played, but I never doubted that I would find her. I made lists of all the clubs I could find, and *arondissement* by *arondissement* I went to every one, asking if they had ever had a young Irish musician called Aoife. Months passed, and my optimism waned.

During the day I painted in the little studio apartment I had rented. I had bought a second-hand easel and some brushes and paints in a dusty old art shop near the Sacre Coeur, and I started to copy scenes from tourist postcards of Paris's famous landmarks. Much of what I had learned was locked away in recesses of my mind as dusty and forgotten as the old shop, but slowly I remembered and slowly I began to blow the dust away. Partly it passed the time, but partly also it assuaged the growing need in me to create something – to do something positive, no matter how insignificant it might be.

Every evening was spent trawling Paris' clubs to find my daughter.

Then it happened. It was called La Caleche, deep in the 15th. I walked in at around 8pm one Friday evening, before the evening's entertainment drew the bustling crowds kicking off the weekend. Like every evening, I planned to visit seven or eight clubs, to be told that nobody by that name or of that description had ever worked there, to finish my demi and walk outside, crossing the club's name off my list.

The barman first shook his head, then stopped. "*Attendez*", he said, waving an index finger at me.

"Claude? Claude?" he called to an old man busy carrying crates of bottles from the cellar. "That girl," he said in French, "the pretty Irish one, who played the violin here last summer – what was her name?"

Claude put down the crate and scratched his head.

"*Oui, oui*, I remember her," he said, "but her name... her name...".

After what seemed like forever, a light went on behind his thick glasses and he beamed a wide smile.

"*Eefa*", he said, clicking his thumb and forefinger. "Oui, *Eefa*." His expression darkened. "Who are you, what do you want with her?"

"I'm her… friend, from Ireland," I responded. I turned back to the barman. "You said last summer – where did she go?"

The barman looked at the old man.

"Claude?"

Claude looked uncertain, suspicious.

"Please," I begged, "it's very important. I mean her no harm, but it's very important that I find her."

Claude went into a small back-room and emerged with what looked like a tattered old photo album. As he thumbed through it, I could see it contained handwritten farewell messages from, it was obvious from the messages, people who had worked in the club. He showed me a page with two messages scrawled almost illegibly, and pointed at the second.

"She went with her friend, Hélène. This is by Hélène."

"Will miss you all!" it read in French. "I'll sing a song for you every night! Come visit, Hélène."

Below she had scribbled her forwarding address.

"That one?" I asked hoarsely, pointing to it.

He nodded. I could scarcely believe what was written before me. After years living in London, and months searching Paris, the address was in Malahide, a town near Dublin, just miles from my old home. The barman handed me one of the pub's advertising cards and, with a shaking hand, I scribbled the address on the back and put it carefully in my wallet.

I looked at Claude, and asked slowly:

"And… I know this sounds odd, but… what was her… her surname?"

The old man stared at me.

"You said you were her friend. And yet you do not even know her name? Who are you? What is this?"

I raised my hands in a plea of innocence.

"You have to trust me. It's not how it seems."

He waved me away contemptuously, picked up the album and went back to the cellar, a trail of expletives left hanging in his wake.

I stood up and offered my hand to the barman. He took it reluctantly. My voice was faint, hoarse.

"Thank you."

The aching in my legs put a stop to my running, and so I made my way slowly back past the harbour towards my hotel. The small foyer of the hotel was full of noisy holiday-makers heading out for the day, equipped with picnic baskets and rugs and sun-cream and over-excited children. I suspect the reason I never challenged Caitríona about having another child was that, if I was honest, I never really wanted all of this. I didn't want to spend my hard-earned time off work in the equally, if not more, stressful environment of the family holiday. And it made me a little guilty to think that, if we had kept Aoife and maybe had more children, this would have been my life and I might have hated it. I went back up to my room and took a long shower. Scrubbed clean and tingling from a few minutes under the cold tap, I came out draped in a towel and lay on the bed.

I pulled the small card from my wallet and flipped it over and over between my fingers. Scrawled on the back was the address, 23 St Mary's Terrace, my destination, the terminus for this long journey. Aoife's address. Of course I didn't know if she was going to be there, but I felt sure she was. After a year of searching, I found myself back in Ireland, in this little fishing village in the holiday sunshine beside a benign sea and I sensed that the stars were aligning. It just felt right.

Now, perhaps inevitably at the culmination of the odyssey, I was scared of what lay ahead. I had thought about writing to her before venturing down here, to at least give her notice, but I was afraid of frightening her off and losing the best lead I'd had. And so I had chosen to take her by surprise. I knew it wasn't really fair. I'd had the chance to prepare, but had denied her that opportunity. I knew I was being selfish. Maybe the search for an adopted child is based on that irony – you began all those years ago thinking only of yourself, and here you are full circle. But if I didn't find Aoife I would maybe lose the chance to hold on to my last remaining piece of Caitríona, and that was too bitter a truth to bear. I got dressed and made my way downstairs.

The hotel foyer was empty, the milling throng of an hour or so before having departed for the beach and the park. The light breeze from earlier had strengthened a little and tempered the heat of the sun. I walked to the train station and bought a ticket. Sitting on the train, watching the coast and the coastal suburbs zip past, I had a sense of an emerging reality. What had for the better part of a year seemed like a hopeless quest had somehow led me here, to where all of the imagining and wishing and dreaming would become, at last, tangible.

The train pulled into the station at Malahide. I looked again at the little map of the town that I had printed from the Internet, although I had long since committed it to memory. Turning right from the station, I crossed the main street, and turned right again and walked along St Mary's Terrace. The odd numbers were on the right, so I kept to the left hand side to give me the opportunity to walk past the house before approaching the door. The house was part of a three storey terrace, narrow and tall. The front door and the shutters on each window were painted a bright blue, in vivid contrast to the grey walls. At each window, brightly coloured flowers grew abundantly from window boxes, spilling over the ledges and draping the wall below. I stood across the street and stared at the house. With a deep intake of breath, I lowered my head, crossed the street, climbed the front steps and rapped on the door. After a moment, I heard the growing echo of footsteps on a tiled floor and the door opened. A young woman looked at me, and raised an eyebrow.

"Yes?"

She was beautiful. Her skin was fair, her eyes dark and wide, striking and vulnerable. Her prominent cheekbones gave her a regal air, accentuated by a strong, aquiline nose. Her long black hair was wet, and cascaded wildly over her shoulders as she dried it with a towel. She was tall, almost as tall as me, but her slender body looked fragile. She wore a plain white t-shirt and denim jeans cut off just below the knee, and simple sandals on her feet.

She looked at me curiously.

"Can I help you?" she said, more forcefully, and this time I could hear her strong French accent.

"I'm looking for Aoife?" I managed to get the words out, but only just.

She stopped towelling her hair, and paused before answering.

"Aoife is not here. She does not live here," she said evenly, eventually. "Who are you?"

In the previous two years, and maybe in the years before that, I had become accustomed to bad news, to disappointment. But I had so convinced myself that Aoife would be here that I had not considered the possibility that she might not be the one to answer the door. Involuntarily, I stepped back from the door, trying to lasso her words and pin them down to make some sense of them.

"Who are you?" she said again, putting her hand on the door and closing it almost imperceptibly.

I couldn't think, couldn't decide what to do. Did I tell this person who I was? But I had no idea who this young woman was and I didn't want to risk all of my progress thus far with one indiscretion. Did I turn and run? Tempting though it was, it would have been ridiculous, the end of my search for sure. I grasped for a reason for my presence.

"I'm a painter," I said. It was half-true and current and the only thing I could think of. "An artist." I hoped the repetition would mask my efforts to construct a story.

"I have a friend in Paris who has seen Aoife play. He suggested that I should paint her. He said she might be willing, said she would be here."

My mouth had taken over, and the words came out independently, unrelated to the muddled thoughts and emotions thrashing around in my head.

"Saw her where?", she asked, her voice suggesting that I amused her, aroused her curiosity.

"In La Caleche." I risked, proffering my half-knowledge of the truth, conscious that at any moment I might blow my tenuous cover.

She paused again, clearly weighing up her response.

"Well, she is not here," she finally offered.

"But she's coming back? Or coming here?" I begged, clutching at any available chance.

She shook her head.

"She is supposed to – was supposed to – come here, but she hasn't arrived yet."

"Do you know where she is?" I asked, an increasing desperation welling up inside me.

"No. I haven't seen her for… for a long time. I don't know where she is now. I'm sorry."

"Do you know if she is still coming here?"

She shrugged her shoulders. "I am no wiser than you."

She began to close the door. I stepped forward and gestured for her to stop.

"Wait!", I cried. "Please. Is there anything you can tell me, anything?"

"You are very eager to find her?" She seemed sceptical.

"Yes."

She shrugged again. "Well, like I said, I can't help you. Aoife is perhaps not the most reliable girl I know, she does precisely what she wants. So she might turn up, she might not. That's the way she is. If I were you, I would not count on finding her. You will probably just be disappointed. I am sorry."

She shrugged another curt apology and closed the door.

I stepped back onto the street, and an old man driving an old Ford Anglia blew his horn at me impatiently. I jumped clear. My head spun. With no right to hope, I had still been sure that Aoife would be here. I had given no thought to a contingency plan. I thought of knocking again on the door, but I had nothing else to say and didn't know what to do. I turned and shuffled slowly back toward the station in a daze. The sun had taken cover behind some dark clouds and the breeze had picked up. I took a seat on the station platform and tried to calm my mind, to come up with a plan. But I could think of nothing. The young woman in the house had been so dismissive of Aoife. I realised that I had never imagined her as unkind, or selfish, or careless. I had been realistic enough to try not to paint her as an angel, not to impose on her my version of perfection. But I had built in my heart a model of such faultlessness that no mortal could possibly live up to my expectations. I just assumed that she was someone whose company I would enjoy and whose character I would admire. I assumed she would be someone whom I would be proud to call a friend. I had worried endlessly that she might not like me. I had come all this way, and maybe I wouldn't like her.

CHAPTER 3

Do you ever wonder if you saw her? Ever spoke to her even? In Dublin for a holiday or a weekend, and walking down Grafton Street on a Summer Saturday afternoon, swept along in the milling crowds, did you see her? Was she there? Was she the girl whose eyes you caught for the briefest second, a lightning flash of intimacy as soon over and immediately forgotten? Was she the girl playing the violin outside Brown Thomas? Maybe when you stopped to listen to her for a few moments, you were spirited away on the back of some melancholy melody that made you shake yourself imperceptibly, drop some coins self-consciously in the open violin case and move quickly on. Was she the girl who served you coffee in Bewleys, overwhelmed by the unyielding pressure of the weekend throngs? You felt chastened by her indignantly, impertinently dismissive response when you questioned your change, and you wished you hadn't made such a fuss over a Euro. Was she the assistant in the clothes shop who helped you choose a skirt or a sweater or a shirt? Who lingered a little too long to help you, told you with a slightly embarrassed and wistful smile that you looked so young in it, that it made your eyes look somehow brighter. Was she the girl with the clipboard, carrying out yet another survey or collecting for yet another spurious charity? When she chased you down, you were disarmed by her questions and opened up a little more than you should or contributed a little too generously. Was she the teenage mother pushing a buggy through the sea of shoppers, furiously fingering the keys on her mobile phone. You were maybe subconsciously critical of her short skirt or that she couldn't hear her baby's crying over the metallic din of the music playing through the ear-phones of her iPod. Was she the self-conscious young lover stealing furtive glances up at the boy whose hand she held as they moved uncertainly through the melée? When you caught her eye, she reddened and smiled and dropped her gaze to the ground ahead. Was she the sullen teenager in designer jeans slouching along beside her perfectly-presented mother, laden with bags from a day-long spree. Your lips tightened with disapproval at her whining protest that all her friends had those jeans and that they were not too tight and that it simply wasn't fair. Was she the girl loitering by the cigarette counter in the crowded newsagents when you went in to pick up a paper? Who beat a hasty retreat under the weight of your frown?

I wonder if you saw ever her, ever had a brief exchange that maybe in some way changed the course of her life. Did she go home that evening and, à propos of nothing, fleetingly recall your face from the crowded city street? Did she wordlessly concede that her mother was only trying to look out for her or wonder if she would ever be as pretty as the woman who bought the blue shirt or resolve never to smoke again, ever? Did you, in a quiet moment on the train or the drive home, recall the innocence in her eyes or the softness of her hands or the urgent passion in her music? Or did you shake your head at the sharpness of her words or the pointless waste of yet another young life?

Maybe Aoife was one of those strangers, casually encountered and as soon forgotten. Maybe she, like those countless others, left her indelible mark on your life, like the initials of children carved into the trunk of a tree. Maybe you inadvertently and innocently deflected the course of her life by even a few degrees. And maybe she deflected yours.

CHAPTER 4

It was late afternoon by the time I found my way back to Howth. On the train back from Malahide, I cursed my own stupidity, my naiveté. I had been so sure that Aoife would open the door that morning, and based on what? On an old man in a Paris bar and a scrawled note in an old photo album from who knows how many months before. And I had leapt aboard a plane to Dublin as though the very fact of my arrival at her door would have her dissolve in tears of joy and collapse into my out-stretched paternal arms. Twenty years of separation could be bridged so easily.

The train pulled into Howth station. I stepped onto the platform and made my way slowly to the exit gate, which spilled the early commuter crowd onto the harbour front. I sat down on a bench over-looking the small working harbour with its fishing boats and lifeboat launches. The west pier extended away from me out into the bay and towards Ireland's Eye. Along its length, proprietors of the small seafood shops stood at their doorways to catch the last of the day's sun. Shouted conversations between fishmongers and the fishermen on the boats, punctuated by swearing and laughter, drifted back along the pier, carried by the gentle on-shore breeze.

"Francie, how're ya' doin'?"

"Arra, Bobby, I thought you were dead!"

"No, that was only the smell of your feckin' pollack."

"Go on ourra tha'! How's that young fella of yours doin' in the big school? Is he still playin' football?"

"He is surely. Payin' more attention to the ball than the books, I'd say. But sure there's no talkin' to these young lads."

"You're right there. Only thing they'll listen to is a clip round the ear. And you can't even give them one of those these days. Political correctness gone fuckin' mad."

And they nodded in knowing resignation, bonded by the afflictions of a common injustice.

On the neatly manicured lawn between me and the harbour's edge, children played on brightly coloured swings and slides while mothers chatted and watched, drinking coffee from flasks and trading biscuits and home-made cakes before going home to make the dinner. Even in these enlightened times, it was an exclusively female club. One of them looked over at me and said something to the others, who stole surreptitious glances in my direction. I could hear their voices hushed in earnest debate. It was my cue to move on – the slight blonde with the twins looked vaguely familiar and I dared not risk a reunion with an old schoolmate or schoolmate's sister. Anyway, I needed a drink.

McGrath's pub was next to the station. Inside, a few early patrons were scattered around, some reading newspapers, some watching the horses on the television, some apparently just taking refuge from the day outside. The pub had been metamorphosised by interior designers and decorators, but it was the same place I had come to with my friends when we had turned eighteen and could legally, if coyly, order pints at the bar. It was where we had grown up, coming home from university and first jobs in the city to cling to what we knew was safe. And it was the place from where we had looked to the future and made big plans.

I've always felt that a pub outside normal drinking hours is a sacred place. I get a slight rush as I enter, the puerile thrill of the innocent misdemeanour. You should be somewhere else, somewhere productive, but you toss a scoff at convention and embrace the indulgence. The faint whiff of cleaning detergent over stale beer confirms that you are among the first. It's your place, your domain. Later, the noisy, jostling crowds will invade and take it from you. But until then, it's yours.

The barman looked up from his glass-polishing as I approached the bar. I thought I caught a flash of recognition in his eyes.

"What can I get for you?" he asked with a smile.

"Pint, please." I nodded at the Guinness tap.

He started pulling the pint and looked up at me. My demeanour must have betrayed my mood.

"Tough day?", he asked, sympathetically.

I smiled a rueful, humourless smile.

"You could say that."

"Four-fifty please."

I handed him a note and he turned to get my change. In the mirror behind the bar I could see his face as he punched keys on the till. I racked my brain to remember his name... Pat, Paul, Pádraig? He must have been working here for, what... more than twenty years? In my youth he had commanded our respect, the guardian of a prize. He treated us with a certain aloofness, like a schoolteacher or a guard. He was never overtly rude, but he made sure we knew our place behind our elders and betters. Now he looked somehow smaller. The years had taken their toll, yes, but it was more than that – while I had grown up and gained experience and confidence and the scars of life's tribulations, he had held his place. I remember when I used to see him outside of McGrath's, on the street or in the newsagents or at Mass. He looked so out of place, so incongruous in jeans or a sweater instead of his barman's white shirt and bow-tie. It had never occurred to me that he had a life outside McGrath's, worries, passions and joys.

Turning back, he handed me my change and set about topping off my pint. He put the glass on the counter.

"There y'are now. That'll take the edge off it for you."

I picked my glass up from the counter, raised it slightly to him in thanks, and made my way into the corner. My head had stopped spinning and I could start to piece together the day's events with something approaching coherence. I took a long draft from my pint, leaned back against the seat's soft cushions and replayed the day in my head. For the months since I had set about searching for Aoife, I had lived by the premise that she was as consumed with her past as I was with bringing it to her. True, she had made no further contact since that first letter to the Agency, but I construed that as a function of the raging and unresolved debate in her head: coming to terms with her past versus disloyalty to the parents who had nurtured her. Now, for the first time, it occurred to me that perhaps there was no raging debate, no crisis of conscience. Perhaps she was living her life in peace, happy to be who she was and not at all desperate to find her other self. She had made only one effort at contact, and even that might have been on a teenage impulse, and not at all the pre-cursor to engagement that I had deemed it to be.

I had been a fool to pin such hopes to the address in Malahide, a folly cruelly made so clear by the French girl in the house. Maybe she had never intended to go there. Maybe she had gone on a whim to some more exotic destination. Maybe she had chosen instead to pursue her musical aspirations in Paris or London or New York. Whatever the truth, it was clear that Aoife was content in the present and not dwelling on the past.

The lounge-girl had wandered over and picked up my empty glass.

"Another one?" Her bright, wide eyes asked the question before it ever reached her lips.

"Sorry? Er... yes, please. And some crisps. Please. Cheese and onion."

"Sure, no worries," she said, in a broad antipodean accent.

She smiled and made her way to the bar. I watched her back as she walked away, languid and careless. Caitríona would have said she was pretty.

I heard his voice before I saw him, the urgent cadence of his Kerry brogue that had in equal part enchanted and terrorised my childhood. I looked up toward the bar and saw the Master talking to two other men, his back toward me. I was getting on for forty years old, and yet he would always be the Master, the headmaster from my old primary school. I would meet him from time to time when I was home from boarding school or during my university days, and I could never bring myself to address him even as Mr. O'Dwyer – or Mac Uí Dhuibhir as his Irish-speaking Gaeltacht heritage would demand – much less Críostóir. And though he and my father were good friends, and though he and I met regularly in a social context, he never invited me to.

Like Goldsmith's village school-children, we had beheld his knowledge and wisdom with wonder. Like the village schoolmaster's charges too, we sat ready with enthusiastic laughter for one of his jokes and shifted uncomfortably at our desks when his morning demeanour promised a stormy day ahead. His relationship with my family predated my schooldays and influenced our pupil-teacher relationship. My childhood memories are full of evenings with him sitting on our back patio with my father, the two of them drinking whiskey, watching the sea below and debating I knew not what. Although my father never included me in these sessions, the Master would often call me if I passed the patio door or played in the garden. I could sense my father's impatience if I lingered too long or answered the Master's enquiries in too much detail, and so I would politely make my excuses and wish them both goodnight. I was grateful for his efforts to include me and for his interest, and while my class-mates feared his wrath, I feared his disapproval, his disappointment. It was difficult for me to join in their play-time gibes at his expense, and I was often dismissed as his pet. He had known my mother before she and my father were married. A bachelor all his life, I wondered in later years if he had loved her, if losing out to my father had in some way determined the course of his life. And I wondered if that had somehow affected his relationship with me.

During our playtime breaks at school we would play football in the school yard. At the beginning of each week we would pick teams, and play for the glory of "winning the week". In a close run week, we were rabid with excitement. In the last class before lunch on a decisive Friday, we could hardly pay attention, minds wandering to last minute winning goals or last-gasp tackles. When the Master finally let us out, we would burst through the door onto the makeshift and ragged asphalt football pitch behind our classroom, ready for the off.

One such day, a group of girls from our class, apparently indignant at being barred from this ritual, camped on the halfway line, playing some inane hand-clapping game and crafting necklaces from daisies and buttercups. None of our best attempts at coaxing or cajoling them from the hallowed ground made any difference. Then, their ringleader, Gemma, grabbed the ball and made off with it. I gave chase and caught her, but she wouldn't let go of her prize. We tussled and she fell over, cutting her knee between her school skirt and socks. Embarrassed and unsure of what to do, I turned back to the field of play, which the other girls had vacated to check on their commander. I put the ball down in the middle and our game kicked off again.

I thought no more of Gemma until lunch-break was over and the bell called us back to class. When we got back to our desks, the Master had still not returned to the room. We laughed and joked and debated the epic clash just finished

44

until he appeared at the door, his face purple with fury. He stormed down to the back of the class where I sat, a trail of copybooks and the contents of pencil cases lying scattered on the floor in his wake. He reached over and grabbed hold of my ear, pulling me to my feet.

"You will never, ever hit a girl again, do you hear me?" he snarled. "No boy in my class will ever, ever hit a girl."

He dragged me to the front of the class and pushed me outside the pre-fabricated building and into the yard.

"You'll stand there until I decide you can come back in here. If I decide."

Even at that age, I understood that hitting a girl was wrong, we all did. My face was blood red with the shame of having been dragged by the ear through the class, but also with the shame of having been accused of such a crime. Across the yard, another pre-fab housed a younger class, all of whom were peering at me through the window, intrigued by the unfolding drama. I glared back, and turned away.

"But I never hit her!" my mind screamed with indignation. "I was just trying to get our ball back and she fell over!"

But I said nothing. Said nothing because I knew it was a technicality that this court would never entertain.

An hour or so later, he opened the door and stepped back to his blackboard. He didn't look at me as I came back into the room and took my seat. Head bowed, I lifted my eyes to peek at Gemma from under heavy eyelids. She caught my glance, and sent back a triumphant, mocking smirk.

I couldn't reconcile his reaction with the nature of the playground misdemeanour. True, he was a guardian of chivalry. True, he believed that education was about development of the character as well as the intellect. But had my crime been so heinous? Slowly, I came to understand that any other deviant might have escaped such wrath. But he expected – demanded – more of me, and I had let him down. In the following days, his demeanour reassured me that I had been forgiven, but my shame lasted much longer and my lesson was well learned.

When the time came for me to leave primary school and move on to "the big school" as we called it with awe, it was my father's wish that I go to his *alma mater*, a boarding school in County Tipperary, some hundred miles away. The Master coached me in preparation for the entrance exams, and assured me that my father was doing the right thing. A great academic institution, it would prepare me well for the world of university and work. I would enjoy it, he insisted. They played football and rugby, even hurling. I would have a great time.

But even my young mind could sense his misgivings. September came around too soon. My friends were all going to schools in Dublin. Some to Parnell Square or Drumcondra or Portmarnock, some venturing to the unknown lands of Blackrock or Dún Laoghaire. Some of the less studious had barely heard of Tipperary, much less of the small town to which the CIE bus would take me the next day. The Master came round to our house that evening as I packed, to share a drink with my father in the twilight. As I passed the patio doors, he called after me.

"Well now, *gosso'n*, big day tomorrow, ha? Listen, you work hard down there now, it's a great chance you have so you make the most of it, d'ya hear me."

I nodded.

"I will, Master."

He pulled a book out of the plastic bag he was carrying.

"Listen now, some of the Irish they use down there is different to what you know. This might come in useful."

Awkwardly, he pushed the bound *Foclóir* – the Irish dictionary – into my hands. He paused a fraction of a second, as though about to say something and then decided against it.

"Good luck now, *gosso'n*."

He turned and walked back out to the patio before I could respond.

"Thanks, Master," I mumbled to his retreating back.

My thoughts were interrupted by a guffaw of laughter from one of the Master's drinking pals, amid much back-slapping and finger-prodding. Chuckling heartily, the Master turned to look around lest they were disturbing any of the other patrons with their raucous banter. His eyes scanned past me in the corner, then stopped, reversed. He looked at me uncertainly for a few seconds, cloaked as I was by the gloom of the corner. He hadn't seen me for some five years but, standing over six feet tall and topped with a mop of unruly red hair, I was hard to mistake. He turned back to his friends, touched the elbow of one and whispered something. Then he turned back and walked over to me.

I stood up as he drew close. He squinted his eyes, and tilted his head slightly.

"Aengus? Is it you?"

"It is, Master," I smiled weakly, and stood up to shake his hand.

"Yerra, *gosso'n* how are you? I didn't know you were home, your father never mentioned you were coming?"

He pulled over a chair, took a seat beside me and set his glass down on the table.

He leaned towards me conspiratorially and said in a quiet voice, "You know, it's my very good fortune to see you here – you've freed me from the clutches of that pair." he smiled and nodded his head towards his two drinking pals, raising his eyes to heaven in mock exasperation. "They've been giving me nothing but abuse since Kerry took such an awful beating at the weekend! And I wouldn't mind only that fella's from Offaly – sure the last time that lot won anything, you weren't long finished making trouble in my classroom."

He smiled broadly and punched me playfully in the ribs. The Master was an avid fan of Kerry football, and his knowledge of the country's most successful Gaelic football team was encyclopaedic.

"Yerra, it wasn't a great game anyhow, there were maybe too many young lads playing. But sure with this new system, we're still alive. And no team will sleep easy in their beds while Kerry are still alive."

He took a sip from his whiskey, and spent a moment looking me up and down.

"You're looking well. As well as can be expected I suppose?" he said quietly, as though arriving at an important conclusion. "It can't have been easy on you these past months. How long has it been now? Nearly two years?"

"Nearly. It'll be twenty-one months next week."

"And you're still working in London? Still living there?"

"I'm still in London, yes."

"Great opportunities there, no doubt? And it's a great city, a great city. And I suppose you must have plenty of Irishmen over there to keep you company?"

I smiled.

"Plenty. Too many, sometimes!"

He was quiet for a moment, pensive.

"And are you happy there? I suppose happy is maybe the wrong word?"

"Honestly, Master? I'm not sure." I looked down at the floor, then raised my eyes again to his. "We were so settled there, it felt so much like home. But now?" I shrugged and shook my head. "Now I'm not so sure anymore."

I hadn't spoken to a single person about my increasing sense of dislocation, and I was a little surprised at how quickly I had dropped my guard. But, perhaps naively, I considered him a trustworthy confessor who would protect my confidence.

48

He called to the lounge girl.

"Ella, there's a man here with an empty glass. We can't have that now, can we?"

The girl smiled.

"We certainly can't, Mr. O'Dwyer," she replied with a grin, a hand on his shoulder. "Another pint?" she asked, as she lifted my glass from the table.

"Yes, please."

"And another whiskey, Mr. O'D?"

"Thank you, Ella, that would be grand."

She breezed away to the bar.

I looked after her.

"In my day, we were all going off to Australia and England and America looking for work and adventure. Now they're all coming here," I remarked. "How times change."

"You'll find Dublin a very different place now, I suppose. We get used to it, the foreign accents and languages, the little ethnic shops, the black men driving our buses! I think some people find it a bit hard. But I think it's good for us. Good for us to learn about them and good for them to learn about us. The world is a different place to when you were growing up – we Irish can't just rely on our old friends if we want to flourish in the future. How many children in China and India and even Russia have ever even heard of Ireland? Why would they think of us in twenty or thirty years when they've grown into the next generation of industrial giants? We need new friends if we're not to get left behind."

He looked after Ella and raised his glass.

"And if they're all as pretty as our Ella, sure isn't that just a bonus!"

The Master had always had a passion for geography. From the small classroom in Howth, it seemed as though we had travelled the world. I remember as a child of ten or eleven years old, we had been tasked with a school project on Sweden. The walls of our classroom were festooned with blue and yellow flags, with maps painstakingly traced from atlases, with pictures of dense pine forests, barren snowscapes, and cityscapes of Stockholm and Gothenburg. To be honest, I can't remember the principal industries or the highest mountain or the largest lake, but ever since, I've found myself with an unexplained wistfulness for the place. I would urge on their footballers in World Cups or European Championships. I would find my eye drawn to newspaper articles on Uppsala or Norrköping. I have never even visited the country, but I have always felt there is an invisible, unspoken bond between the Swedes and me, born in a little classroom in a little north Dublin schoolhouse.

Ella came back with our drinks and set the tray down on the table. She passed me my pint, and handed the Master his whiskey.

"There you go, Mr. O'D. I presume you don't want anything in that, do you?"

"I want nothing in my whiskey, young Ella, except for an 'e'!" he quipped – he would only ever drink Irish whiskey, and never Scotch – and handed her a crisp €10 note.

When she had walked back to the bar, he turned to face me and raised his glass.

"Well, it's very good to see you again, Aengus. *Sláinte.*"

"*Sláinte*, Master. It's good to see you, too." And I meant it.

"You sounded… I don't know, hesitant maybe, about London. Are you having second thoughts?"

I shrugged.

"I don't know, Master. For the first few months after …" I paused. I think it might have been the first time I'd spoken to another person about it, and I wasn't sure I knew how. Wasn't sure I knew the words or how to speak them. I didn't know, I suppose, how they were going to come out. They had been trapped for so long in my head, echoing in that dark place, that they might burst forth unconstrained or trickle out weakly, blinded by the light.

"For those first few months, I just assumed it was going to be a question of time. I knew nothing would ever be the same again, and that I'd have to learn to live all over again in a world I wouldn't know. But I just assumed it would be in London, surrounded by my friends, surrounded by familiar, comfortable things. I knew it would be hard seeing the places and the people we knew together, but I couldn't imagine starting afresh somewhere new on my own. Without her."

The pub was steadily filling up now, commuters coming in for a quick one to ease the pain of the day gone by before going home to husbands and wives and children. The Master raised his hand to acknowledge the many patrons who nodded or called his way. But his attention never strayed from my story.

"And now you're not so sure." It was a statement, not a question.

"No, I suppose I'm not."

"Why not?"

I exhaled, blowing the breath through pursed lips.

"God, I've been asking myself that question for months. I suppose it's a few things really. I just think I need a place to take root. Our life has been – even before Caitríona went away – it's been so transient. It feels like either we've been moving around or other people have moved, gone away or gone home, moved on or moved back. It's felt like we've only known our friends – even our best friends – for a few years at the most. I don't have a history with them, and if I'm honest, I don't really have a future with them. It's hard work." I smiled ironically. "And it's not supposed to be that hard, is it?"

He sipped his whiskey and shook his head.

"In my day, it wasn't like that at all. I moved here in 1962 to do my teacher training, left behind all of my friends in Kerry, thought I'd moved a thousand miles from home. Might as well have in those days. I was so homesick, I wanted to give it all up and go back home. But my father wouldn't hear of it, couldn't afford to have me back home I suppose. 'You've made your choice', he'd say. 'Now it's up to you to make the best of it.' But the friends I made in the early sixties are the self-same friends I have today. I don't hear much from my old friends in Kerry, but the friends I made when I came to Dublin have been with me since. Oh, we fall out from time to time, we might tire of each other or drift away for a period. But when push comes to shove, we're still friends at the end of the day."

I nodded, recognising what he described. "I think maybe that's what I'm missing. When I had Caitríona, it didn't matter because I had… her. But now, it feels like I need some stability, something I can hold on to, something that's always going to be there."

Ella was engaged in some banter with a suited foursome at the table beside us. As she turned to the bar to fetch their order, she gave the Master a knowing, sardonic smile. One of the four said something about her to the others and they laughed loudly.

"And after nearly twenty years of travelling about, I just don't know where home is. It's not London. Then I come back here and I realise I'm a stranger in my own town. It's not any of the other cities I've lived in. Where is it?"

I looked over at the four commuters at the table beside us, with their umbrellas and briefcases. I leaned closer to the Master.

"Take those lads. My age. Jobs in town, mates to have a pint with on the way home, wife and kids waiting in the house. Routine, solid routine. Twenty years ago it would have chilled my blood. Now I envy them."

CHAPTER 5

The Master looked at his watch.

"Sorry, Master," I said, and took a long draft from my glass to finish my pint. "I'm keeping you from something…"

He waved away my protestations.

"Far from it, Aengus, far from it. I put a roast in the oven for my dinner before I came down for a warmer. I need to get back and take it out, that's all."

He hesitated.

"Sure look't, if you're at a loose end this evening, you'd be very welcome to come back and join me. There's more than enough."

"No, Master, I don't want to impose."

My protest was weak.

"Nonsense. I'm enjoying our chat and it'd be a shame to end it prematurely. Come on." He finished his whiskey, picked up his coat and we made for the door.

"Goodnight to you, Ella, *slán leat*." He waved to her as we passed the bar, and put his two hands on a shoulder each of the two pals he'd been drinking with earlier in the evening. They talked briefly in low voices, then he said something, clapped them both on the back and they all laughed. He turned back to me and we left the pub.

We spent the short walk back to the Master's house reminiscing about the school and the children and teachers we had known. It was a balmy evening, the sun still high in a clear sky. The East Pier was busy with people out taking an evening stroll, and with fishermen trying their luck from the pier wall. We followed the road away from the pier, and its winking light-house, along the water's edge until we came to a terrace of small white-washed two-storey cottages, fronted by neat gardens separated by low hedges.

"Here we are now," he said, pulling his keys from his pocket with a bundle of Euros, notes, receipts and coins, most of which fell to the manicured grass under the front window. I helped him scoop up the debris of life in the city, and he opened the door and we stepped inside. In all of the years we had known each other, I had never been to the Master's house. One could almost map the evolution of our relationship by my relationship with his home. As a child, it was out of bounds. The Master dedicated long hours in the classroom, staying late after lessons to mark homework or help a child struggling with spelling or arithmetic or Irish. Once he left the school, his time was his own and he countenanced no intrusion. Not that we would have wanted to go there, but stories of the scowling face and sharp words that greeted those who had been sent by parents to hand in forgotten homework, to pay for a school trip or to report a sick sibling was all the embellished proof we needed that this was indeed our Hades protected by an unseen Cerberus.

As a teenager, it simply wasn't cool. You would only visit the Master's house because either you were a bit thick and needed help with Irish or Maths, or – worse – because you wanted to. And as a young adult, first Caitríona then Aoife then London kept me away. It was different for me, of course. All through my secondary school and University years the master's regular visits to our house for an evening whiskey on the back terrace with my father made sure he never became a stranger.

I stepped into the hallway, and drew an involuntary breath. The neat and tidy but humble exterior belied the cave of Aladdin within. The front door opened into a sprawling open-plan ground floor. The dark flagstoned hall floor led through an open archway to a kitchen bedecked with hanging brass pots and bordered by dark wooden cupboards. To my right, through another open arch, was the living room with its dark wood floor and wide, open fire-place. Dark wooden panelling covered the lower half of the walls in the hallway and living room and up the staircase, their upper halves painted a brilliant white. Above, I could see up the stairway to a vaulted roof with a wide skylight, through which the evening light bathed everything in a golden glow.

But it was the artwork with which he had filled every available space that truly bedazzled. He had carefully positioned paintings on every wall to create a den of perfect proportion into which you were subtly or violently drawn. One was filled with ships and lighthouses against a backdrop of malevolent seas. One with views of Howth and the rest of the Dublin coastline under cotton-puff clouds and watery sun. One with portraits, one with rustic scenes, one with exotic Eastern cities. I could see immediately two from my father's hand, one of a woman peeking out coyly from behind her husband as they embraced, one of the Liffey flowing down through the city to Dublin Bay. I was lost in what felt like another world.

"It would appear that we are just in time," the Master said, raising his nostrils to the wafting smells from the kitchen.

He marched into the kitchen and I followed slowly, still captivated by what hung on his walls.

"Master," I said, "your house is stunning. The artwork is… breath-taking."

He was at first a little taken aback, then he broke into a wide, proud smile.

"You're very kind, Aengus – sure it's just a few things I picked up over the years. Many of them thanks to your father's eye, I should say."

"And the house, you've done a great job."

"With thanks, in this case, to a bit of luck on the horses! 'Twas a few good days at Fairyhouse that did most of the work on this place. And a few bad ones that put paid to any plans I might have had to move!"

He opened a bottle of wine and handed me a glass.

"Take this and have a look 'round," he said, "while I dish up."

I felt like a child in a sweet-shop after closing time. The Master put an old vinyl LP on a record-player as I wandered from the kitchen into the living room, and stood in front of the painting that hung above the hearth. It was a beach-scape, a long strand that stretched way off into the distance beside a rough sea topped with white-caps. Along the beach's edge, the marram grass was bent over in the wind, and there was sand in the air. Despite the wildness of the day, the sky was blue save for a few high clouds chased by the wind.

"The strand at Inch." The Master stood behind me, a glass of wine in his hand. "Beautiful, isn't it? I used to spend every spare minute there as a child, swimming and fishing and playing football on the beach. And 'twas often wild, a gale blowing off the Atlantic and the waves crashing on the shore. This picture puts me in mind of those days, days when just to be there was enough."

"Is that where you grew up, Master?" I asked, reminded that so much about this man was still unknown to me.

"It is indeed, I was born and raised in Annascaul, only a few miles from Dingle and beside Inch Strand. We lived only a skip from The South Pole Inn, Tom Crean's pub. But he died a few years before I was born. I remember his two girls though, still living there I think."

We stood in front of the painting for a few moments without saying a word. I think it is a trait of men like the Master, perhaps of his generation, that does not require every silence to be filled.

At last, he took me by the elbow and led me to the dining room table, which sat between the kitchen and living room. We sat down, he replenished our wine, and closed his eyes in a brief, silent grace. Then he carved thick slices from the leg of lamb, and piled my plate with meat, roast potatoes, carrots and broccoli. It had been a long time since I had had a home-cooked meal that consisted of more than microwaved chicken.

While we ate, we discussed football and horses and golf. We delved into Irish politics, a subject about which I knew embarrassingly little, and debated the state of the world in general. I found his optimism a welcome departure from the wearying and formulaic dinner conversations among my circle in London, which almost inevitably centred on the escalating price of property and child-care, and the trials of life working in the city: commuting, an ever-lengthening working day and a fading sense of purpose. The awe in which the Master had beheld the world of my childhood had not diminished. If anything, the freedom afforded to him by his retirement had allowed him to visit some of the places we had studied as children, broadening his horizons and deepening his fascination.

His years as a bachelor had clearly honed the Master's culinary skills, and I complimented him on what had been a splendid meal. We retired to the living room and the Master produced another bottle of wine, a Rioja from his prized collection. We talked a little about wine and food and about his travels through Europe. It seemed that his itineraries had been determined largely by gastronomic landmarks and by the great wine-producing regions of France, Spain and Italy. He had taken cookery courses from some of the best and most innovative chefs in Europe.

By this time we had enough beer and whiskey and wine inside us to get to the day's important topics, and the Master decided it was time to open the box.

"So now, *gosso'n*," he began, swirling his wine around the big glass and staring intently into it as though it was a source of fascination to him. "I take it your father doesn't know you're home?"

"No, Master, he doesn't. Would you mind not mentioning it to him until I have a chance to go up to the house tomorrow?" In truth, I hadn't planned to go see my father at all, but it was always likely that a chance encounter with a mutual acquaintance would force my hand. This wasn't the encounter I had had in mind.

"Of course I won't, Aengus, of course not. But don't leave it too long, eh? It's a small wee village and he'll find out sooner rather than later, you know that."

"I know. And I'll go see him tomorrow."

"It's been a while since you've seen him, I'd say?"

"He came over to the… when we said goodbye to her. But we hardly had a chance to talk, and he flew back straight after. Apart from that, it's been nearly five years. I can't believe it's been so long, but it has. I've spoken to him of course…"

"But not that often?"

"No, I suppose not." I paused, and looked over at him. "Does he talk about it, ever?"

"Your father's a proud man, as you know too well. He wouldn't ever talk about it. But I know he feels it. Any father would."

I couldn't picture him in that way, in misty-eyed reminiscence craving the prodigal's return. All through my childhood, I had sought his pride, respect, his approval even. Whether through academic success, or sporting success, or through art, my achievements seemed always to leave him cold, uninspired. I inherited some of his skill and much of his passion for art, but from an early age he despaired of the manner in which my talents manifested themselves, in gauche colours and harsh angles and lines. To be fair, he always studied my school reports with keen interest – reprimanded poor marks, acknowledged good grades. But that was just it – acknowledgement. Never enthusiasm, never affectionate pride. I got more encouragement from the Master than he had ever been able to muster.

"I'd say he's got over it," I said ruefully. The stout and the wine had loosened my tongue and I was more forthright than I had any right to be. "You know very well that I don't, have never, really featured in his plans."

The Master went to interject, but I stopped him with raised palms.

"He has always looked after me, no question. He has provided for me, spoiled me I'm sure some would say. I had the best clothes, toys, education – but you of all people must know that we've never been close."

He reached over and refilled first my glass, then his own. The bottle was almost empty, so he went to the rack and pulled out another. As he pulled the cork, he said, "It's often the spectator that has the best view of the game. I know how proud you are of him, how grateful too. And I know how proud he is of you. It's only the pair of you can't see it."

"But look what I've contributed to his life." I counted them out on the fingers of my left hand. "First, I took away the one person he really loved, his one true friend. Second, I went into a career that, for him, is a desecration of my art. And third…" I unfurled a third finger, but stopped with my right hand in mid-air. "And third…"

He looked at me expectantly, but now I realise he knew exactly what my third crime had been.

"And third… Aoife," he said quietly, staring into my eyes.

Hearing someone else say her name hit me like a punch to the stomach. That he knew about Aoife left me stunned. It had never occurred to me that he might know, although now I realise I should probably have guessed. I stood up and walked over to the window that looked out on the front garden, over the low wall, across the road and out to sea. The light had all but faded, and a boat sounded its horn out in Dublin Bay as fog rolled in off the Irish Sea. I could see the light blinking at the end of the East pier. I stood there for a few moments, trying to decide what to do. Thank him for the meal and leave? But the Master had done no wrong, he had simply let me know that he knew. Change the subject? But we were way past talking football or politics. Stay and talk about it? In truth, whether because of the wine or the Master's company, that's what I wanted to do. I drank deeply from my glass, to find strength for the road down which we were clearly headed.

I turned back into the room and sat down again. From the speakers in the corner of the room came the crackling voice of Luke Kelly singing Raglan Road, an old favourite of mine and a song I used to put on our music system at home in London or wherever when I felt like I needed to get back in touch with Ireland.

"Yeah," I whispered, "Aoife."

I had drained my glass and so he filled it again.

"Your father told me," he said, answering my unspoken question, "one evening about, I don't know, maybe fifteen or sixteen years ago. We were sitting on his back porch having a whiskey, and he was unusually quiet, pensive. I asked him if anything was the matter. He paused, and then he told me about Aoife. It was her birthday. For some reason, the realisation that she would be going to school had hit him hard."

Caitríona had acknowledged her birthdays, but no more. I took to going to the pub alone after work on those evenings, just for an hour or so, to raise a glass to her and every year I made a note in my journal where it had been. Just so that I could tell her, if ever we met, that wherever I was and whatever I had been doing, I had always celebrated her birthday. And on one of those evenings, while I had been in a pub in New York or London or Johannesburg, my father had raised a glass to her as well, and shared her story with another human being.

Part of me was bitterly indignant that my father should have betrayed my confidence, should have done that which he had no right to do. But I knew deep in my heart that there was no right or wrong in such instances, no guidebook or Code of Conduct. We simply make it up as we go along. And so the wave of self-righteous fury washed over me and was immediately gone, like a wave breaking on the shore.

"I wasn't sure if I should tell you," the Master was saying, "or just keep it to myself. But it is what it is – I know and it's only right that you know that. I hope you're not too upset."

He was as matter-of-fact as ever, as though he had just broken the news to me that Mullingar and Athlone were the main towns of Westmeath and that Carlow's main industry was sugar. I looked for a response in my glass but there was none, so I drank.

"I'm not upset, or at least I won't be when the shock wears off! I just don't really know what to say. Speechless is such a hackneyed word, but…"

"I'm sorry, I could maybe have broken it more gently. Circumspection has never been a particular forté of mine."

I smiled, and looked out of the window and across the road to the pier and the couples who strolled along it hand-in-hand or arm-in-arm.

"You know, I've been thinking lately about how we've kept it all so secret. Caitríona and I never talked about Aoife even in private, let alone in public. And I wonder how she would interpret that? That we were ashamed of her? Or ashamed of ourselves? And I don't think either of those is true. So I've been thinking about how to introduce her to my world, even though it's a world she might never visit."

I raised my glass to him and smiled.

"And maybe you've pointed me down that road, even taken a first step for me!"

He raised his glass.

"I'll drink to that, Aengus." He made a pretence of picking up an invisible piece of fluff from the carpet, and said, "And is that what brings you home?"

I felt suddenly released by the Master's revelation.

"Yes, it is. We've spent the last twenty years hurtling through life, hungry for experiences and excitement. In the beginning, it was to leave behind the pain of letting her go. But somehow, we got carried away by the wave, lost sight of what we were about and where we were going. It was like we were afraid that someone was going to close the shop, that we wouldn't be able to get the shiny things anymore. And so we kept accumulating experiences and ambitions and targets." I shrugged with arms outstretched. "But sure it didn't matter – there was always tomorrow, we could always sit down and figure it out later." I stopped, and listened for a moment as Luke sang the closing lines of the *Auld Triangle*.

"But then later never came. Caitríona was gone, and all of the landmarks by which we had navigated our life disappeared with her."

The Master stood up to change the record which had finished and now filled the room with its crackle. He sat back down and said nothing, letting me continue.

"And I suppose I just needed a rock, something solid and fast to cling to while all of the transience flooded past me. Caitríona has always been that rock, and I needed to find a way to get at least a part of her back. And there was only one way to do that."

"Finding Aoife."

I nodded. "Finding Aoife. We talked about it before… before the accident, when the Adoption Agency started the contact database. But Caitríona was firmly against it. After she was gone, I agonised over the rights and wrongs of it, especially about betraying her wishes. But I think she'd understand. I think she understands."

He didn't *plamás* me with empty reassurances that she would of course understand and want only what was best for me. Another bottle of the Rioja was already gone, and he walked over to the wine rack.

"It would be reckless to continue unaccompanied," he said solemnly, and brought the bottle and corkscrew back to his chair. "And that led you back to Dublin?"

"Not directly." I told him about her letter, about quitting my job and about the search in Paris. And I told him about the club and about Hélène and about the scribbled message in the old photo album. And I told him about the French girl in the house in Malahide, the girl I assumed to be Hélène.

I reached for the now open bottle and filled my own glass.

"And so now, I'm back precisely where I started. Except that I know she has made no more contact with the Agency despite my posting, and that she has made no more effort to get in touch with me."

He looked at me and I swear there was a shard of impatience in his eyes.

"So what do you plan to do now?"

"I don't know."

It was just past pub closing time and four or five young lads strolled past on the street outside, laughing loudly and shouting at a group of girls further down the street. The girls responded and there followed a bout of good-natured but lewd, expletive-filled banter. From somewhere, a neighbour shouted at them to "Keep it down", at which point the two sides became allies in a lusty attack on their new adversary. The Master smiled. How many of them, I wondered, had spent their formative years in his classroom?

"I don't know," I repeated, to myself more than out loud. "I suppose all I can do now is wait and hope that she contacts me, or posts another communication on the database. There's not much more that I can do here."

"You'll go back to London, so?"

"I suppose so."

He put his glass down on the table and sat back in his chair, hands forming a steeple with finger-tips together, glasses perched on the tip of his nose, and sighed.

"Aengus, it's not my place to preach, nor have I any right to advise you or tell you what to do – but I'll claim the prerogative of an old teacher and I'll do it anyway. You can listen to me or ignore me, that's your choice and I'll take no offence either way."

He put his steepled fingertips to his pursed lips and arranged his arguments, then began.

"I think you're in very great danger of being blinded by this sense of disappointment. You've been on this quest for a long time, and you've invested a huge amount of emotion in it. That's only natural. But this setback comes when you least expected it, maybe, and that's why your view of things is clouded."

I started to say something, but he stopped me with a raised palm.

"Hear me out before you say anything. I firmly believe that we can only be truly happy when we are in control of our own destiny. Ah look't, I know we're never fully in control, we're always at the mercy of fortune or God or whatever power in which you choose to believe. But we have to make every effort to control that which we can control, to leave as little as possible in the hands of chance."

He pounded the open palm of one hand with the clenched fist of the other to emphasise every word.

"Now, I agree with you that this French girl – maybe she's Hélène, maybe she's not – I agree that she's unlikely to tell you too much. She sounds fairly guarded from what you've said, and why would she trust a complete stranger? But the fact is that she's your best bet – your only lead. And that's why you simply mustn't let go of her. Go back to England now and you are, as you say, right back where you started." He smiled and reached for his glass. "Now. That's me done. Your turn!"

"But she doesn't know where Aoife is."

"Or she's not telling."

"You didn't hear the tone of her voice, the look on the face. It was like… it was… it was pure contempt. If they are – or were – friends, then they're having the mother and father of all rows. She's hardly going to go out of her way to pass on the message now, is she?"

"Maybe not, but all I'm saying is this: you have found someone who knows Aoife. Maybe she doesn't know where she is, maybe she doesn't even like her. But she knows her, knows things about her that you need to know. Get close to her. Make her understand that you mean no harm and that it's important, so important it transcends any petty argument they might be having. I'm not suggesting you tell her the whole truth, of course not – that would be a betrayal of a confidence to Aoife. But what harm can it do? It's not like you have any compelling reason to go back to London now, is it?"

"No."

"Well, then."

We sat in silence, the plaintive sounds of an old lament from the record player framing my thoughts. At length, I shook my head.

"You may be right, Master, but even if you are, how can I get close to her? How do I make her trust me? If I could go back to this morning, I'd do it differently. I wouldn't go barging in like a bull in a china shop, blurting it all out. I thought she'd be there you see, I really thought it was her. But now my cover is blown. There's no way back."

"Perhaps. But what's the harm in trying, Aengus?" he said. He emphasised the word "trying", his growing frustration beginning to seep through.

"Look. How about this. You told her you were a painter looking for a model, a young musician. Someone said that Aoife might sit for you. Why not ask her if she'll sit for you instead. Go back, tell her you're really at a loss now, you simply have to find a model and would she be interested?" His eye twinkled, and he reached over to nudge me. "Appeal to her feminine vanity, Aengus – you can surely do that!"

I smiled. "It's a long time since I flirted, Master, and I wasn't much good at it anyway. I'm not sure I'd be that convincing."

"Well then you need the practice!"

I finished the wine in my glass and put it down on the table.

"It's late," I said, standing up. "I should be in my bed."

He looked at his watch, and raised his eyebrows in surprise.

"So it is, where did that evening go at all?" He looked up at me. "You've had quite a day of it, I suppose."

"You could say that. A long day, too much wine – good wine, but too much wine – and a trip through the emotional mill." I smiled.

He chuckled. "True, true. I suppose I should apologise." His face grew serious again. "But, Aengus, you know I have only your best interests at heart, I just want to make sure you don't act blindly. Like I said, the spectator often has the best view of the game."

He stood up and we walked to the front door.

He put his hand on the catch, but before he opened it, he put his other hand on my shoulder and said, "Speaking of which, Aengus, won't you go and see your father in the morning? This is too small a place to hide yourself away, and he would be truly hurt to hear from somebody else that you're back."

My raised eyebrows and tilted head was a sufficient expression of my doubt.

He shook his head. "No, Aengus, I mean it."

"OK, I'll go see him in the morning."

"He goes into the Gallery about eight o'clock. He has some work going on, so he goes to let the workmen in. He'll be there most of the morning."

"Then I'll go see him there."

The Master opened the door and I stepped out into the night air. I turned back and we shook hands.

"Thank you, Master," I said, quietly. "For the meal, but more for the talk. I've never really talked about it all before. I'm a bit surprised I did tonight. That must have been some strong wine you plied me with!"

He smiled the sly smile of a man who had accomplished what he had set out to do.

"Goodnight, Aengus. I'll see you tomorrow."

CHAPTER 6

The rain is coming in sheets, borne by the wind that blows off the Irish Sea. It's cold. Goosebumps cover my little white legs and the rain streams down the bare flesh below my football shorts. Mr. Duggan, the junior infants' teacher who takes the football teams, is wearing a track-suit and an anorak against the elements. He gives us some last advice, and sends us out onto the field. They look much bigger than us, the team from the city school. Much stronger. They seem to snigger and smirk when they see us coming.

But I don't see their big full back. I don't feel the bitter cold. I don't hear Mr. Duggan's words of encouragement. Because he's here. Over there, on the sideline under a big black umbrella. That's my father. Do you see him? He's here to watch me play. For the very first time. He's been very busy.

Mr. Duggan throws in the ball and the game is on. I run after the boy with the ball, but he's bigger than me and brushes me aside. He scores a point, and his team-mates clap him on the back. The ball comes towards me. I run to it and reach out. But a big brute of a boy barges me out of the way. I fall over in a muddy puddle.

And so it continues. Then, the ball breaks loose. I grab it and make off up the field. But one of them gets hold of my jersey and drags me to the ground. Mr. Duggan blows his whistle and reprimands the sneering thug. He asks me if I'm alright. I brush off his concern with cheeks blazing red. I sneak a look over to the sideline. The other fathers are huddled together, calling out advice and encouragement. He stands apart. I can't see his face, the umbrella is down low against the rain. He has to be careful you see. If he gets sick, he'll have to take a day off work and he's very busy.

Mr. Duggan blows his whistle. It's half-time. I think he's maybe blown a little bit early. We gather around him. He says that we're playing well. That they're very strong and that we just need to keep working. We haven't scored yet, but it will come. He blows again and sends us back into the game. I look over to the sideline. He's not there. Maybe he went to get a cup of tea, to warm himself. I feel a surge of panic. He's going to miss the start of the second half. Maybe Mr. Duggan could wait for him? But he doesn't. I'm not watching and the ball hits my back. One of them laughs, and picks up the ball. He scores a point. He turns around and looks at me.

"You're shite," he says.

"No I amn't," is my retort.

My boots are heavy with water and mud, my football gloves sodden and cold. Mr. Duggan tells me to move up the field, to full-forward.

"But I'll never get the ball up there, the ball never goes up there," I plead.

"Ah, you will. Go on, there's a good lad."

I stand alone in front of their goal. I fold my arms to warm my hands in my arm-pits. Their goal-keeper is leaning on the post, talking and laughing with his friend who's a substitute. Mr. Duggan looks at his watch, shakes it, then puts it to his ear. It goes on. Then it happens. Their big gorilla of a full-forward drops the ball and Oran toe-pokes it away from our goal. They're all down around our goal, greedy for scores, and now there's nobody near the ball. Oran runs after it. He's very fast. He pokes it again. It's coming to me. I'm petrified, then I shake free of the invisible chains and run after the ball. I pick it up – I don't think I did it right, but Mr. Duggan mustn't have seen – and I turn to face the goal. I kick it as hard as I can. Their goal-keeper turns around, horror on his face. He dives toward the ball. But it's too late. Through the shower of muddy spray he has thrown up, he can only watch as it crosses the line. I'm rooted to the spot in disbelief. There is silence. Then Mr. Duggan blows his whistle. It's a goal. The huddle of fathers watching from the sideline lets out a roar. My team-mates cheer and whoop and slap me on the back. I break into a wide smile, and turn to the sideline. I scan its length, but he's not there.

My smile evaporates. I stand stock still as Mr. Duggan blows his whistle for the end of the game. I turn to search the other touchline. It's deserted save for a stray dog carrying a discarded glove in his mouth.

I hope he found some tea.

CHAPTER 7

The combination of too much wine, drained exhaustion and a somehow rediscovered sense of inner calm lulled me into a deep sleep, and when the morning sun woke me early, I lay for a while in bed listening to the screeching gulls and raised voices from the harbour across the street. It had been quite a day, the day before, quite a day. In twenty-four almost Joycean hours, I had plummeted from a naïve and heady optimism to a black abyss of gut-wrenching disappointment before clambering back to… to what? Where had I gone in the Master's company last night? His intervention seemed almost planned, choreographed, as though he'd been dispatched by some guardian angel to rescue me from my foundering craft and lead me to a safe haven. And so he had winched me from my black gloom in McGrath's the previous afternoon and pointed out another way, where the waters looked somehow more benign, more navigable.

The evening had given me a sense of release. The conundrum with which I'd been grappling for so long had, I think, taken on a blackness and an insuperability born of my reluctance to discuss it with another soul. I don't know why I couldn't bring myself to talk about it with even my closest friends. I could argue that they wouldn't understand – but who could be baffled by the grief of loss? That I felt guilty about burdening them with my despondency when they all had their own storms to navigate – but I hope that I would be prepared to put aside my petty inconveniences for a friend in greater need. That to unleash my demons was tantamount to an admission that they were part of the problem? Perhaps. That I didn't really understand it myself and could hardly, then, explain it to them? Almost certainly.

I pulled on my running shoes and went downstairs, the over-indulgence of the night before betrayed only by the dryness in my mouth and the faint odour of red wine from my skin. Outside, a petulant sky threatened rain. I turned away from the harbour and along the sea wall towards the cliffs again. I ran past the Master's house and to the end of the road, where the asphalt gives way to dirt and the path narrows, tracks the coastline along the nose of Howth and climbs to the cliff tops. The sea below had lost its rhythm, grown angry and dark and swollen. With the breeze at my back, I found my stride and tempo, perhaps stolen from the sea below. My footfall felt light and I ran with no effort. The path climbed slowly to the top of some steep cliffs that dropped sharply into a little cove filled with angry water. Then it continued on towards the Baily's winking light, past the Casana rock. It was off this point of the peninsula that the Queen Victoria steamship perished on the rocks, losing its passengers to the icy sea during a snowstorm.

The brambles and the gorse, newly abundant after a warm and wet summer, strayed onto the trail and scratched gently at my legs. Then I rounded a bend that took the path up towards the Summit to my right. I stopped. There it was, perched high and solitary. My father's house. I had always considered it an ugly house, so squat was it, so stark and grey against the bright gorse or blooming heather. When I said so to my father, he shrugged and said "I am inside looking out. It's for those who are outside looking in to worry about its appearance."

And to be inside looking out was, I had to admit, dizzying. From the back stoop, the sun rose over the Baily lighthouse. From the front garden, it set over distant Ireland. All around, the sea and its moods seemed part of the house, built into its very fabric. In Winter, its hardy walls resisted howling gales and lashing rain. In Summer, the smell of earth and flora rose on the evening breeze and enveloped it in a magical haze. It was the source of his inspiration, and the root of his pain. He built it for my mother, and shared it with her for only a year. I often thought he should have moved away, but I think for him, part of her was still there and he could never leave. To the side, down a winding path and separated by a line of poplars to keep at bay the prying eyes of the public, he had built a gallery, a smaller version of the house. I remember, when he was given permission to build the gallery, the objections and protests from local officials and environmentalists, who claimed that there should be no further development at the Summit, that it should be protected and preserved. But the view prevailed that my father too was a local landmark deserved of protection and preservation, and the building was completed.

I sat down on a rock facing out to sea. In the cold light of day, the Master's argument made perfect sense. I had spent a long time in Paris digging for clues, and this girl in the house in Malahide was all I had to show for it. But I had come to Dublin only to find Aoife, and if she wasn't here, then there was no reason for me to stay. Except that I might find out more, except that she might still come here, except that... that I had nowhere else to go.

And what would I tell this girl? How would I explain my interest in Aoife to this stranger, who had treated me with such scepticism yesterday? I cursed the lack of composure that had concocted the story of the artist seeking a model. Why would I, who had never seen even a picture of the girl, travel on some wild goose chase to find her just so I could paint her? How would I justify that story under closer scrutiny? And I wasn't even a painter, I was a graphical designer for a marketing agency. Not the sort to give up everything to seek out his muse.

Those might be the actions of an impetuous young Lochlann, but not of his son. But I was unable to avoid the stark truth that she was all I had, and giving her up was conceding to the truth that I had nowhere else to look. I had no job and no reason to be in London nor, indeed, anywhere else.

And yet despite the disappointments of the day before – or perhaps because of them – I found myself atop Howth Head in the rain with a renewed sense of unfounded optimism. Why? Surely nothing had changed since I sat in McGrath's the previous afternoon. I still had no idea where she was and no clues. And I still had only one lead – a suspicious young French girl with no reason to trust nor to help me. But one thing *had* changed. For the very first time, I had told another person that I wanted to find my daughter and they had produced no objections, provided no counter-argument. In my own mind, when I had mulled over the rights and wrongs of my quest, I had always had nagging doubts. That it was a search born of selfish motivations. That it was a betrayal of Caitríona. That Aoife clearly did not want to be found. That she was happy the way she was. The Master had offered no such criticism, rather he had treated news of my intent as entirely natural. And that had, I realised, injected a whole new impetus to my search. I got up and began jogging back towards my hotel, far from clear what I was going to do, but fast arriving at the conclusion that I would stay awhile and do it here.

I got back to the hotel, got showered and walked into the dining room just as the staff were clearing the buffet. Margaret, the maternal head-waitress who had for some reason chosen to take me under her wing, came bustling over.

"Well, good morning – it is still morning, isn't it?" she pretended to check her watch and beamed a broad smile. "Late one last night, was it?" She nudged me. I felt it unnecessary to point out that although it had indeed been a late one, I had already been up for two hours, so I just smiled and said, "Don't suppose there's any chance of a coffee, is there?"

"Sit yourself down here, love," she said, pulling back a chair and waving over to the other waitress who was busy preparing the restaurant for lunch. "Ania, is there any coffee left in that pot? Well, stick on a new one, there's a good girl. I've a man in need over here."

She turned back to me.

"Now, if we're quick, I can get them to rustle you up something in the kitchen. How's a couple of poached eggs and some toast?"

I made the universal symbol of approval with a circled thumb and middle finger and said, "That would be spot on, you're a star."

Ania, a tiny, timid Polish girl who looked like she should be getting ready for school, brought over a coffee, and a copy of the Irish Times that another guest had left behind. She blushed when I thanked her and scuttled off to clear more tables. Sipping the strong, tepid coffee, I flicked through the newspaper. Stories of gangland crime and political scandal competed for column inches with tales of soaring property prices and reviews of fashionable new restaurants in a dichotomous mélange that reflected an equal preoccupation with old neuroses and fascination with new diversions. Everything was different and yet everything had stayed the same.

Margaret brought out my eggs and put the plate on the table.

"There y'are now," she said, "get that inside you."

She hesitated a moment and looked at me again, as though searching for an answer that would not come.

"So is it over for a holiday you are? Or on business?"

"A bit of both, I suppose," I replied.

Another pause.

"You look awful familiar, have you stayed with us before?"

"I haven't stayed, but I've been in a few times."

"Maybe that's it," she said, not entirely satisfied. She patted my shoulder and said, "Well enjoy that now, and if there's anything else you need, just shout."

I dawdled over breakfast in anticipation of what I knew was coming next. Eventually, I had no choice but to allow Margaret to finish the lunch-time preparations and so I made my way back to my room to collect my jacket. With nothing else left to delay me, I went downstairs and out the hotel front door.

Despite the probably thousands of times many times I'd taken the number thirty-one bus to the Summit, it felt that morning like a journey into the unknown. I stood waiting at the bus stop trying to rehearse my lines, trying to think of some lines to rehearse. I had considered phoning ahead in warning, but didn't know what to say. I hoped instead that the words would just come when I was standing face-to-face with Lochlann. The bus was late, adding to the gnawing anxiety in my gut. A couple of times I made to walk away, back to my hotel, but resisted the temptation. Finally, a bus appeared up the main street. The journey to the Summit is short, shorter than I wanted and certainly short enough to have walked. We pulled in at the Summit car park, and I climbed off.

It's odd the things that mark our passage through life, the advance of age. A taste for tea. Comfortable if unfashionable clothes. And a growing appreciation of natural beauty. In all of the time I had lived in this house, I had seldom stopped to take in the vista that was spread out below it. And yet that morning, it was breathtaking. The bracken covered slopes of the Head, the cliffs, the lighthouse and the sea. To the North, on a clearer day, you can see past the Boyne Valley to Sliabh Donard. To the South, Dún Laoghaire, the Sugar Loaf and the Wicklow mountains. To the East, in better conditions, you can make out the distant shape of the hills in North Wales. To the West, Dublin Bay and the city skyline. Maybe to delay the inevitable, maybe to steady my nerves, I walked over to a van selling refreshments.

"A coffee please. And a Cadbury's Snack." Just like old times.

"No bother," replied the vendor, his apron stained and his fingernails black with nicotine and dirt. "Not a bad oul' day now, wha'?"

I agreed and took the polystyrene cup. Satisfied that I was out of sight from the house, I sat on a rock and just looked. What tourists there were were out of sight and the panorama was silent and serene. The brooding clouds and persistent rain from earlier in the morning had drifted off on a fair breeze and the sun had emerged in a pale blue sky. A couple of fishing smacks bobbed out at sea, a large freighter made its way in towards the port of Dublin. The familiarity of it all enveloped me. I drank it in.

Finally, I stood up. Dropping my empty cup in a litter bin, I took a deep breath, turned and walked towards the dirt track that led from the car park to the house. Outside the house was the tell-tale debris of construction – an untidy pile of broken bricks and planks, discarded old newspapers and cigarette butts. There was no sign of activity from the house, and a mobile cement mixer stood idle at the first of two gates, the public entrance to the gallery. A couple of hundred yards further on, the tall, solid wooden gate to the house itself was closed. I reached the first gate and looked through its wrought iron bars. There, standing by a huge oak desk in the little studio attached to the Gallery, was my father.

He was reading the newspaper, a coffee cup on the desk by his right hand. I drew back involuntarily a fraction, so that the pillar afforded me some cover. But I could still see him, and had he looked up, he would have seen me cowering outside.

Always a slim man, he looked, inevitably, more gaunt than when last I saw him, his face thinner, pinched even. His stoop, the curse of tall men, was more pronounced, but he carried the same prim and dapper air that I had always associated with him – dark suit sharply creased, white shirt brilliant against the dark tie, reading glasses perched on the end of his nose. Not a white hair was out of place on his head, though it was just a little less dense, perhaps.

He reached absent-mindedly for the cup, took a sip and put it back on its saucer, then looked up from his newspaper and out the window. He tilted his head almost imperceptibly, removed his glasses and stared at me. Neither of us moved for what felt like an age. He put the newspaper down on the desk, and disappeared from my view through the studio door. A moment later he emerged from the Gallery. I opened the gate and walked towards him.

"Aengus," he said as though greeting the postman, and offered me his hand.

"Lochlann." I shook his hand, and we looked into each other's eyes. I searched for a hint of emotion, for even a hint of surprise, but his eyes gave nothing away.

"You should have told me you were coming, I could have collected you from the airport."

"It's fine. I got in yesterday, I had a few things to do."

"I see."

He half-turned towards the Gallery door and ushered me inside. The Gallery was empty save for a ladder and some tools leaning against the wall. The walls and floor had been stripped back to the stone, and the paint had been stripped from the doors. We walked into the studio. He had planned to work from this studio, but visitors to the Gallery with screaming children and inquisitive stares drove him back to the house. Apart from the huge desk and a chair, the studio was empty.

"You say you got in yesterday?"

"Yeah, I had a few things I needed to do in Dublin, so I flew over. On a bit of a whim really. It was late when I got finished and I didn't want to just land on you unannounced. I stayed down in the Arms."

It was unconvincing and he was clearly unconvinced.

"I see." he nodded. "And how are you?"

"I'm fine. You're well?"

"Yes, thank you."

It was stilted and excruciating, but I was determined not to give in, not to fill the vacuum with the babbling small talk that I was trying to suppress.

"Pauline is in the house. I'll have her bring some coffee."

He called Pauline, his house-keeper of some thirty years, on the phone that connected the house and the Gallery, and then turned back to face me.

"Are you staying in Dublin long?"

"I'm not sure." This answer was at least convincing, because it was true. The Master's insistence that I should try to learn more about Aoife from the French girl in the house in Malahide had thrown a cat amongst the pigeons of my plans. "The rest of the week anyway."

I walked to the door and looked around the Gallery.

"Doing some redecoration?"

"Yes. I have an exhibition beginning in a couple of weeks, and this place frankly needed some work. They've had to go into Dublin for some filler or other, I'm not really sure what."

I walked out into the Gallery, looked up at the high vaulted ceiling criss-crossed with wooden beams. It gave the room a cathedral-like quality, made it feel much bigger than it was, and the effect was enhanced by the stained-glass windows at either end of the room. I stepped back and almost tripped over some string and small plastic sticks that had been left on the concrete floor. The crunching of my feet on the grit that covered the floor echoed in the bare room.

I heard footsteps on the flagstones outside, and Pauline came in tray in hand. She shrieked and broke into a wide smile when she saw me.

"Aengus! Come here to me, you!" She put the tray down on the desk in the studio, and bustled over to me. She threw her arms around me and hugged me vigorously. Then she stood back and pushed me to arms length.

"Let me have a look at you. Are you eating at all?" She shook her head disapprovingly. "When did you get here? How long are you staying? I'll make up your room. You're a terrible man for not lettin' us know you were comin'!"

"Don't go to any trouble, Pauline, I'm not sure how long I'll be here..." I shot a sideways glance at my father.

"Thank you, Pauline," he said, "if you wouldn't mind preparing Aengus' room."

"Of course, of course I will. I'll do it now. And you'll be wanting some proper home-cooked food this evening – needing it, I dare say! I'll go and get your room ready, you can tell me all about what you've been up to later."

She hurried to the door, stopped and turned around. "It's great to see you," she said earnestly. And with that she was gone.

She had just walked out the door when I heard her voice again.

"Arra hallo, Críostóir, and how are you doing? You're not going to believe who's in there – seriously, you're not! Go on, go in and see! I've just brought in some coffee, I'll get you a mug."

The Master walked in and waved his hand.

"Morning all, and what a grand morning it is." Walking over to my father, he put his hand on his arm and pointed his other hand at me. "I came across this hooligan last night, Lochlann. He said he was coming up here this morning – I should have called and warned you so you could have been out!"

"You're looking a bit better today, young Aengus," he said to me, "you were looking tired when I saw you last night, it was a hard oul' day I'd say? You slept well?"

"I did, Master," I smiled, grateful to him for sparing me the need to fabricate further. Grateful also that the tortuous conversation with my father, if it could even have been described as conversation, had been at least temporarily suspended. I think now that he came to the house for that very reason, to play the neutral peace broker.

I looked at my father as he and the Master discussed some story from the village. I tried to remember if there had ever been a time when we had talked easily with each other, shared stories and experiences, debated opinions and ideas. But time blurs the memory so that we remember things either as we want them to be remembered or as inevitably coloured by what came after. I know I loved my father, but what inspired that love, if indeed love it really was? What, after all, is the love of a child for a parent? Isn't it born of the hero-struck infant's dependence on his parents and the certainty that there is nothing they can't do, no obstacle they can't overcome? And as we grow and learn more of the world, we realise that they are neither infallible nor invincible, but with the realisation that the world is a tough place comes an admiration that they have navigated it so surely and a respect for their skills and what they have achieved. And with age and growing maturity comes gratitude for what they have done and sacrificed. And finally, sometimes, comes a friendship borne of shared experiences, shared values, shared passions. And somewhere in the middle of all of that, love is born and grows almost unnoticed, unnurtured.

I think I can remember the awe in which I beheld my father as a young child. This tall man, imposing and handsome even to my young eyes, bestrode my world like Cassius' colossus. And I learned from an early age to admire and respect his art, encouraged by the Master's admiring commentary and the crowds that regularly filled the Gallery. I learned, too, to be grateful. The covetous looks of my school-mates taught me to appreciate that I had more than most. But we stopped somewhere short of warmth, and somewhere short of friendship. We shared a passion, yes, but we had no stories of valiant deeds to recount from the past, and I don't think I ever really shared his values, his motivations. Not that I disagreed with them, I just never understood them.

And what of a parent's love for a child? That love, we're told, is innate, not learned through experience. But what did I feel standing over Aoife's cot in the hospital room? Powerful, almost debilitating emotion, yes – but love? I don't know. I suppose I didn't have long enough to find out.

I had heard stories of women, friends or friends of friends, who found the days immediately after birth the most gruelling emotionally. Conditioned to believe, and fully expecting, that the arrival of their child would trigger a wave of love more potent than any emotion they had ever known, they had been distraught to discover that they felt no bond, no overwhelming adoration or devotion. Caitríona, I have no doubt, loved Aoife from before she made her entry to the world. Perhaps knowing that their time together would be brief, her initial shock and horror gave way to an affection and ultimately to love, a love she was perhaps too frightened to entertain. That's maybe the difference between the paternal and the maternal. Her love was innate. Mine had to be learned. All of which perhaps explains my father's emotions toward me. His grief stopped him learning to love.

A father's love for a son, I think, grows and changes with his child. Every new phase of life must bring new and unexpected emotions and reward. At the start is vulnerability.

This tiny child is so helpless and dependent that a father strives to protect. Then comes reliance, where protection gives way to provision. Then comes investment. Not financial, but the investment of self, the passing down of skills and talents, and the living of dreams that have never quite materialised. And finally friendship, where father and son become equal – the closing equilibrium. A father uncovers yet another new treasure in every change his son goes through. A mother doesn't ever want him to change.

As a child and a young man, I would watch my friends with their fathers, at the school gates or at football matches or in the pub on a Friday evening – fascinated by the ease of their company and all that they so clearly shared. I have watched my friends with their new-born children, besotted and disarmed by a beguiling infant. I watched their need to protect taking over like a primeval instinct. As time went on, I watched their need to provide offer a clear purpose where perhaps purpose had begun to fade. And I watched their investment of self, perhaps as much about celebrating their own ambitions and aspirations as the achievements of the child. I watched but I never understood. Only a father – a real father who has nurtured, protected, provided for and invested himself in a child – can know the true meaning of a father's love. Aoife might not share blood with the father who adopted her, but it gave me hope that he would love her no less because of it.

And I think it's only when this journey has run its course, when the child takes on the mantle of responsibility for himself, that father and child become friends, that they become equal. My own father somehow missed these stages, or avoided them. Protection was out-sourced to child-minders. He provided for me, for sure, but from a safe distance – affording me everything, but giving me little. For a man with so much to give, he invested nothing. And so we had never become friends.

I suppose he gave me a sneak preview of the relationship

I might some day share with Aoife. I had not earned the right to be her friend.

The Master looked around the Gallery, his lip curled, tutting his disapproval.

"Those boys are not the fastest workers, Lochlann, are they now? And where are they this morning?"

"They had to go into Dublin to get some filler. A problem with the far wall, I think."

"And it took two of them to go? Afraid of being lonely were they? I'll tell you now, if it wasn't for Oran you'd have no chance of being ready on time."

My father saw my eyebrow rise at the mention of Oran's name.

"Oran is helping me with the work here. As Críostóir says, we would be at a real loss without him. I owe him a great deal."

Oran was my best friend as a child, we were inseparable throughout primary school. Despite the enforced separation of my time at boarding school, we remained firm friends, sharing the school holidays and growing up together. Then came time to leave school, and Oran failed to secure a place in university. Even though we were both living in Howth, we drifted apart. I think he resented my new life and friends, whom he unfairly considered pretentious and fake. And of course I was spending my time with Caitríona, trying to come to terms with Aoife, of whom he knew nothing. He got a job working in a restaurant in town, working unsocial hours for small reward. Our paths diverged and I saw little of my old friend. Having left to live in London, I had been in contact with him very little, and indeed over the past few years communication had dried up altogether. To be honest, with all of the distractions of the previous days I had hardly thought of him despite being back in Dublin. It would be good to spend some time catching up with him.

"An understatement, Lochlann, if I may say so. Have you told Aengus about the exhibition?"

"I mentioned that we were preparing the Gallery, yes."

"How big is the show?" I asked.

He shook his head. "Not very big, fifty pieces or so."

"What's it about?"

"It will be titled 'Ireland's Changing Women in Ireland's Changing Times.' It explores the evolving nature of womanhood in Ireland."

"Will you have much new material?"

"Some, yes, some borrowed from collectors."

The Master interjected.

"Well, aren't you the master of understatement this morning, Lochlann?"

He turned to me and made an expansive gesture with his hands.

"This will be the most important show by an Irish artist in Dublin this side of the millennium," he said emphatically, pausing for dramatic effect. "The past few years have been barren, just barren. It's time that the changes in this country were reflected in the work of an Irish artist. And this is the man to do it."

My father shook his head slowly and gave him the same despairing look that I had received so many times before.

"Críostóir, that's nonsense as you very well know," he said, quietly. "I appreciate the compliment, but it is simply not true. What about Caoimhghin Ó'Cróidheáin? Or Conor Walton? Or Colin Davidson up in Belfast? Or our own Paul Kelly? Excellent artists producing fine works."

The Master raised his right hand. "That's fair enough, Lochlann, fair enough. Very fine painters all of them and no doubt. But, tell me, where is the art that reflects the enormous changes sweeping through this country, ha? It can't just be reflected in city-scapes with tall cranes and shiny new trams, saying 'now, look at all the building that's going on, isn't it all change?' That's just scratching at the surface, there's so much more to it than that. Our writers are doing it, our film-makers are doing it. Even our photographers are out there capturing the new mood and the new culture of this country. But landscape art that simply records the physical can surely never provide a full record of how much things are changing before our very eyes?" He pointed an index finger at my father. "Make no mistake, Lochlann – what you're doing now is studying one of the ways that Ireland's evolution is manifesting itself, through the evolution of our women. Not the only way, that's for sure. But an important way. That's what you're doing. And it's important for that very reason."

Lochlann nodded.

"It has merit, I'm not denying that. It will be interesting, I hope, to examine how the composition of one section of our community has grown and changed. But recording the physical change has no less merit, indeed it is perhaps more important. In fifty years from now, you and I will be gone. But the fruits of the construction and development that we see all over Dublin and all over the country will stand, redefining the landscape. What came before, and the manner of the metamorphosis, that must be recorded too."

It had been a very long time since I had seen my father so animated, if indeed I ever had. He spoke slowly, deliberately, never losing control, never yielding completely to passion, but there was no doubting the strength of his conviction. Like sparring partners, I could see that they revelled in the verbal joust, each accepting the arguments of the other and respecting his right to express them.

Pauline's arrival with a mug for the master and a fresh pot of coffee enforced a truce. As she left the Master poured himself a coffee and asked my father, "So have you decided how 't will work? The layout I mean?"

My father walked over to the centre of the Gallery.

"There will be four sections, not clearly defined but

separate sections nonetheless. The first will use older pieces and represents Irish woman as depicted in so many stereotypes – the fruit-seller on Moore Street, the old woman sitting sewing nets on the up-turned currach in Dingle, and so on. The second will represent motherhood, and the constancy of a mother's selfless love amid the changing demands of raising children in Ireland." He paused, and looked at me. "It will centre around a portrait of Claire."

My mother. Although he never referred to her as my mother. He had never shown me his portraits of her, although I knew there were many. I nodded, not really knowing how to respond. He continued to look into my eyes for a moment and then carried on.

"The third section will represent the powerful, professional young woman of more recent times. And the fourth will look at the entirely new role of women – women as radicals, women not content to simply conform, determined to shock with their appearance or their words."

He turned full circle and surveyed the Gallery.

"I have not yet determined the positioning, the flow. It remains difficult with the room in this state. Oran and I are going to look at it this week."

The Master gestured towards me. "This man should be able to help too." To me, he said, "You must have worked on this kind of thing in London, for companies and the like?"

"Yes, but I'm sure it's a very different proposition when it's art and not corporate marketing," I laughed half-heartedly, and looked at my father.

"Indeed," he replied.

CHAPTER 8

The gate outside clanged shut and Oran walked into the Gallery. He was the same Oran I remembered from so many episodes in our past. A little heavier maybe, flecks of grey appearing at his temples, but the same Oran. He grunted a greeting to my father and the Master, then saw me and stopped.

"Aengus?" He seemed to double-take, making sure he wasn't mistaken. "How's it goin'?"

I walked over to shake his hand, and went to embrace him. He recoiled a fraction and we compromised with a rough slap on each other's shoulders.

"Good, Oran, thanks. How have you been? Eatin' well by the looks of things," I joked, punching his shoulder.

He hesitated. "Yeah, s'pose so."

He turned to my father, and shook his head angrily.

"Sorry I've been so long. Some fucker hit my car while I was in the shop. Just fucked off. No note, nothing." He was seething. "I tried to see if I could see him, you know, looked around for a car with a dent or something, but he was gone. Fucker."

My father shook his head. "What sort of fellow does that? What sort of rotten so-and-so?" He squeezed Oran's arm. "Don't worry. I know a chap in Ballyfermot who does crash repairs, I have no doubt he'll be able to carry out the necessary repairs at a reasonable cost. Go into the house and get Pauline to make you a cup of tea. And don't worry, it will be ok."

"Ah, those other gobshites aren't back from town yet and I'm way behind now, Lochlann, I better get on…"

My father blocked his path with an outstretched arm.

"Oran, go and get a cup of tea, and sit quietly for a few minutes. Go on."

Oran nodded, but as he walked to the door he noticed something on the floor.

"Ah for *FUCK* sake!"

I looked for what had caused this violent reaction and realised with dismay that he was looking at the pieces of string and plastic that I had trodden on earlier.

"How the *FUCK* did that happen?"

My father walked over to where he was standing.

"What's wrong, Oran?"

"I set out the grid for the tiles here last night with lines of string, and they're all over the place now. Fuck it."

I hesitated, then stepped forward, and said, "Jesus, Oran, I'm sorry, I think I might have stood on them. Here, I'll help you sort it out." I bent down and began to straighten the lines of string but had no real idea what to do.

"Just leave it, leave it. I'll do it myself. Fuck sake, Aengus, only just back and you're already making a mess of things."

The Master intervened with arms outstretched, palms down in a calming gesture.

"Ah now, Oran, take it easy lad, it was only an accident and there's no permanent damage done."

"No, it's not permanent. Just more work and we're already behind. Great."

And with that he was gone out the door, violent expletives left hanging in the air.

I stooped again to try to undo at least some of the damage, but my father stopped me.

"Just leave it, Aengus, leave it to Oran to fix it." His tone was impatient. "He knows what he's doing."

Turning to the Master, he said, "Let's go and have a look at his car, see how bad the damage is."

He walked out of the Gallery and the Master looked at me. I shook my head, and he followed my father out the gate.

The optimism of the morning had faded and, like the sun, retreated behind the clouds. The contrast of my father's reaction to my appearance and to Oran's arrival could not have been more marked. I would have said that he was trying to deliberately make a point, but any intention to do so would have been superseded by Oran's misfortune and I had no doubt that my father's reaction was entirely genuine. It was one of the things I admired in him, his calmness in a crisis, and yet it was his evenness of temper that I found most frustrating when the crisis was mine.

I sat on the bare concrete floor and set to work on the strings. I could scarcely make it any worse and I had nothing else to do. It was like a child's puzzle. The section of floor covered by the makeshift grid was small, perhaps designed to be an island in the middle of… of something. I tried to make out the intended pattern from the undisturbed sections. It looked like Oran was aiming for a mosaic-like composition, so small were the shapes bounded by the lines of string. One or two of the segments were complete, unbroken, and so I set about recreating these where I had uprooted the small plastic stakes.

As I got older, my father's exhibitions had become less and less frequent, and the Gallery was too often bare and empty. It had become my playroom, the place where I could bring toy cars or a train set or my action men and lose myself in their imaginary world. So when Pauline came in to tidy away the cups and coffee pot, it must have been quite a throwback to see me sitting there, lost in the task at hand. I didn't hear her come in, and when she spoke I started.

"Sorry, love," she said. "I didn't mean to startle you."

"That's alright, Pauline," I looked up and smiled without much enthusiasm. "I made a mess of Oran's work, I'm just putting it right."

"Don't mind Oran," she said, "he's havin' a bad day."

She waved her hand over the tangle of string.

"You weren't to know that was there for any reason. If I'd seen it myself, I'd probably have set to it with a brush and pan. Accidents happen to the best of us."

"I'm not sure Oran sees it like that." I said ruefully.

Pauline looked at me, then down at her hands, then back at me.

"It might have been better if you'd let them know you were coming. It's been such a long time, and so much has happened. They probably just need a chance to get used to the idea. But they will, and things will settle down, you'll see."

I imagined Oran's indignant ranting that had prompted Pauline to come down to pour oil on the waters. She and the Master had a lot of work to do.

"What brings you home anyway? Apart from seeing me," she chuckled.

"I just had a few things to do in town, a few things to sort out. I didn't even know I was coming until last week."

"And how long can you stay? You can stay a wee while can't you?"

"I really don't know. But a wee while, yes."

"Good. It'll be good for you to spend some time with your father. He misses you terribly, Aengus. I know he doesn't always show it, but he thinks the world of you, you know he does. I just wish the two of you would stop this pretending and just talk to each other. You won't have him forever, and it'll be too late for regrets then."

I sat up straight. "He's not..."

Pauline raised her hands and shook her head. "No, no, no. Nothing like that. But he's getting older, we all are. Don't leave it too late, that's all I'm saying."

I nodded. No matter how often she and the Master protested that he missed me or worried for me or cared for me, I couldn't fight the feeling that they were acting out of loyalty to him and affection for me, and that their assertions were founded on no more than that. I hadn't discerned the slightest crumb of affection in my father's greeting, especially when compared with his obvious concern for Oran.

"Now," she went on, her tone breezier, "where are your bags? I've made up your room."

"Down in the Arms. I stayed there last night, it was too late to just land up here by the time I got finished."

"Hmm," her response told me my story was gaining no credibility with the telling. "Well, you go down and get them and I'll have dinner ready for you this evening. What would you like? How about a bit of bacon?"

"That'd be…" I stopped, remembering one of her comfort food dishes that had soothed turbulent times often in the past. "Actually, Pauline, d'you remember that thing you used to do with the steak, stuffed with mushrooms I think it was?"

"Stuffed steak? Lord I haven't done that for a long time, not sure I can remember how! But let me see what I can do," she said, elbowing me gently in the ribs.

I arranged the last of the string, and sat back to survey my work. To my untrained eye, it looked all in place. But I didn't hold out much hope. Even if it was a perfect reconstruction, I felt sure Oran would find fault.

The Master and Lochlann came back in, and I stood up quickly.

"I'm just going to pop into the village to get a few things for dinner," Pauline said to my father. "Can I pick up anything for you?"

"No thank you, Pauline," he replied. "I might go down myself a little later."

He turned to the Master.

"Will you join us for dinner, Críostóir?"

"Thank you all the same, Lochlann, but I have a school councillors meeting this evening. 'Twon't go on too long hopefully, maybe I'll come up for a wee nip after."

"Do that, Críostóir, do that."

"Right so, I better be off, see if I can find that recipe!" Pauline winked at me and hurried away.

The Master wandered around the Gallery, then went into the studio, his face and furrowed brow betraying the whirr of cogs in his head.

"Tell me, what d'you use this for these days, Lochlann?" he asked, waving his arm around the small room.

"Nothing really. A store room sometimes, but other than that it lies empty. A pity I suppose, a waste really. I considered knocking down that wall, making it all part of the Gallery, but you never know when that space might come in useful."

"Mmmm." The Master stroked his chin. After a moment, he turned to me.

"Aengus, that friend of yours from France, the girl living in Malahide. What did you say she did for a living?"

I sensed that the Master knew exactly where this train was headed and, despite my reticence, my instinct said I should trust him.

"Well, she's a musician I suppose."

"Mmmm." Another pause.

"D'you know what I was just thinking, Lochlann? And hear me out now, it's just a thought."

He paused to collect his thoughts, though the speech he was about to deliver had been well practised, carefully rehearsed.

"Despite your protests, I firmly believe that this show will go down as a landmark exhibition for Irish art. Wait now, wait...", he raised his hands to quell my father's objections and counted off on his fingers the reasons for the show's importance.

93

"It will be a landmark show because it heralds a return to form for one of the country's foremost living painters, because it is the only show in recent years to chronicle the human aspect of our changing times, and because it marks a return to the traditional in a time where modern and alternative art-forms are taking centre-stage."

The Master's time in education, addressing a sometimes unwilling and often disinterested audience, had honed his oratorical skills, and he was now in full flight.

"What, then, could make this an even more compelling event? What could ensure that this is an event that the art establishment and art-lovers alike simply cannot afford to miss?" he paused, leaned forward and looked at the two of us, eyebrows raised and arms outstretched as the question hung between us. Still he waited. My father drew a breath to respond, but before he could utter a word the Master continued.

"The passing of the mantle from father to son, the coming of age of the next generation!" He was triumphant. "We show to the public, for the very first time, the work of the virgin son in the midst of the work of the established father."

Lochlann and I both just stared at him, trying to make sense of what he had just said. We understood it, but could make no sense of it. Lochlann's eyes, as they always did when he was deep in thought, narrowed slightly, as though to hide the machinations of his mind from the rest of us. I searched desperately to see what I was so obviously missing, what it was that made this proposition even possible, let alone attractive. But try as I might, I could not.

Sensing our failure to follow his thread, he adopted the air of a teacher helping the class laggard. He came over

"Lochlann, I'm simply suggesting that you add just one of Aengus' portraits to the collection."

Lochlann looked at me, clearly deciding on his words but not his response.

"I see, Críostóir, I see. A very interesting proposition. Very interesting indeed. But we are less than a month from the show's opening, there simply isn't time to work through the logistics. Perhaps if we had thought of this a little sooner... Perhaps next time." And with that the case was closed.

But the Master was not to be so easily deflected.

"Now, Lochlann, think it through before we discard the thought. Think of the publicity this could generate. I'm sorry to be a bit mercenary, but just think of the sentimental value. Think of how the galleries would see it, the opportunity it would present to them. There's never been anything like it."

"But, Master," I found my voice having grasped the gravity of his idea, and its implications, "I don't have a portrait to show, nothing that would be good enough anyway."

"And even if he had, there is the question of compatibility with the other works on show," my father said.

"Ah, and that's where your friend in Malahide comes into the picture," he clapped his hands and beamed jubilantly. My blank expression was his cue.

"This show is about the changing face of Irish women, is it not? One of Aengus' works would introduce a whole new angle to the show – the emergence of youth and how a new generation of Irish men have a new perception of Irish womanhood. And crucially..." he paused for dramatic effect, "crucially, Aengus' work reflects an entirely, entirely new Irish woman – those who have come to live here from abroad. Aengus paints this girl, this young French musician seeking to make her way in strange, foreign Ireland with its foreign language, strange customs and unfamiliar culture. She is both teacher and learner, like every foreign migrant come to our shores – with knowledge and experience to glean and to impart. And *that's* the silver bullet."

"But it would take weeks to work on a piece like that, if not more," my father said. "I'm sure Aengus doesn't have that kind of time to spare at such short notice."

The Master looked at me. "What do you think, Aengus?" he asked.

"I could probably find the time, I suppose," I replied, increasingly conscious that his arguments were well-prepared and certain that he would brook no dissent.

Had I been a dispassionate observer, listening to a promoter describe the theme of an exhibition, I would have been in full agreement. It made sense, and in a world where art must compete with a myriad other channels of entertainment, it was indeed compelling. But it was impossible. I could not deliver a piece of sufficient quality in such a short period of time. And even if I could, it wouldn't matter – my father would never deem it good enough.

My father shook his head slowly.

"It's wonderful in principle, Críostóir, a delightful development of the theme. But the fact remains that we don't have enough time to crystallise the thought. We have already produced the publicity material, already briefed the galleries and the press. It's simply too late."

The Master was a study in calmness and perseverance. It dawned on me that he had probably been concocting this scheme since I left his house the night before. He knew exactly what my father would say, what I would say, and we had played into his hands. He sat on the edge of the desk, his face pensive as though searching out a solution already long found. He shook his head in resignation.

"You're right, Lochlann, I know you're right of course, absolutely right. Time is too short. Too short." He appeared to concede the folly of the project, when his countenance brightened and he stood up again. He walked over and took hold of Lochlann's arm, as though his counsel or opinion could not be imparted by words alone.

"But hang on now, how about this. Aengus starts to work on a portrait of this French girl. If he doesn't finish it in time, or if it's not compatible with the other works to be shown, then fine – nothing is lost and at the very worst, sure we have a new piece to show after the exhibition is over. But if it *is* finished in time, and if it *does* fit with the other pieces on display, then we add it to the show. And we use it as an excuse to republicise the exhibition closer to the opening."

It was a master-stroke. We had already denied him once, a denial he had graciously accepted. It would have been mean-spirited to deny him again, to deny so reasonable a compromise.

But I was still reluctant.

"Master, I don't even know if she would be willing to sit, if she even has time."

"Who is this girl, what is her name?" my father asked.

"Hélène. I think."

"You think?"

"Yes," I mumbled. "I don't really know her, she's more a friend of a friend."

"Well, in light of that our debate seems a shade academic. One doesn't simply find models growing on trees. It's a little more complicated than that."

The Master realised that he was losing his position of authority to our analysis of detail.

"Look, maybe you're right, maybe she won't be able or willing. But let's worry about all that when you go and see her, Aengus, when you'll have to put the proposition to her in a way that has both virtue and value. We can think that through, figure out a plan. The important thing is that we all agree that you're going to work on a piece with a view to adding it to the exhibition. Don't we?"

My father and I looked at each other. The Master had succeeded in uniting us, if only in opposition, where blood and circumstance had so often failed. We looked at him, and nodded.

"Well isn't that grand?" he smiled, his work done.

Oran came back into the Gallery, his demeanour a little improved by the tea.

"Oran, we had a wee look at your car, it's not as bad as maybe it looks at first sight," the Master reassured him. "It's fairly superficial. Have you comprehensive insurance?"

Oran shook his head.

"Only third party," he said. "Do you have any idea how much comprehensive would be, even on that old thing?"

He looked at where I had destroyed and then tried to reconstruct his work of the previous night.

"You do that?" he asked me.

"I had a go, yeah."

He looked back at the floor, then back at me, and nodded. "Thanks. Not bad."

"You're going to have some company in here, Oran," the Master said. "Aengus is going to use the studio to work on a piece for the show."

By making it public he brought it a little closer to being a reality, although the look on my father's face confirmed his continued reservations. Only the Master could have pulled off such a stunt and not incurred my father's wrath.

"Right," said Oran, eyebrows raised in surprise as he processed the Master's words. "Right. We'll have to figure out where to put the tools and things while you're in there. Right." He picked up his toolbox. "Well, I better get on with this."

"And I better make a move or the day'll be gone," said the Master, making his way to the door. "I'll maybe see you tonight Lochlann. You'll be here, Aengus?"

"I will," I answered. "Actually, if you're going down to the village, I might grab a lift, I need to get my bags from the Hotel."

"No bother at all, come on and we'll go so."

"I'll see you in a while?" I said to Lochlann.

"In a while then," he replied.

I climbed into the Master's car, moving books and newspapers and leaflets onto the back seat. He started the car and pulled away, and I looked over at him.

"Can you tell me exactly what happened back there?"

He smiled a mischievous smile.

"Sometimes the right course of action is so obvious we are blinded to it," he said. "And we just need a wee steer and a wee push. That's all that happened. A wee steer and a wee push. Now it's up to you two."

"She might not even go for it…" I began to protest.

"Details, *gosso'n*, details," he swatted away my arguments with a dismissive hand. "We've been through all that. If she won't do it we'll find somebody else. But if she agrees, you have your model and your path to Aoife."

We arrived at the harbour front, and he stopped the car and turned to me, taking hold of my arm.

"Look't, you two need one another more than you think, more than either of you thinks. Now you have your chance to make a start."

I nodded slowly, still uncertain but shrewd enough to recognise an argument I wasn't going to win.

I opened the car door and got out, then leant back in and smiled.

"Thanks, Master. I don't know what you've let me in for, but thanks."

He winked at me, pulled the door closed and drove away.

CHAPTER 9

It was like a portal to another world, a sinister, hopeless place. We walked hand-in-hand through the bright city square outside, teeming with life and youthful vigour. Artists peddling their wares from wrought iron fences. Buskers howling soulful laments. Children throwing stale bread to the ducks, running with bravado at the pond's edge, retreating with giggling terror from a too-bold mallard. Dappled sunlight through spring-green leaves. The noise and smell of the city, familiar and safe.

And eventually we passed, timid and alone, through the hospital door. The building wrinkled its nose with disapproval. The first time you were small, so small we might have been visitors come to see your mother or aunt or cousin. The helpful smile at the welcome desk disappeared with a sniff, the finger that pointed the way was accusing. Down endless dark corridors, deeper into the building's belly. To sit on hard chairs at sticky tables with dog-eared magazines. Your turn came; and you went inside with a backward pleading look. And were gone. I have never been so bereft.

That first day at boarding school, lost in a sea of lost faces, instinct becomes your guide and leads you to some common solid ground. That first day at university, far from the insulated security of the school, awkwardly-feigned teenage indifference rescues you from fretful isolation. That first day at work, desperate to impress and prove your worth, the false confidence inspired by the shiny veneer of learning provides the rock to which you cling.

But what ally can save me from a place like this? A place where I have no place, where I am an interloper tarnishing beauty. I have no allies and so I try to make myself small, to fade into the stern background of the institution. Nurses pass me by and I am invisible. Doctors and surgeons and therapists bustle purposefully through vaulted, mosaic-tiled halls, and I see only their coats and clipboards and stethoscopes – in my mind they don't exist outside this place. They have no car and no house, they don't take holidays nor play golf. They don't go home for dinner and dinner-parties and parties. In that place, the world outside evaporates until that place and our plight is all there is, all I have, all I am.

And recently I've had this nightmare that she is sitting alone in some alien place, searching for a way out. But she has no-one, she has no ally. When bad things happen, they remind you that bad things happen. And they remind you how indiscriminate and fickle a foe is fortune. She might be alone. In my dream, she has perhaps abandoned or she has maybe been abandoned, has discarded or been discarded. But in the black night of solitary hopelessness, she has no bond of blood. We denied her that harbour in the storm.

I know you think I'm wrong. I know your reasons and once upon a time I grant you they were right. But that time passed with you the day the world changed. Bad things happen. Not gradually, they follow no convention, they tread no well-worn path. They just happen. And whatever provision we think we have made, however strong we think we are, we are never prepared.

Friends might seek to provide comfort in the white spaces in busy diaries. They will reassure that time heals, that all is inevitably for the best, that life goes on. And on. And on. The bland, beige bullshit of the unaffected and the innocent. And then they will drift away to collect their children from school and pick up the dry-cleaning and make a reservation for dinner on Saturday. While she maybe sits alone and quiet and lost. Lost.

She maybe needs to be found.

CHAPTER 10

Dinner was a quiet affair, both of us treading carefully through the minefield of so many sensitivities and a fractured history. My father was never one for stories. Every son, I think, has memories of tall tales retold and superseded with ever greater superlatives. The school breakfast plate ever larger, the single sausage ever smaller. The wind and rain ever wilder, the free-kick from ever farther away. The dog ever fiercer, the rescued maiden ever more fair. But I have no such memories, no pictures of him in my mind's eye sitting back in his favourite armchair, whiskey in hand, commanding his audience with the embellished deeds of his youth. Or the time he met Thomas Kinkade in Carmel. Or the time he was commissioned to paint the Rock of Cashel as a Presidential gift for the visiting Ronald Reagan. Oh, I encouraged and cajoled, I even tried to draw him out by tossing deliberate inaccuracies into my versions of events. But he would simply correct me and go no further.

The storyteller's legacy is the library of tales that he leaves behind, and his legacy ensures that he is present even where he is absent. He is there when his stories are recounted, and it is often in the retelling that loneliness and longing are diffused. The storyteller is rarely forgotten. My father left me with no such parting gift when I moved to London. He was perhaps never entirely forgotten, but his memory became more and more distorted and my hindsight more blurred.

Regular conversation breeds habit and comfort that a

shared interest or antipathy will always inspire a passionate dialogue. The first exploratory musings of strangers, on the other hand, bring the promise of unknown facts and incredible coincidence. With my father, I had neither.

I didn't tell him why I was in Dublin. I hadn't made a conscious decision to keep it from him, but no door opened that led me down that path. I did tell him that I had left my job and that I planned to spend some time rediscovering and rekindling my desire to create art and not advertising. And although I hadn't thought about it in quite that way, it was true. Even when I had had Caitríona, the thrill of my work had been slowly but surely quenched. I was still content to work on campaigns for clients I had served for years – but what was once exciting and raw had become staid and repetitive. What had once been romantic had been tainted by the realisation that it was all slightly devious and a little disingenuous. And there had been many evenings when, working late into the night to finish a piece and meet a deadline, I stood back to admire the fruits of countless hours only to be slightly disappointed, slightly frustrated. What had started as art had been diluted and manipulated according to the whims of the marketing men. A model's wistful eyes were made to grin, her pale skin bronzed, her individuality sacrificed in the name of uniform, conventional beauty.

But it was only after Caitríona had left me that I was struck by the insipid pallor of what I did every day. Unable to muster the artificial zeal that masked growing disaffection, my corporate days were numbered. My decision to leave only pre-empted the inevitable. And my new-found freedom also gave me back the opportunity and the liberty to create something that was truly beautiful to me and not just aligned with some corporate message. I had started in Paris, in the days before my nightly search for Aoife. And what had started as a way to fill time quickly grew into something more, something that got me out of bed every morning and gave the day a purpose before the night came. And there was the lurking aspiration to create something that would make Aoife proud and the acknowledgement that this was my only avenue.

"And how is your work?" he had asked.

I paused.

"Actually, I quit. A couple of weeks ago."

He put his glass down slowly on the table and looked over my head and into the distance for a moment, squinting barely noticeably so that the crow's feet that had emerged at the corners of his eyes deepened just a fraction, as though reacting themselves to my news.

"I see. You were offered another position?"

"No. I just…" I searched for the words to articulate my reasons, the emotions that drove me. I shrugged. "I just wasn't enjoying it anymore, I suppose." Immediately, I regretted my choice of words. Lochlann had always considered me flighty, unable to stick to a task, short of commitment. Abandoning a career, even one he deemed unworthy, because I wasn't "enjoying" it would simply confirm his view. Life wasn't there to be enjoyed, it was an obligation to be honoured.

He started to say something and stopped himself, but not before the look of disdain flashed across his face.

"And have you thought about what you will do now?"

"I want to paint. I think it's a hankering I've had for a while, but I've never really acknowledged it, never had the chance I suppose. I want to spend some time thinking about it and working on a couple of ideas I've had."

He furrowed his brow with a look of slight confusion. Then the confusion gave way to a barely discernible cloud of anger.

"Is that why you came here?" he said slowly, as though uttering the words only as they formed in his head. "Because of the exhibition?"

It was a moment before I realised that, logically, he had weighed up the day's events and arrived at entirely the wrong conclusion. A conclusion that said I had only become back because of the opportunity to use his exhibition as a vehicle for my selfish aspirations. Even that I had manipulated the Master into opening that door on my behalf. A reasonable conclusion and an ugly one.

I put down my fork and knife and raised my hands in defence.

"No, no, not at all," I protested. "It was nothing like that. I didn't know anything about the show until the Master mentioned it to me last night. I don't even have anything to show, I have no concrete ideas, I've certainly not considered a portrait, and – let's be honest – it's fairly unlikely that I'd have something in time."

"Quite a coincidence then?"

"I guess so. If I'd been planning to hijack your exhibition, I'd be a lot better prepared than this." My initial guilty protestations gave way to indignation. "Look, just forget the whole thing. It was just the Master's way of trying to get us to work together, well-meaning but ill-advised. You don't want me to show, and I have nothing to show. Let's just forget it."

I waved my arm as though petulantly batting the whole idea away with the back of my hand, and set about my beef with a renewed violence. Lochlann was watching me silently, his eyes burning the side of my face as I tried hard to ignore him.

Finally he sighed and said with a hint of resignation, "No. If you are really committed to your art, really committed to rediscovering your voice, then I certainly don't want to stand in your way. I make no promises, of course, no guarantees that I will be able to show your work in this exhibition. But we said we would try it and that is what we shall do." He laid his hand firmly on the table cloth to lay the case to rest, paused, and looked at me. "And I... apologise, for any suggestion that you might have been less than candid."

I nodded, we ate, and the subject was closed.

The Master did not join us for a digestive whiskey – he called to say that the meeting had been a little feisty and he had retired to the pub with some of the parents to try to calm things down. I wondered again if that was all part of his Master's plan.

I woke the next morning in my old bedroom. My room was in the attic, which had been converted when I finished in boarding school and started in University. It made little sense for me to rent an apartment in Dublin – the DART from the village also served the University and the commute was straightforward. On those evenings when I wanted to stay late in town, there were always plenty of friends' sofas and floors to sleep on. And, in time, there was Caitríona's bed. And so my father had offered to build me a suite in the loft, complete with bedroom, study and bathroom. I added a small fridge for beer, and my palace was complete.

Through one of the windows added at either gable end, I could look out on the sea and the lighthouse. That morning, there was a light haze through which the sun shone faintly. I thought of the view from our little terraced house in London, of another grey terrace only twenty metres away and of the high rise block of flats behind it that dwarfed our street, the street that was clogged day and night with stalled traffic.

The house was empty and ghostly quiet when I padded down the stairs to the kitchen. Why do we treat silence with such respect? Why do we whisper in quiet, empty rooms? In the kitchen I hunted through cupboards and drawers to find some coffee and some bread or cereal. Pauline's kitchen was her pride and joy, and she rearranged things almost weekly. She said it was "to keep things proper." I suspected it was more to do with maintaining her indispensability. I'm sure she took great satisfaction from our inability to ever find anything and her inevitably coming to our rescue.

I found eventually a larder full of breakfast provisions, and made myself some coffee and some toast. I didn't think, in my heart of hearts, that I could deliver a portrait in time for the exhibition opening. And even if I could, I didn't believe for a moment that it would pass Lochlann's criteria for inclusion. And yet despite these reservations, I was undeniably excited by the prospect of working on a portrait with a clear objective and a real purpose. Throughout my professional life, any attempt on my part to craft a work for my own sake and not for a client engagement had evaporated amid feelings of pointlessness. There had been no time to dedicate and no real purpose other than self-indulgence. Now I had time and reason, and even if the odds were stacked against me, I felt the stirring of a faint thrill in my gut when I thought about the opportunity to create.

That thrill dissipated slightly when I thought about my first job – to convince the young woman I had met only two days before to sit for me. The thought made me nervous even though I had, on the face of it, no reason to be nervous. I was an artist looking for a model, it was that simple. And yet this girl was my daughter's friend. And that made everything impossibly complicated. This girl – she was a young woman and yet her association with Aoife meant that for me she could only be a girl. Aoife had never grown up in my mind. Forever young, like Oisín's Niamh.

I thought about being completely honest with her. Tell her that I was looking for my daughter and that my search had led me to her. Tell her that it would mean the world to me to spend some time with her and to talk about Aoife. And that sitting for my portrait would afford us that opportunity. It was ridiculous and I ruled it out immediately. For one thing, she might not even know that Aoife was adopted, and I would risk breaking the ultimate confidence. Besides which, I didn't even know this girl, and after years of white lies and careful avoidance of booby-trapped subjects, I wasn't about to entrust so profound a secret to her.

I thought about concocting a great charade, passing myself off as a painter of some renown in Dublin circles. I felt sure that Ireland's art firmament was not so celebrated in the public domain that my obscurity would be immediately obvious to a such a newcomer to the city. But I am a terrible liar, and such dissimulation would inevitably be found out before long. Besides which, such an imposture would require the experience and *savoir faire* of the genuine article, and my fumbling ineptitude would never pass for that. All of which might precipitate tears and recriminations from one person I could not afford to upset.

And so I opted for a diluted version of the truth. I am an aspiring artist, who has been given a once-in-a-lifetime opportunity to show his work at an exhibition held by an established Irish artist, who also happens to be my father. But I need a model. A friend in London saw Aoife play in the club, suggested her to me as an example of a new generation of Irish woman and I had tracked her down to this little house in North Dublin. Initially disappointed not to have found Aoife, it occurred to me that this French woman was an even more powerful example of new Irish womanhood – an immigrant making her way in a strange city, like so many Irish women in the past. It was a story full of holes and one that would bear little scrutiny, but she would surely feel reassured by the association with my father, a well-known personality in Dublin, and my obvious inexperience might even put her at ease.

It was decided. I cleared away my breakfast debris, picked up my jacket and set out for the village and the DART station.

I spent the short journey on the train rehearsing my lines. The old couple in the seats across the carriage elbowed one another, whispered and smirked at "yer man chattin' away to himself." A bit early to have been drinking, their eyes said. The train arrived in Malahide too early, I wasn't ready. But then I was never going to be ready. So best to just get on with it.

St. Mary's Terrace was deserted, its residents long gone to school and jobs and chores in the village or the city. I stood at the end of the street, gathering my thoughts and steeling myself. It had never occurred to me that she might be out, but the empty street made me suddenly realise that there was no reason why she, too, might not be gone to do a day's... what? Did she work, or study, or practise her music? Part of me hoped predictably that she was out. But really I wanted to talk to her. I wanted to talk to her about my portrait. And I wanted to talk to her about Aoife, not today, but soon. And this was the first step along that road.

A young boy was sitting on the step of the first house on the terrace, hidden behind a huge pot-plant, playing with two toy action hero figures. He had stopped his game, his heroes frozen in mid-duel, and was staring at me from behind the ornamental tree.

"Are you lost?" he asked. "Cos if y'are, I can give yeh directions." He articulated "directions" slowly and deliberately, like a treasured word newly learned, and nodded sagely. "Only three... no four euro."

I smiled at him. His enterprise was worthy of that.

"No," I said, "I'm not lost. But thanks."

"Are you sure? Cos you look lost."

"Well, you wouldn't know where I could find some peace?" I said, teasing.

He furrowed his brow, then shrugged.

"No, I don't know. But I could ask me mammy, I know she's always looking for it?"

"No that's ok, I'll have a look down here. But thanks for your help, here's your fee."

I gave him a coin and walked off down the street, again seeking cover on the even-numbered side.

"Thanks, Mister," he called after me.

I came to number 23 and paused, then crossed the street, climbed the steps and knocked on the door. There was silence for a moment, then I heard the sound of heels on tiles and she opened the door. The casual bohemian from two days before had been transformed into a smart young woman in a business suit and subtle make-up, her hair tied up behind her head. She carried herself with the confident, almost arrogant, self-possession that is the exclusive preserve of a French woman – all that was missing was the Gauloise. And yet something – was it the slight frame, or the dark, soulful eyes? – suggested something fragile, even lost.

"You again?" she said, drawing out each syllable in her slow, soft French drawl and tilting her head to put on an earring. "Look, she is not here. I told you. She might never come here. You are wasting your time. And my time."

She went to close the door, but I stepped forward.

"No, you don't understand. I'm not here to see Aoife. I wanted to talk to you."

She stopped, and raised one eye-brow.

"To me?"

I nodded.

"Why do you want to talk to me?"

"Well –" I drew a deep breath and delivered the well-practised lines "– I told you I need a model for a portrait. Look, I just can't wait around for this Aoife, and I wondered if you would be interested? In sitting for me, I mean."

"Sitting?"

"Yes, posing, modelling."

"I am not a model."

"I know, but it doesn't matter. Actually it's better. More natural."

She was silent for a moment, staring almost through me, weighing me up.

"I do not take off my clothes," she said.

"No! No!" I was aghast, horrified that she might think I was some nasty little pervert seeking a cheap thrill. "No! That's not what I do, not at all. Really."

She seemed amused by my embarrassment, and let me squirm in it a little while she pondered the integrity of my motives.

"There is a café on the main street," she said eventually, pointing in the direction from which I had come. "The Crock of Gold. Go there. I will meet you there in fifteen minutes."

She closed the door and left me on the step. I turned, walked slowly down the steps and made my way towards the main street. She might never follow, might leave me sitting there, but then I'd know and at least it saved me the humiliation of a flat-out, face-to-face rejection.

"Hey, mister," called my guide from across the street, "did yeh find it?"

I looked over at him.

"Do you know what," I shouted back. "I just might have!"

"That's good. See ya so."

"See ya." I waved back, and walked on.

I ordered a coffee in the Crock of Gold and took a seat at a table by the window. It was school lunch-time, and mothers with children in reluctant tow hurried along the street amid barked commands and reprimands. I wondered why my new young friend with the action heroes wasn't at school. He had cut a lonely figure, playing alone on the front step, so eager to talk and to help. I thought of the imaginary world I inhabited with my toys in Lochlann's empty gallery, a world he had never sought to enter, its crown prince *in absentia*. He was my father and I had never questioned the cards I had been dealt. But if I discovered that he was not my father, that I had come to him through some artificial arrangement conducted with due legal process, would that change everything? Would I then resent his absence? Would I demand more from him because he had entered willingly into the contract? Would I feel suddenly free of obligation? It was a game I played often. And how would I feel about the father who had absconded? The one who really was absent, who had never protected nor provided? Lochlann might have battled with the finer points of fatherhood, but he had always been there.

The café filled up, and I could feel the scavenging eyes fixed on my table, hovering mothers eager to bed down their young. I looked out the window and sporadically checked my phone and glanced at my watch to assure them that I was expecting company. I caught the eye of an angry-looking woman, her lip fixed in a disapproving curl as she snapped at the child by her side, and finished my coffee. To linger further would be to draw the wrath of the gathering mob, and still there was no sign of her. I looked at my watch – it had been half an hour. Maybe she had better things to do, maybe she didn't trust me, maybe she was on the phone at that very moment laughing with a friend about the painter and his transparent proposition. And yet, despite the folly of my situation, I couldn't bring myself to leave. Not yet. Not now. And so I had put my jacket back on and I was about to go to the counter to order another coffee and leave my table to the circling vultures when she walked in. She scanned the room and waved to me. I waved back and it seemed to me that every eye in the café followed her as she glided to my table. Even the scavengers admitted defeat and withdrew.

"Sorry," she said, "the telephone rang." She waved her hand dismissively.

"No problem," I replied, in what I hoped was an airy tone. "Can I get you a coffee?"

"Yes, please. A double espresso."

I walked smugly to the counter amid the dagger-glares, and I had to shake myself. It was really happening. I hadn't found Aoife, but wasn't this the next best thing? I had broken the ice with the only person in the world I knew who also knew her. A tenuous link perhaps… but no, not tenuous. Real. Tangible. Real.

I brought our coffees back and put them on the table. I took off my jacket, and sat down.

"Thank you," she said, taking a sip from her espresso. "I need a coffee." She smiled. I smiled back.

"My name is Hélène," she said, proffering her hand formally.

"Sorry… of course… Aengus. It's, eh, a pleasure…. Hélène." I took her hand and she shook it firmly.

"Aengus," – n-goose – "that is Irish?"

"Yes. Yes it is."

"So, Aengus. You need a model."

I sighed, relieved even to have got to this point, the point where I could relay concrete facts that required little fabrication.

"I do. My father is an artist – he's very good in fact, quite famous in Ireland. And he is putting on an exhibition in a couple of weeks. He's asked me to paint a portrait for the show, but I have only a few weeks to do it. So you can see, I really need to get started."

"What kind of exhibition?"

"It's about women in Ireland, how they have changed as the country has changed, grown up I suppose." I took a breath and risked a lie. "That's why my friend thought Aoife would be a good subject – an Irish woman doing something that Irish women haven't often done."

She nodded slowly.

"But I am not Irish?"

"I know, and that's why I thought you would be such a perfect subject too. You are one of a new breed of women in

Ireland – an immigrant, like so many Irish women in the past, but you have come here, to make a life in this country. The very fact that you are so *not* Irish makes you a perfect study. You represent how women in Ireland – if not Irish women – have changed."

She was silent, staring at me. Her dark eyes were a screen I could not breach. She sipped her coffee.

"And you have done this kind of thing before?"

I sat back and paused.

"No. Not really. I studied art at university, and I've painted and drawn all my life. But never professionally. I've been working as a designer, for a marketing company, but I left that job a few months ago, to go back to art for art's sake. I'm lucky to have this chance."

"So what would it mean? You would need me every day? For how many hours? And for how many weeks?"

"I don't know really. I suppose it depends on what you can do, on how much time you can spare?"

"I'm free in the morning, most days."

"You don't work, in the day I mean?" I asked, waving a reference to her business suit and office-attire.

"This? Oh, no," she looked down at her pin-stripe jacket and skirt and smiled. "I had an interview today, to be a secretary. I hate offices. I thought maybe you would have a better idea." She sipped her coffee again and smiled from under long eye-lashes.

"I work at night as a musician. I play the violin. Maybe your friend saw me too. But he chose Aoife," she smiled a soft reprimand. "So I am free in the morning. Perhaps."

"I'm really sorry you missed your interview. I'm sorry, but to be honest I'm really glad. I hope you think it was worth missing it too?"

"Well, I have to find a job and now I have missed my interview. I hope you will have a good offer!"

I had expected this to be so difficult, to be painful, excruciating. I had feared flat rejection, ridicule even. And yet here I was, joking and being gently teased, feeling lighter than I had since… since I couldn't remember. Though I could barely process it, the girl sitting across from me had shared a life or part of a life with Aoife. I was desperate to ask her the questions I had hoarded for so long. What does she look like? Is she happy? Is she loved? Does she love dogs and is she afraid of the dark and does she always mispronounce "remuneration"? Does she giggle like her mother?

But I dammed that torrent. Now was not the time. I dared not startle her and frighten her away.

"OK. How about this," I tried to adopt a business-like tone. "We work from 9am to 1pm Monday to Friday. I need a couple of days to get some supplies and set up the studio, so can we start in two days? For three weeks. To start with."

"And how much will you pay me?"

I had no idea.

"I… don't know."

She looked at me.

"You don't know?"

"Not really. How much did the secretarial job pay?"

"Twenty Euros an hour."

"So how about forty Euros an hour." The going rate for a five-year-old Malahide guide.

"Fifty."

She could have asked one hundred.

"OK."

"Done," she smiled her bewitching smile and held out her hand.

"Done," I grinned back and we shook to close the deal.

Activity impersonates progress. Sometimes you are entirely unaware. Sometimes you recognise the deception, but being busy begets optimism. But activity – even treading water –

requires energy. It wears you down, leaves you exhausted so that you can no longer maintain the illusion. The screen drops and the full extent of the deceit emerges – the grail remains as far away as it ever was. My reality had perhaps not been so bleak – the database had led me to Paris, Paris to Malahide, Malahide to Hélène. The illusion of progress, however, had been abruptly shattered that first morning I visited the house in Malahide.

But like a pawn's opening move, meeting Hélène that second time in the Crock of Gold had propelled me forward two squares on the board. Maybe the wee boy playing on the step had been a worldly manifestation of my bearded elf, sent to guide me safely to the end of my rainbow. I felt a new energy surge inside me and a renewed, or perhaps entirely new, optimism. It took me a step closer to Aoife – not only closer, but it allowed me to pass for the first time into her world. And it wasn't only that. Almost in spite of myself, I was now committed to the creative process. For how many years had I searched in vain for a vehicle to make real what I felt compelled to express? But I had never known how. And as so often, I had found what I was searching for where I wasn't even looking.

CHAPTER 11

Injected with a new impetus, I went back to Howth and set about making preparations with a fervour I thought lost. Even Lochlann's guarded responses when I looked for advice and counsel failed to douse the fire, fanned the flames in fact. And so the following morning, I padded down the stairs in a silent house once again to the kitchen, made a coffee and some toast, and brought them to the gallery and my studio. I liked the sound of that. My studio.

I sat at the huge desk, leaned back and looked around the little room. Without the Master and Lochlann and Oran, it was quiet, only the gentle breeze in the poplars outside for a soundtrack. It was early, before Oran and the other tradesmen had arrived – or failed to arrive as was more likely to be the case – and I had a chance for the first time to really think about the piece of work on which I was about to embark.

I knew my work could not bear comparison with Lochlann's. It wasn't just his experience, it was his raw, natural ability. It was the way one of his paintings struck you the first time you saw it. If you never knew the theme of one of his pieces, you would understand it immediately it was unveiled before you. You might not be able to immediately articulate or explain it, but deep inside you would understand because his work touched people on an almost subliminal level.

It was clear that if I stood toe to toe with him, I would be knocked down. If I tried to tell the same story, to deliver the same message, my work would fade into the background. And that was if he even deigned to show it. I had to tell the same story, but from a new angle. Lochlann's theme was the evolving nature of Irish womanhood, how Irish women have grown in strength and influence over his lifetime. How much more prominent a role they play in society than in the generation of his mother and grandmother.

If that was his message, then mine would be its corollary. It was Hélène's dark eyes that sparked the thought, the lost melancholy that first time on her front step – soon dispelled but unmistakeable. A strong, able young woman, yet cowed perhaps by a strange city and its forthright people. And perhaps especially by its strong women. Thousands of Irish women had made the same journey to England and America and Australia, to live in awe and a certain fear of those who seemed so confident, so at ease in their home towns and cities. And those Irish women had rarely made the journey alone, they had gone with their men and had been protected by them. Or terrorised by them? Today's immigrant women were as likely to travel alone.

Of course I knew so little about Hélène. Her pathos might have flowed from an entirely different source, she might well have arrived in Ireland with a boyfriend, husband even for all I knew. But for the thousands of immigrant women who had made their way to Ireland from Eastern Europe and Asia and from nearer shores, this new Dublin must be an uncomfortable place. And Hélène's eyes told me at least their stories.

And what of Ireland's new class of strong, dominant women? Were they too consumed with their new-found status and role to recognise the cries for help, to comfort and welcome the new members of their sisterhood. Were they as guilty as the women of London and New York before them, who cast a cold eye on the immigrant classes and even imposed a new hierarchy to keep them in their place?

That would be my message to Irish women – now that you have assumed your rightful place in Irish society, have you the time and the kindness of spirit to help those who, like your mothers and grandmothers, remain in its shadows?

I could see the image in my head. Hélène sitting in a chair leaning forward, her elbows resting on her knees, her head tilted slightly back so that her eyes stare at you. Eyes filled with the lost melancholy I had witnessed that first day. Her left hand holds a violin by its neck, the right a bow. The symbols of her skill and craft, symbolising the ability and talent which have so far been unable to save her. And her eyes ask for you to help. With these newcomers, the evolution of Irish womanhood turns full circle.

Although I scarcely dared acknowledge it, the portrait opened a new chapter, provided me with a whole new direction. Unlike my job, I felt released and free to chase ideas without the constraints of client engagement and commercial success. Unlike the search for Aoife, it was a tangible goal that, if I applied myself, I could realistically attain. Oh, I knew that Lochlann would probably choose not to include it in the show, and I knew that I would struggle to complete it in time. But in my mind it was a beautiful thing and it spoke on my behalf.

It was, I suppose, the first time in a long time that I had had a spark of passion in my belly. And it made raw and stark the absence of the one person who would have rejoiced in sharing it with me. Caitríona would have been so enthusiastic, so opinionated even! We would have spent hours arguing and debating. She would have asked if I was trying to tarnish the blossoming of Irish women with an accusation of cold, harsh dispassion for those less fortunate? Was I trying to drag women back into the dark days? Was I suggesting that men had no role to play in welcoming strangers? But whatever my decision, whatever message I chose to deliver, I know she would have supported and helped me. And she would have been proud of me. So often, she had encouraged me to break out of corporate life, to give into the yearning to create. And here I was.

I know she would have been pleased that I had finally taken up the challenge. My ulterior motive might not have pleased her so much.

The din of crashing metal from the gallery and the volley of expletives that followed announced Oran's arrival. After a moment's hesitation, I got up to go see if I could help mitigate this morning's disaster. From the door between the studio and the gallery, I could see him stare dumbstruck at his toolbox handle, which had somehow worked itself free of the rest of the toolbox, dropping the box and spilling its contents all over the floor. The dumbstruck phase lasted only a brief moment and gave way to a further salvo.

"Fuckin' stupid bastard of a thing, useless fuckin' stupid bastardin' bollix," he shouted at the handle, which he then threw violently at the pile of tools. "Fucker!"

He sensed I was there and swung around.

"How's it goin'," he said, not at all embarrassed at what I had witnessed. "Fuckin' handle broke, useless piece of feckin' shite!"

"I gathered," I replied, trying to suppress a smile. It was not the time for humour, especially given how our reunion had worked out yesterday. "Listen, I'm just going to make a coffee. You look like you could use one?"

"Yeah. Yeah, I could use one alright."

"Grand. I'll be back in a minute then."

I dallied over the coffee to give him time to cool down, then made my way back to the Gallery.

"Here we go," I said, putting the tray down on the desk in the studio. "I made some toast as well, I'm starving. Help yourself."

The tools were back in the box, and he had at least stopped swearing. He came into the studio, took a coffee and a slice of toast, and sat down on the low sill under one of the two floor-to-ceiling windows that took up almost all of one of the studio's external walls.

"You're in early," he said, as though surprised to see me this side of noon.

"Wanted to make a start, I suppose. Not much time until the opening, I need to get stuck in if I'm going to have any chance of getting this thing done."

"So you're goin' to do it? The portrait I mean?"

"Yes. Look, I don't know if it'll be good enough or if I'll get it finished in time or if I'll even get it started. But I have to try at least."

"Or the Master'll give me a clip round the ear!" I added with a rueful smile.

He grinned. "You wouldn't want to cross Críostóir, that's for sure."

He stared into his coffee for a moment, then looked up at me.

"So have you done this before? Exhibited, I mean."

I shook my head. "Never. No idea what I'm doing, to be honest. I've never really created a piece other than for work. Not properly, I mean."

"So what are you going to do?"

I told him my initial thoughts. He raised his eyebrows a fraction and nodded slowly.

"Sounds like you've got it sorted in your head anyway. Sounds good." From Oran, lavish praise.

"An idea's one thing. You can't hang an idea."

"So who's going to be the model? Have you someone in mind?"

I hesitated, trying to get my story straight.

"A friend of mine happened to mention that he had seen someone who he thought would be a good subject, for a project at work. Turned out she had a friend in Dublin. Long

122

story short, I found her and she's agreed to sit for me." It was a story that wouldn't bear even the most superficial scrutiny, but it was the best I could do and it would buy me time. I cursed myself for not having a story prepared, one that rang true and didn't hinge on the unlikeliest coincidences.

"So you'll be working in here then?" he said, looking around the little room. "Bit small."

I followed his gaze. I had spent many a long hour daydreaming through some client presentation or internal meeting of setting up my easel in a place just like this. To me, it was perfect.

"It'll be fine, just needs a bit of straightening out."

He got up from the window sill and paced the length and breadth of the room.

"Hmm. That desk'll have to go."

He was right, and I didn't need a desk that size.

"But I'll need somewhere to sketch and write and... draw, I suppose, when I'm not at the easel."

"There's a small desk in the store-room, we'll bring that in here and move this monstrosity to the store. Come on." He put down his coffee mug and went to the far end of the desk.

He caught me by surprise. "Now?"

"Had you something more pressing that needed your immediate attention?"

I put down my cup and got into position by the desk.

"On three," he said, crouching, "one, two, *three*." He heaved on that last and lifted his end. I heaved at my end, raised it an inch and dropped it to the floor with a thud that echoed through the empty gallery.

"Jesus Christ," I said, my face reddening with the effort. "It weighs a ton."

Oran just grinned. "Will we try that again, miss?"

"I wasn't ready," I protested. "Is it *on* three, or three and *then* heave?"

"On three, yeh gobshite. Now come on – one, two, *three*."

We lifted the huge piece of oak and scraped, bumped and dragged it out of the Gallery and into the adjacent store-room. My eyes widened when Oran turned on the light in the store. It was a veritable treasure trove. The room was a new addition, and my father's old easels and palettes and brushes and unfinished canvases were piled, stacked and filed neatly on shelves and hooks and racks. Some I recognised. An unfinished oil of a young football fan holding his father's hand among the crowds making their way out of Croke Park caught my eye. He had been working on it when I was born, when my mother died. He could never finish it, but equally he could never throw it away.

"I could find everything I need in here," I said. "I was going to go down to the supplies shop tomorrow, but sure it's all here. Or most of it anyway."

Oran looked around. "Probably. Just be careful. He knows every single thing that's in here," he said. "If he comes looking for something and you've moved it, there'll be war. You might want to ask him before you take any of it." He pointed a warning finger at me. "Do *not* piss the old man off – he's going to get fuckin' stressed enough about this show as it is without you drivin' him mental."

He spoke with a warmth that surprised me, a warmth that the flippant afterthought sought to disguise. It was not only unlike Oran, it was unlike my father to stoke such affection in others.

We carried the other desk back into the studio and placed it in the middle of the room.

"Where do you want it?" Oran asked.

"In the corner. I'll put the easel and the model's chair by the windows. It's the best light."

We pushed it flush against the wall and stepped back to review our handiwork.

"Thanks, Oran, I appreciate it." I said, and I meant it. "I'd better let you get on, you must have a ton of work to do." I was reluctant to let him go.

"My mammy said I should always help old people if I see them struggling," he said. I was born two days before him, and just as I had used my age as a badge of seniority when we were kids, he never let me forget who the old man was as we grew older. "Listen, I'd murder another coffee. Let's get one in and then I can get cracking."

We went into the kitchen and Oran put on the coffee machine.

"So, how long are you going to be staying for?" he asked.

I paused. "I don't know, to be honest."

As long as it takes to find out where Aoife is – but that wasn't a conversation I was ready to have. I had never shared with him the trials of my college days, and how they had ultimately driven me away. A selfish part of me had always wanted to tell him – confidence in a friend would surely make it all easier. But first it was too soon, then too raw, then we moved away, and the opportunity never presented itself.

"And it's not like I have anywhere to go or anything demanding my presence."

He raised an eyebrow.

"I've packed in the job," I responded to his silent question.

"So what'll you do when you go home?"

"To London? I don't know." I shook my head, then paused for a moment. "It doesn't feel much like home at the minute."

The words hung in the air in front of me, demanding to be acknowledged. I was so struck by the revelation, I said it again. "It doesn't really feel like home."

"But your life is there, your mates, your… life."

But a certain kind of friend is attached to a certain kind of life. They come with it, like a free cushion on a sofa. And they suit the sofa, make it comfortable. They complement a passage of our lives, and we complement theirs – a perfect symbiosis. And it's not that we lie or exploit or mislead – we make that passage of each other's lives better. Nicer. Richer. But we grow up and move on and change the furniture. And the cushion just doesn't work anymore.

And if not by reference to our friends, then how do we position our life, how do we fix its location? What defines its geography? Career? Family? A sense of empathy for a place and its people?

Another conversation for which I was unprepared, and so I deflected it with a shrug. "Yeah I know. I just need to sort myself out I suppose."

The coffee machine pinged and saved me further introspection.

"How about you? What are you up to these days?" It was sad, I thought, how little we knew of each other's lives.

He poured the coffee, looked at me for a moment and seemed to reach a conclusion.

"That, now, is a bit of a *scéal*," he said, "but everyone knows it around here, so you might as well hear it from me." And so he began slowly to tell me the story.

It's all too easy, in the midst of our own personal crises and dramas, to assume that the lives of others are serenely unaffected by misfortune and mishap. It's only natural. Like the duck in the park pond, most of our struggles go unseen. I was, I suppose in hindsight, sublimely oblivious to the tribulations of others, even those closest to me. Often the misplaced assumption that others have never suffered serves only to deepen our own despair. The revelation that others know or have known our sadness would be a comfort surely, and yet we perversely choose to make the patently ridiculous assumption that everybody else's life is a bed of rose petals.

Oran's was not. I knew he had worked in the restaurant in Dublin after leaving school, a little family-run Italian. I didn't know that he had discovered there a talent for, and a love of, the culinary arts. He had worked his way up the kitchen hierarchy from general dogsbody to sous-chef to head chef. Oran's family background had not been altogether harmonious. His parents were always either recently split up or just back together. His two older brothers had left to work in England as soon as they could afford the plane fare, and Oran was left essentially to his own devices. Not that he minded. He was just as happy looking after himself and never, as far as I could see, longed for parental intervention. But the lack of a support structure became, for perhaps the first time, an unhappy state when he began to consider his future beyond the little Italian restaurant in which he had learned his trade.

And that was when he had called on my father for advice. Oran and my father had never been especially close, never given to overt affection nor to particular comradeship. But I suppose my father had always displayed an interest in his well-being that I had dismissed as passive politeness. And yet it was to my father that Oran had turned when considering his bold plan – to open a restaurant of his own.

And so, with Lochlann's counsel and guidance, Oran opened The Ketch, a sea-food restaurant in Portmarnock.

"It was brutal," he shook his head, his eyes betraying painful memories. "I just wasn't ready for it. I knew how to cook, and I wasn't bad. I loved that part of it. Designing the dishes, preparing the menus. Loved it. But the rest…"

He looked out the window and, for a brief moment, I had never seen him look so beaten.

"I just couldn't do it, Aengus. What did I know about VAT returns, wages for the staff, cash flow? I hadn't a fucking clue. And so I got deeper and deeper in trouble. Everything started to go wrong. I couldn't afford to source decent stuff, to pay decent staff. It was a shambles. And then…"

He went over to the counter and poured another coffee.

"And then I really screwed up. There's a food critic in town called Alan Joyce. He's a bastard. Bastard. I knew of him from La Bella Cucina, my old boss there had a run in with him a few years ago. Anyway, he came to the Ketch, and he claimed he had a bad meal. Claimed the waiter messed up his order and that the food was a disgrace. The place was nearly full, and he made sure they all knew, called me out of the kitchen and made a huge scene. And then he wrote a review for the *Independent* that made sure the whole fucking world knew. I was a laughing stock. Bookings just dried up. Some of my suppliers were even afraid to be associated with me, stopped taking my phone calls. I couldn't keep it afloat. I had to close it down."

"Jesus, Oran, I'm really sorry. I had no idea." I couldn't quite believe that my friend had been through this whole trauma and I had known none of it. "When was all this?"

"We closed in the Spring. With Valentines night and Patrick's Day and Easter – I thought things would pick up. But it just got worse and worse. I owed suppliers, staff, the revenue. But just when it couldn't get any worse, I made it a whole lot worse. I was in McGrath's one night, having a few pints on my own, when Joyce walked in with a few of his sponger friends, looking for a free dinner. He saw me, and said something to his pals and they all had a good laugh." His lips thinned at the memory, his eyes narrowed. "Something inside me snapped. I went over to him, grabbed him by the front of his jacket, and dragged him out the front door. I shoved him against the wall, and I bashed him."

"Shi-it." The slowly dawning realisation of what he had done caused me to draw out the word. "Christ. What happened?"

He shrugged.

"I just went home. But of course the cops were called and they came round half an hour later. Arrested me, banged me up for the night. Your father bailed me out. I'm up in court in a few weeks."

I didn't know what to say. Oran was robust, quick to argue, slow to back down. But he had never been violent, I had never seen him hit anyone, never seen him fight. But he had been through the mill, and his reaction had been extreme.

"Your father's been a saint, Aengus. Bailed me out, came to court with me, gave me a job. I'd have folded without him."

I nodded. I knew my father was a decent man, I knew he had done good things. Not that he had ever made even the slightest reference to them. Instead, I had learned of them in overheard, hushed conversations in the pub or at the back of the church at mass-time, or from oblique, off-hand remarks from a shopkeeper or a Garda or the local priest. "Tell your father I was asking for him," they might say. Or "Tell your father thanks," with a knowing wink. Or "You're a lucky boy, he's a good man your father." These compliments drifted over my young head, I was oblivious to his generosity.

Oran snorted a wry laugh. "Funny isn't it? After all these years, after all the plans we made and the dreams we had, we never thought the two of us would be here at forty and still sponging off your old man!"

We both laughed, relieved that the tension had been broken.

"So what now?" I said, stupidly.

"Don't know, Aengus. Just wait for the trial, that's all I can do."

"You have a decent solicitor?"

"He's not really interested to be honest, just going through the motions. We both know I'm going down. The only question is how long for."

"They won't send you to jail surely, not for a first offence?"

"You should have heard Joyce's brief in court. You'd think I'd nutted Mother Teresa. 'A decent man assaulted for simply going about his business and doing his job'. My arse. Assaulted for being a prick."

I was struck mostly by the manner in which he handled himself. Dashed dreams, a sense of injustice, likely incarceration – one of those would be enough to destroy a normal person. And yet he continued to display his own brand of abrasive dignity and loyalty, compassion even.

Once, when we were children playing in Lochlann's orchard, I fell out of an old apple tree and hurt my arm. I started to cry but Oran gruffly silenced my sobs, dismissing my pain and mocking my weakness. I got up and the game went on. It was only that night, when my sobbing woke the childminder, that the doctor was called. I had broken a bone – only a little bone, but it was broken nonetheless. I was taken to the Accident and Emergency Department and proudly wore my cast for three or four weeks. Oran now displayed the same phlegmatic disdain for his own predicament as he had demanded from me in mine.

I was struck also, inevitably, by my own father's reaction. No doubt the Master was party to the whole affair, and little wonder that he held Lochlann in such high regard. But why, then, had Lochlann chosen to take so detached a role when I needed him? Was my crime less noble, less deserving? Did I need him less? I was torn between being proud of him, and being bitter that I had enjoyed none of the succour he had given Oran. I felt guilty for bearing a twenty year-old grudge, but there it was.

"Come on," he got up from the table. "That's enough whining for one day."

We walked back to the Gallery. The workmen had arrived and were busy enjoying a cigarette by the Gallery door.

"Fuck sake, lads," Oran protested to them, "were you boys thinking of doing any work today? Or do youse just want to fuck off home and I'll do it myself?"

I went into the studio and sat down at my new desk. The sound of his rant followed me through the door.

130

CHAPTER 12

T hat's your day.

She was from Canada, my second year tutor with the steel blue eyes and a stare as cold as the plains of the frozen Yukon. And an unquenchable passion for the naked, raw beauty of art. Fire and ice. I went to see her as usual on a Monday afternoon. I was angry. Angry and frustrated. I had spent all of the previous day and night trying to finish an assignment that would not be finished, could not. A simple assignment, an urban landscape in pencil.

There was a tree in a quiet corner of the campus, near the lake, surrounded by concrete and steel. Like an old man who refuses to move out of his old house when the developers move in, it stood defiant. Age had bent its back, gnarled its fingers, thinned its thatch. But still it stood, alone and incongruous, resisting the urban spread.

I went there in the morning. It was Sunday. The place was still sleeping off its hangover. It was quiet and peaceful. I sat on a bench and sketched. All day. And into the evening until I couldn't see it anymore. But I could capture neither its spirit nor its dignity.

And so I knocked on her Monday afternoon door, empty sketch book in hand, only the tattered remnants of ripped out pages to show for my weekend's efforts. Tired, angry and beaten. I vented my frustration and she sat, impassive, watching me and listening. On I went, bemoaning all the myriad obstacles that stifled my inspiration, obscured my vision. She listened and said nothing. I finished my rant and still she was silent. For – it must have been – five minutes, we sat staring at each other. Then she spoke.

"Every day, life changes the rules. Get over it. She'll make a nonsense of the plans you made and the road you chose. That's your day. You choose to be here, you choose to learn how to create the beautiful, the inspiring, the uplifting. You choose to do what others can only dream of doing. It's not supposed to be easy. Things will go wrong. You will be challenged. You will be frustrated. But you will learn not to despair. You will learn how to overcome, because that is to excel. Whatever goes wrong, whatever is sent to block you, that's your day. It's up to you to find what it is in every day that inspires you. Then discard the rest. Learn from it, then discard it. We just never learn that when a day is over, it's gone, dead. And in every day is something you will cherish and want to live over and over again. But you can't. So make the most of it before it slips away."

God, how you hated whinging! Your naturally short fuse was further frayed by the moaning you heard around you every day.

"I know life is frantic, and the pressure is relentless, and it's sometimes grey and cold and damp," you used to say, a hand pressed against your exasperated forehead after another evening of gloomy doom-mongering. "I know all that. But we have money and friends and food and fun... does everybody really have to be so bloody miserable? Do they have to complain all the bloody time?"

If you don't like it, you better change it before you've pissed your life away. That's what you used to say.

You'd have been proud of Oran today. You never knew him as well as you should have. That was my fault. The two of you were uneasy with other, mistrusting almost. To you he was unfriendly, unwelcoming, resentful. In his eyes you were opinionated and pompous. I wish you could really have known him. I wish that he had known you, I could share you with him now that you're gone.

He's no longer a little boy, scratched and bloodied and bruised after a fall. He's not a child who's lost a toy or broken a treasured plaything. Now he's a man, but he's the same. Life has made a gratuitous and unprovoked nonsense of his plans. But he's still the same. Still unbowed, defiant.

Like that old tree by the lake.

If you don't like it, change it, you said. But what if I can't change it? What if I don't like it, but it's all there is? What if all of the alternatives are just as bleak, just as hopeless? Because none of them have you. Do you shake your head when you see me give in, despair of me and my despair? What would you have me do then? How do I move on?

When you were with me, everything else was incidental. We kept all of the drama and all of the crises of modern life in a cupboard, a cupboard we carefully locked every night. Our problems and the turmoil they spawned were just one small part of our world, never the dominant force. We never allowed them to take over, to consume what we loved and cherished. And unnourished by our disinterest and neglect, they never had the strength to blow us off course.

We were strong and calm. That was our day.

CHAPTER 13

It was the first time in a very long time that my fitful sleep had been a result of a sort of latent excitement and not of tormenting thoughts that refused to be banished. And so I got up with the cloud-covered sun and ran on the Head. The early morning cold defied the season. So little distance separates London and Dublin, so why is it that Dublin always feels so much colder? Do we strip the west wind of its chill before it reaches the British shore? Climbing back towards the house again, I stopped at an old bench looking over the Baily and started to stretch out my stiff muscles. On a clear day, they say, you can see Mount Snowdon from Howth Head. The soaking mist that hung in the breathless air ensured it stayed hidden from view.

I looked past the lighthouse towards the unseen Welsh coast, and beyond that unseen Snowdon, unseen England and, deep in her bosom, London. And my home. Only months before, that's what London had been to me – my home. The home we shared and the life we had built together. From those grim, bare days in Dublin we had somehow fashioned a life that would have seemed impossible, fantastical. We worked in jobs that, if they failed to inspire us, then at least were tolerable. We endured the mindless trudge from Monday morning to Friday evening because that is what you do. Along the way, we found islands of relief in Tuesday evening dinners or Thursday night sessions in the pub. And they steered us safely through the traffic and the bills and the long days to Friday night and the sanctuary of the weekend.

Ah, the weekends. How we cherished those days. We sucked out of Europe all it had to offer, from Paris and Florence and Barcelona to Istanbul's Asian frontier, the Croatian coast and the frozen snowscapes of Scandinavia. Or we eloped to those isolated gems in Britain's jewellery box: Devon's moors and Cornwall's coast and Yorkshire's dales. In Winter we skied the Alps and the Pyrenees, and in Summer we took holiday homes in the California winelands or the Canadian outback. It was a time to experience new and exciting worlds, to inhale them and to draw inspiration from them. We bought the world's beauty, put it in a bag and brought it home, where we stole furtive glances in that other Monday-to-Friday world. The weekends and holidays that burst at the seams with impossible plans and ended all too soon, and emptied us again into Monday morning.

And carried along by our zest for discovery and experience, we never questioned the unfulfilling banality and covert tensions of that humdrum world. We might never have admired the emperor's new suit, but it blinded us to his nudity. The camaraderie of the afflicted bound us and made us somehow content. And I suppose we were content, with our legion of friends and colleagues who were really strangers. And our world carefully hid from us the startling truth that these were strangers whom, if we looked closely, we would not recognise. Because no matter how many times we had dinner together or visited their homes, we never truly got to know them in the brief liaisons that those abbreviated evenings afforded us. They were nice people, good people in whose company I revelled and who entertained and interested and amused me – but they remained benign strangers nonetheless.

I stretched the lactate out of my aching muscles. Somewhere below me out in the bay, the Leinster sat under twenty metres of water. At school, the Master had taught us the stories of the ships that had been lost off Dublin's shores. The Leinster was the one that captured my imagination. She and her three sister ships, each named after a province, were owned by the City of Dublin Steampacket Company, and carried passengers and mail between Dublin and Wales. It was October 1918. The mutinous and wounded German submarine fleet had taken to picking off the easy targets in the Irish Sea, who sailed without the naval protection of the Atlantic merchant navy. As the Leinster began its familiar journey from Kingstown to Holyhead in heavy seas that day, they could not have known that the battered German leadership had already sent a message to the Americans asking for peace. They could not have known that the war had only weeks to run. They had no sense of the catastrophic irony that placed them in the path of a lone hunter u-boat. Some of the 700 passengers on board, many of them troops heading to England and the front, saw the first torpedo as it waked past their bow. The second hit the port side, the postal sorting room. The captain tried to turn back to Kingstown, but a third hit the starboard side while the crew deployed lifeboats and tended to the injured. To be so near safety and yet so doomed.

Doomed and forgotten. It served neither the leaders of Ireland's struggle for freedom nor the British still chastened by that rebellion to remember that Irish soldiers fought and died alongside the British, Americans and Canadians in French poppy fields. And so the names of many of those who died that October night in the Irish Sea were consigned to the record archives and conveniently forgotten. Forgotten lest the truth should embarrass or obstruct or deflect the chosen course.

Conveniently filed away and forgotten, until it became more convenient to remember. The mist lightened and lifted its shroud from the sea below. What would my reaction have been if Aoife had found it opportune, convenient to remember us? Before we were ready? How would that have deflected us? If she had chosen to introduce herself into our world, to obstruct our path to wherever it was we were going? I remember my reaction to the Adoption Agency letter that my father had forwarded to us, when I thought she had come looking for us and found us. I was excited and thrilled in that first instant before I realised the truth. But if it had been really so, really Aoife, how would I have felt as the realisation dawned and all of the implications became clear? Because when I had imagined meeting her and seeing her and talking to her, it was in romantic soft focus. The crystallisation of responsibilities, pleading justification for what we had done and what we had gone on to do, maybe even coming to terms with who and what our baby had grown into could be, in reality, a much harsher truth.

The nervous couple in the nun's office not daring to hope, holding on tight to each other's hands when we met them, assured us that they would never hide Aoife's adoption from her, that they would be open with her from the outset. And so I had always assumed that she grew up knowing her heritage. Of course they may never have told her, left her to discover it by accident. Filling out a passport application form or applying for university, perhaps. They had promised also not to change her name. Caitríona had been adamant. It was the one thing we could leave her. At least I knew they had kept that promise.

I walked back up the path to the house. In the Summit car park to my right, someone was trying to start a car. The motor coughed like a smoker but refused to start. A car door opened and slammed shut, and a woman's voice swore in exasperation. From inside the car I could hear a child crying. I looked at my watch – still a couple of hours before Hélène was due to arrive. I walked over and into the car park. The woman had her back to me and was stabbing frantically at the keys on her mobile phone.

"Sounds like a flat battery," I said.

"I'd figured that out, thanks," she said, still stabbing at her phone. "Aargh, answer for God's sake," she growled under her breath.

She turned around, looking sheepish.

"I'm sorry," she said, her hand to her brow. "That was very rude. Yes, I think it's the battery. And I need to get this fella to school." She nodded to the sobbing child in the car.

Then she stopped and stared at me for a moment.

"Aengus? Is it you?" she said.

"Niamh?" In another life, in another world, she had been my girlfriend. My first real girlfriend. I was, I suppose, fifteen or sixteen, and in the summer holidays before my last year at school, we had been in the same crowd of hormone-fuelled teenagers looking for something to do in Howth. She hadn't really changed. A few flecks of grey in her hair, a few more lines around her face, but the same eyes. The same bright, open, kind eyes. Niamh was always the quiet one in our gang, the sensible one. The last to take a self-conscious sip from the cider bottle as it was passed around, the girl least likely to steal a box of fags from the newsagent or to leave her mark in graffiti on the DART station wall. She was in my class all through primary school, and we had been friends forever. And as friends, we had never really known how to be more, how to be boyfriend and girlfriend. I remember our physical encounters as embarrassed and awkward experimentation. We had never actually broken up, we just stopped kissing.

"Jesus, how are ya'?" she smiled and hugged me. "When did you get home?"

Funny how those who never left assume it's still your home too, like it was only a matter of time before you saw sense and came back to where you knew you belonged.

"A few days ago. You're looking well."

"Thanks," she blushed. "So are you."

The little boy's sobs grew louder and she looked at her watch.

"God, I'm going to be late for work."

"Come on, I'll give you a push."

"Are you sure? Do you think it'll start?"

I shrugged. "I have no idea, but we'll know in a few minutes and then if it doesn't work we'll go to plan B."

"What's plan B?"

"I still have a few minutes to figure that out! Come on, get in." I opened the driver's door and she climbed in.

"Now," I said, trying to remember. "Take off the handbrake, put it in first gear – no, second gear – and put your foot on the clutch. Oh, and half turn on the ignition, only halfway now. Then as soon as we get rolling, let the clutch out and it should start."

"Will it work?" she asked doubtfully.

"It'll be a miracle," I shrugged, in a poor impersonation of Billy Crystal's miracle-worker from the cult movie of our teens. "But if it does, just keep going and don't stall it. And go straight to the garage down in the village."

"Off you go then, Max," she grinned, and pulled the door closed.

The car park was empty and we had a clear run to the road. With the help of the slight downslope I got the car moving.

"Now," I screamed as we got up to speed. She let out the clutch, the car jerked and then spluttered to life. The engine roared as she revved it hard. Through the back window I saw her waving. I waved back, and she was gone.

I turned and walked slowly towards the house. The longer I spent in Howth, the more my two worlds would inevitably merge. You often imagine that the world you left behind hasn't changed. In your head, its inhabitants stop ageing, like some banal Tír na nÓg. In your condescending mind, they continue to do the same things and remain beset with the same problems that populated your world. Like you were the fuel that powered them. But Oran had opened a restaurant and assaulted a critic, and Niamh had a little boy in tow. Without my permission or agreement, for better and for worse, they had moved on.

I got back to the house and went into the kitchen to make some coffee.

"Well aren't you the early bird! God bless us and save us, Aengus out of bed and it still morning? Wonders'll never cease!" Pauline came bustling and beaming into the kitchen behind me and tousled my hair. "What has you up so bright and breezy?"

"I just couldn't sleep, Pauline, to be honest. I'm starting work on the portrait today and, frankly, I'm shitting myself."

"You mind your language, young man," she said with mock horror. "You're not too big yet for a clip round the ear!"

The coffee machine pinged and she poured a mug for me and made some tea for herself.

"What are you going to do?"

"I don't know. I mean, I have some ideas, but they're just ideas. And I have someone to sit for me, someone who was recommended to me. And that's about as far as I've got."

"Well, himself is around for most of the day, most of the morning anyway. Why don't you sit down with him and tell him what you're thinking. He's done this before you know, might have an idea or two," she smiled.

I smiled back.

"What could he possibly have to tell a man of my experience? But just to please you, I'll do it. I'll humour him."

I paused to drink some coffee.

"Oran told me what happened," I said, changing the subject. "Is he alright, do you think?"

Pauline shook her head.

"Shocking business. God love him, he's got himself in a right mess. Your father's looking after him, but sure what can he do?" Her expression lifted, some of the darkness faded. "You know, it's just what he needs, having you home. Your father's been a great help to him, Críostóir as well. But he needs someone his own age, someone he can trust and let off a bit of steam to."

"Well, he's done that," I grinned.

"I suppose he has!" she smiled a rueful smile. "But keep an eye on him though, Aengus. Make sure he's alright. He's a closed book, that one. He might open up to you more than he would to the likes of us."

I looked at my watch. "I better get a move on," I said. "I need to give Lochlann a few tips for this show."

I winked at her and went up to take a shower, and to mentally prepare for what the day might hold.

An hour or so later and I was sitting at the small desk in the studio, coffee in hand. Hélène would soon be here, and I still hadn't made the most basic decision – the medium in which I would work. It was a mark of my amateurism that I had no particular strength in any – passably adept in each, exceptional in none. I had not had the kind of childhood where smudged schoolwork watercolours or lurid potato-stamps were hung proudly on the fridge door. Such exhibitions were rarely humiliating at nine years old. How vulnerable the adult son in the same position.

Of course I wanted to work in oils. Lochlann had always worked in oils. In his view, it was the only medium of the master, all others being the hiding place of the amateur. But I had no time to dredge up from the distant past some long-dormant experience, and the stark fact remained that an oil canvas would never be dry in time to hang at the exhibition. Acrylics were more practical given the time frames in which I had to work, more manageable and more straightforward. But also unforgiving in their own way – faster to dry but therefore also easier to make permanent a blemish. They demanded that every stroke was true and tolerated no mistakes, no change of mind to follow a change of light or mood. And I hadn't worked in acrylics for so long. My technique could not have held up during the barren, corporate years, and I just didn't have the time to rekindle it with the patience it would require. And even if I could somehow craft a work of passable quality, it would be simply outclassed, overshadowed, disregarded perhaps in the midst of Lochlann's work.

I had never worked in pastels or watercolours and had no real interest in either. Which left me effectively back where I started.

"Pauline said you were looking for me." I looked up to see Lochlann standing in the doorway. His voice was tinged with a faint impatience that he tried to hide but that seeped out with his words.

"Em, no. No, not really," I said, uncertainly, feeling caught out, not sure what to say. "How are you?"

"Fine, thank you. Fine. She must have been mistaken. Well, we'll see you later no doubt." He half-waved his hand and turned to leave.

I stood up from the desk.

"Actually, Lochlann, there is something you could help me with. If you have a moment?"

He turned back towards me and raised an eyebrow.

"I'm battling with this portrait a bit," I said, trying to exude the nonchalant calmness that eluded me, as though I had only a couple of minor questions to resolve. But my mouth betrayed me. "I'm not sure where to start to be honest."

My voice was pleading in spite of my determination to appear in control,

He hesitated, looked curious.

"How do you mean?"

"Well, it's daft really, but... I don't know what to do. I mean, I can picture what I want to do, I really can. And I know what I want my message to be, what I want to say." In spite of myself, I found myself blurting the very weaknesses I was desperate to hide from him. "But what format should it all take? I don't have enough time for oils, I haven't painted in acrylics for ten years." I looked at him. "And I don't want to produce some piece of amateur crap that you might feel bound to show."

His face, usually a screen for the thoughts in his head, couldn't hide tumbling emotions as he stared back at me through narrowed eyes. Vexation begat irritation which gave way to frustration which in turn gave way to his irrepressible urge to contribute. I always thought my father should have been a teacher. Perhaps that's why he and the Master were such firm friends.

He sighed.

"I fear you're starting from the wrong place," he said. "You're basing your decision on what you think others might think of the outcome. Do what your heart tells you, go where your passion lies. Do what you want to do and what you can do, not what you think others expect."

I stared back blankly, and so he went on.

"You have always expressed yourself most eloquently in a medium where expression is perhaps most difficult. And I suspect that medium is the most closely associated with the work you have been doing in London, however sanitised that might have been."

I desperately wanted to trump his conclusion with my own Eureka, but the waters were too murky, the maze too intricate. I waited for the finale.

He shook his head like one who has given every reasonable clue but cannot draw out the blindingly obvious answer.

"Pencil, Aengus, pencil," his outstretched arms and upturned palms betrayed his exasperation. "Coloured if you want to. You have time to experiment, you can easily correct and amend. You could even work on a series. And there would be nothing else comparable on show. You would have your own stage. If that indeed is what you want."

I tried to take it in. Not so much his ideas, but the fact that he had given it such thought.

"You've got it all figured out," I quipped and immediately regretted the attempted levity. "I mean, you... you..." I shrugged. "You've thought about it."

He smiled, then quickly recovered. "Of course."

"Pencil?"

"Yes. I think it is an appropriate compromise of experience and skill."

He was right, of course. Pencil had always allowed me to depict emotion starkly and without the complication of paints. Simple and raw. And in the world of graphic design, pencil-based outlines or their computer-generated equivalents were the basis for everything.

He turned to the door and waved me to follow. He walked out of the Gallery and to the storeroom door. Pulling a set of keys from his pocket, he opened the door and switched on the light inside. I followed him inside. The room developed a different atmosphere, took on a different personality in his presence. What had been a melée of junk and bric-a-brac seemed to stand to attention under his gaze.

"Here," he said, pointing to a pile of materials stacked on a desk. "This should get you started. And if you need anything else, just go down to Johnny Wright's. Johnny will be able to find anything you might want."

Had the neatly arranged pile of paper, pencils, erasers and charcoals been there the day before, when Oran and I had been moving the great old desk? I couldn't remember. I picked up a box of pencils. Turning to him, I asked "You had all these? I didn't think you ever worked in pencil."

"I sometimes work in everything," he said, stooping intently to brush some invisible dust from a box of brush cleaner. "It was just good fortune, I suppose, that we happened to have so much of what you might need."

"Yes," I said slowly, "I suppose so."

Lochlann left to meet a client for lunch, and I set to moving my new stock from the store to the studio. Slowly, what had been an empty shell two days before, began to take shape, to look more like how I had always pictured "my studio". On the little desk in the corner I arranged the pencils and the charcoals and the erasers, and behind it I put a little swivel chair I had found in the store. After two or three attempts, I finally settled on a resting place for the easel, at an angle to the tall window at the back of the room. I had also found, amid Lochlann's props, a high-backed chair carved in a dark wood, maybe teak or mahogany. I swept the stone floor and beat the old rug until its pattern emerged from under months or even years of dust.

A flustered Pauline came bustling through the door.

"You have a visitor," she said, as though she had just had a Marian apparition. "A young woman." She leaned forward and lowered her voice. "French, I think," she said as though Howth had never before seen the like.

"Hélène?"

"Yes. Yes, I think so. She's in the reception room."

"Thanks, Pauline. I'll go and get her."

We walked back towards the house.

"Lochlann was in," I said, with an accusing smile and a knowing tilt of the head.

"Oh?" she replied. "That's good. I'm glad."

"And you had nothing to do with it?"

"No," she said. "Why do you say that?"

"Because he said you told him I was looking for him."

"No, I haven't seen him yet this morning." She shook her head, looking genuinely puzzled. "You must have heard him wrong."

"Er, yes. I suppose I must have."

We walked back to the house in silence, and went to the reception room where agents and clients and journalists were made to wait. She was reading a magazine, flicking the pages impatiently as though looking for a promised truth that she

145

could not find. She wore a blue linen shirt and a black skirt to just below her knees. Her nut-brown legs were bare.

"Here he is, love," Pauline said, reaching down to touch Hélène's arm. "Are you alright now?" she asked softly, her voice echoing with the maternal concern that I knew so well from my childhood.

Hélène smiled up at her and nodded.

"Yes, thank you," she said, "I am fine now. Thank you again, you are very kind."

Pauline squeezed her arm and smiled.

"Not a bit of it. If you need anything else, himself'll know where to find me." She nodded her head to me, and made her way back upstairs.

"Hello," she said to me when Pauline was gone. She gestured down to her shirt and skirt. "I was not sure what to wear? This is ok?"

"It's fine, Hélène," I said, "we won't be doing any sketching today. Just getting set up and working out what we're going to do. Listen, are you alright? Is everything ok?"

She nodded with a slightly embarrassed smile. "I am fine, really. I just didn't feel too good on the bus, but that lady gave me some water and a tablet. She is very nice."

"Pauline? She is, and you'll be seeing plenty of her! Come on, let's go into the studio. Can I get you a coffee or some tea?"

She nodded a touch too vigorously. "Yes. A coffee. Please."

"Me too. Let's get the pot going."

We exchanged nervous small-talk while the machine gurgled.

"The house, it is beautiful," she said. "You grew up here?"

"I suppose so," I said, "a very long time ago. But I was sent away to school when I was twelve and then I went to university and then to London, so it's been a long time since I really lived here."

"Why would you leave this," she asked with a bewildered shake of her head, " to go to London?"

"It's a very long story," I said.

"Maybe you will tell me some time," she said from under her eyelashes with a sly smile.

"Maybe."

We brought our coffees into the studio. I half-spun around and waved my arm extravagantly around the little room. I hoped my air exuded a confidence that would hide my insecurity.

"And this," I said, "will be our home. From now until we have a portrait that does you justice and impresses my father. Neither of which will be easy."

She ignored the compliment and looked around.

"Nice," she said, nodding her head. "It's nice. Cosy."

I followed her gaze around the room. "I hadn't thought about it that way," I said, nodding slowly, "but I suppose it is, yes."

I gestured to the chair. "Please, have a seat."

"So," she said, "how will this work?"

I walked over to the desk and pulled the little swivel chair over middle of the room, closer to her.

I hesitated, then shrugged. "You know what – I'm not really sure. We're kind of going to make it up as we go along, I suppose. But we still have a few weeks."

"Until the exhibition starts?"

"Yes. It goes on for a month, so if the worst comes to the worst, we could add the portrait after the show opens. At least I think we can. I'm not sure what Lochlann would think."

"Your father?"

"Yes."

"And you call him Lochlann?" she furrowed her brow and smiled the question.

I looked at my coffee mug.

"Yes," I said, hesitantly. "We don't have what you would call a traditional relationship."

147

I was used to the reaction of people new to our home. Friends who visited our house, who came from stable, normal families, never quite "got it" when I introduced them for the first time. Either they didn't realise that he was my father, or they thought it was a new-age hippie thing that replaced "father-son" with "equals and friends", or they thought I was being impudent and would get a physical or verbal kicking later. Dublin wasn't ready for our kind of family.

"But you... like each other?" she asked.

"Sure. Of course."

"I looked him up, on the Internet," she said. "He is very famous!"

I smiled. Another reaction to which I had grown accustomed.

"Yes, he is. He's very talented."

When I was young, celebrity had not yet become fashionable in Ireland. Fame was something you kept in a dark room, out of sight. There was, perhaps still is, a secret code in Dublin that prohibited approaching or even acknowledging the presence of a famous writer or actor or musician. As students, we often went to the Queen's Arms in Dalkey. Even in those pre-boom days, Dalkey was monied Dublin, populated by a chic assortment of rock stars and motor racing drivers. We'd often walk into the pub and spy one of their number having a quiet pint with his pals, and would simply nod our heads as we passed and toss a careless greeting. Anything more profuse was simply unacceptable.

And so the weight of my father's reputation was lost on me. I never heard him speak of it, and to my child's mind, the mute, the nodded greetings offered hurriedly by strangers we passed on the street in Howth were just the normal way of things. It wasn't until I reached the Master's class in primary school that his significance began to pierce my consciousness. The Master took it upon himself to gently extol my father's virtues, to remark on a piece in the Irish Times or on a critic's review or on a new commission. Always in private conversations, never in the classroom unless it was directly relevant to our work. And although some of those classroom allusions alerted my classmates to his importance, he occupied a field so far from their world, and even from that of many of their families, that he remained irrelevant. Became even more so. Had he been in charge of the fire station or played football for Dublin, that would have been a different matter. But an artist?

"He's very talented, and this will be an important showing of his work," I said, my voice perhaps betraying my trepidation. "So we better be good!"

She finished her coffee and put her mug on the floor.

"We will be great," she smiled. "What will he do? For the exhibition, I mean."

"I think he's going to use his work over the years to show how Irish women have changed, And there'll be a few new works as well."

"You think?"

"Yeah. We haven't really talked about it yet."

"Perhaps you should?"

I smiled. I was being lectured on art by a twenty-year old violinist, and of course she was right.

"And you will do something different," she continued.

"Yes. I'd like to stake my own claim, establish my own ground."

"I don't understand."

"Sorry. I mean, I don't want to just do what he's doing, more of the same. I can't compete with him, or my work would add nothing to the show. I need to find a way to be relevant but different."

"That's good. That makes sense."

Buoyed by her affirmation, I went on.

"And I want to be different in two ways. First, I want my subject to be different, like I said to you in Malahide. I want to look not so much at new Irish woman but the new woman in Ireland. And second, I need my style to be different."

"What is your style?"

"Lochlann says I should use pencil. It's the least complex, and it's the closest to what I've been doing at work."

"But you don't like it."

I paused, taken aback slightly by her perceptiveness, picking up what I hadn't quite recognised myself.

"Er, no. Not really, no."

Since talking to Lochlann, I hadn't allowed myself to face up to the gremlin lurking behind the curtain, but Hélène's blunt assessment laid it bare. He had clearly given it some thought. He had gone looking for the materials that had miraculously appeared in the storeroom. And his advice was genuine, I had no doubt about that. But maybe he was protecting me. And even himself. Resigned to my inexperience and unproven capabilities, but cajoled by the Master to include my work, maybe this was his damage-limitation solution. That was why he had gone to such lengths. That was why he had dropped by the studio that morning. And despite the undeniable logic of his argument, I couldn't help but feel that it was the safe road to invisible respectability.

"Anyway, I guess he knows best, and it's his show. So pencil it is."

I gestured with a sweep of my hand that the debate, such as it had been, was now over. She nodded as only the French can, at once agreeing and expressing unqualified dissent.

"And what about me?" she asked, "How do you want me to be?"

"Well, I'd really like to make a feature of your music. It's what you bring, almost like your gift to a family you're visiting. And I'd like to..."

I hesitated. I wanted to capture that lost look I had seen in her eyes on the doorstep in Malahide, the fragility, vulnerability.

"When I saw you at your house the first time, you – and please, don't take this the wrong way – you had a look, an almost haunted, fragile look. It was very powerful. And if I can capture it, then this piece will speak."

She looked at me in silence for a few endless moments. Then she smiled.

"Some day you will tell me what that means," she said, quietly. Then she sat up straight and regained her verve.

"So you still haven't told me. How do you want me to be, to sit?"

This was perhaps the only element of the project that I could see clearly in my mind's eye. I leaned forward in the chair, elbows on my knees.

"I'd like you to sit like this, and in your hands will be your violin and bow. I need you to stare straight ahead. And I'd like your hair untied, falling down either side of your face in front of your shoulders. A bit wild." It was clear in my mind, but I wasn't sure if it translated readily into words. "Does that make sense?"

"I think so. Like this?" She slouched forward in the chair.

"Exactly. Perhaps your shoulders a little more hunched, your back not quite so straight. You should look a little lost, a little confused. And your eyes, wide and looking for an answer."

"And what do you want me to wear?"

"A plain white, long sleeved shirt, and a long, black skirt. To the floor. Like a member of an orchestra might wear. Is that ok?"

She nodded. "Yes, I think so. I think I have things like that."

I pointed to the chain around her neck, with the silver cross. "And that would be good too. It's nice, simple."

She lifted her hand to touch it, and nodded.

I was suddenly worried that this was too much, too proscriptive, that she might not be comfortable.

"Look, I don't want to sound like I'm giving orders. You have to be happy too, comfortable I mean. Is that all ok?"

She started to speak, then stopped and drew a deep breath.

"Yes, it's ok. I mean, it's fine. But... you want me to look sad. Why do you want me to look so sad? You think we are sad?"

She could be so disarming, she could strip the wind out of my sails.

"I think maybe we're all looking for something. Searching."

"It sounds like you are."

I didn't know what to say.

"I need a coffee."

CHAPTER 14

The kitchen was my sanctuary. Making coffee gave me an excuse to talk but not to engage in uncomfortable conversation, to look at her but not to get locked into her gaze. If I hadn't found another way, I'd have died from caffeine poisoning and killed her. Hélène had gone wandering in the garden and I could see her from the kitchen window, leaning on an old garden bench, looking out over the Irish Sea.

I brought the two mugs and the pot out into the garden. She didn't hear me approach and she jumped almost imperceptibly when I said her name.

"Here you go, Hélène," I said, handing her the mug and putting the pot down on the bench.

"Thank you."

We stood in silence a few moments, sipping coffee and getting lost in the vista spread out before us.

"It is beautiful," she said, eventually.

I nodded.

"So where are you from, Hélène?" I asked.

"Biarritz," she said, "on the Atlantic coast."

"You must have the ocean in your blood then," I smiled. "A bit wilder than the Irish Sea though, eh?"

"Yes, I suppose so."

"Why did you come to Ireland?"

She looked at me and smiled.

"It's a long story too! And you have to tell me yours first. Why you left this place."

I waved an index finger at her.

"Oh no, I'm not that easy. You need to do a whole lot of sitting before I go there."

She shrugged and laughed the laugh of a child that knows she's been caught but isn't afraid to be caught.

"Touché," she said.

The door to Aoife's story was ajar. I stepped up to it, my senses straining for any sign of trouble on the other side, and gently nudged it further open.

"Seriously though, it'd really help me to understand why you came here," I tried to pick my words, like a parent explaining some sensitive truth to a child. "What was it made you leave your home for a strange place, with a different language and a different culture? It's almost a way of life for the Irish to go to London and America and Australia, but not many French men come here, and I'd say even fewer French women come here alone."

She shrugged again.

"It's no big secret. We came to play music, we wanted to play exciting music, to play for real audiences. When you play the violin, there is nowhere better than Dublin." She smiled.

"We?"

She didn't understand for a moment, then realised that she had recounted in the plural. A cloud of faint annoyance passed over her face.

"Yes. Aoife and me."

And I was in, through the door and in. Aoife might have been who knows how far away, but I was closer to her than I had ever been.

I couldn't trust my face to keep my secret, and so I turned to pick up the pot and fill my mug again. From under eyelids that were focused on the pouring, I stepped carefully on.

"So this Aoife, she's a good friend?"

She didn't answer straightaway, her face took on the look of someone who has asked themselves the same question and hadn't found an answer.

"Yes, I think we are friends. At least, I thought we were."

"But...?"

"I don't know," she said, with a hint of resignation, "some people are hard to predict I think."

I tiptoed forward in my mind, afraid to push too far but desperate to see what lay beyond.

"Did she... let you down?"

Hélène's face darkened, then brightened again as though clouds had been dispersed by a gust of wind.

"We all have dreams," she said finally, her dark eyes fixed on mine intensely, "and we must chase them. Nobody can stop us and nobody should, especially our friends. She has a dream and she is chasing it."

"What is her dream?" I asked, carefully.

"I don't know," she said with an air of finality, clearly unwilling to continue the conversation.

But I couldn't turn back now, and foolishly pressed on.

"Is that why she isn't here, in Malahide?"

"Maybe," she threw up her hands with the frustration of one who has looked for the answers already and found none. "I don't know." She stood up. "Can you tell me where is the toilet please?"

"Er, yes, of course." I pointed into the house. "Go through the kitchen and it's the first door on the left."

The nagging fear that had haunted me after that first time I had spoken to Hélène sneaked again into my head: what if the angel I had constructed in my head was far from the truth, what if she was less than perfect? Of course she was. It was ridiculous and naive to expect her to be the paragon whose image I had so lovingly sculpted. And it was unfair, grotesquely unfair. I, who had deserted her, now expected her to somehow comply with my standards, to live by my mores? It was arrogant and it was obscene, and I loathed myself for thinking it. But I couldn't dispel it.

Hélène came back into the garden, her face brighter again, but there was something a little forced about the smile she wore.

"So when are we going to start painting?" she asked, with an outstretched left hand. "Or drawing?" she offered, with the right.

"Tomorrow," I said. "If that's ok with you? Say nine thirty? I need to go into Dublin this afternoon, to the art shop, to get some supplies."

"OK. And I should wear what we talked about?"

"Yes, please. If you want, you can bring the clothes and get changed here? You can always leave them here if you want?"

We walked back to the studio in silence. The sound of angry voices crashed across the garden from the Gallery as we approached. Oran was berating one of the workmen in the Gallery, his colourful language filling the room. Once in the safety of the studio with the door closed behind us, Hélène turned to me.

"Who was that?" she asked with wide eyes.

I laughed.

"That is Oran. Don't worry, he's a good man and his bark is much worse than his bite."

Her eyes asked for a translation.

"I mean, he shouts a lot and loses his temper, but he wouldn't hurt a fly."

Then I remembered the critic, but shook the thought away.

"He's a good lad, really. He's been my friend since we were kids." I hoped that was still true.

She looked unconvinced as Oran's angry diatribe reached fury-pitch again.

I ventured again onto unsafe terrain.

"You know what friends are like, you only ever see their good side."

I laughed a laugh that had no mirth. And went again where I had no right.

"So what's she like, this Aoife?" I asked, carelessly.

Her brow furrowed and her eyes narrowed a fraction.

"She's...she's... I don't know," she said, clearly frustrated to be back on this track. "She's very determined – but she's not always a very good friend."

"How do you mean?"

She shrugged.

"I don't know. I think honesty is the most important thing, you have to be honest, especially with your friends. Even if the truth is not what they want to hear or what you want to tell."

"Has she not been honest?"

"We all tell the lies we need to tell, I suppose."

"What does she look like?" I tried to make it a throwaway question, like the answer was of no real consequence. But my voice cracked – it actually broke mid-sentence – and betrayed me. Laid bare the importance of the question and my preoccupation with it.

Her forbearance ran out.

"Look," she said with matter-of-fact impatience, "if you want Aoife for your painting – drawing, whatever – then fine, I really don't care. You haven't even seen her, but she is obviously the one you are interested in."

She picked up her bag.

"I didn't ask for this work," she went on, pointing a finger at me, "but I maybe lost a job because of you..."

She stopped abruptly, stood still, her accusing finger still suspended in mid-air. The annoyance and irritation that clouded her face gave way to brow-furrowed puzzlement which was slowly replaced by a dawning realisation.

"My God," she said, her voice lowered to a whisper. "You'... her father."

We stood forever on the edge of an abyss, she on one side, I on the other.

"You're her father," she said again slowly, barely audibly. The significance of the revelation took a few moments to unfurl. Nothing I could say would soften its impact.

"You're her father. You betrayed her, and now you think you can use me?"

I stepped forward and reached out to her, started to deny and object but the words were a rag-tag mob, unruly and disorganised, and they would not be spoken.

"Get away from me," she spat, recoiling.

With that, she spun around and strode out through the door past an opened-mouthed Oran and his workmate.

I started after her, but then thought better of it. She was gone. And she had taken Aoife with her.

I slumped into the chair and held my head in my hands. There was a crushing sense of inevitability about the scene that had just been played out. I had spent so long searching, so long following the trail that had ended here, how could I still have been so hopelessly unprepared? Like a bad soap opera, I was lurching from one shambolic episode to the next, not knowing what to do or how to react. If it had just been my life on the line then I could have – would have – ignored the perils of this self-focused mission. But the danger was that I would blunder in on Aoife's life as I just had on Hélène's, with who knew what implications. For her and for me.

"That's the problem with you artistic types, all temperamental."

I looked up to see Oran leaning against the doorframe. I said nothing.

"I take it that's your model?"

"Was."

"Still smooth with the ladies, I see?"

I shook my head, willing him to leave.

"Ah sure, I'll sit for you. How do you think Lochlann would feel about this: the role of the handyman in the world of Irish women? Mind you, it's been a while since an Irish woman had a roll with this handyman, or any woman for that matter. Not too handy in that department, by the looks of things."

In spite of myself, I laughed.

"You talk a huge amount of shite, don't you?" I said, looking up at him.

"Guilty as charged."

"Fuck it, Oran, now what am I going to do?" I buried my face in my hands. He could have no sense of how desperately I asked the question, no idea how desperately I needed an answer.

And he didn't.

"She's just a model," he said, scoffing despite himself at the depth of my over-reaction, "sure there has to be more where she came from?"

The irony reminded me starkly of the role I had to keep playing.

"Lochlann will fucking love this, eh?" I said, with genuine bitterness.

"Ah, now, give him a chance. He'll understand – sure if anyone knows what a gobshite you are, he does."

I stood up.

"Yeah, well gobshite or not, I'm going to finish this fuckin' painting," I growled, stabbing an emphatic index finger in the air, "and he's going to fuckin' hang it."

My despair became anger and sought out a new target.

"Fightin' talk, eh?", he grinned, with a clenched fist. "You go get 'em, Tiger!"

"Tomorrow." I picked up my jacket. "Right now I'm going to get pissed. You coming?"

He looked at his watch.

"No, some of us have real work to do. Might come down later."

"See you later then," I nodded and walked out the door into the early evening air.

McGrath's was full of the same commuter crowd as it had been a few days before, when I had gone to drown my sorrows after finding Hélène. Now I had lost her, I was back to do the same again. But something had changed. The resigned despair of that evening had given way to the seeds of a bloody-mindedness that had set my face in an angry scowl that parted the assembled throng as I made for the same quiet corner. I was, I suppose, tired of losing, tired of coming off second best.

Ella, the young New Zealand barmaid, spotted me and came over.

"Hello again," she smiled. "How are you doing?"

"Not too bad, thanks," I said.

Lochlann used to complain at length about people who, when he made a polite enquiry as to their well-being, replied with a detailed answer based on the true facts in which he had little or no interest. With that in mind, I was always sparing with the truth.

"But I'll be better when I get a pint inside me."

"Coming up," she said with a wink and a grin, and she floated away to the bar.

I sat back and sighed a long sigh. It might not have been an inevitable course of events, but hardly unimaginable. If they were as close as it would now appear, then it was hardly a surprise that Hélène would know about Aoife's past. And a man of my age, in Dublin, asking so many questions – well it didn't take Holmes and Watson to add together the two and two. I had cautioned myself against pushing too hard too soon, lest I should frighten her off. But true to form, I had ploughed on and screwed up.

Ella arrived back with my drink.

"Here you go." She shook her head. "Looks like you could use some happy pills."

"I don't think drugs are the answer," I replied, sternly.

She was aghast, horrified at my interpretation. She leaned forward, eyes wide and darting around to see who might have heard. She gestured denial with a sweeping downturned palm.

"Oh Christ, no, you don't understand, I didn't mean..."

She caught my smile and realised I was pulling her leg. She put her hand to her chest and blew out her cheeks with relief.

"Bastard," she giggled, "you know what I mean."

I smirked.

"I bet you've never offered the Master a few poppers to liven up an evening."

"Mr O'Dwyer doesn't need them. You, on the other hand...!"

I handed her the price of a pint and raised my glass.

"Well, let's start with this and see how we go," I said.

"Fair enough," she winked and was gone.

I looked around the pub filled predominantly with a homogeneous crowd of my contemporaries in business suits or the new smart casual uniform of chinos and open-necked Ralph Lauren shirts. That might have been me if I had stayed here. Just off the train from the city, ready to drown the day's stresses in the evening's first pint. My hair might not be thinning, but perhaps I would be a portlier, more ruddy version of my current self. Maybe Caitríona would have left her job; maybe she would be waiting for me at home, my dinner in the oven, the house sparkling and bright and my little boy – boys? – playing obediently in the lounge, ready to rush to the front door at the sound of my key in the lock, shouting "Daddy! Daddy!".

That's the way we see the lives of others – like showhomes, perfectly constructed, beautifully accessorised. Would we in fact have grown apart under the stresses of family life? Would Caitríona have resented the loss of her career? Would she ever have agreed to that in the first place, or would we have been forced to juggle two careers and a family, each trying to fit domestic responsibilities around work diaries? Of course we would probably never have had a family, even if we had stayed in Dublin.

But for some reason that I couldn't quite understand, I didn't find myself wishing we had stayed – even though the course we chose was destined for such pain. And even though, at that moment in my life, I could scarcely have been less content.

"Now, *gosso'n*, I hope this isn't how you plan to spend all of your evenings while you're back!" I looked up, and a smiling Master was waving an admonishing finger. "Do you mind if I join you?"

"Please," I said, taking my jacket of the chair.

He took a seat with the muted groan of an old man and a sigh.

"And how are you doing this fine evening?"

I laughed.

"Now that's quite a story," I said, ruefully.

"Oh?" he raised his eyebrows.

"Yes. Where to start?" I took a long draft from my pint and put it down on the table. "Hélène came round this morning for our first session."

I paused, trying to get the sequence of events straight in my head. It had only been a few hours, but so much seemed to have happened that day. The Master waited, didn't fill the silence, just kept his eyes on me.

"It was all going so well. She seemed very comfortable with my ideas for the pose, what she should wear. She thought maybe I wanted her to be too sad and we talked about that a bit, but no problems. Then I asked her about Aoife again, and she got annoyed. I think I've made her feel like she's second choice, a substitute that I only asked because I couldn't find Aoife. And then it hit her. Somehow she figured it out, she realised that Aoife is my daughter."

The Master sat back in surprise, in shock almost. It took him a few moments to process what had happened.

"But how on earth did she arrive at that?" he asked, eventually. "Did you let something slip?"

I shook my head.

"No. I don't think so. She obviously knows about Aoife's past, and I had obviously dropped enough clues, however obscure. And *bang* – she hit me with that and stormed out. Said I'd betrayed Aoife and now I was just using her."

He was quiet again, shaking his head in shocked disbelief.

"Well that's not the way we thought events would unfold, and that's for sure," he said, almost to himself. "So what will you do now? Can you go see her tomorrow, maybe?"

I shook my head again.

"Don't think so. She was pretty angry. She might cool down I suppose, but I can't see it happening." I raised my glass to him in mock salute. "Welcome to square one. Again."

We sat a few moments in silence, then the Master beckoned to Ella to bring us two more.

Silence again.

"I don't know what to say, Aengus," he said at length, leaning forward to put his hand on my shoulder. "I'm truly sorry, honest to God I am. I just wish I could tell you what to do next."

And I knew he meant it, as sincerely as a vow.

"What about the painting?" he asked.

"You know, I think I'm still going to try to do it," I said.

I felt, I don't know... mistreated that this chance had been taken away from me, and I could almost feel the determination rising in my chest.

"I want to, I really do. It's the first thing that I've been excited about for so long, I don't want to give it up." My voice threatened to shout and I had to take a breath to calm my frustration. "And anyway, I need to think about where I go now to look for Aoife, and maybe I can do this at the same time, while I'm trying to figure out the whole sorry mess. It's like you said – I need to take control, and this is maybe the first step."

"Good man." He nodded his approval. "I'm glad. Good man."

"Actually, Lochlann came into the studio this morning."

"Did he now?" The Master looked a little surprised. "And what did he have to say?"

"Gave me some advice, pulled some supplies out of the store-room for me. Thing is, deep down, I don't think I want to do what he suggested."

"And what was that?"

"He said I should work in pencil. It would be easier and quicker." I shrugged. "He's right, of course. But it feels like a cop out. I just don't think I'd ever really get into it, might never be really fully committed, you know?"

I took another long draft.

"All academic now, maybe" I went on with a dark ironic smile, "given I don't currently have a model."

"But you can find another model. Sure isn't Dublin full of girls who'd give their eye-teeth to be models. Plenty of them too who'd love to get paid for it, I'm sure."

"I know, but her background was perfect, she personified exactly what I want to say."

"But your model doesn't have to be an immigrant, surely? It's not like anyone's going to know? The story you tell can still be the same."

"Maybe. But I think she would have inspired me. When I looked at her I knew exactly what I wanted to do, knew exactly how I wanted it to be. I won't find that again. And I'll never find a better way to Aoife."

"Well, all you can do is give it a try. I'm glad to see you're not giving up. I'm proud of you, Aengus."

I actually blushed under the unexpected compliment.

"Thanks, Master." I said, taking a drink to mask my embarrassment. "Thanks."

CHAPTER 15

She said I betrayed you. Is that what you think? I expect so. Who else could have led her to that conclusion if not you. Now that I've met Hélène, I have created a picture of you both in my head that lives with me every day, like a painting hanging on the wall of my imagination. You are sitting with her at a café, somewhere in the 6th. Maybe the Café de Flore or Les Deux Magots. It's summertime and you are at a table on the pavement in the still-warm early evening sun. You have come from a class and your violin case is at your feet. Your light, white summer dresses flutter in the gentle breeze, or in the draft of a bus as it trundles along the Boulevard St. Germain. You draw admiring glances from the men walking past on the street, and from the *"m'as tu vu?"* boys riding past on their scooters with carefully crafted nonchalance.

I want your face to beam and glow with a healthy *joie de vivre* inspired by the city around you – but I can't get it right. Instead you look angry: your eyes are narrowed and your brow is furrowed in deep annoyance. Your arms are waving in irate gesticulation. Hélène is sitting quietly, allowing you to vent your ire, all the while nodding sympathetically. She feels your pain, I think she wants to make it go away. She is your friend and she loves you but are you too blinded by your own anger to see or reciprocate? An anger that is my fault.

I think you are talking about me. One morning, did your mother hand you the brown envelope with the Harp? Did she take it from her pocket, where it had been secreted while she agonised over what to do? Her eyes were wet, I'd say. She said that she and your father only wanted what was best for you and that they would support you, always love you, whatever you chose to do. You took the envelope and turned it over and over in your hands.

And even though you feared a betrayal of your own, of the very people who had cherished and nurtured you, you reached out to find me. Me, who had betrayed you. And for months, for a year, for longer, you waited for me to respond. Checked every day for a sign, for some signal that I was out there, that I cared. And then finally you gave up. You angrily deleted the web-site address from your computer's Favourites, perhaps? And you never went back. Why should you? I had forsaken you once, abandoned you. Betrayed you. Is that what you said to Hélène? That I betrayed you? And now when you had given me the chance to redeem myself, I had ignored it. Ignored you. Was that my last chance?

I want to explain, to defend myself – but I can't. You see, I've spent years trying to build my case with logic and reason. We were young, I argue. We had nothing to offer you. We could never have provided the secure home that you deserved. But there is no reason that justifies leaving you with strangers. So I appeal to the judge for clemency, beg him to understand. But he just shakes his head with a withering look. He picks up his gavel and brings it down with a final crack. Guilty of the worst treason. Now I can only hope for mercy, that you will find it in your heart to forgive. But why should you.

So when Hélène accused me of betrayal, I had no response. She is your friend, loyal and true. And yet I, your father, could not dredge from my being the merest fraction of that fidelity. She has nothing for me but a bitter loathing. I cannot seek her out or follow her because I have nothing more to say.

And so now I stare at the painting in my head, but something has changed. Hélène is not looking at you anymore.

Now she is staring intensely out from the canvas. She has seen me looking in and she is staring out at me. And in her eyes I see a new spark, a new emotion. I lean in and peer closer to make it out, and realise with a jolt that it is anger. I try to change it, paint over it, retouch her eyes with understanding or sympathy or pity even. But I cannot even temper the contempt.

Contempt for a betrayal.

CHAPTER 16

The rain swept across the headland in sheets so dense that I could barely make out the sea below, like the curtain closing on an Ibsen stage. The wet stones that bordered the narrow path were so treacherous that I slowed to no more than walking pace lest my old running shoes should lose their grip and send me sliding down the heathered slopes above the cliffs. On days like these Howth had always seemed to me its own secret kingdom, isolated and removed from the rest of Dublin and the country. The city's high rise buildings and bustling streets, the lights that blinked on top of the Pigeon House, the distant Sugarloaf, were all hidden and ceased to exist in my dominion.

My head was filled with the fug of too many pints in McGrath's, and the rain was in truth a relief. The Master's robust support for my pursuit of a work to hang at Lochlann's exhibition finally convinced me to look for a way to go on in the face of Hélène's abrupt departure – because despite my bullish refusal to give up, I had in my mind no real strategy to continue. And despite his assurances that Dublin was filled to creaking with beautiful, haunting-eyed subjects, I had not the first idea how to go about finding one.

Oran had joined us later, in surprisingly buoyant if typically caustic mood and the three of us talked about football and rugby and old schoolmates and well-embellished tales of childhood skullduggery from long-gone schooldays. I nestled in the cosy camaraderie of conversations that meandered well clear of Aoife or Caitríona or food critics – not deliberately, but naturally. It was the kind of impromptu *session* that is invariably the best kind.

It was already late when the Master made his excuses and bade us goodnight, in what even my stout-addled mind could plainly see was yet another of his ploys to mend my broken bonds with the past. The barriers lowered by what we had already drunk, Oran and I sat there until closing time, the tone of our banter dipping innocently below the threshold of what would have been acceptable in the Master's company. When the barman questioned for the umpteenth time the existence of our abodes, we shuffled to the exit and planted manly slaps on each other's shoulders.

"See ya tomorrow then, Aengus," he said, pulling up the zip on his jacket against the rain that had already started to drift in from the sea.

"Yeah, see ya, Oran."

And with that the chasm's closure was complete.

I was back at the house and pulling off muddy shoes in the doorway when Lochlann appeared from his study. He looked surprised to see me.

"Did you have a good run?" he asked.

"In that?" I said with a sceptical snort, gesturing out to the rain that darkened even a summer morning. "You must be joking."

"Indeed," he nodded distractedly. "I was just about to make some coffee. Would you like some?"

"That'd be great. I'll just go and have a quick shower, back in a few minutes."

The steaming water in the shower stung my frozen skin and I shivered involuntarily in the heat as I tried to figure out how to break it to Lochlann that I no longer had a model. I couldn't, or didn't want to, explain to him why she had left, and so I probably wouldn't be able to explain what had happened. He would think me flighty, no doubt, as unreliable as always. He might call a halt to the whole project. But even if he did, even if he pulled the plug on my work at his exhibition, I realised with some surprise that I was resolved to go on, to finish this thing anyway.

I towelled myself down, threw on some clothes and went back down to the kitchen.

"There you are," said Lochlann with a hint of impatience, glancing at his watch. He poured me a coffee. "I hope that it's still hot."

I took a gulp.

"It's grand," I said.

"We missed you at dinner last night," he said pointedly. "Perhaps in future you might tell Pauline if you plan to eat elsewhere."

I inwardly slapped myself for the indiscretion.

"Shit, sorry, Lochlann," I said with a shake of my head. "That was really stupid. I'm not used to my plans affecting anyone else. Sorry."

"Hmm," he nodded what I took be acceptance of my apology. "You went out I suppose?"

"Yes, yes I did. To McGrath's." I took a deep breath. "I needed a bit of time to think. You see, Hélène – the girl who's sitting for me – she, er... walked out on me yesterday."

My father, to whom a show of surprise was a display of weakness, could hardly mask that this was, to say the least, unexpected. He looked out the window for a moment, then back to me.

"I see," he said. "Might I ask why?"

"We couldn't agree on the pose," I lied. "The look I wanted, she thought it was too sad, too weak, I think."

I immediately regretted the fabrication that made her the flighty, unreliable one.

"Well, that's the end of that, I suppose."

I looked for the hint of relief or of smug self-congratulation that I expected, but to my surprise there was none. If it had been anyone else, I would have said there was even a touch of disappointment in his voice. If it had been anyone else.

"Look, I'm sorry to have messed you about," I said, slowly. I paused, looking for the right words to make my proposition. "But if it's ok with you, I'd like to keep trying. To find someone else or to do it without a model? At least try to get it done in time. And if not, well then fair enough."

"Time is not on your side, Aengus," he said, with a despairing shake of his head. "I would have to change the literature, amend the floorplan... It's not simply a case of making the decision the night before we open."

"I know, and I won't ask you to wait too long," I found myself pleading in spite of myself. "Just a few days to see if there's any way. Maybe you know where I could find another model?"

He paused.

"Speak to Johnny Wright," he said. "He may know of someone. If you go through the agencies, it will take too long."

Johnny Wright was a long-time friend, confidante even, of Lochlann's. He owned an art supplies shop in Dublin where Lochlann had sourced his materials for as long as I could remember.

"OK. Thanks." I looked at my watch. "I'll go in now. Will he be there, do you think?"

"I expect so, yes."

"OK." I drained my coffee and picked up my jacket from the back of the chair. I looked back as I pulled open the door.

"Thanks, Lochlann," I nodded, and left.

The DART trundled its way along Howth head's northern shore, across the isthmus and into Sutton. The rain rattled off the windows and the roof like a continuous blast of pebbles and grit. I had bought a newspaper for the trip into town but it sat unopened on my lap. I was preoccupied by Lochlann's reaction to news of Hélène's desertion, as I had inadvertently painted it. I had been prepared for him to be condescending, to smugly remind me that he had told me so. I was ready for him to take the opportunity to call a halt to the whole project, to cite time constraints and my obvious inexperience as justification, if indeed any was needed. But his objections had been weakly made and he had left the door, if not open, then at least ajar.

Johnny Wright's shop was on the east side of Parnell Square, in the centre of the city, so I got off the DART at Tara Street, crossed the river at O'Connell Bridge and made my way up O'Connell Street. When I was a boy, I thought O'Connell Street must be one of the grandest city thoroughfares in Europe. In the world, even. Wide and straight and proud, steeped in history and culture, it was our Champs Elysées, our Fifth Avenue. Guarded at either end by Parnell and O'Connell, its statue-lined length is like a passage through our history. From Smith O'Brien's futile rebellion and Larkin's lockout to the GPO and the vacant spot where Nelson used to stand, it remembers a violent history of bloody defiance.

In the school holidays of our childhood, Oran and I would get the bus into town to buy new football boots or socks or gloves in Arnott's, or a book in Easons, or to marvel at Clery's Christmas window. Later, we would take shy girlfriends on the DART to the cinema – the Carlton or the Savoy. But then O'Connell Street fell victim to another invasion, one that it couldn't repel. Now fast-food shops, amusement arcades and Euro-shops line its pavements and the boorish crowds that spill from its pubs hold hostage its night-time hours. And so now she roams Dublin's heart like the homeless that beg coins from strangers – a once proud woman reduced by the greed of others to rag-clad poverty.

Johnny Wright's shop was old and old-fashioned. The shop-front was of dark wood, with his name in ornate, intricate script painted over the shop-window. I lingered a moment outside, surveying through the window the neatly ordered floor-to-ceiling shelves inside that held the shop's vast array of stock. Johnny himself was sitting on a high stool behind the counter, reading the newspaper. He was an instantly recognisable older version of the man I knew from those days when I had been able to persuade Lochlann to take me with him on his trips into town to replenish his stocks. Lochlann always drove into the city – not for him the indignity of the bus – and I beamed with giddy pride until my face ached as I peered out of the window from the front seat of his car, willing everybody to see me and take note. Johnny always had a toy or a comic for me to pass the time while Lochlann selected his wares, but the wonder of the treasures on display was beguiling diversion enough to pass twice the time.

I pushed open the door and walked in, and an old bell above the door tinkled gently to announce my arrival. He finished the piece he was reading before looking up to see who had come in. He looked at me a fraction too long.

"How're ye?", he said with the faintest of nods.

"Hi, Johnny," I replied.

So I knew his name. He looked at me again, his brain racking behind impassive eyes, but couldn't dredge me from his memory. I stepped forward and introduced myself.

"Aengus, Lochlann's son," I said, hand outstretched. "It's good to see you again. How are you keeping?"

The impassive eyes glinted with recognition.

"Ah Jaysus, it is too," he said softly, rising from his seat and coming around the counter to shake my hand, clasping it firmly in both of his.

"It is too," he repeated. "How are ye, son? God, sure it must be what, fifteen years?"

"And the rest, Johnny," I smiled, standing awkwardly with my hand still in his.

When he finally released me, we chatted about where I had been and what I had done – a sanitised, abbreviated version of the events of almost twenty years – and we talked about his business and the boom in artistic endeavour in Dublin.

"Your father's a busy man these days," he said, his face getting serious. "The exhibition is important to him, eh?"

"Yes, I think so," I said, suddenly embarrassed that I actually didn't really know if it was or not. "Yes."

"He was in the other day, getting a few things," Johnny continued. "He's lookin' well all the same, thank God."

"He is," I said, suppressing a sudden urge to smile at the universal need of Irish people of a certain age to issue a health bulletin – invariably negative or, if positive, then positive in spite of everything.

Johnny straightened himself .

"So, to what do I owe this pleasure?" he asked.

"Well, I'm actually looking for some supplies – and for a bit of advice. I'm going to work on a portrait to show at Lochlann's exhibition."

Johnny's face inadvertently betrayed his surprise, and a fleeting shadow of doubt.

"Jaysus, that's fantastic," he said, recovering his composure. "Fantastic opportunity."

He cocked his head slightly and the doubts peered out again from behind his eyes.

"Big commitment though, big responsibility" he said. "How much work have you done on it?"

"I haven't started. I've scoped it in my head and I know what I want to do, but…" I let it hang, the implication needed no elaboration.

Johnny exhaled with a long whistle.

"Jaysus, lad, you've got your work cut out, so you have. So what are you thinking of doing?"

I explained the girl with the violin and what she represented, and he nodded kindly.

"The problem is –," I started, "actually the first of a long list of problems – is that my model walked out on me yesterday."

"D'ya have to have a model?" he asked, skipping past the obvious but pointless question why.

"I think so. I think I need the face in front of me. And I need the inspiration of a real person, if that doesn't sound too pompous."

"No," he said, as though considering it and arriving at a conclusion, "I know what you mean. So you need another model then?"

"I do, and Lochlann said you might know of someone."

He rubbed his chin and nodded slowly.

"I might alright, I might. And you're going to sketch in pencil?"

That he had so pre-empted my next question took the wind out of my sails, and I stared at him with a frown for a moment.

"Well," I fumbled, "that's the plan I suppose. Why do you say that?"

"I just assumed that's why Lochlann came in, to get those pencils and charcoals?"

The stock that he had apparently found in the storeroom. Suddenly my determination to work in paints seemed somehow ungrateful and duplicitous.

"Yes..." I said, my mind distracted. "I suppose so."

My stuttering vagueness did nothing to persuade Johnny that I could deliver a work of any quality in the time available, and eventually his patience ran out.

"So," he said with an air of finality, "is it different pencils you're looking for, or more of the same?"

I took a deep breath before answering.

"Actually, Johnny, I want to paint, not sketch. It's too late for oils, I know that – but there's still time to work in acrylics. And I'm going to work in monochrome."

If I had shown myself to be naïve, then at least I hoped I had shown also that I could be decisive.

"And Lochlann's happy with that, is he?" he asked, knowing full well that he would be anything but happy.

I thought about making up a story, but I've never been a convincing liar.

"We haven't talked about it yet. I wanted to get another opinion, and…" I waved my arm towards him and smiled a sly smile from under uncertain eyelids, "… I thought you might have one or two!"

He didn't answer straightaway, but held my gaze and let out a long breath of benign exasperation.

"You young fellas, honest to God…!" he raised his eyes to the roof. "And you should be old enough to know better!" he said, lifting his voice and prodding a gnarled, paint-stained finger at me.

"But you'll help me?"

He shook his head. "Of course I will. Lochlann'll have me guts for garters, but sure I can't stand in the way of genius, now can I?!"

He went round behind the counter, brought his stool round to where I was standing and sat down.

"Right. Tell me everything."

I told him about Hélène, about her music and about the sadness in her eyes, and I showed him the pose I envisaged.

"I want to capture the fear and loneliness of a young woman who has come here with great talent to share, but who is still a bit lost, still feels like an outsider," I said, almost pleading with him to understand. "Do you know what I mean?"

"And why do you want to work in black and white?"

"It's a stark message, she lives in a stark reality. I don't think it needs embellishing."

I stood in front of him like a man waiting for his girl's response to a proposal. He made me wait while he mulled over my vision, his eyes once again impassive and giving no advance clue to his conclusion.

Finally he stood up.

"It's a beautiful concept, Aengus," he said sincerely, "but you're never going to get it done in time."

I should have been deflated but whether by virtue of arrogance or naïve optimism I was undeterred, buoyed even by his praise for the idea.

"I know it's going to be tight," I said, with a sharp cut of my hand for emphasis, "but I just think it's the way I want to say what I want to say. I've thought about it, I really have – agonised even – and it's the right style for this piece. If I can't make it work or if I run out of time then so be it. I'd rather hang nothing than show something I'm not proud of, something out of place in an exhibition like this."

Johnny was quiet for an age, staring up into the high ceiling, his darting eyes giving clues to the silent unilateral debates going on behind them. Suddenly, the little bell over the door tinkled. Johnny looked over and, with a broad smile, climbed carefully down from his stool and went over to welcome the visitor. They chatted for a few moments amid loud guffaws and back-slapping, and then Johnny went into a backroom and emerged with a package wrapped in brown paper and string. The man thanked and paid him, shook his hand again warmly and left.

Johnny walked back over to the stool and sat down again.

"Look – I've seen a lot of painters come in here, son, and fret and wring their hands just like you," he said, his face suddenly serious and his tone business-like. "And if there's one thing I've learned from them it's this: there's no right or wrong way to paint. You have to treat every subject as unique," he brought the side of his hand down lightly on the counter-top to make his point, "human, animal, inanimate – whatever it is. You're telling a story. You…" his finger prodding my chest, "…have to make up your mind – what's the best way for me to tell this story?"

The gently drumming hand on the counter kept time with his words and he paused for dramatic effect before going on.

"Yeah, there'll be the snobs who turn up their noses at anything that's not oil, just like the wine snobs who won't drink anything that comes out of screw-top bottles."

He waved his hand with dismissive contempt.

"Gobshites. Good artists – really good artists – will use different styles for different work. They might choose to use oil or acrylic or charcoal or a mixture of all three if they think that's what the story needs. At the end of the day, acrylic was designed to look and feel like oil and if you mix it with other stuff like retarders and glosses it really can look and feel like oil. And since the fumes from oils will give you a right feckin' headache, most people can only work in oil when it's warm enough to have the door open – and round here, that leaves about three days a year!"

I smiled and nodded, trying to take it all in, to let slip no pearl that could prove defining.

"Your ideas for the portrait are clear, well thought out," he went on. "That's good. You know your story. If you want my opinion, you might want to start it in charcoal and bring it together in acrylic. Maybe leaving the charcoal in some places to come through. If you want to give it a bit of atmosphere, you could wash it in a burnt siena acrylic, thinned with water. That'll give it an old, almost sepia feel."

He paused, and looked at me with raised eyebrows, as though checking that I was still with him.

"And you might," he said, a new thought clearly forming in his head, "want to give it a splash of colour, something bright and strong – after all, in her heart, she is bright and strong, isn't she, this girl?"

"I think so, yes. Yes, she is," I nodded, thinking about Hélène's angry departure and pausing a moment while my mind tried to catch up with him. "And you think I can get that done in time?"

He blew out his cheeks dramatically again.

"Look – it'll be hard. No doubt," he said. "But in some ways you've already done the hard work. Putting paint to canvas or board is the easy bit. You might be able to finish a piece in a week – but only if it's a technique you're happy with, you've perfected. If it's experimentation you're thinking about, you might as well pack it in now. And bear in mind that a portrait that has to look like someone in particular can take you more time. But if it's a made-up person then it could be less. Maybe you should rethink the model?"

Apart from the Master who, to be fair, had ulterior motives and a tenuous grasp on the reality of painting, it was the first time anybody had given me both reason to believe I could produce something worthwhile in time and had given me a tangible set of instructions.

"Thanks, Johnny, I can't tell you how much that helps."

He waved away my gratitude.

"That's only the start, son. The hard work comes next and now you're on your own."

He climbed again deliberately from his stool.

"We'd better get you some stuff to get started then."

He spent the next few minutes pulling out brushes and palettes and cleaners and paints. He found retarders – "this'll stop it drying too fast, give you a bit more margin for error" – and gloss – "dab this where you want sheen, the layman'll mistake it for oil!". Finally he disappeared one last time into the backroom and reappeared with three canvas boards.

"You might only need the one," he said, "but sure just bring back any you don't use. They're small enough, but you'll probably want to cut them down a bit. The charcoal you should already have, Lochlann got some when he was in."

He put the whole lot in a big old canvas bag that had appeared from somewhere, and handed it to me.

"There you go now. If there's anything you think I can help you with, you know where I am. And just sleep on what I said about the model. If you still want me to find someone tomorrow, let me know."

"I will. What do I owe you for all this, Johnny?" I asked, looking into the bag like a child looking into an over-sized Christmas stocking.

"I'll have to tot it up. Will I put it on Lochlann's account?" he asked.

"No," I said, slightly shame-faced. "It's bad enough ignoring his advice without making him pay for the result!"

"Well look, I'll set up an account in your name and I'll send you an invoice. You're staying at Lochlann's?"

"I am. Until he chucks me out when he sees all this!"

I shook his hand again and ignored his protests at my gratitude. I knew how close he and Lochlann were and, though I had faith in Johnny to talk himself around any of Lochlann's moods, helping me fly in the face of Lochlann's counsel could damage their friendship and even their business relationship.

I walked out onto Parnell Square. O'Connell Street looked suddenly longer with the big canvas bag on my back, so I hailed a taxi to take me back to the station at Tara Street.

The afternoon traffic through the city was dense and we sat in endless queues as we inched down the street. The driver was unusually quiet, deterred perhaps by my monosyllabic responses to his initial attempts at conversation. O'Connell Street was a window into a new Dublin. Earthier and simpler than the money-lined Grafton Street or Leeson Street or

Baggot Street, it retained a sense of grounded reality that other parts of the booming city had perhaps lost. It was a reality that reflected the city's losers as well as its winners. Teenaged pram-pushing mothers with sad eyes, aged vagrants with wild eyes, immigrants from east and farther east – non-nationals in Ireland's new lexicon – with a stranger's eyes, local lads in hoods selling fake designer bags and watches on corners with hardened, knowing eyes watching out for lurking Gardaí. O'Connell Street was like Dublin's staff quarters.

We must encounter hundreds or even thousands of people during a day in the city, in any city or any town of any size. Even though we are from the same place and occupy the same narrow stratum of the world's population, we will never share a drink or a meal or even a conversation with the vast majority of them just because we are so different. And we seem to shy away from contact with even those who do conform to our parameters, walking head down in the street, treating an unsolicited greeting in a pub or on a bus with incredulous suspicion.

How do we know whom we should get to know? We have access to such a tiny fraction of the human race, and yet we shut out the majority of even those who share our cities and towns. If we welcome only those already related to our circle, then the circle falls victim to inbreeding and shuts out infinite possibilities. We're a little bit afraid of welcoming in strangers, nervous of outsiders with no references. The media has made us paranoid with paper-selling stories and high-rating exposées of conmen and the deranged who lie in wait for us at every turn. But maybe we risk more by exclusion than inclusion. Maybe we could have found fulfillment or excitement or love or friendship behind the outsider's eyes. But we have trains to catch and friends to meet and work to do and sure how could we fit any more people into our already over-crowded worlds? Maybe we could have found a daughter.

Once back in the studio, having ensured that Lochlann was not around to witness my brazen slight on his advice, I set the bag down on the desk and began to unload its treasure. I placed one of the canvas boards on the easel and carefully pulled out the palette as though it were made of fine china. I held it and looked at it. I hadn't had my own palette since I left university, having lost it in the move to London. It was to me what a *camán* must be to a hurler, a pen to a writer – a powerful symbol of my craft, albeit I had scarcely earned the right to the possessive. More than brushes which are disposable, temporary, the palette was to me the real symbol of the artist. A borrowed palette from Lochlann's store could never have cast the same spell.

My mind's eye picture of Hélène's portrait now had the substance of an expert's support, and I could see a path for the first time. Even when she had been sitting in front of me, even when I could look into the eyes that inspired my vision, I didn't know how to make it real, how to bring it from my mind to the canvas. Now that I had that map, all that remained was to find a face to paint.

CHAPTER 17

The expletive shower that usually announced Oran's arrival burst through the door to the gallery. He was, as the Master used to say, one of the few people who could make asking for the time sound offensive. The two labourers with him scurried out to fetch or carry as instructed, eager to escape his attention, and I wandered out into the gallery.

"Sweetness and light personified as always," I greeted him.

"It's all your shaggin' fault," he retorted, "leadin' me astray on a school-night. I had the head from hell this morning, and I had a site meeting at eight. While you were still tucked up in your *leaba*, no doubt."

"I was out for a run actually," I said smugly.

"A run, is it? Yeah, that's how you masters of the universe usually start the workin' day," he said. "I tell you, the day you have to do some real work'll be some shock to your system."

Anything involving a desk and a computer fell way short of his definition of work, unless it involved moving the computer or building the desk. I exhaled a quiet chuckle.

"So how's it going with the Gallery? Are you on track?"

He looked around the empty room with a despairing shake of his head.

"No, not really," he said. "There was a lot of work to do just to get this room up to standard – fix holes in the walls, fix a leak in the roof, replace lengths of wood in the floor that had gone rotten or had nails stickin' up out of them."

He waved his huge hands around the gallery to emphasise the size of the task.

"This room hadn't been used for years. You couldn't just set it up and open the next day." He lowered his voice conspiratorially. "To be honest, I don't think your father had any idea how much work it was going to take. If he had known, maybe he'd have pushed the opening back a bit."

I nodded.

"But it's looking good now, the bare room I mean?"

"Yeah, it's grand. I give the boys a bit of a hard time—"

"D'ya think?" I interjected, and he ignored me.

"—but they're not bad lads really. They've done a good job, so they have."

He nodded like a proud father.

"But next we have to design the actual exhibition, and these lads haven't a clue about that. Sure, how would they?"

"So who's going to do it?" I asked.

"Lochlann, I suppose."

"Is he not getting an event organiser to help?"

Oran rolled his eyes and shook his head.

"He's got an exhibition manager that he used to work with, guy called O'Leary, to design the venue and organise getting the pieces in from collectors. But to be honest with you, I don't think he has it under control at all. Maybe he was a good man one time, but I can't see it, I really can't. I'm no expert, but his ideas for the design are a bit…well, he doesn't really seem to *have* any ideas."

I walked into the middle of the room and turned around slowly, trying to get a feel for the shape and dimensions and the flow, trying to remember what my colleagues in event management used to do for corporate clients and their marketing departments while I designed the graphics for the venue and literature. All I could remember was that it was hard to imagine a bare empty room fully decked and full of patrons.

Oran, who had been watching with a puzzled look, suddenly let out a loud snort.

"So have you found your feng shite then?" he said, and guffawed loudly.

I smiled a concession of defeat.

"Fair enough," I said, "fair enough. But he's going to need some help. Especially this late in the day."

I gestured to the door behind me.

"So they come in there and... what?"

"And those who have been invited are greeted with a glass of champagne and a programme setting out the works on show."

I swung around to see Lochlann standing in the doorway, a look of curious amusement playing on his lips.

"Those who have not," he continued, "are invited to pay the admission price which entitles them also to a glass of champagne to enhance the experience they are about to enjoy."

I didn't know how long he had been standing there, and I was embarrassed that he might have witnessed what must have seemed pompous and condescending.

"Sorry," I mumbled to the floor. "I was just... Sorry."

Lochlann looked at me, at Oran, back at me.

"I would be interested in your thoughts," he nodded quietly, his tone suddenly serious.

"I'm really not qualified."

"Perhaps. So, what would you like to know?"

I looked at him, at once afraid he was mocking me but wanting to believe that he was genuinely seeking my advice. I stepped carefully.

"Well, I was just wondering how the whole thing would work, I suppose."

"Indeed," he brought steepled fingertips to pursed lips and frowned slightly. "Where to begin?"

He came into the room.

186

"Well, as I said to you the other day, the exhibition will be made up of four distinct sections, or eras – Irish women of days gone by, Irish women as mothers, Irish women in new positions of influence, and the new Irish woman of today. The exhibition will be in the form of a corridor, leading from the entrance here –" he gestured to the door "– and winding through the four sections. We will have serving staff at intervals along the corridor to provide refreshments. At the end, after the final section, there will be a small open area with seats where I can give talks or seminars for groups and for the press."

He seemed almost embarrassed by the presumption.

"The challenge is, I suppose, the construction of the route. Then the positioning and lighting of the pieces. Have I missed anything, Oran?"

"I don't think so, Lochlann, no,"

Lochlann's eyes turned back to me, an expectant look on his face as though awaiting some great wisdom. I searched for the right words – not because I didn't know what to say, but rather because what there was to be said had to be carefully fashioned.

In short, I hated it. This would be Lochlann's first exhibition for years, years in which styles had moved on. But this was old school. Herding people through exhibits like cattle in an abattoir was from the past. It made the thoroughfares dark and narrow, and building the corridor would be materials-intensive, time-consuming and expensive. It denied people the choice to skip ahead or revisit, as though they were not really to be trusted to make such a decision. It gave no sense of scale. It denied Lochlann the opportunity to superimpose on the entire proceedings a message or a theme and denied him the chance to evolve that message. It fragmented the whole and it lost something because of that.

"I see," I nodded, too vigorously. "Yeah, I see."

Lochlann's eyes stayed on me, waiting as though for an explanation like when I had committed some childhood misdemeanour. Oran, I could sense without looking at him, was enjoying this. Lochlann's silence had the desired effect.

"Would you think about something a bit different?" I asked with transparently false lightness of tone. "Maybe?"

"What did you have in mind?"

I scurried off into the studio and came back with a sketchpad and pencil. I put it on the floor and crouched down to outline an alternative. It took me a few moments, then I stood up and showed it to Lochlann.

"Oran, come here and look," I said, beckoning him over to us.

The three of us were in the middle of the room, hunched over my sketch as I started to explain.

"I'd maybe put the sections in four rooms, chambers if you like, in the four corners of the gallery. The doorway is in the middle of that wall, so you could still use that as the access point coming in between room one, on your left, and room four, on your right. The welcome desk is here, between them, and the welcome staff direct you to room one and in a clockwise direction to rooms two, three and four."

I was, for a moment, transported back to my world. It was the world in which I was most comfortable, and its familiarity dispelled my initial nervousness.

"It has a few big benefits, I think. First, it gives a sense of space and light and scale. The Gallery is a beautiful room, with the vaulted roof and the beams. This way, rather than seeing only one small piece at a time, you can see the whole thing and that might be more impressive."

I tried to be moderate in my suggestion, tried not to assert.

"Second, it gives you a central space where people can gather, a social space. That might be a better place for seminars – you can point to the rooms as you speak, people can better picture what you're saying – and it's a good place for any central theming that you want to do – banners with quotations from poets or writers that reflect your thoughts, supportive critical reviews maybe? It's also a more efficient food and beverage point."

The more I spoke, the more I could picture the Gallery resplendent in its show finery, the more immersed I became. Lochlann's face was a blank screen, but at least he was paying attention.

"And third, you give people the chance to revisit sections they've seen before, go back to look at pieces again." I looked at Lochlann who was staring intently at the pad. My nerve almost failed me. "Look, it's just a thought. I'm sure you've thought this through more than me. Anyway…"

I was out of words, and so I stopped and drew breath, stepped back a fraction and waited for the reaction.

"How would you preserve the integrity of the flow?" Lochlann asked without looking up.

"You would have to brief the welcome desk staff carefully so that they can make it clear to people when they arrive. And you'd have to make it very prominent in the programme and make sure the signage is clear."

"Hmm. And this central area. How would you set that up?"

"Well, it could be a fairly flexible space – with seating and tables that could be set up for seminars or in a *café*-style."

"Oran?" Lochlann turned to him.

Oran said nothing for a moment, then looked at Lochlann.

"It'd mean less work," he said, eventually. "The corridor is going to be a bastard to build. This –" he pointed at the pad "– would be a lot easier."

"It would probably mean fewer staff too," I suggested. "You'd be able to cover a bigger area with fewer people."

"May I take this?" Lochlann asked, pointing to the pad.

"Yeah, yeah – of course," I stuttered, taken aback momentarily. I tore the page from the pad and handed it to him.

"Thank you. I will need to think about it, of course." He paused. "But you make a strong case."

He nodded what I took to be his approval and left. I stood where I was and watched him leave the Gallery. For a few moments I didn't move, trying to make sense of the unexpected course events had taken. At last Oran could indulge me no longer and woke me from the trance, but his voice had none of its usual brusque cynicism.

"Good man." he said. "Will we get a coffee?"

Pauline was on her way to the shops when we went into the kitchen. Seeing her reminded me of my *faux pas* of the previous evening, and the frostiness of her greeting told me I'd have to work harder to regain her favour. Pauline and I had a history of falling out but we always seemed to put it behind us and this time would be no exception. I made a mental note to get her some flowers in the village and to be even more than usually effusive when it came to praising that night's dinner.

Oran put on the coffee machine and sat down on one of the high stools in the kitchen.

"That went well," he said, "the old man really liked it."

"I don't know – I didn't do a great sales job, I'm afraid. But it's up to him. I think it'd work."

"So do I. I can't believe I'm saying this, but so do I!"

He laughed and punched my shoulder as he got up to pour the coffee.

"So is that what you've been doing these past ten years?"

"Thanks," I said, taking the mug, "Not really. I was more involved in the artwork that goes with events – the brochures, the posters, the invitations, sometimes the graphics for the venue. It was the events boys that looked after this kind of stuff, but I spent so much time around them that some of it rubbed off, I suppose."

I had always envied them. I loved creating, loved seeing my work finally adorning walls and literature – but I always envied them the adrenaline rush and the thrill of watching a venue fill with hundreds or thousands of people doing exactly as they were expected to do without being told or asked, just by virtue of clever organisation. I envied them the satisfaction of watching the crowd's reaction when things went just right, when the impact was powerful and the hairs on the nape of your neck would stand up. Of course there was always the risk that things would go wrong, and when they did it was the events people who were exposed to a client's wrath, with nowhere to hide. But that fear only heightened the euphoria of success.

"Do you like London?" his sudden change of subject caught me unawares. "You didn't sound so sure before."

"I don't know," I said matter-of-factly. "I think I liked the life we had there."

"But not now?"

"It's funny. Before, if you'd asked me the same question, I'd have said yeah, for sure I like it. But I think now I liked the life in spite of London, not because of it. I never felt like I belonged, and everything felt a bit superficial. The best thing about living there was the time we spent somewhere else. Even the good friends we had, it was like we only occupied a small part of their lives. I didn't know what they were like as kids or when they got married. I didn't know why they started supporting Chelsea or why they didn't like people from Wales. My friends were just nice strangers whose company I liked and who I could have a drink with. That was just it – when you just meet people for dinner or a pint, you don't really get under their skin. The last few months have made me realise that our friends were really just nice people we knew. And when you realise that, it's hard to go back to the way things were."

"So will you go back?"

"I suppose I will. But I don't know how long I'll stay. Maybe it's time to try somewhere new. Australia, America, or South America maybe. I don't know."

"What about back here?"

I shook my head.

"Here's not home any more either. I've been away too long, missed too much. I met Niamh yesterday, with her kid – Niamh with a kid, for Christ's sake!"

Oran nodded.

"She has two actually, a boy and a girl. But you know her husband left her?"

"No. Who did she marry?"

"Fella from Portmarnock, Clancy his name was. Bit of an arse to be honest, really messed her around. So she's back livin' with the parents for a while."

"Poor Niamh. See what I mean though? I've missed a lot, I'm not sure I'm really *from* here either."

There was a soft cough from behind me. I turned around to see Hélène standing uncomfortably, framed by the doorway. Oran stood up.

"Well, I better get to work," he said. "Excuse me, love."

Hélène smiled an apology and stood to one side to let him past, then came uncertainly into the kitchen.

"I went to the studio but you weren't there," she said. "I thought you might be here."

"It's nice to see you again," I said, awkwardly. "Did you… forget something…?"

She shook her head. The next thought that crossed my mind was that she had come to be paid for the previous day's debacle, before it suddenly dawned on me that she was back. She had come back.

"I came to apologise. I was very rude yesterday, and I am sorry." She looked down at the floor, then back to me. "And I came to ask if you still want me to be your model."

"Yes," I blurted, getting up from the stool, "yes, absolutely! If you will, if you really want to?"

She nodded.

"That's great! Fantastic!" It was almost too perfect. After talking to Johnny, I had a real picture of what I wanted to do – all that was missing was a muse. I could probably have concocted something from photos, but I felt since the day I saw her that Hélène's was the face I wanted to paint. The face that might take me to Aoife.

"Come in, have a coffee."

I took her jacket and handed her a mug.

She looked ill at ease, which I took to be a function of the awkwardness of the situation. But there was more, beneath.

"Are you ok?" I asked.

"I'm fine, thank you." She smiled. "This is just difficult for me."

I spoke slowly, selecting my words carefully, desperate not to lose her a second time.

"Why… why did you come back?" I asked.

She shrugged.

"It is between you and Aoife. I have no right to judge or to take a side. But I have listened so many times to Aoife talking about finding you and her mother, and you never came looking for her. It was like you were hiding from her. And that is why I was angry yesterday."

Her voice quavered slightly and I was afraid she was going to cry, or to run out on me again. But she took a moment and composed herself.

"But it's not my business."

She looked up into my eyes, and the look in hers winded me. That was the look I was desperate to capture.

"Look, let's go into the studio and we can make a plan. When can you start?"

"I can start tomorrow? We are playing tonight in… I don't

remember where. But not in Dublin and so we have to drive there this afternoon."

"That's ok, tomorrow is fine. Come on."

We walked back to the Gallery and into the little studio in silence. I opened the studio door and ushered her in, and Oran raised his eyebrows to me as we passed. I answered his unspoken question with an almost imperceptible nod.

I closed the door behind me and beckoned to Hélène to take a seat.

"I went down to the art shop today," I said, gesturing to the pile of supplies on the desk. "The man there is a friend of my father's. We had a good chat, actually. He gave me some great ideas for the portrait."

I picked up one of the paint tubes.

"He says I should start the portrait in charcoal but then bring it together in acrylics. In paint. But not in oils."

Her face was a blank.

"It means I don't have to do a pencil sketch. And I don't really want to. So it was a good conversation. And he sorted me out with pretty much everything I need."

"So we will start tomorrow?"

"Yes, yes. What time can you make it?"

"Nine? Eight even?"

"Eight would be perfect – we have a lot to do and not a lot of time."

"And you want me to bring my violin, and to dress as we said?"

"Yes, please. What time will you finish tonight though? Won't you be late home?"

"A little, maybe. But it's ok. I like to get up early."

Out in the Gallery I heard Lochlann talking to Oran, and his voice drew nearer until he came through the studio door, still talking to Oran over his shoulder. He turned around and started to talk to me, then noticed Hélène.

"I'm sorry, I didn't realise you had company. I'll come back."

He turned to leave.

"No Lochlann, I'd like you to meet Hélène. Hélène is sitting for my portrait."

A puzzled look briefly passed over his face, but he recovered immediately and, always the epitome of decorum, greeted Hélène as though ignorant of the events of the past few days.

"It's a very great pleasure," he said, proffering his hand in greeting. "Aengus has told me about you. If there is anything I can do to help, please do not hesitate to ask."

"Thank you," Hélène replied coyly, getting to her feet. "I have read a lot about you since Aengus told me about you. It is a pleasure for me, too."

"Please, don't get up. I just came to speak to Aengus but it can wait until later."

"No, it's ok, really – I have to go anyway," she said. She turned to me. "So I will be here at eight tomorrow, yes?"

"Yes." I walked her to the Gallery door.

"And, Hélène?" I said quietly, "I'm really glad you came back. Thanks."

She nodded, walked down the little path that led to the garden gate, and was gone.

I walked back into the Gallery.

"So what's the story," Oran asked eagerly. "Is she back?"

I nodded and smiled in spite of myself.

"Yeah, she is."

"Deadly," he grinned.

"Did she simply come back?" Lochlann asked.

"Yes, just an hour ago."

"You must have been surprised to see her. What was it that led to her change of heart?"

"I don't know," I shrugged. "She just lost her temper yesterday, I think. Today she thought about it and said she over-reacted. Whatever the reason, I'm just glad she's back. I'm not sure I could have done it without her."

"Not the set of circumstances to inspire confidence," he warned. "Just make sure you manage her properly in the future."

He let his admonishment hang in the air for a moment before speaking again.

"I couldn't help noticing the paints on your desk," he said and my heart sank. I was going to have to talk to him about it sooner or later, but I wanted to be at least prepared. "I take it you went to Johnny Wright?"

"Yes, I want to talk to you about that actually."

"Indeed."

"Look, I really want to work in paints, and Johnny had some great ideas. I know you think I won't get it done in time and, to be fair to him, Johnny said the same, but I really think I can get it done. And you'll know whether or not I'm going to be done in plenty of time for the final programme print, so it'll be your call."

"And how are you going to work?"

"I'm going to start it in charcoal and finish it in acrylic, in monochrome except for a splash of red, leaving the charcoal exposed in places. Johnny had an idea to give it a more texture – washing it in thinned burnt siena acrylic to give it an older feel."

I bit my lip and waited like an accused waits for the pronouncement from the chairman of the jury. He made me wait.

"And you're starting tomorrow?"

"Yes."

"Well, I have made no secret of the fact that I think your inexperience and the lack of time will make it difficult for you to prepare something of the requisite quality in time. And you know that I will only hang a piece that truly merits inclusion. But if this is what you want to do then you must follow your instinct. Working on something to which you are not fully committed is almost certainly doomed to failure."

Not guilty.

"Thanks, Lochlann," I said. At the back of my mind I still doubted that he would hang my work, but at least this was a licence to continue.

He nodded.

"And as for your thoughts this morning on the structure for the exhibition," he went on, "I have given it some thought and, I agree, you raise some valid points. I admit, I still have some concerns about maintaining the integrity of the flow, but that can perhaps be managed."

He turned to Oran.

"Oran, discuss it with the exhibition manager, have Aengus explain his ideas. If it is feasible in the time available and not more expensive, then have him put together a proposal for no later than the end of the week."

"Will do, Lochlann," Oran replied.

"Have you thought about music at all? For the show, I mean," I asked Lochlann.

He looked a little surprised by the change of subject.

"Yes. I'm putting together a play list of music at the moment and we will have a sound system in place."

"What would you think of having live music, musicians playing in the central space? Not every day, just on special days, opening day for example. I was thinking of a string quartet, all women. Hélène is a violinist, and plays in Dublin. She might know some others. Irish women of the new generation."

He rubbed his chin thoughtfully and considered it for a moment.

"Let me think about it," he said.

"It would just be another feature, a talking point for the press maybe," I offered. "And it might help Hélène too," I added quietly, slowly.

"Let me think about it," he said again, and left.

Oran turned to me when he was gone.

"Well aren't you the golden bollocks all of a sudden, ha?" he said with a laugh.

His reaction seemed genuine, but I was conscious that Oran might be aggrieved that I had sauntered back in and taken over what he had built. He would have every right to be, but I didn't think for a moment that I had suddenly become a prodigal son. My work was still a long way from hanging, and my observations on the exhibition flow were simply born of common sense that might save time and money. Lochlann hadn't killed the fatted calf just yet.

"It's not far from golden bollocks to just bollocks," I said with a rueful smile. "If I don't make this portrait work or if I screw up his precious 'flow', he'll be quick to unleash his venom. I'll be out on my arse and you'll be left to fix it!"

"Well you better get to work then. I have enough to be doing without cleaning up after the likes of you!" He waved me away in mock dismissal. I gave him a solemn faux-military salute, and went back into the studio.

I sat down behind my desk and picked up the palette, turning it over and over absent-mindedly in my hands. Since I had arrived in Dublin, I felt like I was standing in the middle of a busy motorway at rush hour, fending off the unexpected, the uninvited, like I was avoiding speeding cars. Now, for the first time, I felt brave enough to peek out from behind the raised arms that shielded my face. Now I felt that I could maybe stop the traffic, or at least step clear.

I had somehow overcome Oran's initial antipathy, and maybe I had arrived at an opportune moment to help him through what was going to be a difficult time, if I could. I had found and lost and refound my path to Aoife and my muse. I had perhaps softened Lochlann's contempt, although I knew that to fail him, to let him down again, would serve only to plunge me even deeper into that hole. The complexity of life, of managing its twists and turns and surprises, had always been a little beyond my grasp. I had often wondered how Caitríona and I would have coped if we had chosen to have children, so difficult did I find managing a life with just two of us. I marvelled at my friends who negotiated a life irrevocably complicated by the educational and medical and developmental and emotional, never mind the quotidien logistical, responsibilities hurled at them by their children. Up to now, Dublin had thrown at me more questions than answers. Or maybe it was throwing me a lifebelt while behind me my ship went down.

CHAPTER 18

There will be a portrait of Claire at the show. I've never known what to call her. Some childish title of affection would sound like a denial that I never knew her, like a claim that I did and so have some right to familiarity. I started calling him Lochlann out of some sense of angst-filled teenage rebellion – to call her Claire suggests the same and that's not true.

So I have always called her "my mother". I say always, but I rarely speak of her. You tried to persuade me to learn more about her, to make her somehow a part of my life. But Lochlann and I never talked about her and where else would I learn about her without seeming to go behind his back?

We looked at pictures of her, you and I, and you said she was beautiful. And you said it not in that way girls have of only complimenting women who are not so beautiful as to cast a shadow over their own fairness. You said it as though you meant it and were a little surprised. We're always surprised to find that older generations were beautiful in their prime.

A son's relationship with his mother is the most natural, normal thing in the world, but I have no idea what it's like or how it feels. I didn't miss it because I never knew it. That which others could not countenance losing, to me was nothing more than a concept, no more tangible than the theorems we learned at school. I tried to make it painful, like a self-abuser tries to hurt himself as punishment or retaliation, just so that

I could bridge the gulf between Lochlann and me, give us some common ground. But I could find no guilt, no cause for punishment. I could feel no pain, squeeze out no tears.

A mother's relationship with her daughter is just as precious, just as natural, yet you denied it to yourself, denied yourself the right to be called a mother. In your heart, did you think we would have a child again some day? Did you pass it up because you were sure you would have another chance? Or did conception and pregnancy quench any curiosity, any desire that was in you to mother a child? I don't think you ever thought of yourself as a mother. I think, in your mind, the physical experience of bearing a child was not enough to qualify you. You could never join in those exclusive conversations between girlfriends at parties about pregnancy or labour or birth. You could never offer advice over coffee to a newly pregnant friend. Even if they had known, even if you had shared that secret, I don't think you would ever have presumed to join their club. Not, I think, that it would have upset you – in time you came to terms with that, as much as you could – but because you felt you had no right. The day they took her away, they also took away your entitlement to recall the experience and recount the story.

I see mothers every day with their children, with babies and toddlers and kids and teenagers. I try to imagine you in their shoes, but I never can. You don't fit, you have no place in that picture. If every woman is a mother in waiting, then why is the impact so profound? Proud, powerful, capable women seem so often lost in the mothers that emerge from the maternity ward. Flustered, frightened and newly focused in a new reality. Or betrayed by a promise broken? Drawn in by the light and the comfortable certainty that it's the right way. From where there is no retreat.

I nearly saw motherhood at first hand. Twice. I never knew my mother and never knew you as a mother. How different my life might have been. Lochlann would be different, would be Dad, maybe. We'd play golf or go for a pint or watch the football on television. I would be a different person, surely. You might still be here, the same but different. Our little girl would be all grown up and gone from home, probably. We might have another child, or two perhaps. Our life's priorities would be incomparable.

I had never had a mother and so I never missed her, never felt that grief. Is it wrong to sometimes wish I had never had you?

CHAPTER 19

Hélène arrived promptly at eight o'clock the next morning and we made the mandatory pot of coffee before going to the studio to at last begin work. She seemed less anxious than when she had come back the day before, but she was not as entirely at ease as she had been when we talked in the coffee shop in Malahide. Whether it was down to the events of the days before or simply to nerves now that we were starting in earnest, I wanted to try to make her as comfortable as I could, for her own sake as much as for the sake of the work we were setting out to do.

She was dressed as we had agreed, in a simple yet formal white shirt, open at the neck to reveal the little silver cross, and a floor length black skirt. On her feet she wore simple black shoes with no heel. Her long hair was pulled back and tied in a pony-tail behind her head. She laid the violin case on the studio desk.

"How was the gig last night?" I asked.

"It was good, I think."

"So, what kind of music do you play?"

"Everything, really, whatever I can. Last night I was with a band that plays rock music, but in an Irish style. Trad rock, I think you call it. They are very good. The lead singer has a wonderful voice, deep and strong."

"Where were you playing?"

"In a town called Carlow – that is how you say it?"

I nodded even though that was how nobody had ever said it – the small country town dominated by the sugar factory had never sounded so romantic.

"It was in a hotel, in the night club."

"What time did you get home?"

"About three, I think."

"Jesus, you must be shattered?"

She smiled.

"A little. But, this is ok?" she asked, looking down at her clothes and shoes.

"It's perfect, Hélène. It's exactly as I pictured you."

She smiled briefly, then her face became again serious.

"One thing," I said, hesitating to suggest that anything that might be construed as criticism. "Can we change your hair, just a little?"

She put a hand to her head.

"Yes. How? You would like it loose?" She frowned as though she didn't quite understand.

"No, I like it tied up. But could we make it less tidy, less neat? Could you, like, pull a few strands loose and let them fall over your face and hang down by the sides of your cheeks? And just, maybe, loosen it a bit, without letting it fall free. Does that make sense?"

"Yes, I think so." She looked around the studio. "Do you have a mirror that I can use?"

"No, I don't," I winced at the omission. "I should have though, you're right. I'll get one next time I'm in town. There'll be one in the bathroom, at the back of the Gallery." I pointed out through the studio door to the far wall of the big room.

"OK," and she walked out into the Gallery. I took out a notebook and scribbled "mirror", then busied myself with positioning the easel and stabilising the canvas board, and with arranging the charcoals and erasers for the umpteenth time.

When she came back in I was scrabbling about with the foot of one of the easel's legs, but the transformation stopped me in my tracks. I stared at her, and the sad, dark eyes of a latter-day Cosette started back at me through tumbling locks, as though from behind the makeshift barricades.

"So," she said. "This is ok?"

"This is…" I was momentarily lost for words. "Jesus, it's fantastic. It's just perfect. It really is perfect, Hélène."

My concerns about appeasing and encouraging and reassuring were momentarily put to one side – the look she had created was at once disabling and inspiring. My reaction needed no embellishment, and this time the gratified smile played on her lips a little longer.

I moved the old wooden chair into the light that was streaming through the long window and offered her the seat. She went to the desk and took her violin and bow from the case. She sat down in the chair and leaned forward with her forearms resting on her knees. She held the violin by its neck in her left hand and the bow in her right so that they hung just off the floor between her feet. Her head was tipped back so that her eyes looked straight ahead, filled – whether by virtue of her nervous uncertainty or by design – with the lost look that had so captivated me the first time I met her.

"May I?" I asked, reaching for a strand of hair that had fallen across her eyes.

"Yes, of course."

I brushed it back so that it fell down the side of her face.

"Perfect," I said, almost to myself.

I went to the desk and took my camera from the drawer.

"Can I take a photograph?" I asked. "I just want to make sure we don't ever lose this. It's so right."

She nodded her head and I had to brush back the hair that fell again across her eyes.

I took two or three shots from different angles, and then looked at them in the camera's digital screen. I stepped over to her and handed her the camera so she could see.

"What do you think?"

She didn't answer for a moment, but scrolled through the pictures once, twice, three times. Finally, she nodded.

"Yes, I think it is what you want."

All that week, we began our days the same way. Hélène would arrive at eight, always on time, we would make a pot of coffee and make our way to the studio. The charcoal sketching began to slowly take shape and Hélène's features began to emerge. The canvas board gave the charcoal a grainy texture that gave it an old look, as though it had been started years ago and only now rescued from some dusty box in the attic to be brought at last to its conclusion. And it gave Hélène's face an elusive mystique, so that you couldn't quite catch her eye, nor place the expression.

It was slow progress, painstaking almost. I knew that I should build the broad base first and worry later about minor corrections or refinements. But I couldn't move on until it was right, and so I wasted hours on fine amendments that would make little difference to the final work. I was constantly surprised at what I found difficult and what came almost naturally. Her eyes were easier than I imagined, their dark lustre almost designed for charcoal. But her hands, her hands… How they frustrated me. The fingers were too long then too short, too thin then too stout. The nails were too big then almost disappeared then became claw-like, like a hawk's talons.

Hélène's coolness of early in the week gradually thawed and she became a little more animated. She was engrossed by the process and patient while I reworked and revised. Every so often she would come around to my side of the canvas to see what I had done. Her insights and suggestions belied her artistic inexperience, and her very naïveté was innocently eloquent. Still she remained a little distant, not entirely comfortable in my presence, I suppose, now that she knew who I was.

At two every day she left to prepare for that evening's performance in Dublin or Kilkenny or Wexford or Navan…

her itinerant band taking her to towns that I couldn't even remember ever visiting. When she was gone, I would spend the rest of the day, often into the night, retouching or erasing, or often just staring in quiet awe at what I had done. Look, it was no master-piece, I knew that, I had no pretensions nor delusions nor aspirations to acclaim. But it was mine and it was better than anything I had ever done or even imagined doing.

It was later in the week and we were taking a late morning break over a coffee in the garden, looking out over the calm sea below. It had been a tough morning. With the sketching of Hélène's body almost complete, I had struggled to get to grips with the backdrop that framed her, to represent in the base monochrome the colour of the sky outside and the sunlight coming through the window, and the rough-hewn Wicklow stone walls of the studio. I was still lost in my frustration, trying to find the stroke of genius that would capture the background to set-off her frame, when she asked the question.

"Why have you not asked me about Aoife?"

I didn't know how to respond. All week I had been fighting the overwhelming urge to ask the questions that had been gnawing at me since we had first met. But conscious of the bumbling, crassly insensitive foray into that domain that had almost driven her away already, I resisted and forced myself to bide my time, literally biting my tongue until I could taste the blood.

I looked at her, trying to gauge where the question had come from, what reaction my answer would provoke. Eventually I shrugged.

"I nearly screwed up last time, I don't want to risk losing you again. There are so many questions I'm desperate to ask you, but... I don't want to make you angry again, I just don't want to upset you, I suppose."

"I'm sorry that I reacted badly," she said, and I felt that she was finally saying what had been on her mind all week, perhaps at the root of her distance.

I shook my head.

"You have nothing to apologise for."

"I do. It's not my business. What is between you and Aoife is between you and Aoife. I should not judge, I should not hear only one side of the story. Aoife thought that you didn't care, that you could not care to respond to her or to look for her. But maybe you had reasons. I do not know the story of your life and I do not have the right to judge."

She spoke as though reciting a well-rehearsed speech, perhaps one she had been preparing since the day she stormed out of the Gallery. I looked down at the ground.

"Thanks, Hélène," it came out as a hoarse whisper. "I'm going to make more coffee."

I almost ran to the sanctuary of the kitchen. I stood at the window, and leaned on the counter and my head hanging. I realised that I was breathing heavily, as though I had just run back up the hill from the Baily to the house.

"Fucking hell," I whispered to myself, shaking my head slowly. "Jesus."

Absent-mindedly, I flicked the switch on the coffee machine. I had stored so many questions behind the dam I'd built, the dam she had now she had breached, and they cascaded through my head in a torrent I couldn't control. All of the carefully orchestrated imaginary interviews that I had conducted in my head, the subtle, sensitive questioning, the calmly rational justifications, were smashed by the surge and lost in the foam, their wreckage bobbing and swirling in the eddying water.

The coffee machine coughed to an apologetic stop. I looked at it, then reached past it to take a bottle from the little wine rack on the counter that Lochlann used to hold his "every day" wine. I took two glasses from the shelf, pulled the cork and went back into the garden.

"I need more than coffee," I said, pouring two generous glasses.

"Me too, I think," she smiled uncertainly as she took the glass. "Thank you."

She sipped the wine, and drew a deep breath.

"How did you find her, the address I mean?"

My eyebrows lifted involuntarily at the memory of the dark old bar buried in Paris' core.

"The message Aoife left when she contacted the agency, she said she was playing music in Paris. I went to Paris and searched every club I could find. Eventually I found La Caleche. I saw the message you left."

She furrowed her brow.

"The message?"

"Yes, in the old photo album. Claude showed it to me, although I think he probably wished he hadn't. I think he wanted to throttle me!"

I smiled, and she smiled back and nodded.

"Ah yes, of course. Claude is quite protective!"

I swirled the wine around the glass and stared at its sweeping spiral.

"What's she like?" There was no other way to say it, no way to introduce the subject or ease into the discussion. Like a sky-diver, either you jump or you don't. There's no easy way down.

There was a pause and I didn't even try to fill it. Hélène said nothing for a minute, two maybe. Just took a long, slow drink from her glass. Finally she spoke.

"She's pretty, I guess," she said quietly, as though conceding that she had thought otherwise and had been finally convinced. "She is dark, her skin I mean. Her hair is long, she is tall..." she sub-consciously acted out each description with her hands, putting a finger to her face, touching her hair, raising her hand over her head. "She is a little bit too thin maybe... I don't know." She raised an eyebrow. "She looks nothing like you."

We both laughed nervously.

"Well, thank God for that at least," I said awkwardly, predictably, with a hollow laugh.

Thank God she looked like Caitríona.

"She's not so reliable, like I told you. She doesn't like to stay somewhere or to do something for a long time, and sometimes when she makes promises, well, she does not always keep them." She shrugged and her face was conciliatory. "She worries about a lot of things, about everything. And I think she tries to run away."

She drank more wine and emptied her glass. I poured her another and filled my own.

"It is too early for a lot of wine," she joked, weakly.

"Extenuating circumstances," I said.

"She is a good musician," Hélène continued. "In her first year, she won the prize for being the top of her class, although I think maybe she was not the best. But she is very good. Very good." She nodded and opened her eyes wide to make sure I understood.

Neither Caitríona nor I could hold a note, and I could think of no musicians in my family, no uncles who sang at family get togethers or at Sunday mass. But then we weren't really a sing-song family.

"Is she happy?" I asked quietly, "Do you think?"

Another silence.

"I do not think she is unhappy, not all of the time," negatives tripped over negatives, and she was unconvincing. "But I don't know if I could call her happy. I think she is looking for something." She shrugged again. "But she doesn't know what it is so she can't find it and that makes her sometimes sad."

"What about her family? Do you know her family?"

Yet another silence, which I was starting to understand always preceded what she thought I might not want to hear.

"That is difficult," she sighed a long sigh. "Her parents both worked at the University in Paris. When Aoife told them she wanted to look for her natural parents, they were angry a little bit – no, they were disappointed I think. They didn't shout or argue, but it became difficult, like they became strangers. Then her parents were offered a place at a university in America, and Aoife decided to stay in France. When they went away, she decided to leave school, to try to find work."

It was my worst fear, that she might be unhappy and alone. No wonder she thought I had abandoned her.

"They still talk, of course, on the phone and maybe they are not so angry now, they understand a little bit. But it is not like when she was young and it is a little bit sad."

Out at sea, a swarm of gulls followed a fishing boat headed back to Howth harbour, diving and swooping in futile unison.

"What does she want her life to be?" I was searching for the words, but I couldn't quite frame what it was that I wanted to know. "What is she going to do?"

"I don't think she knows. Like I said, she is searching for something, but she does not quite know what it is that she is searching for. I think that is why she wants to come to Dublin. She says it is for our music, that we will discover new ways to play here, but I think there is something else also. I think she has always wondered what it is like to be really Irish, to live here, to be a part of it. It is like she knows she is Irish, but she doesn't know how to be Irish." She clenched a fist as though grasping the very essence of Irish-ness. "I know the music is a part of it, but it is more than that. And with her family so far away, there was no reason not to go now."

"But she didn't come to Dublin? Why didn't she come?"

She shook her head, and sighed.

"Suddenly, she wanted to take the chance to travel before

she came to Ireland, before she settled down again. She asked me to go with her, but I didn't want that. We had made all of our plans, made all of the arrangements, and I just wanted to come here, to make a start. So she went and she said she would come here when she was finished. So I'm here, and she will come when she comes."

So close and yet so far away.

"How about friends? Apart from you. Does she have good friends?"

"She is my best friend – but I don't think she is the best friend of anybody else. She has friends, for sure, but she keeps them at a distance. She won't let anybody get too close. People don't like that, maybe." She looked and me and paused, perhaps looking for an answer.

"Is she…" despite all of the times I had practised this very conversation, the words failed me. "…nice? I mean, is she a nice person?"

Hélène's brow furrowed, surprised, as though she hadn't ever considered the question before.

"I don't know," she said slowly. "What is a nice person? She is not a saint, but she does not try to hurt people. It's just that sometimes she is careless with people."

"How do you mean?"

She blew out her cheeks and her expression was one of benign exasperation.

"She frustrates her friends, I think. She agrees to do something and then changes her mind, it seems sometimes for no reason. I think she seems a little bit wrapped up in her own world, with her own problems. And she is always afraid that the worst will happen, she is… how do you say it in English?"

"Pessimistic?"

"Yes, I think so. She is pessimistic."

"Does she frustrate you?"

She hesitated, then nodded slowly.

"Yes. A little." She grinned. "She is stubborn also, so stubborn, even when she knows she is wrong! And she has an opinion about everything, I mean *everything*, even things she knows nothing about!" She shook her head as though irked, but her eyes exposed a warmth, a friend's affection.

Hélène looked at her watch. She was playing in Naas that evening and it was almost time for her to go. I was drained by the conversation, more drained even than after any morning's work.

"Can we just go back to the studio for five minutes?" I asked, sensing that she was anxious to wrap up for the day.

It was nearly the end of the week, and Hélène's charcoal image grew bolder on the canvas board. But still the background wasn't right. It would be better when the paint was added, I reassured myself, adding the impression of light through the window. But the shapes and the angles were still askew and the pencilled texture of the stone walls didn't create the atmosphere that it should.

"Sure," she said.

As we walked back to the studio in silence, she looked up at me.

"Are you ok?" she asked.

I looked back at her, once more surprised by the question.

"Yes, " I said, after a moment. "Yes. Thanks."

Hélène sat down in the chair, and I pulled a sketch pad from the drawer in the little desk. With a pencil, I roughly sketched her outline and the dimensions of the shapes behind her – the window, the ceiling line, the corner where the walls met, the floor. Then I held it up beside the easel to compare the two and to see where I had gone wrong on the canvas board.

"I need to go, Aengus," Hélène said after a few minutes, apologetically.

"Shit, yes – sorry. Of course, you go ahead and I'll see you tomorrow."

CHAPTER 20

I picked up the empty bottle and glasses from the desk, walked with her to the gate, and went into the kitchen. I was putting the glasses in the dishwasher when Pauline came in with a basket of laundry. I had only just been forgiven for my non-appearance at dinner earlier in the week, and Pauline had remained a little bit cool with me. Still, she was warming again and she recoiled in mock-shock at the sight of the wine bottle.

"Bit early for that, isn't it?" she laughed. "Still, drinking wine in the garden with a pretty French girl – nice work if you can get it, eh?" She nudged me with an elbow and, giggling at her own wit, started loading the washing machine.

"Very funny," I smiled. "I'm about to make some coffee – would you like some?"

"D'you know I've been dying for a cup of tea, Aengus," she said. "Good lad."

I made Pauline's tea and some coffee for myself to offset the effects of the wine and made my way back to the studio. I picked up the sketch pad and held it up again to the easel and the canvas board. The easiest thing for me to have altered would have been the window, but its scale looked fine relative to Hélène's outline and the room's dimensions. The ceiling height, too, looked in balance with the room. But somehow the walls and the window looked too close to her back, like she was in a cell. And that in turn gave the walls an ominous appearance, as though they were closing in on her.

I thought about Hélène's veiled criticism of Aoife – that she was perhaps wrapped up in her own world – with a pang of guilt, and about my own tendency to intolerance of those who seemed preoccupied with their own travails, to the exclusion of any concern for others. It was, I think, an intolerance that had lain dormant during my university years, but took firm root when we moved to London. Dublin, or that piece of it that I inhabited, was a small enough city – and Howth a small enough village – that people knew you, or they knew your parents or your grandparents. And they asked them about you or you about them. Maybe it was a feigned interest, I don't know, and maybe it got a bit irritating from time to time when their earnest concern seemed more like nosey curiosity. But it was a reassuring trait of community to feel that people cared. It was, I suppose, part of my father's almost-celebrity status, particularly in Howth, but I could not walk down the street in the village without fielding enquiries as to his well-being.

The corollary was also true: a consistent humility, a determination not to trouble others with one's own difficulties. An expression of concern or a simple enquiry would rarely uncover a problem, even when you knew all was not well.

"Grand, grand – sure you know yourself," they would reply to a "how are you?".

Even when you knew of a problem or misfortune and expressed sympathy or concern, the response was as likely to suggest guilt or justifiable comeuppance as bitterness or rancour.

"I heard your car was robbed," you might say.

"Ah sure, wasn't it my own fault to leave the feckin' door open. How are you anyway?"

I was always conscious that my cosy, hearty reflections on Irish life might be naïvely inaccurate, the emigrant's tendency to romanticise. I knew, I suppose, that it was hardly a universal truth of the Irish national psyche, this compassionate strength of character, this stoical indifference to adversity. In Dublin, bemoaning was often dressed up as indignation. I remember the story about a Dubliner who was passing a fire station while the firemen were conducting a practice drill. He stopped and looked on very approvingly at their industry, until one of them pulled a wrong lever and unleashed a powerful jet of water that hit him square in the chest, knocking him over and leaving him saturated. Brushing himself off, he stood up and shouted at the errant fireman, "Jaysus, you wouldn't feckin' *do* it to me if I was on fire!"

But our London was a bigger, more impersonal, more transient place. We lived on the same street for almost ten years, and yet fostered no close friendships nor even neighbourly acquaintances. People I passed every day on the street or saw at the tube station would walk by with diverted or downcast eyes. Even when I went running in the park, other runners would give the lie to our supposed bond of suffering by looking the other way rather than returning my nodded greeting.

I think it was a lack of empathy that permeated those relationships that we did forge, too. I got the sense that people didn't care. No, it's not that they didn't care – rather, they were preoccupied. They had drama enough in their own world and had no time to pay any real attention to ours. I often found myself recounting stories to people who would listen with avid, active interest, and I knew I had had exactly the same conversation the last time we spoke. And I knew that this time, too, they were listening but not hearing, and they would forget again. It wasn't even that they forgot. That is too harsh, suggests an active decision not to care. It was just that their lives and minds were full, there was no room for more. Like an overflowing bin, the things I tossed in would just fall out. Other people's problems just didn't fit.

And it didn't make London a bad place to live. We had friends whose company we heartily enjoyed. We had good times and good experiences, we laughed and we had fun. But without ever admitting so much, we knew it was skin deep. Even though we never let it bother us to the point where we acted, I could not shake a nagging pique that people's troubled progress through their own lives left them little capacity to really care about ours.

When times were good, perhaps it was relief that prompted them to openly broadcast their successes and good fortune. When times were bad, they were careful to dress up their failures, quick to lament the injustice of their misfortune. It was never malevolent, never malicious, just self-preserving. But the protective barricades we throw up around our own worlds often just isolate us, and keep out the very people who might help or alienate those who would share our happiness. And the more we do it, the less we communicate. And the more walls we build. Maybe it's why big cities can be such lonely places.

Maybe it was just because it was Aoife that I felt the twinge of guilt. Had Hélène been recounting the story of some unidentified friend who had let her down, who had gone travelling when they had agreed to go to Ireland, whom others found frustrating because she was too self-absorbed to care about them, maybe I would have nodded with knowing contempt. I had done it so many times before. And how many of those whom I might also have dismissed as "careless with people" had legitimate reasons for their introversion? How many had failing relationships or hidden illnesses? Difficult children or financial worries?

But it was Aoife. And whether it was because I could never imagine her as flawed or because I blamed myself for any flaws she might have had, I could never have been contemptuous of her. Does a parent have to, by definition, love his child? Surely there are children so vilely unpleasant or viciously unkind to challenge even a parent's love? I suppose it's the important distinction between to love and to like – it is the fate of a parent to always love their children, even if they can't bring themselves to like them. And maybe in those instances, is it the child that the parent loves, or the vision they had for what their child could be? Wouldn't that be the worst punishment? A life sentence.

I remember one time we went away for a weekend with some friends and their two young children, who were – if it is possible for there to be more than one – the anti-Christs. They dedicated the weekend to weaving a tense misery around everything that we did and, when we could take no more and made a hastily transparent excuse to get away early on Sunday afternoon, we sat in silence in the car until Caitríona turned to me and said matter-of-factly:

"I'd kill myself. If I had those two, I'd kill myself. I'd kill them, only I'd go to jail. So I'd just kill myself. And you for doing it to me."

Maybe that was why I never truly questioned Caitríona's insistence that we would not have another child. Because the lottery of it scared me. That you could end up with a child you didn't actually like, or that your child could be unhealthy or disabled. I'm not sure anybody ever really believes the former – we think that no spawn of ours could be so bad or that we will be able to mould the child of our dreams. But that latter possibility truly terrified me.

In my daydreams of meeting Aoife, she was perfect. Of course she was. She was funny and kind, pretty and engaging, positive and bright. Over the years, I would play with the child Aoife in the park and then sit with the growing teenaged Aoife in the cafés in my mind. We would laugh loudly and unself-consciously and play happily with a ball or on swings, or linger over coffee and deep conversations while she joked and teased me and touched my arm and listened intently to my every word. Although strong, she would tell me about her problems, seek out my advice and gratefully accept my help.

But sometimes, when I saw a misbehaving child scream at a ragged parent in a shop or on the street, I wavered. What if Aoife was like that, not a perfect angel at all but a child-demon? And later, when I saw surly teenagers slouching angrily down the street, it made me wonder again and imagine an altogether different Aoife, until I guiltily threw the treacherous thought away.

Now the creeping doubts were back, but this time supported by the substance of a reality I could only have imagined up until now. Now, the picture emerging in my mind's eye was based not purely on my imaginings, but on the weary reports of a good friend who knew her well. And the question loomed starkly: you might find her, but what if you don't like her? In some ways, I conceded in my mind's debate, there was no reason I should like her. There was, for a start, the generation gap. She probably communicated only with abbreviated tappings on a keyboard rather than by talking, watched reality TV rather than football, and listened to hip-hop or boy-bands on her iPod rather than U2 or Dylan. Her character would surely have been shaped by her parents. She was almost French, for Christ's sake, all pouting affectation and Gauloise cigarettes. And she was given to self-obsession. A chasm of age, culture, technology and gender.

But she was my daughter and, more importantly, she was a little piece of Caitríona. Despite all the nagging fears and suggestions to the contrary, deep in my heart I knew I would like her and love her and she would be charming and perfect. I knew she would.

I sat back and stared at the canvas, trying to see a way to undo and repair the work. I thought about going into the house to see if Lochlann could give me some advice, but I wasn't really in the mood to talk to him. And I had a childish determination not to show him he was right and that I was out of my depth after all.

The sound of voices grew louder as Oran and some of his charges approached the Gallery door. To give my addled mind a break from its deliberations, I got up and went in to talk to him.

"How're ya?" he said when I came out of the studio. He turned back to his two workmates. "Listen, lads, them tiles have to be finished tonight, end of. So get crackin' and nobody leaves here this evening until I say so. Right?"

With mumbled assent, the two men shuffled off to get tiles and grout and to start work.

Oran turned to me again with a grimace.

"Snowball's fuckin' chance," he said under his breath, raising his eyes to the roof. "How're you anyway? I saw the French bird leavin' earlier. You haven't pissed her off again, have ya?"

"No. The 'French bird', as you so eloquently describe her, is playing a gig down in Naas tonight, so she had to go and get ready."

"Right." He nodded with a mischievous smile. "So let's see this paintin' then." He pushed past me and into the studio. I followed him in. He was already standing at the easel, nodding almost undiscernibly.

"So, do you approve then?" I asked.

His tone became suddenly serious.

"Not fuckin' bad, Aengus," he said, looking at me then back at the canvas. "Not fuckin' bad. So when do you add the paint?"

"Soon. Next week I'd say." I shook my head in frustration. "But I just can't get the background right. It's driving me fucking mad."

"Yeah," he nodded. "It's a bit on top of her, isn't it?"

I nodded. He never ceased to surprise me, this oafish thug with a streak of artistic sensitivity.

"Exactly right. When did you become a critic?"

"I've been around your father for a long time. Even a monkey learns eventually."

"And your solution would be…?"

He shook his head.

"That's the great thing about being a critic – you can criticise, but you never have to actually do anything! Have you asked Lochlann?"

I shook my head.

"Fuck sake, Aengus," was all he said.

We studied the canvas in silence for a few minutes to the strains of a tiler's plaintive whistling. Then I had a thought.

"Maybe it's not so much that it's all closing in on her – maybe it's because it's dwarfing her?"

He said nothing. I went on, sensing a crack of light in the blackness.

"If it was a bit smaller, or not as high even, it might look further back."

"Deeper?" he ventured.

"Exactly, Oran." Once again, he hit the nail on the head, and I stabbed a finger into his chest. "Deeper."

"So how do you do that?"

I pointed to the top of the wall on the canvas.

"If I take this a bit lower –" and then pointed to where the wall met the floor "– and take this up a bit, then I can maybe make the wall shorter, so it dominates less. What do you think?"

He struggled for a moment to see what I was saying, but then nodded.

"Yeah. Yeah, I think so." His voice was not fully convinced. "But then the bricks'll look huge?"

He was right.

"So I'll have to make the layers of stone thinner, make it look a bit farther back in the room."

"Right. Might work. Do you think?"

"I think it might, yeah."

"Look, I'll leave you to it then. Get it done before the thought goes away."

"Thanks, Oran. Really, thanks."

"No bother." He made for the door, then turned around. "Listen, I'm going down to Parnell Park this evening, there's a Minor Football challenge match, against Laois. Brian Molloy's young lad's playing. You want to come down?"

"I'd love to. If I get this done." I pointed at the canvas. "Give us a shout when you're going."

He nodded and left.

I set to work on the portrait with a new-found vigour.

It was a couple of hours later when Oran came back into the room. So engrossed was I in what I had to do that he was in the room and standing almost beside me before I heard him. I looked at my watch.

"Jesus, is it that time already?"

"Are you comin'?" he asked with a backward toss of his head.

I looked at the board. I had made some progress in the painstaking task of shifting the wall backwards, and it wouldn't take me long to finish the job. Besides I was tired and needed a break.

"Yeah, sure. Let me wash my hands. Two minutes."

I made for the washroom at the end of the Gallery. When I came back, he was standing in front of the easel again.

"Looks better," he said.

"Thanks. Did the boys finish the tiling?"

"Would you believe they did?" he said, shaking his head with a smile of exasperated disbelief. "And it's not a bad job either."

"Airborne bacon?" I said.

"Exactly," he grinned.

Parnell Park, or "The Nell" as we knew it in the mandatory abbreviation of children-speak, is on Dublin's North side, beside the church in Donnycarney. On a big day, it might hold over 10,000 baying Dublin fans, but that evening's less tantalising prospect drew only a few hundred. Oran and I, with our old friends, used to go there regularly to watch club games and the odd inter-county game. I hadn't seen the place in nearly twenty years, and it had clearly benefitted from the success and growing affluence of the GAA, and in particular of the sport in Dublin. It was summer and championship time, and I had been surprised to see so many people of all ages and both genders walking around town in replica county colours. As children, we were proudly decked out in the football shirts of our English footballing heroes, but today's plumage was of a decidedly more native hue and the colours of Dublin or Galway or Kildare vied with those of Arsenal and Manchester United and Liverpool.

Oran had arranged to meet Brian and another friend of his at the ground, both of whom I knew from our school-days but neither of whom I had seen for years. I wouldn't have recognised either of them. Blessed, predictably and inevitably, with more weight and less hair, they reminded me immediately of so many fathers of my childhood who watched us play football and took us to the Nell on days and evenings just like this. Surroundings and circumstances might change, but maybe little else really does.

The game was a drab affair, and we spent much of it distracted by Oran's lewd observations about three young women in Laois shirts sitting not far from us and who glanced back at us from time to time, huddling in giggled conspiracy. Whether their giggling was borne of derision or attraction mattered little, it was good entertainment. Half-time came and Brian pulled four cans of lager from his back-pack. We drank them and a few more that he produced from his tardis-like bag, and settled down to watch a second half that was as turgid as the first.

A poor game of football, in an empty stadium. Four grown men behaving like adolescents and drinking warm beer. It was good. We have access to so much entertainment in our modern lives that the very abundance of choice is overwhelming. I sometimes think that the breadth of what's on offer just adds to the stress of our lives – the nagging fear of having devoted scarce and precious free time and money to the wrong option takes away from our enjoyment of it in some self-fulfilling circular reference. It is a fear that is exacerbated by people's immutable determination to be luckier or better, their intense anxiety that somebody else might have done or seen or experienced something richer. And yet in the face of the exciting and expensive delights offered by far-flung destinations, lavish restaurants and luxurious getaways, often the greatest satisfaction comes from the simplest pleasure.

Dublin eventually ran out undeserving winners, and we all trudged out of the ground.

Brian and Terry made the usual excuses of children to put to bed and work the next day and declined our invitation to join us in the pub. So we shook hands and said our goodbyes and Oran and I headed for the DART station at Killester.

"Good lads, aren't they?" I said to Oran as we crossed the road.

"Yeah, they are. Hard workers, the pair of them. But not obsessed, you know what I mean?"

"I do. But it's hard not to be, it seems."

"Too right."

We got the train back to Howth and couldn't quite resist the lure of McGrath's as we left the station. Oran stopped to talk to someone and I took a seat at my already regular table in the corner. It was surprisingly quiet and Ella came straight over.

"Hey there, how are you doing?" she asked, wiping the table and throwing down some beer mats.

"Good, thanks. Just been up to watch the worst game of football we've ever seen, so we deserve a couple of pints I reckon."

"Sounds fair," she grinned. "You having a good time in Dublin?"

"Yes, thanks. It's nice to be home"

"So you're sticking around for a while then?"

"For a while, I suppose. Yes."

"Where is it you live?"

"London."

"Oh right," she said. "But you're from Dublin? Originally, I mean?"

"Yes. From Howth, actually."

She was surprised for some reason, then more animated. She leaned towards me and whispered conspiratorially.

"I spent a year working in London. Bloody hated it." She was suddenly contrite. "Shit, sorry. That was a bit rude, slagging off your home."

I held up my hand.

"It's where I live. I never said it was home. Don't worry."

"I know exactly what you mean," she said, her voice rising as though she had found an unexpected ally. "It's so hard to settle down there, don't you think?"

She put a hand on my shoulder and smiled a mischievous smile.

"Come back to Dublin. It's great here, I promise!" She winked and nodded towards the bar. "I'll get your beers."

Oran came over and sat down. Another DART had just pulled into the station and the pub was suddenly buzzing with its discharged cargo of thirsty drinkers.

"Sorry. Bit of business," he said, mysteriously. "Shite match, eh? Sorry I dragged you out."

"Don't be daft," I replied. "I enjoyed it actually – not the football, mind – but it was nice just to go to a match again. And they're good lads, Brian and Terry. And a minor football challenge match this time of year is never going to be fantastic now, is it? Anyway, I needed a break."

"Did you get anywhere, do you think?"

"I think so, yeah. I think I should be able to finish off the changes in the morning, before Hélène arrives."

"How is she? To work with I mean. She seems like a good girl."

"She is, she's great. I've been very lucky to find her, to be honest – and lucky to keep her."

"Where did you find her?"

We used to joke that, when someone said something stupid or asked an awkward question, a silence would descend and you could hear the tumbleweed rolling down the street outside. It was one of those moments.

For no reason, I was suddenly emphatically tired of the secrecy, of twenty years of hidden truths. Caitríona and I had carefully crafted answers to so many simple, natural questions that I sometimes felt that whole relationships were fraudulent, built on fabrications. And just in that moment, I had had enough. I wasn't ashamed of Aoife. I wasn't going to endanger her or expose her in any way, and I had nobody else to protect anymore. Lochlann had confided in the Master, and so I wasn't breaching his confidence. In that moment, I felt free of a burden I had carried my whole adult life.

I looked at Oran, whose face had become puzzled by my delay.

"That," I said, with a spontaneous grin that I couldn't quite control, "is quite a story."

He raised his eyebrows, his curiosity piqued.

I drew a deep breath and herded the story's loose ends in my mind.

"Do you remember," I set off, not really sure where the road would lead, "when I was in University, in first year, and I met Caitríona?"

He nodded.

"Well, Caitríona got pregnant." I paused, more to recover than to let him catch up. When I started speaking again, the words came tumbling out and I could barely keep up. "We had a baby. In the Summer after my first year. I got a flat in town so she could come back to Dublin to have the baby. We couldn't look after the baby, so she was adopted." I paused again. "Apart from Lochlann, you're the first person I've ever told."

He looked at me and was silent for a couple of minutes. He seemed to be processing the information in his head, formulating a response. I searched for an emotion, a reaction in his face.

"Aengus," he said eventually, then paused, trying to find the words. "Aengus, I know. I've always known. Everybody knows."

As his lips moved and the sound came out in slow motion, I heard the words I expected to hear. For a nano-second of reality but for minutes in my head, he said what I knew he would say and I nodded in knowing appreciation of his comradely concern.

"Jesus, Aengus, you poor bastard," he was saying. "I can't believe it. How did you cope? That must have been tough. Why didn't you tell me?"

Then, like a cartoon car screeching to a halt, the flow of imaginary words stopped and I heard the real Oran. I heard what he said and I frowned. Then I closed my eyes and laughed quietly and with no humour to myself. In that instant, everything seemed so ridiculous and I laughed at the absurdity of it all. But it was also, maybe moreso, a laugh of relief that released years of pent-up tension and angst.

Ella came over with our drinks and we shared a joke about something or other, then she left us be.

"How did you know?" I asked him, taking a long draft from my glass.

"I actually don't know, Aengus," he said, shaking his head. "I mean, I don't remember how it came out, or even when. It just seems like it's one of those things we've all always known, and that was that."

"Why did you never say anything?"

He shrugged.

"At first, because it was a bit of a dark thing, you know? Like a dirty secret —" he raised a hand in apology, "sorry, like — but you know, something that you didn't talk about. And we were all young and easily embarrassed. And it just wasn't right. And sure I hardly saw you then for ages. And afterwards it was old news and awkward and you obviously didn't want to talk about it. And then the pair of you fucked off to England." He shrugged a QED.

"And did people talk about it?"

"A bit. For a while. Then something more interesting came along. Like a paint drying competition!"

We laughed, then went quiet. He broke the silence.

"Listen. You didn't know 'cos you never asked. But I was there for you, man. You only had to ask."

I nodded, because I knew, or had always hoped so.

"I know."

A pack of suits near the bar had clearly been in the pub for most of the afternoon, and had begun singing a selection of bawdy songs. Ella was in the middle of the group collecting glasses, and asked them to pipe down, but her plea was met only with wolf-whistles, puerile quips and loud sniggering. Oran glowered at them, and finally put his glass down on the table. He was about to go over to confront them, when the barman came round from behind the bar and jovially diffused any trouble.

Oran muttered a few obscenities in their direction and resettled himself.

"Listen," I said, "I know they piss you off, but you can't afford to go getting involved. Not with the case coming up."

"I wasn't going for a fight, just to shut them up."

"Yeah, because your self-control in inflammatory situations is the stuff of legend."

"Jaysus, hasn't fatherhood made you all mature, eh?"

"Am I going to have to put up with Daddy jokes from you from now on?"

"Too fucking right!" he retorted, pointing a finger at me and grinning, recovering his composure. "So what's all this got to do with the French bird anyway?"

I had forgotten where this trail had started.

"Well, I've started looking for Aoife…"

"Aoife?"

"Our daughter. Her name is Aoife."

He looked at me and was quiet for a moment, and nodded gently.

"Nice. Nice name."

I was surprised to feel flattered, and I smiled sheepishly in spite of myself.

"Thanks. Anyway, I think it's time, and I've started looking for her." I told him about the Adoption Agency website and how it had led me to Paris, about the club and the scribbled farewell in the photo album. "And that convoluted trail led me to… Malahide. Of all places, to Malahide for fuck sake!"

I told him about going to the house and finding Hélène, and finding that Aoife was not there.

"I was going to give up and go back to London, but then I got talking to the Master and it turns out Lochlann had told him about Aoife and he convinced me to stay, to get Hélène to sit for me and to stay." I turned my outstretched palms to the ceiling. "And that's where we are."

"So where's Aoife now?"

"Don't know. Hélène doesn't know. She went off travelling, she was supposed to come here but that was months ago. I get the feeling that they fell out, or that there's a bit of bad blood. But I don't know how serious it is."

"Does she know who you are?"

I nodded.

"I didn't want her to know, but she figured it out. Like an idiot, I kept asking about Aoife even though I'm not supposed to know anything about her. Hélène knows Aoife was adopted, and she realised where all the questions were coming from, I suppose. That's why she walked out last week. She got really angry, accused me of betraying Aoife. Whatever row they've had, she still obviously cares about her."

Oran sat back and drew a deep breath.

"So are you going to stick around then? Wait for her?"

"I suppose so. But I don't know how long for – depends on how long I can afford to stay I suppose, and how long Lochlann will put up with me. She might never arrive, I might need to start looking all over again."

"You really want to find her?"

"More than anything."

He nodded.

"Good man."

CHAPTER 21

I never liked Áine, your friend from Tipperary. I had no reason not to nor a shred of evidence that she reciprocated my antipathy. God knows, I gave her enough ammunition over the years, enough justification for petty loathing. And yet she never rose to take the bait. First, I kept you from her for those passionately introverted first months after we met. Then, it must have seemed to her, I lost interest so that you hid away in Wexford mourning that whole Summer, and never even called when you came back to Dublin. And then, just when shallow student frivolities were giving way to the adult maturity she must have craved, I took you to London. And you never came back.

Or did she know all the time that it was the shame of unmarried pregnancy that drove you to Wexford? Was she poised, ready to help and support you when you called? Did she despair that I had abandoned you? Did they all know, all the time?

She was never one for frivolity, Áine. Serious and studious, she lived student life with the earnest devotion of one who didn't think she ever really deserved it but was determined to repay its permission to take part. She was unbearably, excruciatingly grateful for everything. If you invited her to join us for a drink, she gushed like you had bought her a puppy. If you remarked on her grades – always good – or her appearance – always neat – she blushed until I needed to open a window. I naturally assumed it was all a deceit-based master-plan –

nobody could be that saccharine without ulterior motive. And yet I was the only one to see it.

Of course I was wrong. I look back now with a splinter of shame when I think about how I treated her, tried to marginalise her. I wasn't vicious or deliberately hurtful – I just didn't want her in my world and nor, therefore, in yours. But she was just a girl trying to get through life with the baggage of whatever that life had thus far dealt her.

If Ireland was populated by one hundred people, or one thousand, we'd have to make the effort. We'd have to accept that the thousand people of Ireland were in our lives and that the course of our lives to some extent would be determined by them. And so we'd try to fathom them, to understand what made them the people they were. What fears and neuroses filled them with dread. What small things excited and enthralled them.

But we don't. The population, by its very size, overwhelms us like the choice on supermarket shelves. If a tomato looks too red, take another. So it is with people. If they are too funny or too dry, too loud or too quiet – take another, plenty to choose from. So we do. And we accept that immediate gratification might come at the cost of finding a kindred spirit, a soul-mate. And even if our interest is prodded by a stranger whose conversation we overhear, there's no time to make his acquaintance and no obvious advantage to accrue from so doing.

If I walked into McGrath's and bumped into Oran or accidentally spilled his pint, how would I find him? Witty, accommodating, relaxed? No. Bellicose, belligerent, unforgiving? Almost certainly. Knowing him as I do, I know that to dismiss him would be to discard a gem. But few will take that chance and so few will have that chance. And yet I fell under your spell, and all too readily. Does that mean that we are destined to find the one who is meant to be found? Does that mean that I am destined to find you again? In another student bar on some obscure parallel plane, or in some other common haunt on a faraway sphere? Will you be my friend or my sister or my nemesis? Or will you once again be my soulmate? You know that I scoff at the romantic humbug that promotes such philosophies, but I still wonder.

So how would we react, I wonder, to Aoife? This slightly aloof girl with her search for who knows what and her fixation on, I suppose, herself. A bit distant, hard to get to know, none too reliable and frankly a bit uptight. Would that be our conclusion? And I wonder how I would react if I heard such a conclusion drawn? How would Áine's brother or father have reacted to my unkind and unwarranted dismissal of her, borne of no more than a shallow and careless disrespect for what she was, a failure to take the time to understand her? To understand the forces that had buffeted her young life so that she was now so timid and so grateful and so in awe.

I find myself now, for the first time in my life, looking for the good in the people I come across, guilty that for so long I have been too ready to see the bad or too preoccupied to care. I'm frightened, I suppose, that I would just see a cold, self-absorbed young woman. Where my beautiful daughter stands.

CHAPTER 22

I suppose I started running every day to find a way to escape.
I needed to get away from the pressure of living and working
in London, to run away from it, maybe. We need our own time,
time to break free of the endless prying attentions of others
and to just indulge in some selfish introspection, self-pity and
self-congratulation. Among the pressing throng of the city,
there is no personal space, nowhere to go to be alone. And
yet running along a crowded river tow-path or through parks
crammed with people, you can feel somehow solitary in your
own head, insulated by some invisible shield from the world
outside. I did some of my best work when out running, finding
an imagination and a creativity that managed to elude me in
the confines of the office.

For a while after Caitríona left me, I couldn't bear to run.
It was the knowing that she wouldn't be there when I got back.
I felt that if I went out, I would have to run forever to avoid
coming back to the vacuum she left behind. Rather than an
escape, running became a prison. In time, I started again,
slowly overcoming the pain of coming home with nobody to
ask how it had been. I cried the first few times, racked with a
desperate emptiness that made my gut ache, the tears trickling
down my cheeks as I ran.

Now, once again, it's an antidote to all of my life's ills.
Whether overcome with lethargy, fighting despondency or
even riding a rare wave of positive feeling, pounding the streets
under dark clouds or blue skies is where I feel I belong, at home

on the road. Maybe it's because we never ran together that I feel it's a sanctuary, somewhere I can pretend that everything is still ok. But still, as I turn the key in the lock when I come home, I feel the same debilitating ache in my stomach, and still I have to fight the urge to cry. Sometimes I don't fight it at all.

Coming home to Lochlann's house after running on the Head had proved a blessed and unexpected relief. Pauline's incessant chatter or the sound of Oran berating a workman or of Lochlann answering the phone in his study was a far cry from the empty, quiet chill of our London home. And I basked in it a little every time I came in.

And while I was out, my mind was filled more with positive thoughts than at any time since Caitríona went away. In those first, pain-filled days in London's parks or on the banks of the Thames, I had to work ceaselessly to push my thoughts out of the negative places they always wanted to go. Like a teacher corralling children on one of our school tours to Skerries or Bray, I had to keep my mind away from the cigarette shops and one-armed bandits of self-pity and lonely despair. But whether it was the passing time or the familiarity of the Head and the comforting sight of the Sugar Loaf and the Mourne Mountains, the fight to keep the blackness out of my head seemed a little less intense and a little less fearsome.

That is not to say that the loneliness was dispelled. In the quiet moments, like in all of the quiet moments whenever I was on my own, Caitríona would be with me and I had to shake off the small devils on my shoulders and their temptations to just give up, to surrender. When the only sound was the waves and the gulls and the weight of my breathing, the blackness might still descend and the demons would linger and goad me with whispered suggestions of doubt.

That morning, the early chill heralded imminent Autumn and the trails had lost their Summer hardness. I kept the black emptiness at bay with thoughts of painting and the exhibition, but a new shadow was cast long over my consciousness. Although I wanted so desperately to find Aoife, the emerging prospect of seeing her brought a new and altogether unexpected emotion. Maybe it was acknowledgement that I was doing what Caitríona had expressly asked me not to do. Maybe it was a fear of rejection – that she would reject me or, worse, that she would not – could not – be what I dreamed she would be, what I craved. Because if she failed to meet the wildly unrealistic expectations I had crafted, it would be my fault. But I think it was a fear that finally reaching that destination would lay bare again the pain of losing Caitríona, but without the distraction of the search for Aoife. And I had no other seam to mine.

I got back to the house and leaned against the gate-post, out of breath and sweating hard after an ill-advised final assault on the hill-side trail that led up from the Baily. It was almost eight o'clock, and I could hear the reassuring sound of Pauline's chatter and kitchen clatter. As I stretched the acid out of my aching muscles, the door from the kitchen opened behind me and a voice said:

"Thought I heard you back – you're turning into a right action man, aren't you?"

I turned around, and Niamh walked out of the house and down the path towards the gate that still propped me up. There was still that old vulnerability, a sort of uncertainty, about Niamh that had been there throughout our childhood and teenage years. Maybe she had once outgrown it and found a place in life where she was comfortable, only to be torn from it by the failure of her marriage. Or maybe she had always remained so, the same timid Niamh that we gently mocked but whom we would have fought to defend from the unkindness of anyone outside our clique.

"Hi, Niamh," I smiled, a note of surprise in my voice. "What brings you up here? Were you up with the wee lad again?"

She shook her head.

"No, not today," she said. "His father had him last night."

"Oh right. I'm sorry," I said, then immediately winced. The child wasn't dead, for God's sake, and sticky pity was probably not what she wanted to hear. I was surprised, without having any reason to be so, at the matter of fact way she said it. I suppose I was expecting a tremor in her voice, a quiver in her lip when she referred to the break-up – in the patronising way that we so often expect people's lives to be the clichéd soap operas we imagine for them. Although timid and seemingly vulnerable, Niamh had never proven weak and I should not have assumed that she would be so in the face of this latest adversity.

She smiled at my awkwardness.

"That's alright. I take it you've heard then?"

"Yes. Oran told me."

"Hard to keep a secret round here!"

"Always has been, I suppose. Small town and all that."

I shivered involuntarily.

"Sorry, Aengus, you should get inside before you catch cold."

"I should. You'll come in for a coffee?"

She hesitated.

"Ah, I won't. I'm sure you have things to be getting on with."

"No, really. Come on, I'm going to make one anyway."

She shrugged with a faint smile.

"Alright then."

I ran upstairs to pull on a fleece top and came back down to find Niamh making the coffee.

"Listen I just wanted to say thanks for rescuing me the other morning," she said, pouring a cup for me. "You really did save my life you know!"

I smiled.

237

"No problem. You're just lucky I remembered how to start a car – not the most technically competent, remember?"

She grinned. "True! So how long were you out running for?" she asked.

"About an hour I suppose. It's beautiful out there, I'd forgotten how beautiful."

"Do you run much?"

"Every day if I can, if I don't get a bit lazy. How about you? Ever get bitten by the running bug?"

"God, no! Running after Micheál is about all I'm good for, and I won't be able to keep up with him for much longer!"

"How old is he?"

"Nearly five," she said, unable to hide the quiet smile in her voice.

"And you've another little one, Oran was saying?"

"I have. Ciara. She's just gone two."

She handed me a mug and I used the coffee to camouflage my loss of words. How did I broach the subject? Was it taboo altogether? Or could I offer condolence or encouragement or congratulation, even? There must be cases where the end of a poisonous marriage is a thing to be celebrated. Or would I risk breaking some unwritten code of marital break-up enquiry?

Niamh rescued me from the edge of the precipice.

"So, what did Oran tell you?"

I shrugged.

"Nothing really. Just that you had broken up with your husband." I paused, looked at her for a trace of upset, but there was none. "I really am sorry, Niamh. It must be hard."

She looked down at the floor before answering.

"It was, I suppose. Hard for Micheál especially. He didn't understand, of course. He still doesn't, I think. But he misses his Daddy."

"How long ago?"

"We split just over a year ago." She sighed. "He was travelling a lot with work, and the temptation just got too much for him, I suppose. It became final at the start of the Summer."

"Do you see much of him?"

She shook her head.

"Not really, just when we have to. He doesn't come round much, doesn't even want to see the kids that often, which is a blessing I suppose in some ways. Although they miss him. Especially Micheál."

"And you? I mean, are you ok? Moving on?"

She nodded.

"Yes," she said, simply. She was about to continue, but stopped and looked at me, a question in her eyes. She tossed a mental coin and it landed heads. Heads you venture into the uncharted ground...

"Aengus, I heard about Caitríona," she said slowly, as though prodding tentatively with a stick, afraid of the response. "I'm so sorry."

My lips narrowed and hardened in the stock defensive position, set against fear of crumbling. As time went on, it seemed that people felt less obliged to broach the subject, there was less chance that they would. My friends in London had already expressed their sorrow and their pity and they knew that I still couldn't really talk about it. So they steered clear, sometimes painfully, obviously clear, of any reference to Caitríona, like stepping gingerly over a pool of murky water. Of course she came up in conversation from time to time, inadvertently finding her way into a story or a reminiscence. But though I had started to try, I still wasn't able for the conversation, I couldn't carry on talking or listening. And so my friends would stop talking abruptly, steal a guilty, concerned look my way, and change the subject. There were very few people now that I hadn't spoken to or been with since Caitríona left, but that somehow only made it worse.

"Thanks, Niamh," I whispered at the floor.

And yet, for the first time, I felt something else stirring, something else fighting to take over from the customary onset of tired weakness. I realised for the first time that I resented the pain. I resented it. Just like when, with Oran in McGrath's, I had found myself suddenly tired of the pretence, I was at that moment explosively weary of feeling hopelessly lost and seeing no end to the torment. I hated the weakness of it, my own weakness. I loathed that I had lost the run of myself, lost control. But I had no bold move that could cut out the cancer, no revelation on the back of which I could clamber out of the abyss.

I took a deep breath, counted to five, trying to regain control enough to speak. I must have known that asking Niamh to share a coffee, to come inside to talk, I must have known that it would inevitably lead me to this place.

"Thanks," I managed to muster, again.

"Oh, Aengus, I'm sorry, I shouldn't have..." Niamh couldn't bear to be the cause of pain, and she was aghast at having blundered thoughtlessly into still painful memories.

"Jesus, we're a right pair," I said with a snort and a rueful smile, wiping away stray tears with a rough sweep of my sleeve. But with almost a smile.

Niamh came over and put her arms around me.

"God, Aengus. I'm sorry, I'm so sorry," she whispered.

We stood there holding on to each other in silence, punctuated by quivering intakes of breath and long, deep, resigned sighs.

Eventually Niamh stood back, embarrassed slightly by the unsolicited display of affection, and reached for my hands, squeezing them hard.

"I was going to say 'are you ok?'" she said. "Why do people always say that when ok is so obviously the last thing you are?"

"Because there's nothing else to say, I suppose."

We smiled.

"Thanks, Niamh," I said, again. "Christ, I think that's the first time I haven't had to run away. Whenever someone talks about it, I just panic. I can't be in the same place as the words. Do you know what I mean?" I was clutching for a way to express the feeling, and I shook my head in frustration. "Sorry, I'm talking shit. Sorry."

I pulled a tissue from a box on the counter, and handed her the box.

"No, I do know what you mean," she said, quietly. "I think I do. At first, it's all too much, too much to handle. So you run away and hide from it. But eventually you know you have to stop running. You know it's going to hurt you, but to even begin to face it, you have to be able to stand up to it. If you don't stand up to the bully, the bully'll keep beating you up."

I nodded. That was exactly it. Eventually I would have to stop turning tail and taking emotional flight. Even if I was going to get badly beaten up, eventually I would have to stand and fight.

"I just battle to see the future, Niamh, you know?" I said. "It's not like we had it all mapped out or anything, but I knew it would be fine because I knew she was going to be in it. Standing up to it means facing up to a future that doesn't have her, and I can't even begin to imagine what that's going to be like."

I suppose she knew exactly what that felt like.

"They say time is a great healer, but sure it's just wishful thinking," she said, with a rueful shake of her head. "It doesn't really heal anything, you just get used to the pain. Your leg is still broken, but you learn to limp faster. I think you have to stop waiting for the pain to go away and just accept that it's always going to be there. Learn to live with it and get on with building a future. What else is there?"

The clock on the window-sill chimed, and Niamh looked at her watch.

241

"Oh God, I'm picking Micheál up and I'm late," she said. "I have to go. Are you going to be ok?"

She looked up into my eyes to search for a sign of life.

"Look, I'll come back," she said. "I'll drop him at nursery and I'll come back."

"No," I said, "I'm fine, really. You go ahead, I have to get to work and, anyway, Hélène is going to be here soon."

Her eyes asked the question.

"Hélène," I said again, "I'm working on a painting and she's sitting for me."

"OK," she said quietly.

"Listen," I said, "some night, let's go for a drink or something. I promise I won't cry like a girl again, honestly." It was a weak attempt at humour but a genuine offer. It was never going to be easy, I had no doubt about that. But somehow I felt that the pain, although heartbreaking, had stopped somewhere short of hopelessness for maybe the first time.

"That'd be nice," she nodded, softly.

I walked her out to the car park and she unlocked the car.

"I feel terrible leaving you like this," she said. "Some friend I am."

"It sounds daft," I said, "but I meant what I said. It... I don't know... helped. Or something?" I shook my head, unable to express a headful of emotions.

She nodded.

"I'll see you soon, Aengus, yeah?"

"Yeah."

She reached up to kiss my cheek, got into the car and was gone.

Only the most naïve of us think that we are immune from fortune's cruelty, the way it has of blindsiding you. It knocks you off track so that no matter how well you plan for life, no matter how you insulate yourself against fate, these is no assurance that you will not be subject to some vindictive trick. Just the opposite.

Niamh and I were proof, if proof were needed. We were never gamblers of fortune, nor speculators on fate's markets. We never entertained thoughts of an adulterous fling that might rent our world asunder. We never bet our house on a sure thing investment, nor took holidays in exotic but dangerous locations. We never even drove too fast, for Christ's sake. And yet, somewhere along the way, we must have made a bet and lost. I just don't remember when. And lose we did, and our safe, solid, stable worlds were obliterated without reason.

I was left with part of a daughter, the part that is intriguing and interesting and beguiling. A young, independent woman in my mind, full of promise and potential, a world of opportunity at her feet. Sure, it was a part that caused me pain and longing and frustration, and for sure it was a part that would never banish the pain of Caitríona's loss. But it was the part that was – if any part of a child is – easiest.

But Niamh was left with two young children who depended on her totally, two small children to raise alone. Her time would never be her own, not for nearly twenty years. She would fetch for them and provide for them and nurture them, and she would shuttle them through their young lives. Never daring to be late for a pick-up, never wanting to refuse them a pleasure. Resenting their father, perhaps, but careful not to turn them against him, never wanting them to be without a daddy, even an absentee one. She would bear the brunt of their tantrums and irrational moods and the invective of the child denied. Although she would never admit it, she was trapped. She couldn't take a job in Cork or New York, couldn't spend Christmas on a Pacific Island, couldn't take up guitar classes at night school or join a drama group or a film club. She couldn't even hold out much hope that she would find love again.

Her job consumed seven days a week, she was on duty twenty-four hours a day. And the quiet moments, just after bed-time or during the school-day, must have been where guilt lurked. No parent can ever deliver the perfect world for their child, because the world is so far from perfect. The best they can ever hope to do is to deflect the pain, decorate their children's lives with pretty things that paper over the ugliness of the world, sing a happy song to drown out the sound of weeping. And on those days – and there will be lots of those days – when they're not there to block the pain, or when the paper is ripped to reveal the darkness below, or when they're just too tired to sing a happy song, the stunned, uncomprehending pain in a child's eyes will trigger remorse and self-loathing. Until the next time.

We're not all naïve, and yet generation after generation thinks that for them it will be different. The pure hope that comes from the programmed human need to nurture is stronger than any threat of hopelessness. Caitríona knew it. I never really understood.

I got back to the house to find Hélène waiting by the Gallery door, reading the newspaper. I asked her to make some coffee for us both and ran upstairs to shower quickly and change my clothes. When I came back down, she was waiting for me in the studio.

"Sorry about that, Hélène," I said, "I got waylaid. An old friend came up to see me."

"Yes," she replied, "I saw her, at her car."

To my surprise, she was clearly annoyed that I had kept her waiting. Of course, she had every right to be. She came in from Malahide every day, had never been so much as a minute late, and I couldn't even manage to travel the fifty metres to the studio on time.

"I am sorry, really," I said. "I should have been here. Sorry."

She dismissed my apology like a wronged teenager.

"You have to look after your girlfriend," she said.

I laughed, shaking my head.

"No, no," I said, "Niamh's not my girlfriend. We've been friends since we were children. Just friends."

"Oh. So you just had a sleepover then?" she said, her voice laden with a sarcasm I hadn't heard from her before.

It suddenly struck me that what Hélène had seen, a woman kissing me and leaving my home so early in the morning, suggested more than friendship. She was, I suppose, justified in leaping to the conclusion. If it made me seem nonchalant about the work we were doing, seem to be taking her for granted, then her annoyance might have been justified. But worse than that, sleeping with another woman, a woman who was not Aoife's mother, might suggest not only contempt for our work but, worse, a carelessness for the mother of the child I professed so desperate to find.

I cut the air with a flat, sweeping hand to stress my denial.

"No, no, no – you've got it all wrong, Hélène. It's nothing like that," I said. "She comes up here with her little boy in the mornings."

"But there was no little boy?"

"Not this morning, no," I threw up my hands to emphasise my innocence, conscious that I was making it sound so much more far-fetched than it should have appeared. "But a few days ago she was up here with him – on the Head – and her car wouldn't start and I got it going for her. And she just came up to say thanks."

"She could not have called, she had to come here before eight o'clock in the morning?"

"She had to pick up her little boy from his father's – they're divorced – the little boy spent the night with his father, and she came here on the way – that's where she was going."

My words were racing in my attempt to explain the innocence of it all, but succeeded only in making me sound desperate and thus guilty. I had nothing to explain, and no reason to explain myself nor justify my actions to Hélène, and yet for some reason here I was pleading for her to believe me.

"Look," I held up my hands to halt the careering words that threatened to knock me down. "Niamh is a friend. She came to say thanks. There's nothing more to it than that."

"It's fine," she stood up, put her mug on the desk and settled herself in the chair in front of the easel, ready for work. "It's none of my business anyway, what you do." She tossed the words at me in attempted nonchalance, but couldn't quite disguise her irritation. "But I leave my home at seven, I walk to the station, I take two trains and one bus – so just please try to be here when you say you will be here."

I nodded, suitably chastened, and we got to work.

The backdrop to the painting, the window behind Hélène and the stone walls around her, was a little more consistent with the figure in the chair, and I had decided to leave it alone for the time being to focus on putting the finishing touches to the pencil sketching of Hélène's form. I was finally satisfied with her hands, too, and was working on the shading of the shadows cast on her face.

We worked in silence, born partly, I suppose, of a little bit of lingering strain from the misunderstanding about Niamh, but partly also of a growing comfort with the process of painting. We had been working like this now for over a week, and we no longer felt the need to fill silence. For me, it was a chance to focus on my work. I don't know what passed the time for Hélène.

Around mid-morning, we took a break and made our way into the kitchen to get some coffee and toast, as had become our daily ritual. Hélène went to the bathroom and I put on the coffee machine. Pauline had left a note on the fridge door to say that she had gone into Dublin and would be back later in the afternoon.

Hélène came back in, twisting the ring on her right hand and looking a little sheepish.

"I'm sorry," she said, quietly. "I was wrong to say what I said. I jumped to the conclusion and anyway it's not my business. So, I'm sorry."

"Don't worry about it," I said, relieved that the episode was over. "The important thing is that we sorted it out. And there's no chance of me being late again – I wouldn't dare!"

She smiled, relieved too, I think, to close the chapter.

I made the coffee and Hélène made some toast and we took them back to the studio and sat around the little desk.

"Are you guys playing tonight?" I asked her.

She nodded, munching on some toast.

"Yes, in Dublin. We are in Dublin for a week now, we play five nights."

"It'll be nice not to have to travel so much, eh?"

"Yes. And Gerry – who drives? – I think he is not a very good driver. So I sit in the back and close my eyes and try to sleep." She shook her head, a faint smile playing on her lips at the thought.

Despite Gerry's questionable driving ability, I detected a change in the tone of her voice when she talked about him, a softness.

"What does he play?"

"He plays guitar, acoustic usually. And he sings."

"Is he any good?" I asked, trying to draw her out.

"Yes. He is very good."

"And what's he like? Is he a nice guy?"

She nodded and smiled again.

"Yes, he's a very nice guy. He has been very good to me, they all have. But especially Gerry. He helps with the songs, you know? Explains them to me and what they mean so I can really feel them when we play them. I think he makes me better, you know? I play better because of him. I don't think I would have found a place to play music if Gerry hadn't offered me a place."

There was a knock on the door and Lochlann came in.

"I'm sorry to disturb you," he said. He nodded almost undiscernibly to Hélène. "Good morning, Hélène, it's very nice to see you again."

Hélène smiled and nodded. "Hi. It's good to see you again, too."

"There's coffee in the pot – would you like some?" I said, standing up.

"No, no thank you. I've just come to see if you would be available to meet the exhibition manager tomorrow afternoon? He is going to be here at three o'clock. I thought perhaps you could share your thoughts with him."

"Sure, I'd be happy to."

"Good. Three o'clock then." He made a move to leave, then stopped, his eyes on the back of the easel.

"May I?" he said, his tone suddenly less sure, less business-like .

I nodded, and my stomach lurched at the thought that rejection now might put an end to all of this. And I was starting to feel comfortable in this persona, to be inspired by the work, to enjoy it even.

He came around the front of the easel and stood square in front of the canvas board. For what seemed like an eternity, he stood almost motionless, one hand slowly caressing his chin, the other behind his back. Still his expression betrayed no emotion. I looked at Hélène, her wide eyes even wider, filled with raw suspense. Still he said nothing, didn't move.

Finally.

"What colour do you intend applying?"

"Very little," I replied slowly, searching for the right answer, checking my words carefully for any indiscretion or error, like a child having his homework marked by a devious tartar teacher. "Monochrome, mainly. And a vivid red for the sash across the back of the chair."

"Hmm." Still silence again.

Then.

"You might think about browns. To bring out the earthy hues in the stone, the textured wood of the violin, her hair. They would merge with the burnt siena wash, when you apply it."

He was right, of course. The monochrome image I had pictured would be clean, but might be cold, lacking atmosphere. The earthy tones would make it warmer, maybe even bring it to life.

For a moment I forgot my nervousness and that he was delivering a verdict. For a moment we were friends collaborating, or he was a benign mentor.

"You're right," I said, with growing excitement as the image formed in my head. "That's a great idea. Make it real – turn it from a photograph into a window into a real room…"

"Indeed."

He made for the door to leave, then turned.

"Three o'clock tomorrow then, in the Gallery," he said. There was a long pause, then the faintest of nods. "Well done."

And he was gone.

We said nothing for what must have been two or three minutes after he left, then I couldn't contain a quiet, relieved laugh. Hélène looked at me and smiled.

"We did ok," she said, "yes?"

"You never know, I suppose," I rubbed my eyes with a smile that dared not to hope, "but yes – I think we did pretty well. We're still in the game anyway, that's the important thing."

We set back to work with the renewed vigour of affirmation. I put on some music and hummed out of tune to some of my favourite old rock classics – most of which had made it onto greatest hits compilations before Hélène was born. In that place, with Hélène, with work for which I had a real passion, with Lochlann's tacit approval, I felt infinitely less empty, less desolate. And, somehow, even a little less guilty for it.

CHAPTER 23

After Hélène had left for the day, I spent a couple of hours putting what were to be the final touches to the pencil sketching before "bringing it together", as Johnny had put it, with acrylics. I was terrified of the damage I might do with the paints. Quick-drying acrylic left little margin for error, and far from bringing it together, I was afraid I might tear it apart. But if it was to be finished in time, then now was the time to move on.

Oran came into the studio as I was tidying up for the day.

"Did Lochlann tell you he's meeting O'Leary tomorrow?" he asked.

"He did."

"Good. He's a lazy bastard, and he won't want to change the design. So it'll take the three of us to bully him."

"If he's used to fighting with you and Lochlann, he's not going to be too scared of me."

He winked conspiratorially.

"The more the better. And you're new and you're a big-shot designer from London. Or at least we'll say you are. He doesn't need to know you just draw pictures for a living!"

"Thanks very much!"

He grinned and looked around.

"She gone home?"

"Hélène? Yes."

"Fair dues to you," he said, "you've a good eye on you. I saw her on the train Tuesday evening and I swear, everyone was just staring at her. She is a bit gorgeous, isn't she? Too gorgeous to even notice me, by the way."

"I suppose she is."

"You suppose? You're standing staring at her every day – if anyone should know, it's you!"

"Alright. In my professional opinion, she is very attractive. Satisfied?"

"Oh right, and it was your *professional* judgment that picked a gorgeous French girl for you to work with one-on-one, six hours a day. Nice work if you can get it, I suppose."

I sighed and shook my head – this was a primary school playground discussion that I didn't really want to have

"You know why I asked her to sit for me. And you know that she's my daughter's best friend. My daughter's best friend, for fuck sake."

He put his hands up in mock self-defence.

"Jaysus, you were a lot more *craic* before you had kids, you know that?" he grinned.

I grinned back and pointed a warning finger at him.

"And while we're on the subject, she is *far* too good for the likes of you – so don't you even think about hanging around Hélène, do you hear me?"

Oran looked at me askance.

"Yeah, that's right. In case you'd forgotten, I'm about twenty years older than her as well, I have no job, no money, and a smashed up car. Oh, and I might be spending a wee while in jail. How could she possibly resist that, eh?"

"Isn't it what every girl dreams of?" I laughed, and slapped him on the back. "Anyway, I think she's got a soft spot for the guitarist in her band, and even twenty years ago, we'd never have been able to compete with a musician. We were never that cool! So having established that Hélène is way, way out of your league, come on – it's been a tough day and I'd murder a pint."

The DART hadn't yet started tipping glazed-eyed city workers into McGrath's, their ties like nooses strangling them slowly. So we sat in the pub in the blissful peace of a late summer evening, a golden light from a dipping sun streaming through the terrace doors. When I worked in London, I used to relish these little trips to the pub before heading home. On the last working day of each month, basking in the smug satisfaction of having done my daily run in the morning, I would meet Caitríona to pay tribute to the small triumphs of the thirty days gone by. Neither dead nor fired. Or if she wasn't able to make it, maybe just some colleagues or a friend. Or sometimes just alone with the paper and the crossword. Our lives are so fraught with targets and goals and things to be done that we don't often take the time to acknowledge the small achievements of the everyday. I was determined that, in the face of growing lists of things to do, I would always take a moment to quietly celebrate the things that were done.

We chatted about nothing for an hour.

"Was that Niamh's car I saw coming out of the car park this morning?" Oran asked me then, wiping away the moustache of creamy stout from his upper lip.

"Yeah. She came up to the house."

"How is she?"

"Good, I think. She's tougher than we think is Niamh, I think she'll be ok."

"It's hard though – bringing up two kids on your own." He shook his head. "I don't know how you'd do it."

"I know. I said I'd meet her for a drink some night."

He looked at me.

"Careful," he said, and took a drink.

I waited for him to continue, but he let the word hang in the air.

"Of what?" I asked.

"You know what. Rebound City."

In despair, I put my hand to my forehead.

"Oran, do you think I have nothing else on my mind? Do you think I'm going round all day on a woman hunt?" I shook my head and leaned forward in my chair. "Oran, listen to me alright – it's the very last thing I'm looking for. I mean it."

But his tone wasn't the playground chaffing of before, rather it was uncharacteristically contemplative, grave even.

"I'm not saying you're on the hunt. I just don't want to see either of you doing anything stupid. You two have a history. I'm just saying be careful, that's all."

I nodded and accepted that his motives were sound. I changed the subject.

"Listen, Hélène's band is playing in town for the next few days. Will we go see them?"

"What do they do?"

"I don't really know – trad rock I think."

He shrugged.

"Sure, why not. Where are they on?"

"Don't know. I'll ask her tomorrow."

"Fair enough."

He looked at his watch.

"I'd better get off," he said, picking up his glass to finish the pint. "A couple more of these and I'll be here for the night, and I've to be in early in the morning."

"By the way," I said, as we put on our jackets. "You said you saw Hélène on the train on Tuesday evening? Are you sure it was Tuesday?"

"Yeah. I was coming back from the builders' merchants. Why?"

"No reason. Just, I thought she was playing down in Athlone on Tuesday night." I shook my head. "I must have got it wrong. Doesn't matter."

The next morning, I finally had to put aside my fear of the damage I could do with the acrylics and begin the end of the painting. I looked at the pencil sketching, and I had to admit that Lochlann might have been right. If it was to have been an image in charcoal, then with a few finishing touches it might well have stood the test of hanging at the show. It was a reasonable attempt to capture Hélène cast adrift and disoriented. But he was right, too, that the addition of earthy shades would give it an atmosphere and an ambience that pure monochrome could not and so that was what I needed to do. I just hoped it was not beyond me.

"You look tired," I said to Hélène, as she stifled a yawn.

"A little," she admitted. "We rehearsed until late last night, and it was hard."

"Why?"

"These gigs in Dublin, they will be bigger than anything we have done before. More people, professional equipment." She drew a long breath. "And Gerry says that there might be record company people there one night."

"Jesus – that'd be fantastic!"

She couldn't contain the nervous smile, couldn't hide her thrilled trepidation.

"Yes, it would. But we have to be so good, so perfect in fact."

"Where are you playing?"

"At The Arena."

I was impressed – it was the kind of place that had refused us entry as students, and so retained a mystique that had survived the twenty years.

"Well, Oran and I are going to come see you play. What night should we go?"

She smiled again, for some reason flattered.

"Friday, maybe? That will be the busiest night and the best atmosphere. Thank you."

"It's a pity Aoife won't be here to see you," I said.

It wasn't an opportunistic manipulation to drag the conversation back to Aoife for my own motives – it was a genuine sense that it was a shame her friend would not be there for what might be a pivotal moment in her life.

She nodded. "She would be excited, I think."

"I guess she'd love the chance to do what you're doing?"

"Yes, I think she would. She dreams of making beautiful music, new kinds of music that change the way people feel. And she dreams of having something Irish – some little piece of Ireland – in what she creates. But she dreams too about being on stage with thousands of people screaming her name, or of having a record deal and CD's on the shelves in record stores and signing autographs. Maybe all art is vanity, but we all have dreams."

I nodded.

"We all do. But I hope it's not just ego. If I ever finish this piece – and if I'm truly happy with it and with what it says – I think it would be enough for me to hang it in my house so that I could look at it every day, get lost in it and in its story. And if I hang it proudly for everyone to see, I hope that it's because I want to tell them the story and to make them think about it and maybe be better for the thought. Or is it just because I need everyone to tell me how talented I am? I don't know."

"When we rehearse, we love to just play and make music – I love when we play the last notes of a song and rise to a big finish, it thrills me. But nothing is the same as being on stage, looking at people who love what you are doing. We say it is because we want to make people happy, to entertain. But isn't it really because we want to show off? It is the same for Aoife, I think."

"I can only imagine what that must feel like. I guess for a painter, there is no live performance. Only watching people looking at your work and reacting to it." I smiled. "You don't tend to get much hysterical screaming at an art show!"

She looked me for a moment, assembling the words, then said softly:

"I think maybe you would be proud of her, if you saw her play."

I stopped short and looked at Hélène. So many times I had dreamed of just that, of seeing her do whatever it was that she loved to do. And Hélène had seen her play. And Hélène was here with me in this room. For an instant Aoife was so close that I could almost touch her.

I shook my head slowly.

"I don't think I'd have any right to be proud, Hélène," I said, softly. "I'd be happy, so happy that she was happy and that she was good at doing what she loved doing. But I didn't put her in that place, didn't teach her or encourage her or share her frustrations and her successes."

I paused, searching for the words.

"A father is someone who has created a place for his child to develop and succeed. He has every right to be proud. I would have none."

Hélène looked at me and said nothing. Still she looked at me. Finally, she stood and laid the violin and bow on the chair.

"I need to fix my hair," she said, pulling it free from the band that held it and shaking it loose. "Excuse me for a moment." I walked over to the window and stared out at the Head. I had no right to feel proud, I knew that. And yet I had no doubt that I would. No doubt that I would see my daughter and that I would be filled with an uncontrollable pride until I would burst. Pride? No, not pride. Love. I would love her. I didn't know her, had never met her, knew nothing about her. And yet I knew beyond any doubt that, the moment I saw her, I would fall in love with her.

Hélène came back into the studio, and I shook myself free.

"So do you think you might get a record deal then?" I

asked, changing the subject and running away from the thoughts in my head.

She shrugged.

"I think we could, maybe we should – but it is so hard, there are so many good bands playing here now, it is hard to even get noticed. If we do get noticed, if the right person comes to see us and we play well, then we have a chance, I think. Gerry's friend got us the gigs at The Arena. It's our best chance."

"Why?"

"It is nice to play in small towns, but you do not get noticed there. But we have to play there because we need to make some money! But venues like that in Dublin, that is where people see you, people who can make a difference."

"I guess so."

I thought about what Oran had said, about seeing her on the train. I wasn't checking up on her, nor accusing, it was just a throwaway remark.

"Weren't you supposed to be playing in Athlone last Tuesday?"

She thought a moment.

"Yes, we did." She looked at the floor as she said it, aware after years of experience that her wide eyes provided poor cover for a lie.

"Oh. That's odd."

"Why?"

"Just that Oran said he saw you on the train on Tuesday evening." I immediately regretted what sounded like an accusation, felt guilty for doubting her when she had done nothing wrong. What she did was none of my business, and my curiosity was shallow. "He must have made a mistake. Hardly the most observant man I know!"

My attempt to throw the subject away on a joke was weak and it failed. She was silent, still looking at the floor. She was out of position, twisting the bow in her hand, but I didn't correct her.

"I'm sorry, Hélène, I didn't mean to suggest... I wasn't saying... anything."

She looked up at me at last, those dark eyes betraying the revolutions of her brain.

"I didn't go to Athlone," she said, slowly.

"It's fine, Hélène, it's none of my business," I said, in desperate retreat.

She continued to stare at me. The bow turned over and over in her hand, a mirror to the churning thoughts behind her eyes. Then she sighed deeply.

"I was at the hospital. I go there every week."

I waited for her to elaborate but she was quiet.

"Shit, Hélène, I'm sorry. I had no idea," I said. I paused, not sure how deeply to probe. But hadn't she volunteered the information? Even though I had perhaps led her down that path, it was as though she didn't mind. Maybe she wanted to talk about it, maybe she needed an outlet. "What's wrong?"

She sighed and shrugged and shook her head wearily.

"They don't know. They do tests and give me medication. But they still don't know. I get sick too easily, I seem to have been sick a lot recently, small things, but a lot. They say it's something to do with my blood count. But I don't understand." She shrugged again. "You know, I am afraid that it is maybe a cancer. I think they are afraid too."

As simple as that. No drama, no hand-wringing, no plaintive howling and no bitter claims of injustice. An honest response phlegmatically delivered, as was her way.

I couldn't find words. Every response that came into my head was so useless, so horribly inadequate. I walked around the easel and knelt down beside her, and put my arms around her, holding her close. She didn't respond at first, then she slowly put her arms around my neck and sighed again. It was only then that I realised how small, how fragile she really was. Fragile and alone.

We stayed that way for four, five minutes maybe, until my knees ached from the hard stone floor. Then I stood up slowly, pulled round a chair from the other side of the desk and sat beside her.

"Are you ok?" I stuttered, stupidly. "I mean, shouldn't you be resting or staying in hospital? You should be taking it easy, shouldn't you?"

She shook her head.

"They say I can stay at home, that I can continue to play music. I just have to be careful, of course, not try to do too much, not get sick. But until they know for sure what it is, they want me to continue to be as normal as I can."

I nodded.

"And are they treating you ok, I mean are you happy with what they're doing?"

"Yes, I think so. I am not a doctor so I just have to trust them."

"Don't you want to go back to France? To your family?"

She shook her head.

"No. I don't want to have to talk to them about this."

Why, I wondered.

"Listen, why don't you come and stay here? There's loads of room and Lochlann wouldn't mind?"

"No," she said, firmly. "Thank you."

"Look, Hélène, I know you hardly know me and I know you might think I've done wrong things in the past – but I hope we're friends and I really do want to help you. And Lochlann is well-connected, he knows lots of doctors and medical people. He can help too. I'll do anything I can. I mean that. Not just because you're Aoife's friend. You're my friend too, I hope."

And I did mean it. This girl, whom I had met only a couple of weeks before, had touched me somehow. I admit that I had gone to find her to use her, in a way – to use her to get close to Aoife. But now I cared about this enigmatic, calm young woman. I cared about her and for her for reasons I couldn't quite explain. And I didn't feel the need to try.

I couldn't understand why she would choose to be alone. Why did she spurn the warm familiarity of her friends and family? What upheaval or fight could have been so final as to push her to lonely isolation just when she most needed support? I didn't pursue it, I had no right and I knew nothing of the circumstances. And maybe the sea below Howth Head rekindled some distant emotions and fond memories of the ocean around Biarritz. Maybe it provided some comfort.

I was in no mood to tackle the application of the acrylics. Already nervous, the morning's tidings had filled my head with other thoughts and the distraction made me useless. So we ended the day early and went down to Howth village for lunch. She spoke candidly of how she had at first become concerned that something was amiss and how she had first visited the hospital assuming that it was an uncomfortable, inconvenient triviality that would be dismissed with antibiotics or some other medication. I was humbled that she remained so even, without so much as a suggestion of the histrionics that others would surely display in her circumstances. That I had displayed, perhaps continued to display?

The world is a dark place. A dark place filled with black-souled people with scant regard for others and a rabid lust for power and wealth. A dark place filled with virulent disease that destroys even the most innocent, the most pure. A dark place at the mercy of fortune, a cruel, ambivalent force that strikes for no reason, based on no pattern or plan.

And yet we choose to bring children into this world, aware of the darkness, aware of the pain that lurks throughout. Why? Why does any man or woman think that it will be different for their child? Why do they think that they uniquely can protect their child from the world? They can't. Nobody can. And why do they see a future that is bright and hopeful when the evidence all around us points to ever greater violence and greed?

We are programmed to perpetuate the race and to continue proud family lines. We think of the good things that we have enjoyed, and we want to pass them on. But when we think about the uncertainty and the fickle chance that would define our child's life, that should at the very least raise a question. To bring a child into the world, and to raise that child and to send it out into the world prepared and able – that involves surely the greatest sacrifice that we can make. And for what? So that our children can struggle through the daily mire of life and live just to stay alive. If we are so desperate to bring our children into the world, why are we so unwilling to make it a place that will protect them and inspire them and give them joy?

"I need to go back to the Gallery," I said to Hélène as we finished our coffee. "I'm meeting the exhibition manager with Lochlann to talk about the design for the exhibition hall. Are you going to be ok? Why don't you come back with me – the meeting won't take long, we could do something afterwards?"

"No, Aengus, thank you. I will be fine, really. I have handled this from the beginning, nothing has changed. You go, and I will see you tomorrow. Anyway, we are rehearsing again tonight and it's important to be ready."

"Just take it easy, eh? Don't overdo it."

She laughed at my pointless caution.

"I am fine! Just go, go!"

She waved me away good-naturedly and I stood up to leave.

"OK, but please call me if there's anything you need."

"Aengus – go. I am fine and there is nothing for you to do. I will see you tomorrow."

I nodded, awkwardly squeezed her shoulder and headed back for the house.

Oran and Lochlann were already talking to the exhibition manager when I got to the Gallery.

"Sorry I'm late," I said. "Aengus." I reached out to shake his hand.

"Stephen O'Leary," he said formally, "Pleased to meet you. I hear you have a few ideas for the exhibition?"

"Er, yes. Yes, I suppose so," I said, trying to keep my mind on the conversation and the subject at hand, trying not to think of Hélène sitting alone in the café as I left.

Lochlann laid out the sketch I had drawn on the table.

"Why don't you talk Stephen through your thoughts, Aengus," he said, a familiar note of impatience in his voice.

"Sure, sure."

I described my vision for the Gallery space and the four rooms, one in each corner, which would house the four sections of the exhibition. I talked about the central area and how it would lend itself to formal or informal gatherings, a social space. And I talked about exploiting the physical beauty of the room and making it a part of the show.

O'Leary nodded throughout, then stroked his chin thoughtfully when I had finished.

"It's an interesting idea, I'll give you that," he said in a condescending tone, "but I'm not sure it's very practical. Have you done an art show before?"

"No," I said.

He screwed up his nose and nodded knowingly as though to a child that has made a reasonable effort at tieing a shoelace or writing their name.

"Well I've done quite a few of them, and the thing you're forgetting is the flow – how people will get through the show," he explained slowly, lest I didn't understand the concept of 'flow'. "We have to make sure that people follow the sequence, and the corridor design does that very effectively."

He waited smugly for my epiphany and acknowledgement of his genius.

"I see," I said, suddenly offended by his very presence.

"Oh yes," he continued. "And of course the other thing is time. Your 'four rooms' – " he wrinkled his nose as though I had suggested strippers and a tattoo parlour, " – would be a lot more work. And that's hardly what we need just now, is it?"

He nodded knowingly to Lochlann, who said nothing.

"So I think maybe you should stick to what you do," he winked and patted me on the back, "and let me do what I do. Isn't that right?"

I weighed up my choices. I didn't really need the additional complication of getting involved in the show design, and I certainly didn't want to engage in a debate with this man. But I wanted the show to be the best it could be, and I believed in what I had suggested. And my affronted pride got the better of me.

"So, Stephen, what you're saying is that the people who come to this exhibition are idiots who can only be trusted to follow the show if confined to a narrow channel that herds them along and makes it almost impossible for them to go back to an exhibit that they might want to see again. Yes?"

He was taken aback by my candour, and looked at Lochlann for support that was not offered.

"Well, that's a… that's a very…" he began, but I cut him off. The morning's news had evaporated my tolerance.

"You're ignoring the ergonomics of the room, the logistics of serving refreshments and the impact of exposing people to a wide open space framed by a beautiful building. You have dismissed the possibility of a central social space. It hasn't occurred to you that this has to be a very human experience, an experience that touches our guests through the art and the atmosphere, through the sound of music and the impact on other people."

I was angry that Hélène had been made to suffer for no reason, angry that she should have been so unfairly treated, And I vented my spleen on this patronising, inflexible sycophant because he was the first target I had found.

"But you've always done it this way, and you're afraid to change because you don't have any other ideas. And you keep going on about 'the flow' because you know that that's what Lochlann is concerned about and if you keep banging on about it you think you'll keep him onside. Is that a fair summary? Stephen?" I spat out his name. It had been an entirely excessive outburst, but I felt much better.

He was lost for words for a moment, but regained a modicum of composure to blurt a stuttered response.

"Well, Lochlann, I'm sorry but I think you'll agree that that was out of order. Very much out of order indeed," he could barely get the words out in his red-faced anger. "I have never, ever been treated so rudely. Never."

Lochlann ignored his indignation.

"Aengus is right, Stephen. I want to see his ideas in the form of a revised plan. We will reconvene here tomorrow evening at five o'clock to review it. Thank you for your time today. Now if you will excuse me." He nodded to O'Leary and walked out the door.

O'Leary took off after him immediately and I could hear his desperate protests fading as they walked away from the Gallery.

Oran, who had been watching the unfolding debate with a growing smirk that he tried to hide, burst into peals of laughter and bent double.

"Jaysus, lad," he said, when he finally caught his breath, "I'd have paid a lot of money to see that. A lot of money."

He slapped me on the back and we went in search of coffee.

CHAPTER 24

Would you not be curious? Would you not even want to see what they look like, your parents? I think you could probably live without that knowledge. I think the you before Aoife might even have done so on some bloody-minded principle. But I would want to know. I'd want to know if they were tall or short, fat or lithe, handsome or gruesome. I'd want to know what colour was their hair, and was it long or short, thick or thin. I'd want to know how they spoke, how they walked, how their presence was felt when they walked into a room.

But more than that, I'd want to understand more about myself. I'd want to know if they wore glasses. If I was left-handed, a *citeóg*, I'd want to know what hand they wrote with, what foot they used to kick a ball. If I was a beautiful singer, could they hold a tune? Were they happier with numbers or words, science or art? Were they honest and generous? Or were they devious and mean-minded, and did I see some of that in myself sometimes? Would they leave a legacy that enriched the world they left behind, or a hole where they had taken more than they had given back?

I might want some guidance on how I should live my life. Recklessly seizing every day because all our men die young? Or shunning the ski *pistes* and the football pitch because my mother's side is cursed with brittle bones? Maybe I should be wary of the drink, we have a weakness for it. Maybe we're obsessive and compulsive and I need to calm my ardour sometimes. Maybe I should avoid stress, it might stop my fragile heart.

And I would want some sense of history. I would want to know what part we played in 1916 and the War of Independence, what side we took in the Civil War. Did my uncle play at Croke Park or Lansdowne Road, or did my grandfather pen a classic tune? Around a friend's dinner table, I could join in the chatter and talk fondly and proudly of a heritage not adopted, but coursing through my veins. A heritage that made me the hero or villain that I was.

Of course, it wouldn't matter. In the heel of the hunt, it would make no real difference to my success or failure, could neither inspire a virtue nor cure a vice. I am what I am, and knowing the origin of my self would change nothing.

But I might like them. There might be siblings, hewn from the same stone as me, or even just half of me. And we might be friends. We might share a passion or a dread, we might think the same thoughts at the same time and simultaneously blurt out the same words, and then laugh at the good of it. We might wink knowingly in a crowd, hearing each other's unspoken words. We might visit each others' houses or spend our holidays together. I might stand for their child, or they for mine, closing the circle and rebalancing the world. Maybe I could help them or they could help me, provide some missing skill or knowledge. But maybe that's all because I have no siblings and I'm just curious.

I suppose the adopted me might be angry or bitter, waiting for an opportunity to release the long-festering tirade at the self-serving injustice of it all. Or maybe I would be sensitive to the parents who had raised and looked after me, unwilling to spurn them with treacherous curiosity. Maybe I would be afraid of what I might find or too consumed with the reality of my life, good or bad, to care about the past and the irrelevant truth. Maybe I would have cares more urgent, more important or just more interesting in my world.

Maybe she is a little bit curious or searching for a past or searching for a key to herself. Maybe she is looking for a solid foundation from which to launch her crusade through the world. Maybe she is looking for guidance or just for a friend? Maybe she's angry with us or just protecting them?

Or maybe she just doesn't care.

But where is she?

CHAPTER 25

The butter yellow tones of the sandstone walls emerged slowly like the colours of waking. Warmth bled from what had been cold, life from where there had been none. My eyes could feel the gritty texture of the sandstone. The charcoal beneath betrayed the rock's impurity, hewn from Wicklow hillsides that were abashed at its imperfection. I was working with hands that were not my own. Every development of the canvas made me catch my breath and shake my head and smile, and I watched the results unfold from outside myself. The stone floor rose out of itself and a creamy sun peeked in through the tall windows behind Hélène. The dark eyes of the slight, grey figure with the violin pleaded for colour.

Hélène came round the easel to look.

"My God!" she let out a quiet exclamation and brought her hands to her face, her mouth open. "My God, Aengus, it is like a different painting!"

She looked at me proudly, proud that what we were doing was finally becoming the treasure we had both hoped it would. Even if only to us. We looked at it in silence, eyes drinking in the honeyed infusion.

She looked at the palette in my hand, then at me, holding my gaze a moment before speaking softly.

"Where is your wife?" she said, like she was asking if I wanted a coffee.

Not at the palette, then. At the ring on my finger that I had never taken off. How could I? I let Caitríona put it on my finger as a symbol of commitment and belonging. She was gone, but I still belonged to her. And I was still committed to what we believed in and stood for. Except maybe in pursuing this search.

At her question, I felt the familiar desperate ache, felt myself start to crumble into weakness as was my way, and prepared to be submerged. But the wave broke on some new reef out to sea, whimpered in to shore and lapped at my feet. It reminded me of the pain and the desolation, but didn't drown me in them. I waited for the blackness to descend but it lingered just out of sight, casting a shadow but not plunging me into bleak, weak night.

"She's not with me anymore," I said, my voice just staying afloat.

She nodded gently.

"I'm sorry," she said, after a few moments. "When did you break up?"

I was a little taken aback by her directness, and it was a moment before I recognised her misunderstanding.

"We didn't break up," I whispered. "She isn't with us anymore."

Euphemisms. I had found so many to replace the words I couldn't bring myself to say, even still. It was ridiculous, of course. But if I said the word, I might lose her again, lose what I had left of her. I might wake up one morning and not be able to hear the sound of her voice or the pitch of her laugh. Not really. Nor see the detail of the laughter lines around her eyes. So I clung to what I still had, guarding it jealously.

Hélène looked at me blankly for a moment, assuming perhaps that it was language taunting her. Then the realisation dawned and she reached out involuntarily to touch my arm, her other hand reaching to cover her mouth. The guilty pity of the insulated, who don't know the real nature of grief, just how we represent it. The reaction of the grief-stricken is different. The resigned and knowing nod, the momentary, almost indiscernible flight to a dark corner of the mind behind eyes well-trained to mask the pain. Their pity is not the tactile kind. Not for them the embarrassed search for words, nor hollow assurances that passing time will heal the wound. Like Niamh, they know it heals nothing, just makes you used to the pain. It never hurts less, you just bear it better. As Niamh said, the wound won't heal, you just learn to limp faster.

Somehow, after talking to Niamh, I felt ready to limp just a little faster. It was in part the solidarity that shared misfortune brings, the forced acknowledgement that my own heart-ache was not unique. But it was also her strength, her determination to stand up and face her troubles, that made me embarrassed by my own weakness. Niamh's defiance, Hélène's robust acceptance that she was ill – I took strength from their strength or was shamed by it. I knew Caitríona would have applauded their stoicism and she would have belittled my frailty if she had seen it in someone else.

"What was her name?" she asked.

"Caitríona."

"Was she Aoife's mother?"

"Yes."

She twisted the ring on her own finger.

"Aoife talks a lot about her. I mean, about what she might be like. I think that is what she is sad about. I'm sorry. She wonders what her mother is like, not so much her father. I am sorry, that sounds terrible."

It didn't sound terrible, although it should have, I suppose. I didn't feel hurt or slighted – how could I bear any resentment, having done what I had done? It was right that she wondered more about her mother. That is why I was looking for her, to share Caitríona with her. Far from hurt, I was actually pleased – really pleased, elated almost – that she thought about Caitríona, that Caitríona in some way was a part of her consciousness. I couldn't really have asked for more.

"What was she like?" she asked, carefully.

It wasn't ok. Everything wasn't fine. I didn't feel a weight suddenly lifted, didn't emerge from the jungle to see a better life open up before me, didn't arrive haggard and exhausted at the mountain top to marvel at the vista of opportunity spread out below. Drums didn't roll nor trumpets blow a fanfare. It still hurt, my life was still robbed of its centre, my moments of joy would forever be tempered with a desolate sadness.

But it was better.

It was better because the pain had a purpose. It wasn't a mournful response that I didn't want to give to a question that someone hadn't really wanted to ask, but felt duty-bound to inquire. It wasn't a plaintive recital of how my life had plunged into a chasm of darkness accompanied by embarrassed consolation that could never understand. It was a story that might find its way to Aoife. Just as the euphemisms stopped me losing any more of her, this might actually win some of her back.

"She was beautiful." I described her hair, her eyes, her tall, imposing litheness. I described her smile and how her eyes danced when she laughed and how every laugh seemed uncontrolled, like it took her over and would let her go only when she had drawn every last ounce of joy from it. I told Hélène how she had bewitched me that first week in university in Dublin, how I almost feared her and was entirely under her spell.

I told Hélène about her contempt for the pompous, the disingenuous and the selfish. For anyone who would hurt another person just for their own gain or for no gain, just out of laziness or disinterest. Her disdain for the self-absorbed. How she could not suffer the stupid, nor tolerate the tedious. How she loved the silly and the serious just the same, fun and philosophy, pleasure and the profound. How she could find the plain-some awesome.

I told her about the work she did, defending people she believed in who fell foul of society's norms doing what they believed in. That she was strong, often fearsomely so. That people were sometimes intimidated by her and often missed the softness below the hardness above. That she was undiplomatic, indiscreet and impolitic but never nasty. I told her about our "time-out" system, how with a T-signal of my hands I was allowed to dam one of her rants if it had gone on for more than five minutes over dinner or in the car or while I tried to watch television. How she often missed out on the pointless pleasures of life because there was almost always a fight to fight. She was sometimes too preoccupied to even see breathtaking scenery, or sometimes fidgeted impatiently when we walked through Richmond Park on a frosty Sunday morning or spent a winter afternoon lounging by the fire while the rain beat the window and the wind played tuneless music on the chimney.

I told her how bad she was at sport, how she could find no purpose in games, and how her short-tempered frustration often became violent, a trail of broken clubs or racquets cast aside in her oath-strewn, arm-flailing wake. How she cheated at cards and Scrabble and quiz games, not to win but to bring the hushed torture of the tedium to a quick end so that she could talk without being shushed impatiently.

How she lived to socialise, loved a party or a night out or any gathering of her friends. She loved conversation, to simply sit with a bottle of wine or over a coffee and just talk and discuss and debate and imagine. How her eyes would widen at some exciting new plan or scheme or dream, because there was always an exciting new plan or scheme or dream. About her obsession with books, how there was always a dog-eared volume in her tow, a train ticket or a cocktail-stirring stick taken from a bar acting as a makeshift bookmark. About her discreet kindness that was never ostentatious but that always spotted a need and was always ready to quietly help.

I tried to tell Hélène how much I loved her, but none of the clichés worked, none of them could explain how she filled my life, but completely. Describing the way we love is surely the oldest, most common form of human expression. Little wonder then that we can rarely find an original, authentic way to say it. The simplest words delivered with intensity are always the most emphatic.

I love her.

A tear trickled slowly down my cheek, but there was no darkness. And I think I was smiling.

Hélène smiled at me kindly, then shrugged.

"But you did not want her child?" she asked, gently.

I shook my head.

"It wasn't like that," I said quietly. "I don't think we ever even had the conversation about whether we wanted a baby or not. It was beside the point. We couldn't look after her, so there was no point even talking about it."

"Why not?"

"Because we were just so young. We didn't have a clue. We grew up in sheltered, protected environments. We'd never had to fend for ourselves – never had to claim social welfare or go to a job centre, or get an electricity account or a phone. I didn't even know how to cook or to wash my clothes. Stupid, simple things, but things that, combined, were as frightening as illness. Caitríona – for all her good intentions and best efforts – well, she wasn't much better. Look after a child? We hadn't the first idea. No jobs, no money, no prospects. What sort of a start in life could we give her?"

"But people do, if they want to," she pressed, her voice soft but sure. "They learn, if it's what they want."

I nodded.

"I know they do, and I take my hat off to them, I really do. But you have to want it. You have to actually want it. I think there's a huge difference between, between…" I searched for the words in vain "… between knowing it's what you want and just not knowing that it's what you don't want. Do you see what I mean?"

She furrowed her brow and thought for a moment, then shook her head.

"No. I'm sorry."

I sighed in exasperation, not with her but with myself, because this was at the heart of how I felt and I just couldn't articulate it.

"Look. Suppose you go to a restaurant and order a pizza. A ham and cheese pizza. And the waiter brings you a chicken and pineapple pizza. If you hated pineapple, you'd just send it back, because you don't want it. But if you like pineapple, and it's going to take fifteen minutes to get a new pizza, and actually it looks quite tasty, maybe you'd just take it anyway. It wasn't what you came for, but it's fine. It'll be grand. That's what I was afraid of. I never said I didn't want a child. It just wasn't what I came for. And that wouldn't have been enough to get us – all three of us – through the hard times. And there would have been a lot of hard times." I looked at her, silently begging her to understand. "Does that make any sense?"

She said nothing, stared at me, her mind whirring behind the deep, dark eyes. At length, she took a deep breath and nodded slowly.

"Yes, it makes sense. I just don't understand it. Maybe you cannot understand until you are there." She shrugged, then was silent again.

"Every child deserves be the most precious thing in the world, at least to someone. It's a hard world and that's the least we owe our children – that they are at the very centre of our world. It just couldn't be right to bring Aoife into an unhappy home, a place cobbled together that could never really be a sanctuary. We would have tried hard, I know we would, but what if we just couldn't do it? What if we just couldn't react with spontaneous pride and unbridled joy at the wonder and excitement that every new experience would bring? What if we never nudged each other or hugged each other tight at the first steps or the first feel of snow? You should react with real, honest joy at every new episode in a child's life, it's only what they deserve. No child deserves apathy. We would have tried to be a happy family. We would have taken on parenthood with the determination to do it right. But we could never have disguised the fact that it wasn't what we wanted. And if somebody was desperate to raise a child, had gone through endless heartache and pain to find a child – wouldn't they give her a better place? Even if it wasn't where she came from?"

Even as the words came out, they echoed with apology, and I hated their very sound. The sentiment was sincere, why could the words not sound the same?

Hélène furrowed her brow, as though tackling some opaque conundrum in her head.

"But, growing up is always hard, there is no easy way, no easy place?" she said, shaking her head and shrugging her shoulders. "Nobody has all of the answers, maybe you just have to learn as you go?"

Even though I knew our reasons were genuine and always honest, that it was in the best interests of the child somehow always sounded hollow. I could never make that argument even to myself without wincing at what sounded to me like seeping insincerity. Part of me accepted it, understood that growing up is hard and requires the dedication and love that come from a parent's unwavering commitment to a child. But every family has its challenges and few lives follow a well-planned path. Not even the luckiest child grows up in perfect idyll, with their every emotional and physical need catered for – but doesn't every child assume that theirs is the norm? Growing up in Howth, I accepted Lochlann's cool distance as normal. I accepted that he didn't come to every football match nor help me with my homework even though I knew other fathers did. Not once, even in angry adolescence, did I ever honestly wish that I had a different father. Sure, I sometimes wondered wistfully what it would be like to have a mother but, truthfully, I could scarcely wish for what I didn't know, didn't understand.

She thought for a moment, and went on, almost recharged by the reflection.

"Growing up is hard, of course it is," she said, batting away the obvious with a dismissive wave of her hand. " But, for most children at least, there is a confidence that comes from knowing for sure that where you are is where you belong, where you were always meant to be. It might not be perfect, but you can handle whatever life throws at you and you know –" she punched the open palm of one hand with a tightly clenched fist to ensure there was no doubt "– you know that your place in the world is no game of chance. The journey of your life begins, at least, on solid ground, not on shifting sands of never really knowing for sure, shifting sands that, every day, present new possibilities out of different realities. The journey, and the choices you have to make, would be so much harder for that, no?"

The passion in her voice left no doubt as to her conviction, and for a moment I said nothing, trying to catch the machine-gun fire of words that came hard and fast, catch them so that I could digest them and make sense of them and understand where they had come from. It was Hélène standing in front of me, but were they Aoife's words? Is that why she was so passionate, because she had so often heard her friend say the very same?

"I know, Hélène," I said, eventually. "I know, and it's what I'm most afraid of. You told me the other day that you think

Aoife is pessimistic, that she keeps her distance, that she is searching for something. Look, I don't buy the pop psychology that claims everything we think and do has some profound hidden reason. The fat man is only jolly to hide low self esteem. The pretty girl only smokes because she's scared of getting fat. The young man stays single because he used to listen to his parents scream at each other. But maybe the fat man's just happy? Maybe the pretty girl is just hooked? Maybe the single guy is just having a good time. We don't always have to find a reason. Some things just are."

I paused to put the words together, and the silence was broken only by the breeze that rustled in the trees outside the studio window.

"But is she searching or distant or pessimistic because of what we did to her? I have always prayed that I would find her living a happily balanced life, doing well at school or at work, with lots of different and fascinating hobbies, surrounded by dedicated friends and loved by a devoted family." I threw them out like trinkets tossed from a parade float. "We thought we were giving her a better chance. What if that was a mistake?"

I paused and looked into her eyes.

"Was it a mistake?" I whispered.

She stared straight back at me, not breaking eye contact for even a second.

"I cannot tell you that," she said, quietly. "Only Aoife can tell you that."

I nodded.

"I know," I said, "I'm sorry. I don't mean to ask you to speak for her, to break her confidence. Sorry."

She nodded, and changed the subject.

"It must have changed your life, too?"

"It was like a bomb," I said, the word dropping from my mouth like one of those dull explosions on the evening news from Belfast when I was a child. "It hurt everyone in its range.

For Caitríona and for me, it changed the course of our lives completely and forever. We took it with us every day, we slept with it every night. But that was our choice and we deserved no better. It affected our parents, too. For Lochlann, it brought disappointment – I didn't let him down by getting Caitríona pregnant, I let him down by abdicating my responsibilities and disowning the consequences. He didn't just lose a grand-daughter, I think he lost the son he had hoped he had."

I think she drew a sharp but barely audible breath at that brutal truth, but she said nothing.

"For Caitríona's parents, it brought shame and they never forgave Caitríona for doing that to them. Ireland twenty years ago was a very different place. The Catholic church ruled everything, especially in the countryside, and to have a child outside of marriage was maybe the greatest crime." I smiled, but bitterly. "It's so ironic given everything else that was going on. So her parents were faced with the worst ignominy and the fear of losing everything they had worked to build up in a small country town."

I thought back to the rushed and hushed conversations on pay-phones that Summer, and about the blissful relief of the days together again in that tired little flat in Dublin.

"Even for our friends, it changed things. For Oran, even. We've been friends since before we could even talk, and suddenly I just wasn't around anymore. He'd say it was a blessed relief, I'm sure!"

She smiled, and it lingered, but there was something else in her eyes.

"Some had made the choice to be part of our lives," I said, "and so maybe they were legitimate targets. But Aoife had no choice, she had no part in the decision. Yet she is the one who took the greatest impact, who lives with it more than even us. She was the innocent, so she deserves the best. I just wish I was able give that to her."

"And you met the people who adopted her?" she said, after a pause.

I nodded.

"Yes, we did," I replied quietly. "They were desperate for a baby, it was what they wanted."

"They were older than you."

It was a statement, not a question, and I remembered that Hélène knew these people. She had perhaps eaten in their home, maybe she embraced them when they met and parted, they probably took an interest in her music and in her life. The anxious couple whose dreams we had held in our hands in that stuffy little room in the convent, whose trappings of modest success had so intimidated me – she knew them.

I nodded.

"If you had been older, do you think you would have made a different choice?"

"Maybe," I nodded, "probably. Yes. Yes, I think we probably would. We would have had a foundation to build on, more experience of the world, more confidence maybe. We would at least have had something to pass on to her."

Something to give her. I had always wished we'd had something to give her.

"Do you ever regret what you did?"

"No." I shook my head emphatically. "No, I don't ever regret what we did because it was the only thing we could do. Do I regret that we put ourselves in the position where we had to make that choice? Yes, every day. If I could change anything, it would be the choice we had, not the choice we made. I wouldn't change what came after because I still think it was the best thing for her, I still think it gave her a better life. Jesus Christ, I hope it did."

Her face took on an expression that betrayed her doubt, her scepticism even.

"It gave you a better life, perhaps."

279

And so we came to it, the natural, distasteful corollary to all of my logical, rational justifications. I sighed deeply.

"It gave me a different life, yes. It gave me back the life I had planned and imagined. And maybe you're right – maybe I have had a "better" life. But if we had kept her, and if my life had been a miserable struggle, then so would hers. And whether you believe my motives or not, *that* was what I was desperate to avoid." I raised my voice a fraction then fought to rein in the frustration that was threatening to explode. "But better? Who can ever say? Who can say that I wouldn't have got more from that life? Maybe Caitríona would still be here. That would be better."

It had been a barbed remark and left an awkwardness between us. She eventually broke the silence.

"Do you have other children now?"

"No, we never had another child."

"Why not?"

I shrugged, because it was a question I had never been able to answer. I didn't think we had made a mistake, I just couldn't answer the question.

"I suppose for the same reasons. We never said we didn't want kids, but we never decided we did. I've seen so many people fall into the trap of having children because that is what we do. We reproduce, that's what we do. We perpetuate the race. It's in our blood. But too many of those people looked shell-shocked by what that choice brings. Too many of them struggle through a life that they didn't think fully through. Maybe Aoife reminded us that it's never a decision to take lightly. Caitríona always said that women have a natural, almost irresistible need to feel a baby growing inside them, to nurture and give birth and nurse. And Aoife somehow satisfied that need in her. And she never felt the urge again."

"And you? Did you feel the urge?"

I hesitated, but the momentum carried me on.

"Now and again, yes. But never so much that it became an obsession."

"Do you regret not having a part of your wife now?"

Her candour and pragmatism had struck me since we had first met, but this was a brutally frank invasion of my darkest despairs. And yet either because this was my doing or because I needed this outlet for months or even years of pent-up emotion, I entertained it.

"Yes," I whispered. "I do, every day. And that's why I'm looking for Aoife."

I stood up, not sure that I could bear more questioning or probing, and brought the impromptu session to an end.

"We need to get a move on," I said, looking at my watch. "I'd like to make a start on your hair before we finish today."

She took her seat and we started again.

By the time the almost black brown of her hair eclipsed the charcoal's grey and her complexion had been warmed with a tinge of tan, it was time for Hélène to leave to prepare for the first of her Dublin gigs at the Arena. I walked her to the gate, and then I set about retouching strands of her hair so that they shone in the window's sunlight. But I stopped and dropped wearily into the chair in front of the easel. I stared at the picture and she stared back.

Her merciless, unrelenting questions had come unannounced and I had been ill-prepared for the assault. But they had afforded my first opportunity to express to another soul the thoughts that had chased each other around my head since I had started to look for Aoife, perhaps even before. I had often recited the words to myself along the towpath by the Thames or along the cliffs of Howth Head, but maybe they seemed to belie my sincere assertion that leaving her behind was best for her. But whether or not we were too young or too feckless to look after her, that is how the world looked to us and that was therefore our reality.

My mobile phone's shrill, pointlessly cheerful ring tone wrenched me abruptly from my thoughts.

"Hello, this is Aengus."

"Hi, Aengus, it's Niamh. How's it going?"

"Hi, Niamh. Good thanks. How're you?"

"Ah sure, grand. Listen, I'm going down to the village later and I was wondering if you fancied a coffee?"

I needed to escape from the studio for a little while, ideally in the company of someone who I didn't think was judging me or trying to decide if I was telling the truth.

"You've no idea! That'd be great."

We agreed the where and the when, and I tidied away the paraphernalia of my new trade.

CHAPTER 26

The Front Room was a new coffee shop near the church and had replaced the old café where we used to have breakfast after mass on Sunday mornings. It was a microcosm of all that Ireland had become in my absence. Gone were the homely old ladies who waited on tables, replaced by young girls from Eastern Europe with thick Slavic accents and a barely disguised *ennui*. Gone was the simple breakfast menu, replaced by a catalogue of Italian coffees and herbal infusions and *pains au chocolat*. Tables of middle-aged ladies draped in designer clothes and accessories chattered excitedly over pastries and the remains of long lunches, leaning across tables and into secrets with pursed lips and knowing nods. I listened in on conversations about holidays and the price of schools, the cost of houses and how you simply couldn't live in Dublin these days without a four-by-four.

And yet there was a nervousness in the air, an uncertainty and a sense that this might all have been an all too short-lived dream. The tone was almost one of loss, as though accepting that they would soon revert to the old lives that they had been able to dismiss with nostalgic mockery.

Niamh walked in and, spotting me in the corner, smiled and waved. I stood up and leaned over to kiss her cheek.

"Hiya," she said. "Sorry I'm a bit late."

"No bother," I replied. "What can I get you?"

I ordered from a reluctant waitress whose career aspirations, I could only assume, lay far from the hospitality industry.

Niamh looked at me intently.

"Are you ok?" she asked, real concern in her voice. "I'm really sorry about the other morning. I never meant to upset you."

"I know, Niamh, and don't worry." I reached across the table and squeezed her hand, then pulled it away it little too sharply, remembering Oran's stern advice. "I'm fine. I have to take my life back. I have to stop crumbling when I talk about her or when other people talk about her. I don't know that I can, or how long it'll take. But I think it must be time."

I nodded to confirm that I believed what I said.

"And I should really be thanking you, Niamh. You wouldn't think it maybe, but it was progress. It was better."

She smiled and looked around the café.

"Do you remember coming here when we were kids?" she said.

I nodded with a grin.

"God, it was a bit of a dive, wasn't it," she went on, then leaned closer as though about to divulge a shocking secret. "And that oul' one who did the cooking? I don't think I ever once saw her washing her hands! It's a wonder we weren't all poisoned."

That Niamh's abiding memory was of hygiene and not of under-aged hangovers or scandalous liaisons or misfired pranks was a glimpse into the soul she tried hard to hide. She was one of us and yet one apart.

"Seems like two lifetimes ago," I said. "And look at it now? Who'd have thought, eh?"

The waitress delivered our order with a well-honed gruffness.

"Thank you," Niamh said to her back. "I know, big changes. But sure it's like that all over Dublin, and it's all going to change again, probably."

"An uncertain future?" I said.

"Looks like it." She raised her mug to me. "To the future. It can only get better, right?"

"The future," I smiled. "Let's hope so."

"So what's in your future, do you think?" she asked, over the top of her coffee.

I exhaled long and hard, and raised my eyebrows.

"Jesus, who knows. But," I tried to find a way to express my cautious optimism without sounding twee or trite, "I think it's about taking your life back. You know what I mean?"

She nodded.

"I do. I think that's what I've tried to do," she said, unusually animated. "I just got fed up accepting things, and I think I've tried to push back, to take back control."

"You know, the first night I was back I met the Master in McGrath's. And that's what he said. Take control. And he's right, you know."

"Críostóir? He usually is," she said, with a grin. "Or at least he usually thinks he is."

"Some things never change?"

"Exactly!"

The gaggle of lunching women rose as one to leave, and diners at the adjoining tables had to take evasive action to avoid swinging coats and scarves and handbags. Amid the overpowering fragrance of disturbed cosmetics and the crescendo of kissed cheeks and hollow compliments, they swept to the door and were gone.

We smiled and shook our heads at the departing crowd.

"He is right though," I said, when their din had faded through the door. "You have to decide what you want and go get it. I've been too willing to sit back and absorb the pain. I don't think it ever goes away, but you have to live your life and make the best of it. Otherwise, you might as well give up."

"I know what you mean," she said, slowly, "but I'm not

sure it's that simple. I have to put Micheál and Ciara before anything else – not "have to", I want to. They didn't ask for this and it's not their fault, but they're the ones who stand to suffer most. And that can't happen. I'd love to just follow a random dream, but I want always to be there for them."

I nodded.

"Of course. I can't really imagine the responsibility that children bring."

She smiled ruefully.

"It's a lot of pressure, that's for sure. But sure that's what you sign up for, isn't it. No point in complaining about it."

I thought about Oran's revelation that the whole world had known about Aoife. I wondered if Niamh was in that world. If it had passed anybody by, it would surely have been her.

"Did you really know what you were signing up for?" I asked, with a grin.

"God, no! Does anyone?" she laughed.

"But you wanted children though?"

She hesitated.

"Yes, we did. I suppose we did. Brian wanted a son, someone to take to the football and go fishing with." She paused, trying but not quite able to suppress the barb in her voice. "I don't think he ever really thought about everything else that goes with it. And in the end it just got too much for him."

"And you? Did you want children? When you had Micheál?"

"Me?" she seemed surprised by the question, as though I'd asked if she liked puppies or chocolate. "I suppose I always thought I'd have a family. But you can't plan for these things, and it's never the right time. So we had Micheál. I didn't want him to grow up on his own, so we had Ciara after."

When it's never the right time, it's maybe not the right thing.

286

"But I love them now more than anything else," she went on quickly, afraid I would misconstrue, and I had no doubt that it was the truth. "Watching them grow up and get stronger and more confident and more capable, that's been everything I could have hoped for. I'd never let anything happen to them, I swear to God I wouldn't. And I'd do anything for them."

"But you can still take control, though, can't you?" I said. "You have to. Or you get buffeted around by the world's randomness. Everybody is scrambling to stay afloat, sometimes at your expense. Some are malevolent, some just don't care. But if you spend your time just reacting to what other people do, I don't think you can cope. You have to set a course that's right for you – and for your kids – and fuck the rest of them."

"Sounds like a voice of experience?"

I paused, then nodded.

"I suppose it is, Niamh. I've spent too long just trying to survive every day, surviving to live another unfulfilling day. I have to take charge. I want to have something to lose."

"You used to dream about being a painter, didn't you? Like your father?"

I think I blushed.

"I did. God, I was a pretentious arse, wasn't I? The great artist! Some chance!"

"Well, you're doing it now aren't you?"

I grimaced.

"Hardly. One portrait for my father's show. And he might not even take it? Hardly the impact I imagined making on the art world." I looked at her. "What about you? What did you dream of?"

She laughed, her turn to blush.

"You'll only laugh," she protested. "But, I always dreamed of being a fashion designer."

"I never knew that," I said, genuinely surprised. "But yeah, you used to make your own stuff didn't you?"

287

I remembered from somewhere deep in the archives of my mind that Niamh would turn up to a disco or a party in some of her own creations, to predictably catty jibes from some of our number but to nods of genuine approval from others.

"You used to come up with some pretty funky stuff, didn't you?"

Her blush deepened.

"I used to love making that stuff. And I'd love to have taken it further, but it wouldn't have paid the mortgage!"

She finished her coffee.

"I'd have another one – you?" I said.

She looked at her watch.

"Yeah, that'd be grand. Thanks, Aengus."

I called to the waitress who took time out from the detailed fingernail inspection that had her so engrossed and motioned for two more of the same.

"So what are you doing these days?" I asked.

"I'm a part-time accountant for the hotel. Book-keeper really. But the hours are good and it means I can pick up the kids from school. And I can do a lot of it at home, so I don't have to pay a fortune for childcare. I'm very lucky really."

Lucky, said the lion-tamer who lost only one leg to his beast.

Where does it all go wrong? As we get old, so our dreams are diluted until they fizzle out unnoticed. As little children we dreamed of being astronauts and super-heroes. As teenagers it was footballers, artists and fashion designers. In our twenties it was to find a great job that would be our vehicle to make the world a better place and make ourselves famous or celebrated or just blissfully content. And we dreamed of things outside of that world – that our band would hit the big time or our team would win its league or we might win a medal or a cup or even a mention in the local newspaper. Then came our thirties, and it all came back to making the best of the job we'd found and maybe climbing the ladder doing something that we would have dismissed and mocked in our teens, but somehow now it's comforting and it's safe. There's suddenly no time for the band or training or playing and without even noticing, we've stopped. In our forties, it will just be to keep paying the steadily rising bills, raising our children the best way we can and saving for the future that will never work out quite as we imagined – all the while snatching moments of joy and inspiration where we can and wondering when it was that we stopped wanting the things that we always wanted so badly. When did our vibrant dreams turn into grey aspirations? We're not racked by regret and we're not unhappy, but it's all such a waste and we'll never get the chance again.

"Do you think you'll ever go back to it, give it another try?" I asked her.

"I'd love to, really I would. I make some of the kids' things now, but it's not really what I dreamed of doing." She stopped. "Bit like you!" she realised, and she laughed.

I raised my mug to her.

"Well, here's to us for at least keeping the dream alive. It's flickering, but the candle is still burning."

She grinned and clinked my mug with hers.

"To us," she said.

It was late afternoon when I got back to the studio. I sat down in front of the easel, and stared long at the picture. I had passed the point where a mistake would be an inconvenience. To err now in unforgiving acrylic would probably be irreversible – the best I could hope for would be to cloak it in some fudged cover. All that was left was to add some depth and colour to her face, bring out somehow the vulnerable warmth that was punctuated by those eyes.

The noise of voices outside jerked me from my reverie, and they grew louder and more animated. I recognised Oran's angry tones, but not the other voices, whose strong Dublin accents sounded ominously calm. I got up from my chair and went outside to see what was happening.

Oran was standing by his car with two broad-shouldered men, shod in Doc Marten boots and clad from impossibly-thick neck to toe in black. They were the sort of men with whom you didn't argue if they refused you entrance to a club, no matter how long you had been in the pub nor how affronted your male pride. It was unlikely to be a courtesy call.

I walked over, trying to affect a nonchalance that might disguise the very real fear that made my legs shake. There is no reason why we should ever feel threatened in our own homes nor even on city streets, but it is a vile fact of our wretched race that, no matter how strong we are, we are always under threat of intimidation from the next strongest. And they had come as a pair.

"Oran," I said, fighting to keep a tremor from my voice, "can you give me a hand in the studio?"

"Bit tied up," he said, his eyes never leaving the closer of the two thugs. "Be in in a bit. See ya."

"Oh right," I said. "Anything I can help you with."

The goon closest to me turned, and I could see his upper lip fixed in a snarl.

"He said 'See ya'," he growled. "So we'll see ya."

He cocked his head toward the gate to suggest where I should be headed.

"Why?" I said, gaining courage from I don't know where, "are you boys off?"

He turned his body fully to face me.

"Do yourself a favour, don't be a fuckin' smart-arse. Just fuck off and maybe I won't rearrange your fuckin' face."

"Don't threaten me," I said quietly, now genuinely and perilously offended by their presence. "This is my house, so why don't you fuck off before I call the guards."

He loped toward me, stopping just short of me and leaning over so that his fetid mouth was half an inch from my face.

"This has fuck all to do with you," he said slowly, emphasising each word. "So get the fuck out of here while you still can."

If the formulaic delivery of b-movie clichés was intended to terrify then it had the desired effect on me. But still I stood in front of him, not trusting myself to speak and not, in any case, sure what to say. He stabbed a stubby, nicotine-stained finger into my chest and I took an involuntary step back. I was about to voice my indignation, when he looked toward the lane beyond the gate from where the sound of a car engine approached. A surge of relief coursed through me when I saw the blue Garda car amble quietly down the lane. It stopped at the gate, and two gardaí climbed out, donning their caps as they did.

"How's it goin', lads," said the older of the two in a thick country accent. "Everything ok?"

"Grand thanks, guard," said one of the goons slowly, in a voice that dripped with menace. "Everything's grand. Good luck, so."

"Everything ok, Oran?" said the guard, ignoring him.

"Actually, these lads were just off, guard," I said, stepping forward. "Weren't you, lads?"

The bigger one stared straight into my eyes with a look that chilled me. But I smiled back, hoping the fear didn't show. Still staring at me with a vice-like grip that wouldn't let my eyes move, he spoke to the guard.

"We were, guard. Just off." He turned to Oran. "But we'll be back to finish that bit of business. We'll be back alright."

He eventually turned for the gate. His accomplice followed him and they lumbered up the path. At the gate they turned, stared at Oran for a moment, then one of them opened the gate and they left.

The guard watched them leave, and walked over to Oran.

"You should maybe reconsider your choice of friends, Oran," he said.

"I wouldn't say we were close, Pádraig," Oran replied, with a watery smile.

"But closer than you'd like all the same. Be careful, Oran. These lads have a way of getting the job done, you know that."

"I know. Thanks."

The front door opened and a wide-eyed Pauline emerged from the house.

"Are they gone?" she said, eyes darting up and down the lane outside.

"They are, Pauline," said the garda. "Thanks for the call. You'll be fine now."

He turned to Oran.

"Well, we'll see you so," he said. He turned to Oran and lowered his voice. "Don't do anything daft now, Oran, d'ya hear me? Give us a call if you need us, but you'll have to sort this out. You know that."

"I do. Thanks, Pádraig."

The two gardaí raised their caps to Pauline and strode down the path and out the gate. The car pulled away, and Pauline looked over at Oran.

"Who were they, Oran?" she asked, all wide-eyed disbelief. "What did they want?"

"Nothing, Pauline," he replied, "nothing. Thanks."

He nodded to her and headed for the Gallery.

"Don't worry, Pauline," I said, when he was out or earshot. "It'll be fine. Don't worry."

I squeezed her shoulder and walked after Oran to the Gallery.

He was quietly and systematically venting his anger on a long plank of wood that he was sawing into pieces. He didn't look up when I walked in.

"They came for the car." He sawed through the plank and another short piece fell off the end.

"I guessed," I replied, quietly. "Who do you owe the money to?"

"Guy in Clondalkin. You wouldn't know him. I hope you never do."

"What are you going to do? I'm guessing they'll be back?"

"They will." He stopped sawing, looked up at me and shrugged. "I'll have to let them take it, what else can I do. It'd be hard finishing this place with a broken leg." He sighed and shook his head. "Won't be enough though. I still have to find the rest."

He set to work on the plank again.

"How much?"

"I owe him five grand. Car's only worth three. On a good day."

Another block of wood fell from the work-bench and into the growing pile of sawdust. I tried to do some quick mental arithmetic based on what I could remember from my own chaotic financial situation.

"Listen, I can lend you the…"

He looked up and put up his hand to stop me.

"Aengus, just leave it. My mess, I'll sort it out. Thanks, but don't get involved, alright?"

"Oran, look…"

"I said leave it, Aengus." He stood up straight and pointed at me with the saw. His tone brooked no further discussion.

I shook my head, but didn't pursue the point. I turned and left the Gallery. At the door, I stopped and looked back.

"Pint later?"

"Yeah."

I walked out into the golden light of the late-summer evening.

I should have gone to the Studio, but I was too distracted to risk putting brush to canvas. So I went up to my room, pulled on my running kit and headed out on the Head. The sea below was calm and gleamed in the evening sunshine through a sheet of soft haze. There was hardly a breath of wind and the hillsides were alight with vivacious gorse. The heather too was in bloom, covering the ground in its calming purples and blues. A car ferry ploughed silently out of Dublin port on its way to Liverpool or Holyhead, and sailing boats from the yacht club bobbed about out to sea.

What had become of the three of us, I thought as a I pounded the trail. Oran was such a talented chef. Niamh had had a flair for design even in her naïve, untrained youth. I had had my moments with a brush or a pencil. And yet here we were, dreams long forgotten, just trying to survive. Swimming frantically against the strengthening tide. And I resolved then that we would make it ashore. And we would rekindle those dreams.

I was meeting Oran in McGrath's at seven o'clock, but I got there at half past six and settled into my favourite corner. I had picked up a copy of the Irish Times at the newsagent and turned straight to the crossword, pulling a biro from my pocket. The pub was quiet, no more than half the tables taken by a mellow crowd.

"Hey Aengus, how are you going?" Ella wiped the table clean with a cloth, and threw down a couple of new beer-mats.

"Good thanks, Ella. You?"

"Not bad actually, not bad." She sounded almost surprised to find that her life was in order.

"Ella," I said, suddenly, "do you have a dream? Something you've always promised to yourself?"

She looked at me as though I had asked her to quickly take her clothes off.

"Sorry," I raised a hand and shook my head. "Sorry, that was rude, personal. Forget it."

She smiled at me.

"You really do need a drink, don't you? Pint?"

I smiled back.

"Please. Sorry."

She looked at me again as though I were a little removed from the real world, smiled uncertainly, and walked back to the bar.

I turned back to my crossword, but I couldn't concentrate. Words capered gleefully around the edges of my consciousness, teasing me from behind the pillars of my mind. I couldn't shake off the image of Oran and his two nemeses standing by the car. Whatever the situation, I had never seen Oran subdued, never tame. And yet he was now so obviously out of his depth, not able even to rely on his own brand of devil-may-care brusqueness to save him.

Ella reappeared with my pint. She put it on the table, and to my surprise took a seat opposite me.

"You know what? I do," she said. "I do have a dream."

"Go on."

"I want to open my own bar in Queenstown, on the south island. For people who want to ski and jump off cliffs and ride the white water." She looked around, leaned forward to me and lowered her voice. "None of these suited assholes, you know what I mean?"

"Nice! Do you think you'll ever do it?"

She paused and then nodded as though arriving at some dramatic conclusion.

"Yeah, you know what? I will. I haven't really thought that much about it recently, but it's why I'm here, working in a bar, trying to earn some cash. Probably won't be able to do it for a few years, but maybe I will."

"Good for you. Take a piece of advice from an old fart – don't lose hold of it. Because you'll wake up one morning in a house in Portmarnock or Auckland or London with the kids screaming, your husband moaning and your head throbbing and you'll suddenly remember that you're meant to be in Queenstown and it'll be too late. Don't ever let it get too late.

Hold on to it like it's gold."

She said nothing, just looked at me for a moment. Then she nodded.

"I will." And she got up to go back to work. As she started to walk away, she turned. "Maybe you're not too late?" she smiled, nodding her head at me.

I smiled back. "Maybe."

It was after half past seven when Oran walked in. I was struck that, far from angry and belligerent as I had expected, he looked tired and somehow at a loss. For the first time I could remember, he looked spent. He went to the bar, looked over to see if I needed a pint, and ordered one for himself. I watched him while he waited for his stout to settle. He leaned with his elbows on the bar, one foot upon the rail at its base, his forehead resting in the palm of his right hand. The barman topped off his pint and he wandered over to me.

"I think you could've had him," I said, as he sat down.

He looked at me blankly.

"What?"

"The big fucker. I think you could've had him. And I could definitely have had the other one. No bother."

He laughed a somehow relieved laugh, and let out a long, weary sigh.

"Fucking hell, Aengus, how did it get to this? How was I supposed to know, the night I opened the restaurant, that it would end here?"

He took a long drink from his glass and put it back on the table.

"Look, Oran, these bastards won't stop until you've either paid up or you're dead. You know they'll keep coming back."

"They won't be back."

I looked at him, waiting for the obvious to dawn on me so I could clasp my forehead in relief. I had no epiphany.

"What are you talking about?"

He sighed again, and looked at me.

"Your fucking mad father is what I'm talking about," he said, unable to stop his lips curl in a smile that betrayed at once his incredulity and deep relief. "Pauline must have told him about them. Lochlann gave me the money. Insisted that I take it. I tell you, I'd have been more scared of what he'd have done if I'd refused than those two fuckin' animals."

Then I understood. I picked up my glass and raised it to him.

"To Lochlann," I said.

"Lochlann," he replied and clinked my glass.

We each drank, and he put the glass down and wiped his mouth with the back of his hand.

"He's a really good man, Aengus. I know you two have had your arguments, but he's a good man. The best. I'd be fucked if he hadn't taken me in. And now he's saved me again."

I felt like a child again, sitting in a pub or in the golf club being told by an earnest friend of my father's that I was lucky to have such a great man to look out for me, and warning me with a wagging finger to make sure I was good to him. And I was proud of him, I always had been, even when I was too young to fully understand what he was doing. I just wished he had been a little more proud of me, wished I could find what it was that would make him proud.

"I know, Oran," I said, nodding. "I know he's a good man."

There was no more to say, no elaboration that would have clarified nor superlative that would have emphasised.

"Listen," I said, looking at my watch. "Hélène's band is playing in town. They're on at nine or half nine. Do you fancy it?"

"Where?"

"The Arena."

He laughed.

"It'd be the first time they ever let me in there!"

"Well then, if Hélène can't get us in, we'll never get in. Will we go so?"

"Yeah, why not."

We finished our pints, waved goodbye to Ella and ran out to catch the next DART.

The Arena was not far from St Stephen's Green and the small queue at the door was full of fashionable bright young things. I remembered our teenage selves and the self-conscious nervousness that accompanied us to clubs and venues. And yet these youngsters looked entirely at ease with themselves and their world. And this was their world, there could be no doubt.

It was a relatively quiet night, the holidays were as good as over throughout the city and Dublin had settled into its back-to-school routine. The queue moved steadily, and before too long we found ourselves in the dark atrium of the club. We went into a small bar just off the atrium, ordered a couple of pints from the barman and took them into the little auditorium where the stage was set up. It was a small venue – the smallest, I guessed, of the three that made up the Arena. The little dance floor in front of the stage was surrounded by tables. It wasn't even close to full, although a steady trickle of newcomers slowly swelled the crowd.

A guitarist – whom I assumed to be Gerry – was playing with a foot pedal tuner and calmly tuning his guitar. An electric violin stood in its cradle beside a high stool, but Hélène was nowhere to be seen. Gerry left the stage. The piped music stopped, the lights went down and the crowd hushed. The short silence was broken by the plaintive strains of a lone violin. After a moment, the lights went up, the strong chords of a guitar and the beat of drum and bass joined the fiddle and the crowd roared its approval. A shiver ran through me and a smile danced onto my face.

Hélène was sitting on the high stool, one foot on the floor, the other on the stool's footrest. She was staring at the floor, eyes sometimes open in intense concentration, sometimes closed in apparent reverie. Her arm and her fingers moved at impossible speed as she followed the drummer's breakneck beat, and her whole body swayed and dipped and rose on the music's wave.

They reached the end of the first song and the crowd again shouted out and whooped and screamed. The four musicians smiled nervously at each other, then the drummer tapped out *one-two-three-four* and the music started again. They played their own material, along with tracks from my student days by In Tua Nua and Stockton's Wing and Christy Moore. Their early nervousness gradually disappeared and they clearly enjoyed the crowd's enthusiastic response, whipped up by the fiddle's frantic rhythm. Hélène too gained in confidence, standing up from her stool and walking around in front of the crowd. She looked lost in the music, carried away by it. The little venue filled with late-comers and the crowd grew louder and ever more excited, singing along enthusiastically to the songs they knew. The band kept up the momentum and we were all carried along on the heady wave of their rhythm.

Too soon, it was the last song of the evening's set. The band took their bows, the noisy crowd bayed for more, and the stage lights went down. The house lights did not come on and the crowd didn't move.

Then the stage lights came back up and Hélène was standing in front of the microphone, without her violin. The band started to play and I recognised the opening bars of *Double Cross*, the old Mary Coughlan song. Hélène began to sing, the words sounding eerily romantic and almost unbearably soft in her French accent. I was transfixed, standing stock still amid the gently swaying crowd. Her eyes were closed again, her two hands on the microphone in its stand, Gerry's guitar weaving a trance. She repeated the chorus one last time, her voice rising, shedding its vulnerability and finishing with a powerful defiance. She stepped back from the microphone, took the faintest of bows to the cheers of a bewitched crowd and they left the stage again. The house lights came up and the show was over.

Oran looked at me and raised his eyes with a smile.

"Jesus, eh? She's amazing. Never expected that, did you?"

I shook my head in undisguised wonder.

"No. No, I surely did not," I grinned back at him, shaking my head again. Grinned because, for some reason, I was so proud of her.

We stood finishing our drinks while the crowd filtered out into the Dublin night. As we were about to leave, Gerry came back out on to the stage and began gathering up his equipment. I walked over to the stage.

"Gerry?" I called over to him.

He looked over, trying to place my face, but couldn't.

"How're ya," he said.

"Great job," I said, "you guys were fantastic."

He smiled.

"Thanks very much."

"Listen, could you tell Hélène that Aengus is here?"

He hesitated, then recognition flashed across his face.

"Oh right, Aengus is it?" he said, putting down the pile of cable he was rolling up. "I've heard all about you. I'll tell her, hang on there."

She bounded out from behind the stage, beaming. She came over to the edge and hopped down from the stage, throwing her arms around my neck. She was still sticky with the night's sweat, and still high from their success.

"Aengus," she squealed, "you didn't tell me you were coming tonight?"

"I know," I grinned at her excitement. "We made a late decision." I pointed over at Oran, still standing by the dance floor's edge.

"Oran too!" She ran over and hugged him. Not one for such physical public displays of affection, he was caught unawares and just smiled awkwardly, his huge hands hovering behind her back, not sure where to land.

"Thank you so much for coming," she said, "I'm really glad you could be here. It means a lot to me."

"I'm glad too," I said. "You really were fantastic tonight."

"Hélène?" Gerry called from the stage, "We need to get this stuff in the van."

"OK, Gerry," she called back. "I have to go," she said, "But I'll see you tomorrow?"

"Yeah, see you tomorrow," I nodded. "And listen – well done, eh?"

She smiled an embarrassed little smile, waved and headed backstage.

Since I had met her, she had been so calm, never ruffled nor extreme. It was good to see this side of her – passionate, overcome. And it was good to witness her triumph. We turned for the door and walked out into the night's late summer chill. I felt an inner glow and a warmth that the late night's cold could not pierce. One dream at least was perhaps coming true.

CHAPTER 27

Did we ever have time to dream? Or did we just assume the dreams that the world told us we should have. I'm not sure we ever dreamed, not really. Aspired, perhaps. But every day was too full of the things we had to do so that we ran out of time and we always had to leave a task or two undone. Pay the television licence or entertain a dream? You can't get a fine or a court summons for forgetting to dream, so that will have to wait for another day. But I think we were still guilty.

We were guilty of not squeezing every last drop out of our lives. Sure, we travelled and socialised and played, but we didn't do the inspiring things, the things for which we had a real passion. We enjoyed the world that we had built for ourselves – maybe we enjoyed it especially because it had at one point in our lives looked so unlikely, so beyond our reach. But I worry that we aspired to and built a world that we felt expected to build, and then filled every moment of every day putting and keeping it together. We followed the rules but we never really challenged them. We never really dreamed.

Too often, we confuse aspirations with dreams. Actually, they come from two different worlds. The world of aspiration is the world we inhabit every day. We know and understand it, its rules are simple and we can recognise its pitfalls and its perils. We simply aspire to make our little world a better world or to make our place in it a better place. Dreams live in a world that doesn't yet exist outside our imagination. It is ours to construct, based on our own passions and codes.

The usual rules do not apply, and there are no parameters to guide us. And that makes it hard, too hard sometimes. It's easier just to deal with what we know and to make it the best it can be. But a bigger house is just more of the same world. A faster car just allows you to navigate the same world more quickly. A luxurious holiday is just the same world by a different name in a different language. We refine everything and change nothing.

We are extras on a film set. We participate, contribute even, but never shape the performance nor feel the rush of adrenaline that comes with a well-delivered monologue or a great display of emotion. We should be the lead in our own film. Of course we can't all star in big screen blockbusters, but we can find our own indie movies, we can aim for our own Sundance, and we can be the stars. We can shape the art and we can revel in the result.

You lived every day with people who dared to dream. You saw the pain and the hardship they brought on themselves and the people they loved, and I know you felt some of that pain. I know you ached for the people whose insatiable desire for justice led only to anguish. When you came home in the evening from work, and collapsed on the sofa under the weight of all the world's troubles, you took refuge in the sanctuary of our home and our world. The simple, the everyday, the mundane – they were your escape. And so you couldn't face the prospect of losing them.

I had no such excuse, but I was blinded by convention so that I couldn't see beyond the boundaries of the world in which we lived. I couldn't see past what had to be done to snatch a glimpse of what could be done, what was possible. My never-shrinking list of tasks and errands only maintained the status quo and I couldn't see past them to the things I could do, the things that were within my compass and might open the way to a whole new reality.

I don't think we were unhappy, nor do I think the life we would have gone on to live would have been cheerless or pained. I'm just afraid that it could have been better and that we would never have made it what it could have been.

CHAPTER 28

An autumn chill had crept quietly in when I ran out onto the Head the next morning. Approaching winter is felt first on the pale, fleshy, goosebumped skin of the still-bare thighs, then in the sharp air that invades the windpipe and the lungs. I drank it in, feeling cleansed as I did, purged of the contaminants of the real world. Despite arriving home in the early hours of that morning, I felt invigorated. My every footfall stroked the ground rather than pounding it and every step seemed spring-loaded. My breathing was easy and light, my legs were strong and loose and free.

The school holidays were over and the cold breeze kept people indoors and off the head, despite the blue sky. I didn't pass a single other person, and the solitude was empowering. I ruled what I surveyed, a modern day Fionn MacCumhaill, whose head lay buried beneath my feet. When I got back to the house, and had thrown a careless glance into the car park lest Niamh's car was there, I prepared quickly for a day in the studio, excited that my work was near its end and that today might see it done.

Hélène was more effervescent than I had seen her on the morning after any other gig. I smiled at her and applauded as she came into the studio. She smiled and took a bow, and I noticed her wince ever so slightly as she did so.

"Are you ok?" I asked, all at once concerned given her revelation of earlier in the week.

She nodded.

"I am fine. It was a late night, that's all. But it was such a good night!"

She smiled again.

"You guys were brilliant," I said, shaking my head as I struggled still to understand how this waif-like girl could be so powerful and commanding. "I really mean it. I never knew you could sing. It was beautiful."

"It's a wonderful song. It's very easy for me to sing when the guys play it so well," she said, warmth in her voice at the thought of her band. Or at the thought of Gerry, perhaps.

"The band is great alright. Gerry's got a great voice too, hasn't he?"

She nodded vigorously.

"Yes, he does. He doesn't really think so, but he has amazing talent. On the guitar too. And you know he wasn't ever trained properly, he taught himself?"

"Do you think there were any record company people there?"

She shrugged again.

"I don't know. The club manager said there were, that his people let them in. But maybe he is saying that because it makes his club sound better."

She paused, and allowed herself a hopeful smile, embarrassed at the presumption.

"But we hope so. We really hope so. It's what we have all dreamed about for so long."

"But you have to look after yourself," I said, trying to balance caution with reluctance to sour her mood or bring her down from her euphoria. "Just be careful."

She raised her eyes heavenward and smiled.

"Of course I will, I am not an idiot, you know," she admonished.

"I know, I know!" I said, shuffling the easel so that the canvas caught the best of the bright morning light. I turned and pointed my brush at her. "You really should be proud of yourself. To have a passion, and a talent, and to have the courage to pursue it, to make it real."

She flushed slightly and looked at the floor, then looked back at me doubtfully.

"Perhaps. But I am chasing a dream that might come – will probably come – to nothing. Only such a small number of people ever actually make it in this business," she said, squinting through her thumb and forefinger at the tiny odds. "And then what? I have no career, no other qualifications, no experience. And there is not much joy in teaching violin to naughty children who would prefer to play football!"

I shook my head.

"You'd find something," I said, "if it didn't work out. You'd think of something. But you've had a go – more than that, you've given yourself a real chance – before it's too late."

I thought of all the days I had sat in the office in London, sat with an army of jaded colleagues, and dreamed of something better, because believing in a dream that might one day come true was the only way to get through the humdrum.

"Christ, so many people are unhappy with what they do, unfulfilled and discontent," I said. "They don't like what they do or what they've become, I really think they use their dreams to define who they are. They work in a grey office, pushing paper around and just trying to avoid failure, but in their minds they're athletes or artists or singers or explorers or inventors... I think their dreams reserve a place for them in the world, an interesting, rewarding place, and a place to which they might otherwise have no right."

"But the world is full of people who followed an impossible dream, and of course they failed," she said. "So now they wander the streets with a crazy look in their eyes." She laughed. "That might be me, some day! You will find me begging on the street and maybe you will throw me a coin!"

I sighed because it's such a mixed-up world – we condition our young to be suspicious of their dreams, and we get old regretting the loss of our own.

"But if you wait too long, the dream shatters," I said. "And when you reach out to catch a shard, it floats away on the breeze. Sometimes it shatters on the realisation that it is just hopelessly unrealistic. Sometimes it shatters simply because we try and we fail. But sometimes it shatters because we're afraid to fail, and that's the saddest of all. I nearly lost my dream because I was afraid of losing it. I let it go because I was afraid of having to give it up."

I thought back to the endless, soulless Monday-to-Friday world that was my home. Or my prison?

"When we went to London and I got a job at the marketing agency, I never for a moment believed that it was my destiny, never expected to be carried along on some wave of corporate inspiration. But we were all doing the same, and I forgot to question it. And as time went on, *my* dreams became *my* refuge too. They reserved for me a place to which I really had no right. In my own mind, I was an artist passing time until my greatness was unleashed on the world. So I let grey career aspirations take priority, and I let them crowd out the things I really dreamed about. Not because I stopped dreaming, but because I was afraid of failing, because to fail would be to lose the dream. If I failed, I could no longer take refuge in that place, I would lose the right."

The brutal irony became suddenly, starkly clear.

"And it's taken all of this," I waved a hand at all that had happened, "for me to take it out and dust it off."

She leaned forward and took my hand in both of hers.

"But you have a chance now to make that dream come true. Your father has given you this chance, so don't waste it. And you will not waste it. Maybe some people never live their dream, but you are right – we *are* lucky. I get to play music I love with great musicians, to people who love to hear it. And you have the chance to hang a great painting at an important exhibition."

She squeezed my hand with a broad grin, then straightened her skirt and took the violin and bow from their case.

"Now," she said, with a flourish, "that is enough talking – let's make something beautiful!"

It was a day for great things. My mood was buoyant, her enthusiasm was contagious. The sun cast its autumn gold over the Head and gently chased away the chill of the morning. On the canvas, Hélène was coming to life. The cold grey shadows of a week before gave way to a figure that radiated warmth but remained vulnerable and fragile, and lost. It was in her eyes. The softness of the browns and warm ambers in her hair and in the room and in the faint hint of tan in her cheeks were in stark contrast to the frightened, lonely isolation in those big, dark eyes. The strong and confident Hélène on stage was in such stark contrast to the girl who had opened the door that morning in Malahide and who lived with uncertainty in a strange place.

We worked for hours without stopping other than to gratefully gulp down the coffee that Pauline ferried to us throughout the morning. Lochlann's earthy browns had brought a new richness to the image. A sandy roughness to the stone walls. An auburn softness to the hair that tumbled wildly over her shoulders. The light brown of dry clay dust to the studio floor. Shades of the charcoal came through in places, in her eyes and her hands and in the little shadows on her face, and through them she retained an aloof detachment, a mistrust of the viewer.

I mixed the burnt siena acrylic with water – enough water to make sure it was transparent, not so much as to over-dilute its sepia effect. And then, with a deep breath, I wet the brush and swept it across the canvas and watched as the picture was transformed, from clear reality to something uncertain, ambiguous, like a dream remembered.

By morning's end, we were exhausted, but I was entranced by what we had created. All through the preceding weeks, I had been pleased with our progress and happy with the way the painting had evolved. But always in the back of mind I knew that until it was done, the final spark that would illuminate the piece would be invisible. It was a function not of a single brush stroke, but of everything we did and every idea we put on the canvas and every fine adjustment and revision in the night-time hours when Hélène had gone home and I worked alone in the dark quiet of the empty gallery.

And with the last stroke of the brush, it emerged from its hiding place. I can't tell you what it was or how it manifested itself, but it took my breath away. The emotion was powerful, intense – I suppose I might have deemed it affected and pretentious in others, but it was very real to me. Hélène stared out from the canvas and her sense of isolation was tangible, I could hold it. Despite her fragile frame and heart-rending vulnerability, somewhere beneath the disappointment there lurked a latent passion, violently expressed by the vivid red sash draped over the back of her chair.

It was no masterpiece, I kept telling myself. And it surely wasn't. But I had set out to craft something of which I could be proud, something that was the very best I could do with the talent and the wherewithal available to me. And I never dared dream that it could be like this. I never dared dream that it would speak to me and tell its story, even if only to me. And for no obvious reason, I somehow felt sure that Lochlann would approve, that he would hang it.

I sat down into the chair, suddenly exhausted. I looked at Hélène and nodded gently. She got up from her seat, laid the violin and bow on the desk, and came round to my side of the board. She stared at it for what seemed like forever. Then she leaned down to me and kissed my cheek.

"Before, when I looked at it, I couldn't really say that it was me." she said, softly. "But now, I know that it is. I can feel that it is. I recognise this girl. I know her."

We sat and stood there for an age, just staring. And she stared back, telling an epic tale of hope and dreams and loss and defiance. I hope it was defiance, and not just a charade, because I wanted so badly for this girl to rise from the ashes and prove everybody wrong. My own Cosette.

I stood up and started putting away my brushes and paints. All that I had read offered the same advice: when you think it's done, leave it alone – you can only do mischief, so come back with a clear mind and a fresh perspective before you tinker and tamper with it. I could see a dozen things that I wanted to rework, repair, rearrange. But I shackled my eagerness and my ego and left the last of the paint to dry.

I picked up a tube to check the drying time of the last tones I had added, but it was a Spanish brand and the instructions meant nothing to me.

"Shit."

Hélène looked over at me.

"What's wrong?" she asked.

I handed the tube to her, pointing to the minute text that, I assumed, set out the drying time.

"I don't suppose you read Spanish by any chance?" I asked. "I need to know how long I have to let it dry?"

She shook her head and shrugged, and handed me back the tube.

"Sorry."

"Never mind, I'll check with Johnny. I just want to know how long I have to make any last changes."

"Next time, you should buy French paints!" she said, with a grin.

"I'll make a note!"

She turned her head to look again at the painting.

"Do you think that he will put it in the exhibition?"

"Lochlann? I don't know." I puffed out my cheeks and blew out a long breath of quiet hope. "I hope so. I really think it works, you know? I don't think I have any more in me, I really don't." I looked at her. "I hope I've done you justice, Hélène. I hope I've told the story in your eyes. I really do."

She looked back at me and nodded.

"I don't think you can ever really tell another person's story," she said, and squeezed my shoulder gently. "But I think we have done well."

We were still staring quietly at our creation when there was a cough from the door and Lochlann came in.

"Good afternoon to you both," he said, the barest bow of his head to Hélène. "I'm sorry to disturb you, but I wonder if I could have a word?"

"Of course, Lochlann," I said, getting up from my chair. "You're not disturbing us at all."

Hélène picked up her handbag.

"Excuse me," she said to Lochlann, "I will leave you to talk."

"Actually, Hélène," he said, "it was you I wanted to speak with."

He had taken her by surprise, and she was momentarily at a loss. But she recovered and put her bag back on the desk. She said nothing but looked at him and waited.

"I was speaking with Oran this morning, and he told me about your concert last night in Dublin. Congratulations – it was quite a triumph from what he tells me."

Hélène smiled, even glowed a little at the unexpected praise.

"Thank you," she said. "That is very kind."

He shook his head.

"On the contrary – it is rather self-serving I'm afraid. I don't know if Aengus has told you about the exhibition layout, but I have a proposition for you. More a favour to ask, really."

She shook her head, entirely in the dark, and waited for him go on.

"Well, the centre of the exhibition area will be a communal social area, where people can gather to meet or take refreshment or listen to a seminar. I wonder if – and this was Aengus' idea, I take no credit – I wonder if you might provide some musical background for the opening night, based in the central area? Perhaps you know some other musicians who could form a string quartet or some such ensemble? I was thinking of perhaps some violin concertos – Vivaldi, Mendelssohn, Mozart, pieces of that nature?"

Hélène raised her eyebrows in surprise, looked at me, and then back at Lochlann, letting out a silent laugh of delighted surprise. You would think he had offered her a record contract or a date at the National Concert Hall.

"Of course, it would be an arms length arrangement in terms of fees and so on, I wouldn't expect you to agree to it for any less than your normal rate," he said, perhaps construing her smile as one of gentle ridicule.

"Thank you, Lochlann," she said, stepping over to him and kissing him on the cheek. "I would love to play at the opening night. My friend Gerry plays violin–" was there no end to his talents? "– and his sister plays also. I am sure they would be excited to play. I will talk to them tomorrow. Thank you so much."

"Well, that, that…" he was uncharacteristically lost for words in his embarrassment at her enthusiasm and unexpected display of affection. "That is wonderful, excellent. Very good indeed."

He turned to leave.

"Very good. I will leave the arrangements to you and Oran, but please come and talk to me if you have any questions. Have a good afternoon, both of you."

And he left the studio.

Hélène and I looked at each other for a brief moment, then broke into a fit of excited, childish laughter.

"Did you know about this?" she asked me.

I shook my head.

"I honestly didn't," I said. "We talked about music options, but it sounds like Oran was blowing your trumpet this morning. It's him you need to thank."

She nodded.

"He is a nice person," she said, almost to herself.

"Oran?" I smiled. "He has his moments!"

"And the first time I saw him, when he was shouting at those men, I thought he was a nasty man."

She sounded almost guilty.

"He has a short fuse, but he has a good heart."

She nodded, and looked at her watch.

"Do you mind if I go home?" she said, apologetically. "It's been a big week, I'm really tired."

"Of course, you get yourself home. Actually, let me get a cab for you."

She began to argue, but then stopped, perhaps thinking of the bus and two-train trip back to Malahide. We went into the house so that I could call the taxi company.

"Are you ok?" I asked her, afraid that I had asked too much of her and that she was trying perhaps to prove that she was still strong when she might not be. "You do look a bit drained."

She smiled.

"I'm fine. We have a night off tonight, I think I will go to bed and have a quiet night."

"OK," I said, happy that she at least planned to take a break. "And look, you don't need to come here early tomorrow,

314

I'll just be retouching. So take it easy, have a lie-in. Just come down whenever you're ready. And listen, if you need anything, anything at all, just call me, yeah? Promise?"

"I promise. Thank you."

I wondered again why she chose to be alone, to stay alone in that big old house just when she surely needed the comfort of company. Some of us need the reassurance of support. Some, I suppose, recognise that there is nothing anybody else can do and just want to avoid the well-meaning but cloying concern. I could understand that, I suppose.

A horn blew from the end of the drive – you would think that cab drivers would relish the chance to get out of the car, stroll up to your front door and stretch their legs, so why do they insist on summoning you rudely from a distance, like a diner clicking his fingers at a waiter? – and she left.

I walked back to the studio, stopping in the kitchen on my way to make some coffee, and pausing in the garden to look out over the sea below. Away to the East the sky darkened and ominous banks of black cloud gathered like troops on the front poised to invade. Looking over the sea and towards England, it struck me how little thought I had given to London in recent days, and to my friends and my life. I missed it not at all, but more than that, I didn't care that I didn't miss it, didn't even think about it. And for the first time, I didn't want to think about when or how I would go back.

But more than any of that, I felt guilty that Caitríona had not been, for a week or so, at the exclusive epicentre of my world, at the forefront of all of my thoughts and at the heart of everything I did. Nothing had, since she left, distracted me in the same way, nor provided a focus that dragged my mind away from the desolate place that it inhabited. Nothing – and nobody. None of my friends had drawn me out of my refuge – and they could not, because there was no pretext that allowed them to do so. But here, it was ok that people had lives outside my reality and it was right that they carried on with Caitríona on their minds, if not at the centre of their world. It would have been pointless to feel guilty because I know Caitríona would have only contempt for such self-indulgence. But nonetheless it all made me somehow uneasy.

I wandered slowly back to the studio, and when I walked through the door, Lochlann was sitting in my chair, fingers steepled to pursed lips, staring at the painting. So intent was he that he didn't hear my entrance, and I thought fleetingly of quickly leaving before he saw me. But I couldn't leave. I was desperate to hear his verdict, desperate and terrified.

He looked up at length.

"Aengus. I didn't see you there," he said, standing up and gesturing to the easel. "I hope you don't mind."

"Of course not, Lochlann," I said, walking over to where he stood. "Of course not."

We stood in silence for moments that felt like hours, both looking at the canvas board. I silently begged him to speak, but couldn't bring myself to ask the question.

"I cannot quite see where it fits into any of the four sections of the show," he said, suddenly. "She is clearly not one of the old generation of Irishwoman, nor is she an Irish mother. She is not a strong professional woman, nor is she the radical non-conformist."

So that was it. True to form, Lochlann had gone straight to the point and not bothered to patronise me with flannel. No faint praise, no words of consolation nor encouragement. He had considered and decided, and I could not have reasonably asked for any more. But I was crestfallen. My assertion that the important thing was for me to be happy with the result, regardless of whether he chose to hang it or not, was exposed for the transparent fabrication it was.

"So I have decided to hang it in the central area, just after the exit from the fourth section. Visitors will pass it after they have been through all four sections, and it is therefore a logical place to hang a piece that asks 'What comes next?' What comes next is in the hands of artists of your generation and young women like Hélène. I find that symmetry appealing."

I had all but tuned out in my disappointment, and so I couldn't trust myself that I had heard correctly. I stood there stupidly trying to replay his words and to make sense of what couldn't be, of what I had clearly misunderstood.

"So… so you're going to hang it? At the exhibition?"

He looked at me as though I had said something so patently obvious as to be ridiculous.

"Of course," he said, a hint of impatience in his voice. "Why would I not hang it?"

"No, no reason," I stammered, "I'm just pleased you're going to. More than pleased. I'm really delighted. Thank you. Thanks."

"Are you alright, Aengus?"

"Sorry, Lochlann," I said, regaining my composure. "It's just that when you said it didn't fit any of the four sections, I thought you meant you weren't going to include it. You don't know how much this piece means to me – I don't think I knew myself until about half an hour ago. And it means more to me than I can tell you that you're going to put it on display."

It was the closest to emotion that I had displayed to him since I was a boy, and it took both of us by surprise.

"Good," he said, composing himself. "Good, I'm glad it means that much to you, I'm glad I can do this for you."

"Is there anything you think I should do, any last touches?"

He looked at it thoughtfully.

"It is often in the finishing touches that we spoil a piece," he said, pensively, "so take care not to attempt too much."

He stepped over to the easel.

"You might darken this window frame a shade to provide a greater contrast with the sunlight outside," he said, pointing to the window behind Hélène's image, "so that it blends less with the interior walls. And you might add a little texture to the walls on this side, bring out the surface of the stone just a shade more here." He waved his hand over sandstone walls that bounded the picture.

He paused, examining every piece of the canvas carefully, shaking his head slowly, deliberately.

"But other than that, no. I would do nothing to the girl, nothing to the violin or the bow. They are not perfect, of course – they never are, but the risk of damage is too great. You will always feel you can make it better up to the point where you make it irredeemably worse, so make sure you let it be, in time."

I nodded, greedily absorbing his wisdom and eager to show that I valued his words. Because I did.

"OK. I'll do what you suggested and maybe I'll just leave it at that. You're right – I can see a dozen things that I think I should touch up, but I'm actually not sure what I think I should do."

"That is the acid test, Aengus," he said, pointing a serious finger at me. "If you're not sure what it needs, then it really needs nothing."

"God, you're on fire with the old aphorisms today, eh?" I said, with a grin, and he smiled back.

"Hélène is a wonderfully expressive subject," he said, looking again at the picture. "How did you say you found her?"

CHAPTER 29

I took a deep breath, and considered how to explain – to tell the truth, to concoct yet another lie, or to craft a compromise story? Lochlann had made a great concession by including my work, even though it was out of context and, despite his assessment, unquestionably amateur in comparison with the works he would display. He had helped Oran, reacted evenly when I had rejected his advice on media and been kind to Hélène. It would have been, I decided, unfair to lie to him again. I steeled myself and prepared to bare my soul.

"You might want to sit down," I said.

He cocked his head with an unspoken question, but stayed on his feet and stared into my eyes, waiting for my explanation.

"I've been looking for Aoife."

He raised his eyebrows, was still for a moment, then nodded his head slowly.

"I see," he said, after a moment. "Perhaps I will sit down."

He took a seat across the desk from me, and his expression bade me continue.

"The letter you forwarded to me from the Adoption Agency was a notification that they had set up a database to help adopted children and natural parents find each other. I registered, and found that Aoife had also registered, a year earlier. She gave no contact details, but she said she was in Paris, playing music in a club. And so I went to Paris and searched for her in every bar and every club I could find."

Memories of the tawdry nightly trawl of Paris' best and worst neighbourhoods and bars came flooding back, and the feeling of hopelessness that had grown as time went by.

"Finally, I found the bar where she had worked and where Hélène, her friend, had worked too. There was an old cellar-man there who knew them, told me they had left together to travel the world, and showed me a farewell message from Hélène scribbled in an old photo album. It gave an address in Malahide, of all places. Can you believe it? And so I went there. Aoife was not there, but Hélène was. And that's how I found her."

He said nothing for a few moments, didn't move, but I could hear his mind processing the story.

"And where is she... I mean, where is Aoife now?" He spoke her name slowly, as though caressing it.

I shook my head.

"I don't know. She was to come to Dublin with Hélène – they were going to play music together – but she went travelling on her way and Hélène doesn't know when she's going to arrive. Or if she'll arrive, even. She expects her still, but she is not holding her breath." I paused, reluctant to appear disloyal, but somehow indignant on Hélène's behalf. "She's not, according to Hélène, the most reliable. Hélène isn't putting anything on hold while she waits."

I shuddered a little at the strange, and somehow perverse, logic that offered that my sympathy and loyalty to Hélène, a stranger whom I hardly knew, and not to the girl and woman to whom I had displayed such a lack of reliability, such a selfish disregard.

"Will you continue to look for her?"

I nodded.

"Yes. To be honest," I said, almost embarrassed to reveal my hidden agenda and selfish motives, "that's why I'm still here. I don't know where else to look."

"And when you find her?"

I took a deep breath. This was the question I avoided every day. I was sure that my motives were pure, that the deed was born of the right reasons. If I merely used Aoife to recover a piece of Caitríona, if this was all some knee-jerk reaction to losing her, then there was no merit in my quest. But if I had, as I was sure I had, her welfare in mind, then this was the right thing to do.

"I want to make sure she's ok," I said, shaking my head at a loss to explain exactly what I felt, what I feared. "There's so much pain, so much loneliness and despair, I want to make sure she's not alone. That she has a sanctuary."

"And you think you can be that sanctuary?"

"I wouldn't dare to assume that but I can only give her the choice."

He nodded, tacit approval in his eyes.

"If there is any help you think I can offer, any support whatsoever, please come talk to me." He got out of the chair and walked deliberately to the studio door. Then he turned and looked at me. "Aengus, I know you and I have not always lived by the same rules but, for what it's worth, I think you are doing the right thing."

He nodded as though agreeing with himself, turned and left the studio.

I spent the rest of the day following his advice, darkening the window frame, deepening the texture on the far wall. He was right, of course, I knew he would be. The touches added just a shade of depth and definition that warmed the piece and centred her even more at its heart. And I resisted the urge to do more, to retouch her hair, her hands, the lines around her eyes. The sun was already going down by the time I finished, and I cleaned my brushes and rags and tidied away for the evening.

I hadn't seen Oran all day and he wasn't in the Gallery when I was leaving the studio. My mind was buzzing with thoughts

321

that flitted about like evening fireflies so that I couldn't catch one and hold it down to find a conclusion. Hélène and Aoife and Oran and Lochlann all agitated about my head, competing for space that only Caitríona had occupied for the last months. I needed a pint and, in Oran's absence, I'd have to go alone.

McGrath's was bustling when I arrived, the evening crowd crossing paths with those city workers who had been there since their train dropped them in Howth, some of them getting red-faced and loud, ties askew and shirts stained with drips of beer. Already on their third or fourth "just one more", they had missed the crucial last flight out and were in for the night and in for a cold welcome when they finally fumbled through the door in clattering, stumbling silence. And yet despite the frosty breakfast table, there will remain a twinkle in the eye because, sure, wasn't it a great night, the way impromptu sessions always are?

My regular table was occupied, and so I stood with a pang of petty annoyance by the bar with my crossword and ordered a pint from the barman, who nodded his curt recognition. Ella flitted like a tray-toting Tinkerbell between groups of men in various stages of lechery, flirting and playing them for tips like a professional entertainer. And standing at the far end of the bar among a group of his cronies, the Master was deep in earnest and animated debate. A compilation of Irish rock music played in the background just below the din of conversation punctuated by the occasional explosion of laughter and raised voices vying for airtime.

Where is the line, I wondered, and why does it define places for some of us and not for others? The line before which a local pub is a warm, comfortable place with familiar faces where you can scrape away the day's travails with talk of football and women and music and dreams. The line after which the same pub takes on a claustrophobic sameness and seems to contract around you so that you feel restricted and violated. It's the same with places – if you are cursed with the wanderlust, what was once ideal is ultimately never enough and you drift unconsciously from belonging to resentment.

Ella came to the bar to order drinks for a particularly rowdy group of suits and raised her eyebrows to the barman.

"Keep an eye on those boys," he said to her, checking her list and pulling a pint of lager. "They're puttin' it away at a fierce pace altogether."

She smiled and winked at him.

"No worries, PJ," she said over the noise, "just a bunch of big pussy cats! I'll be back for these in a minute."

He nodded, and she set off again around the floor. As she did, she saw me, smiled and came over.

"Hey ya," she said, putting one arm around my shoulders. "Good to see you." She pointed at my crossword. "If you need any help with that, just shout." And like a sprite, she was gone.

From the far end of the bar, the Master caught sight of me and waved. He excused himself from his company, and came through the crowd to my end of the bar.

"Quite the Lothario you've turned out to be, eh?" he grinned, nudging me in the ribs. "Watch that one though – she's like fire."

"I've figured that out, Master," I grinned, "and I've also figured out that she probably doesn't go for old men like us! Tell me, does it happen to everybody? I woke up one day and I was twenty years older than when I had gone to bed the night before."

"*Gosso'n*, when you get to my age, come and talk to me about getting old. Until then, would you ever *whisht*!"

I put my hands up in mock surrender.

"Will you have a drink, Master?" I asked him, noting his almost-empty glass.

He looked at it and nodded.

"I will, thank you, Aengus."

I motioned to the barman and pointed at the Master's glass. He nodded, knowing well the Master's favourite whiskey, and drew a dram from the optic.

"Thank you, PJ, and thank you, Aengus," the Master said as the barman handed him a replenished glass. "Now, *gosso'n*, tell me what you've been about. I haven't seen you these past few days."

I told him about the painting and its imminent conclusion and that Lochlann would hang it at the exhibition. He beamed and raised his glass in salute.

"Well done, boy!" he enthused, putting his whiskey on the bar counter to clutch my hand and shake it vigorously. "Well done! You must be delighted?"

I allowed myself a little smile of self-congratulation.

"To be honest, Master, I am," I grinned, stupidly. "I didn't realise how much I wanted him to hang it, I'd convinced myself that it didn't matter. But it really did – really does."

He nodded with a knowing smile, the sparkle in his blue eyes even more vivid.

"The last few months," I went on, "whenever anyone has asked me what I do for a living, I haven't been able to say 'I'm a painter' or 'I'm an artist' – I had no right. But now… now I feel like I've earned at least some right, some vindication. And if I'm being honest? It feels great!"

He clinked my glass again and took a swig of his whiskey. Then he waved to PJ and gestured for a couple more.

"This calls for proper celebration – we can't have you drinking on your own on a day like this!" he said. "I have to admit, I had lunch with your father today, and he told me the *scéal* – I'm telling you, Aengus, he was glowing, he was that pleased. He'll never tell you himself, of course, but make no mistake – he is very, very proud of what you have done. And proud too that you've persevered when, to be honest, you might easily have thrown in your hand."

He paused and looked at me, considering his next words. His voice became serious.

"And he's pleased too that you are looking for her, Aengus," he said, quietly. "Very pleased, I think." He nodded, to reinforce the words, and I nodded too, hoping earnestly that the Master was right.

"I wasn't sure how he would react, to be honest," I said with a shrug. "But he said I was doing the right thing and offered to help, even. In Lochlann's lexicon, that is strong support indeed."

"He told me as well about Oran," the Master said with a rueful shake of the head. "That lad seems to have no luck at all, God help him."

"He's lucky to have Lochlann," I said.

"He is and no mistake. But Lochlann can't keep him out of jail, and that's where he's headed, unless there's a miracle."

"Do you really think so?"

"Aengus, in full public view he hit a man without provocation – or at least none that a judge will recognise, although we all know the bugger had it coming. The judge he's been assigned, Tobin his name is, he's a hard old hawk." He threw up his hands in desperation. "Look, I would normally support Tobin entirely, Dublin needs some discipline and he's got that in spades. But he won't see the Oran that we see. He'll just see some lout who needs to be taught a lesson. It won't be long – he'll take account of character references and the like – but he's going to spend a wee while cooling off." He shook his head again and let out a long, defeated sigh.

"What about his solicitor?" I asked.

He shrugged.

"He's doing what he can, I suppose," he said, "but he's not a fool. He's just concentrating on limiting the damage."

The thought that crept into my mind was impossibly

grotesque, so I chased it out and slammed the door behind it. But back it came, peering in through a window in my head, pleading to be heard. It was the right thing to do, and I wanted to help in any way I could. But there was a limit, wasn't there? Was there?

"You've gone very quiet," the Master said, plucking me from the depths of my thoughts. "What's on your mind?"

I had to try.

"Caitríona has this friend, a colleague from her office in London, who moved home to Ireland to practise. He specialised in criminal defence for people who, in his view, had a claim to lenient treatment on account of some incitement or provocation." I paused, but it was too late to go back. "Like Oran. I could try to give him a call, see what he thinks. He's the best, supposedly, and well-respected. He might add some weight to Oran's case."

The Master perked up at Oran's potential salvation.

"Lord God, Aengus, if it has a chance at all it'd surely be worth a try." Then he recognised the reticence in my voice and identified its source. He tempered his enthusiasm. "But it would be a hard thing for you to do, wouldn't it? Hard for you to go back there?"

I shrugged.

"I have to try, don't I?"

He nodded silently, then spoke.

"Yes," he said, quietly, "I think you do."

His name was Pearse Turner, part of a prominent Waterford family steeped in legal tradition and with connections across Ireland's political spectrum. Any address books or journals of Caitríona's that I had kept were in London, and so I had none of his contact details nor the name of his firm. But it was for eventualities such as these that the internet was created and so, later that evening, with a belly-full of Pauline's stew inside me and a glass of red wine at my hand, I put my tenuous grasp of technology to work and set about tracking him down on the computer in Lochlann's study.

The search proved easier than I had expected, such was his celebrity in his field. He was based near the city's new financial services centre, and his stern features gazed out from his firm's website. I scribbled down his contact details and folded the piece of paper into my wallet. Then I shut down the computer and sat back in Lochlann's big leather swivel chair, swilling a mouthful of red wine and mulling the strangely circular nature of the world that drives us along ever-intersecting paths. Before I met Caitríona, I knew little of the law nor of those who practised it. When I met Pearse Turner, he was no more than a shadow on my consciousness from a world I never expected to visit. And when Caitríona left me, I expected never to see nor hear from him again, once the obligatory message of condolence had been acknowledged. And yet here I was, about to call him on behalf of my oldest friend. A part of me berated the mischievous spirits who mocked me. And a part of me thanked whatever power had given me, and Oran, this faint chance.

I called his office early the next morning. I dialled the number on my phone and then stared at it for what must have been five or ten minutes before summoning the courage and the fortitude to press the call button. I was put through to a fraught woman who had little time and no desire to talk to me. He was very, very busy she told me two or three times, wasn't there anybody else who could help me? And so I left a message with little confidence that it would ever find its way to his desk nor that he would recognise or remember the name even if it did. I went into the kitchen to make some coffee, and Pauline was busy folding sheets and bedclothes that she had ironed to flat, hard-creased perfection.

"You're up and about early today," she said, smoothing out a rogue flaw in a pillow-case with a silent tut. "Do you want a coffee?"

"I'll make it, Pauline. You'll have one? Or a cup of tea, maybe?"

"Oh, Aengus I'd murder a cup of tea, there's a love."

I put on the kettle and set the coffee machine into action, then sat back against the counter-top and we talked about the shortening of the evenings and the sharpening of the air.

"Lochlann tells me you're finished your painting?" she said, handing me back her cup of tea. "You wouldn't put just a drop more milk in that, would you."

"I am," I said, taking the milk from the fridge. "He warned me about trying to make it too perfect, so I think I'm going to leave it be and hope that it's ok."

"Oh now, from what he was telling me it's more than ok, Aengus," she said, dismissing my concerns with a careless swat of her hand. "He's proud as punch, I'm telling you."

I smiled.

"I hope so, Pauline."

"I know so," she said, firmly.

She was quiet for a moment, before asking:

"But you won't be heading off, will you? Just because you're finished?"

I shook my head.

"No, Pauline, I'll stay for the exhibition anyway. After that, don't really know what I'm going to do, or where I'm going. Bit sad for a fella my age, eh?" I snorted an ironic laugh.

She was thoughtful for a moment, then shook her head.

"I don't know why you don't just come home, Aengus. This is your home, where you belong. Oh, you might not want to live in this house, you'd want your space I'm sure. But Howth – or Dublin at least – that's where you should be. I'm only saying, now."

"I know, Pauline, and I've been surprised how quickly it's started feeling like home again, I really have. But I have a whole life in London and I can't just walk away from that."

I didn't tell her that that life had already started to disintegrate and that there wasn't much left to walk away from.

We were interrupted by the ringing of my phone, which still chimed with the irritating tone that I had not yet discovered how to change.

"Hello, this is Aengus," I answered it.

There was a second's delay and a click on the line as the caller picked up the receiver having dialled from the speakerphone.

"Aengus? Hi, Pearse Turner. How are you?"

I gestured to Pauline that I'd take the call in Lochlann's office and I closed the door behind me.

"Fine, Pearse, thanks, fine. And thanks for getting back to me so quickly. How have you been?"

"Oh you know, busy, busy. Lots of people doing things they shouldn't be doing, luckily for us!"

He was silent for a brief moment.

"And how have you been, Aengus?" He paused, and his voice softened. "Tough times, I'm sure?"

The only times I had met Pearse or spoken to him, she was at my side. At a function or Christmas party or drinks after work. He and I had shared a slightly irreverent sense of humour and she would stand with us and chuckle at our jokes, hushing us with one hand and egging us on with the other. And it was with that helpless, almost girlish giggling that I associated Pearse Turner, and the sound of his voice ripped at my gut. I had come a long way, perhaps, in the days just gone, but not that far.

"Aengus?" he said, to my silence. "Are you there?"

I fought the urge to hang up.

"Yes, Pearse, sorry," I croaked. "Tough times. Yes."

"Are you still in London?"

"Yes. Actually, I'm back in Dublin at the moment, but still based in London, yes."

"Really? Look, I understand that it might be hard for you and I'll take no offence if you say no, but maybe we could meet up, for a pint or something, while you're home?"

"Actually, Pearse," I spoke slowly and deliberately, afraid that my voice would fail me. "I was calling to ask a favour. I have a friend…"

I explained Oran's predicament to him, the circumstances that preceded it, our long history and how both Lochlann and Críostóir had taken him under his wing. I talked about the work he was doing in preparation for the exhibition, even the visit from the two thugs who came for his car.

"He knows he did wrong," I said, in conclusion. "And he knows he was a fool, but this guy destroyed what Oran had taken so long to build, and then goaded him for it. He deserves better than a spell in jail."

There was silence from the other end of the line, and I could hear the scratching of pen on paper.

"Would you say, in confidence of course, that he is a headstrong character then?"

"Yes."

"It seems likely then that a prison environment might encourage his darker side," he said, more to himself than to me. "And your father and the schoolmaster would provide strong character references? Testify to that effect?"

"Yes, they would."

"Times have been good here, Aengus, lots of people have made lots of money. There is a certain sympathy for those who have made honest efforts to make an honest living, and a certain distaste for a new element of Irish society that has taken their good fortune as justification for some very unpleasant behaviour. Tobin is an old sparring partner of mine, but our relationship is amicable at least. And despite his reputation, he's got his priorities in the right place."

"Oran hasn't a lot of disposable income right now, Pearse,"

I said, "but I'll speak to Lochlann and see if we can figure something out about fees. If you'll agree to take it on, I mean?"

"Caitríona would take it on, I think, and she would haul me over the coals me if I turned it down." His voice was even, candid. "I'm no sentimentalist, Aengus, so know that when I say I'll do it because she would, I'm doing it out of genuine affection for her."

His respect for her brought a smile to my face and filled me with a warm pride.

"Thanks, Pearse. On both counts."

We agreed that I would talk to Oran – no foregone conclusion in itself – and that we would meet to discuss tactics a couple of days later. He waved away my efforts to discuss fees, but I made a note to myself to talk to Lochlann lest the bill be beyond Oran's and my budget.

I drew a sigh of relief after I hung up the phone, as much that I had managed to get through the conversation as that Pearse had agreed to help Oran. That his references to her had substance, based in a mutual respect, and were not the vague clichéd sympathy of those who didn't have anything else to say about her, had given me strength, I think. It made her feel a little closer, as though she was at my shoulder as she had been every time before.

She would have pestered and bedevilled him to take a case like this, I had no doubt, but I had no doubt also that she would have scolded me for even putting off the call to Pearse, whatever the grounds. And particularly where those grounds were based on sentimentality. I was glad that the Master had been on hand, and a little embarrassed that I had needed him, to gently steer me in the right direction. I don't know if I would otherwise have had the strength of will.

In my halcyon vision of a past I didn't know, I imagine that neighbours gathered around their own in times of hardship. The *meitheal* mentality symbolised a sense of community and maybe people's lives were less congested so that they had time for each other. We don't. We have no time and too many choices, and how often, then, do we leave a neighbour to his struggle – not from apathy nor from callousness, but from just not knowing how to go about helping. It's a skill we have lost. We recognise his pain and we speak about him in muted sympathetic tones and wish there was some way we could help – we just don't know how. But there is always a way.

I went back to the kitchen to get more coffee, and took it with me to the studio. Oran and the workmen were feverishly hammering nails into a wooden frame that would form the archway into one of the rooms. Others of them were painting plasterboard partitions or laying carpet tiles or securing the boards on which the paintings would hang. The Gallery was taking shape.

To my surprise, Hélène was already in the Studio.

"Good morning," I said. "I didn't expect to see you here this morning?"

"I know," she replied. "I wasn't sure, so I thought I better come. I didn't know if you still had some things to finish."

"I talked to Lochlann, and he warned me about over-doing the finishing touches. He said I should increase the contrast here and bring out the texture more here –" I pointed out the window frame and the walls on the canvas board "– but that I should resist the temptation to do what cannot be undone. So I've locked my brushes away and I am, for now, resisting temptation."

She nodded her assent.

"He is right, of course. And I think it's perfect!" She beamed her approval.

"He is a good man, your father," she said, her tone becoming serious and her eyes searching mine for their unspoken response. "I don't know him, of course, but he seems to me like he is a good man."

332

"You know, I've spent my whole life hearing that, Hélène," I said, smiling and shaking my head with a frustration that I had become used to, "from people desperate to point out to me that I don't appreciate him or that I underestimate him. But what nobody seems to realise is that I *know*. I *know* he's a good man. I've always known it. He just hasn't always seemed to like *me*, and that's what's made it hard. I…"

I stopped the juggernaut of my rant – this girl was still a stranger, it wasn't right to air family quarrels. Not fair to her and not to Lochlann.

"I know he's a good man."

"That's alright then," she said, with a sly smile. "Aoife will like him, I think. And I think he will like her."

I looked at her, thrown slightly by her change of tack.

"Why do say that?"

She shrugged.

"Aoife does not suffer fools. I think neither does he. They will be friends, maybe."

I nodded.

"I hope so, Hélène, I really hope so. There's so much that I want to show her, so much that I want her to know. Because it's a part of who she is. And I worry that she might not be interested, or that she might just hate it all. I don't think Lochlann ever really understood what I did, never really forgave me. I want to give them both that chance."

I stood up, looked out the window for a moment.

"I never knew my mother, but my father took me to see my grandparents often and they told me about her and how she grew up and what she was like and how much I looked like her. It was hard for him, I know that now, but he did it. And of course the truth was embellished and of course any unpleasantness carefully avoided, but I knew that and I didn't care. I want to give Aoife that history. What she does with it, well, that's entirely her choice."

333

I shook my head.

"These last few weeks, I've had to admit that belonging brings a comfort that I had been denying for so long. I thought it would be claustrophobic and cloying. But in your self-centred state, you forget that everybody has a life and problems and things they want to do and they can't spend all of every day pandering to your desolation. And when you realise that, having got over the fact that they're not going to be all about you all day, it's a relief. You can get on with healing. It's been quite a revelation. And I want to make sure that she has that, that she has that somewhere to go."

I looked at her, hoping that what I was saying made some sense, because Hélène might be my mouthpiece to Aoife and I had to get it right.

"I'm not so arrogant as to think I could replace her family," I said, conscious suddenly that I might sound as though, after all this time and betrayal, I expected to return to tears of joyful welcome. "I have no right to and I don't want to. But I want to share some of this with her and give her a place to go in case she ever needs it. Pauline and Lochlann and Críostóir and Oran – they've given me that. She deserves at least the same from me."

CHAPTER 30

We used to have music on in the house every Saturday morning, as we pottered around doing all the things we hadn't had time to do during the week. Blaring out of the living room, the sound distorted through our old speakers, because we were adults now and we could. And we tunelessly sang along as we went about our chores, occasionally cranking up the volume to hum along to a chorus or a guitar riff or a drum solo, bedecked with the rock star's gurning face.

And we'd rush to the stereo at the CD's end, and fight in giggling determination for the right to make the next choice. And you'd always win and we'd always have a dose of whining Dylan. And I would mock and raise my eyebrows while you despaired of "philistine young lads like me with their Rick Astley's and their Duran Duran's!", like some sage old-timer from a golden musical age.

And amid my teasing, there was always one song that silenced me, one Dylan tune whose nasal solemnity was above derision. "What good am I?" it asked. What good am I if I just ignore all the injustice and misery around me, all the pain and the hardship that, if I could be bothered, I could stop or just make better. It was like your anthem, the soundtrack to your world and your every day. And though you couldn't be any better, you never stopped asking yourself that question because the bar you set for yourself was too high, almost out of sight. And even though, in coming close, you did more than most of us would ever even attempt, it was never enough.

You were there this morning, while I stared at Pearse Turner's number on my phone, my thumb poised over the call button. I couldn't do it, but you were there and you put a hand on my shoulder and you said "Go on, love. It's the right thing. You know it's the right thing, because the right thing is always hard." And I nodded, and put my hand on yours and squeezed.

I know you're proud of me now. I know you are. And it wasn't a big thing, it was no real sacrifice or virtuous gesture, but I suppose it would have been easier not to. And without you to say it was the right thing to do, I don't know that I could have done it. But Pearse and I both know that you would have done the same and then castigated yourself for not doing more.

I see people give in to a new norm, and it tells them to live their lives by reference only to the personal gain their actions bring. They pay lip service to the right thing, but the mobile phone generation has perhaps become focused only on what's best for them, what enriches their own lives and to hell with everybody else. You used to see it in our circle's social plans and it made you angry. Arrangements were always tentative, right to the last minute. Our friends would never commit to being in the pub or at the restaurant or at the cinema, just in case a better offer came along. And if it did, sure they could always give you a call on the insidiously omnipresent mobile to postpone or cancel or rearrange. Because they treated their time as a scarce resource to be carefully allocated so that it generated the greatest return. And if, at the last minute, a better offer came along, then they grasped it and made the all too easy excuses, and afterwards fretted that they had missed out on something even better. In seeking to find always the best opportunity, they succeeded only in creating a never-attainable nirvana and being always disappointed at falling short.

I'm going to find that Dylan song. And I'm going to play it every night before I go to bed. And I'm going to ask myself, what good am I? I don't have your lofty aspirations, nor your zealous belief in justice and a fair world. But if I can feel your hand on my shoulder and know that I've done any small thing to make you proud, then some good will have come of the day.

CHAPTER 31

O ran had suggested that we meet Pearse in a coffee shop near his building. The prospect of actually going to a law firm's offices was, perhaps, too daunting, too ready an admission that this was serious and not a boyish scrape that would lead to a smacked arse from an irate father and bed with no tea. Too grown up.

The café was in a small, smart new complex by the river, all urban industrial beams and vaulted ceilings and interior design shops filled with the pointlessly desirable accoutrements of people for whom the menial on its own is simply tedious. It was eleven o'clock and the centre was all but empty save for a few misplaced tourists and housewives filling anxious time before appointments or careless time before rendezvous or guilty, thrilling time before dangerous liaisons.

Oran had taken less encouragement than I had feared to meet with Pearse. The gravity of his predicament was emerging ever more starkly with every day closer to his day in court, and Lochlann had rudely awakened him to the need to take this seriously. So he had agreed – on the proviso that we meet on neutral ground and that he wasn't going to take "any pompous shit from any up-his-own-arse solicitor." With those ground rules clearly established and understood, I had arranged a time and a venue with Pearse and the date was set. Oran had been quiet on the DART into Connolly Station, intently focused on a tabloid newspaper whose pages he didn't turn. I didn't try to break into wherever he was lest I cross a hidden line and risk him storming off the train at Sutton or Raheny or Killester.

Pearse was sitting at a table in the café when we arrived, his phone caught between his shoulder and his ear as he bashed frantically at the keys of a laptop. I didn't look at Oran, but I could feel his eyes raised to the roof. I nodded to Pearse, and went up to the counter, holding back the surge in my gut at the sight of Pearse, fighting it with quiet insistence that this was not the time and the distraction of the immediate.

The nervous-looking young girl at the till went off to make our coffees, fumbling with a snarling, steaming machine that she didn't really know how to operate and that seemed in no mood to co-operate .

"You ready?" I asked Oran,

He nodded. "That's him, I'm guessing?" he said, nodding sidewards at the still-engrossed Pearse.

"Yeah. Look, he's a good man, alright? Don't get arsey."

He shot me an impatient look, and was about to retort when Pearse came over, his call obviously finished.

"Sorry about that, Aengus," he said without further explanation, reaching out to shake my hand.

"No problem, Pearse," I replied. "This is Oran. Oran, Pearse."

"Good to meet you, Oran," Pearse said, holding his stare and drawing a professional first impression.

The girl came back eventually with three coffees and an apologetic smile, and we took a seat in the corner, away from the only other customer in the café.

Pearse got straight to the point, addressing Oran directly and ignoring me.

"I've done a bit of digging around, Oran, I hope you don't mind," he said, stirring some sugar into his coffee. "I talked to an old friend of mine in the Garda station in Howth. You must have bought a few tickets at the Garda raffle last Christmas – you have some friends up there. They didn't want this to go

339

as far as it has, but they have no choice and you haven't given them a chance to kill it. Bobby McGrath is an old golfing pal of my father's, and I had a chat with him yesterday as well. He doesn't want to see you in trouble either – you're a good regular – but he has an interest in a few restaurants around town and he can't afford to make enemies out of the likes of Joyce."

He paused to drink some coffee, and I could feel Oran's fidgeting under the table, waiting impatiently for him to get to whatever point he was trying to make.

"Now, I also know Judge Tobin, who's hearing your case. He's got a bee in his bonnet about what he sees as a rise in loutish behaviour in Dublin and he's determined to stamp it out where he can. Public disorder is his red rag, and he treats it with zero tolerance."

Oran raised his hand to stop Pearse's flow.

"Look, Pearse, I appreciate the work you've obviously done, I really do," he said, calmly. "But if this is a lost cause, there's no point me wasting any more of your time, is there?"

Pearse shook his head.

"It's not a waste of time, Oran," he said, firmly. "With your record, you'd usually expect to get away with a fine and a sharp rap on the knuckles. But Tobin has been going to town recently, and he's been handing out a lot worse. And Joyce is making a real song and dance out of the whole thing." He drew breath and his furrowed brow betrayed his concern. "You might even be looking at a short stretch here, and I think I can help you. I can't promise to keep you out, but we can keep it to a minimum."

I had expected to play the arbiter, to calm an over-wrought Oran, but Pearse was in control and didn't need my help.

Oran clenched and unclenched his hands, caught in two minds and taken aback by Pearse's undisguised admonishment, and nodded slowly.

Pearse continued, unfazed by the interruption.

"Joyce, from what I hear, is determined to see this through. An affront to his professional integrity, an attack on the freedom of the press, the usual self-important crap from a hack with an inflated view of his own kudos. It's a restaurant column, not Watergate, someone should remind him. But he has a right to go about his business without being attacked in the pub – apparently!"

He shook his head as though perplexed by the world's obsession with political correctness and smiled at his own joke. Oran had to laugh in spite of himself, perhaps warming just a little to a man who might just be an ally.

"With all of that, I've seen Tobin hand out three or four months."

Oran's smile disappeared and he looked as though winded by a sucker punch to the stomach. He had always known that he was in trouble, that this was serious. But to have it spelled out in such stark terms by one qualified to express an opinion – that made it very real and very, very frightening.

"Now look, just as Tobin is on a one-man warpath against anti-social behaviour, so a positive social contribution goes a long way with him. And as I said to Aengus the other day, he's not a big fan of Dublin's nouveau chic. He has some sympathy for anyone who shows some enterprise and a willingness to graft, and who doesn't assume that the world owes them a living. Character references from Aengus' father – whose celebrity in the arts world will do no harm at all – and from a long-time school-master be very important. Do you think your old boss at the Bella Cucina would speak for you?"

Oran was visibly impressed at the thoroughness of his investigation – he knew more than he had ever expected.

"He might, I suppose. We parted on fairly good terms and he always treated me well."

"Good. We just want him to say that you started at the bottom, worked hard and got to the top. And that you took that experience and left with his blessing to spread your wings and go it alone."

Oran raised his eyebrows and puffed out his cheeks.

"Well, you might have to write it down for him, but yeah, he might say that."

"Leave it with me," Pearse said, scribbling a note in his monogrammed leather-bound notebook. "OK, I'll get started preparing our case and we'll talk again in a few days. Time, as ever, is not really on our side."

Oran nodded, looked nervous.

"Listen, Pearse," he said, uncertainly, "I need to know what all this is going to cost?"

Pearse put the notebook back in the inside pocket of his jacket, and looked at Oran.

"Let's just call it a favour for an old friend, Oran, and leave it at that."

Just then, Pearse's mobile phone rang, and he pulled it from his jacket pocket.

"Sorry, Oran, I thought I turned it off," he said, with a grimace. "Do you mind if I take this?"

Oran nodded, and Pearse walked out to a quiet spot in the concourse.

"Jesus, he doesn't pull his punches, does he?" Oran said when he was gone.

I shook my head.

"What would be the point? Might as well call it like he sees it."

He nodded and rubbed his eyes with both hands.

"I know. Four months in jail though? Shit. I should have hit the little prick harder!"

I laughed and snatched a brief moment of relief at the frankness that was Oran's trademark and that he would have to control if he was to make any sort of good impression on a judge.

"I'm not sure Tobin would see that as mitigation – 'but I could have hit him harder, your honour.'"

He grinned a rueful grin and rubbed his eyes again. He was worried now, as though he had underestimated the trouble he was in, or closed his eyes to it in the hope that it might just go away.

"He knows his stuff, though, doesn't he? I mean he seems to know what has to be done, what buttons to push and all that?" he said, searching for some reassurance.

I nodded. But although I really wanted to, I just couldn't find the optimism to be convincing.

He shook his head.

Pearse reappeared with a contrite smile.

"Sorry about that," he said, "but I've learned not to cut off a call from the boss."

"No problem," Oran said. "Listen, I have to get back, there's a load of work to do and I've learned that it doesn't ever get done if I'm not barking at someone!"

He stood up.

"Listen, thanks, man," he said, looking straight into Pearse's eyes.

Pearse nodded, and Oran was gone.

"Would you drink another coffee," Pearse said to me, "I'm gasping for one."

I smiled and nodded, and he went to the counter.

The centre was getting a little busier as lunch-time approached, and flustered men in the new uniform of suits and bare, open collars hurriedly picked up coffees and sandwiches to bring back to their desks, mobile phones attached to their ears. Despite the swelling crowd, the stores seemed empty and I wondered if anyone ever actually bought anything, or if the shiny silver and stainless steel follies were just expensive ornaments in a huge display case that decorated the centre.

Pearse arrived back with two coffees and sat into the seat.

"Thanks, Pearse," I said, peeling the plastic lid from the cup. "So what do you think?"

Pearse drew a long breath and blew out his cheeks.

"It's not great, Aengus, to be honest," he said, "but let's see what we can do."

"You make it sound a bit hopeless?"

"Not hopeless, no – but we could do with some help from Jude!" he said, with a quiet laugh.

My face told that I didn't understand the reference.

He paused.

"Sorry, Aengus," he said, softly, slowly, uncertainly. "In the office, when a hopeless case came in, we used to... we used to shout over to Caitríona, 'Hey, Jude'. We all knew that, as long as there was justice at stake, she would never turn down a lost cause."

He looked at me, and we said nothing for a moment. And then another. And then another. He looked down and stared into his coffee as though it had just revealed some great secret.

Then, involuntarily and spontaneously, my face broke into a broad smile. I think I might even have laughed.

"Hey Jude, eh?" I grinned and cocked an eye. "And they say lawyers have no sense of humour?"

"I know!" he said, arms outstretched in mock disbelief, and genuine relief. "You should hear us when we get a few pints inside us. Friday night down at our local is like the Comedy Store!"

His face grew serious again.

"She was one of a kind, Aengus, I've never known anyone like her. I'm not a sentimental person, and this has nothing to do with morbid reminiscence – she just commanded that we remember her that way."

He raised both hands.

"Right, that's me done. I've been reciting it for hours and I'm glad I got to say it. Sorry, Aengus – thanks for indulging me."

I shook my head, and drew a deep breath.

"Don't apologise, Pearse," I said, quietly. "I'm just learning how to be proud of her again, and it's good to hear people talking about her and the way she was, not mourning her."

"Do you remember the Rollins case?" he said, and took a drink from his paper cup.

I looked up into the centre's vaulted roof and tried to catch a vague memory that was flitting around my head. Caitríona talked a lot about her work, but never gave me enough detail to commit some indiscretion or *faux pas*, and yet the name sounded familiar.

"It rings a bell, but..."

"Johnny Rollins was a fifteen-year-old kid from west London. Just a normal kid – from a good family, went to a decent school. But for some reason, he had been ridiculed by a bunch of other kids because he had the wrong trainers, you know what kids can be like. But the ridicule got nasty, and became a sort of abuse. Whatever got into his head, he attacked another boy and stole his trainers. But he attacked him with a knife, and he stabbed him. The kid was pretty badly hurt."

He paused while one of the staff cleared empty cups from our table.

"Thanks very much," he smiled at her, and she smiled back. He turned back to me. "Caitríona heard about the case, and asked – well, demanded, really – that we took it on. We used to do a certain amount of *pro bono* work and so she got her way. She was so desperate to help that kid. She was always committed, always threw herself fully into any case she was working on – but this was different. It was as though it was personal, almost. She was like the proverbial dog with a bone. She had every junior in the firm digging out precedents, called in every favour she was owed, and some she wasn't. The case cost us a fortune – only she could have got away with it, and nobody dared question her."

Some coffee dribbled from his cup and down his chin as he drank and he wiped it away with a napkin.

"I came into the office late one evening to pick up some files, and her light was on. She was working on her closing remarks, and I swear she was nearly in tears. The kid had really gotten to her. He wasn't a bad kid, just did something stupid out of desperation. And now the rest of his life was at stake. The whirling dervish that used to sweep through the office barking instructions and organising the troops, she was gone, and there was a quiet, almost desperate woman in her place. 'Why do we spend so much time and effort punishing the act,' she said, 'when we should spend our time dismantling the motivation?' She said that, if he had been insane, they would have found him not guilty. But because he was driven by an ugly obsession that we created, a set of celebrity culture norms that we allowed to become a kind of social law, he would be condemned. 'I wish he really was insane,' she said. We worked on it for hours. She knew he was going to be found guilty, of course he was. But she wanted to make sure that his life wasn't torn asunder by it all, that he still had a chance. And she did. The Judge was more lenient than anyone expected, than any of us could have hoped. Caitríona didn't get him off – it's not a fairy story – but she gave him back a chance in life. She really did."

I nodded. So much of the abrasive, aggressive outward appearance that she put on for the world was a cover for the soft Caitríona, the Caitríona that couldn't bear sadness or hurt, the Caitríona who only wanted to protect. It was the same in her private life, she used a devil-may-care toughness to mask what she perceived to be weakness. It served her well, but it also did her an injustice. It presented to the world a harder, colder Caitríona, and hid from everyone the girl that they would surely have loved.

Pearse's phone chimed, and he checked the message.

"I really have to go, sorry, Aengus." He stood and gathered his things. "It's been really good to see you. Listen, I'll get to work on Oran's case, and I'll give him a call in a couple of days."

He shook my hand, and left.

I got back to Howth late in the afternoon and went to the Gallery to see how final preparations were progressing for the exhibition's opening night, which was only a couple of days away. In only a week or so the Gallery had undergone a metamorphosis. The four chambers, as Lochlann had taken to calling them, that would house the four sections of the show had been erected and were in the final stages of decoration and completion. Entrance and exit archways had been cut in the chamber walls to guide visitors in and point them out in the direction of the next chamber. Along the floor, coloured carpet tiles marked the path from chamber to chamber and through the chambers themselves. The welcome desk was in place by the entrance door, with its refreshment counter and coat-stands.

And at the heart of the vast room, the central gathering area was marked out by ornate roping and a hedge of small potted trees and shrubs. There were sofas and armchairs around its perimeter, and high tables and bar stools at its centre. At one end, a small dais and lectern had been put in place, raised on a small platform, a gantry of lights and speakers above it.

The finishing touches were intricate and elaborate. Each of the eight huge windows in the Gallery walls had been decked with flowing curtains, tied back by silk bands, and closed to the world outside by discreet sheer blinds. Every light had been fitted with an identical, simple shade, and every flower box bound with identical cream ribbon. The effect was simple and dignified, considered and complete.

As I arrived, Oran was marching deliberately through the Gallery checking every minute detail from one end to the other, his face set in its customary growl. He went through each of the chambers, shaking the archway entrances to ensure they were sturdy, kicking at the carpet tiles on the floor to make sure they were properly stuck down, pulling gently at the satin wall coverings that draped the hardboard walls on which the paintings would hang.

Then he made his way to the centre of the auditorium, and stopped. He stared at the dais and the lectern and his hand went to his forehead.

"Stephen!" he shouted, impatiently. "Stephen, where are you?"

O'Leary appeared from wherever he had been nervously surveying Oran's progress through the Gallery.

"Oran," he said, with hollow bonhomie, "how are you doing? Listen, I was just—"

"What are you going to do with those cables?" Oran cut him off, pointing to a mass of electrical wiring that ran from the floor behind the lectern up to the gantry, hanging in a chaotic tangle.

"Ah, don't worry about that, Oran, that'll be fine," O'Leary said. "There's no more we can do with it. They'd usually run the cables through piping across the floor, up the walls and across the gantry. But it's too far from the walls, you'd need a mile of cable. Trust me, there's no other way – they have to go straight up. I don't think it's a problem."

"I don't trust you, and it is a problem." Oran stared at him, his patience with the exhibition manager and with the world dangerously frayed and nearing its end as the opening approached. "Those wires cannot be visible from the floor. They will not be visible. Do you hear me? Now sort it out."

He stalked off shaking his head in frustration, the air thick with his mumbled oaths, leaving a wincing, grimacing O'Leary scratching his head.

"How high is that gantry?" I said to O'Leary, walking into the centre of the communal area, looking up at the wires.

He was no more pleased to see me than he had been to see Oran.

"About fifteen feet," he said gruffly, without greeting.

"And how wide?"

"About twenty feet."

"Well here's what you're going to do..." I raised my hand to stop the interruption he was about to make. "Just listen, will you?"

He stared sulkily at me.

"Measure the height and width exactly. Then get two black crepe sheets, two sets of curtain rings – enough to put a ring every fifteen centimetres – and two strong curtain poles. We're going to fix a pole to each side of the gantry and drape a curtain from each pole. If you can't move the wires, then we'll just hide them."

He opened his mouth to argue, then stopped and nodded grudgingly.

"Just make sure the curtains are the right size, and heavy enough to hang straight without moving, even if there's a breeze."

He sloped off without another word to me and barked at a young workman to fetch him a measuring tape.

"Is there a problem?"

I turned around and Lochlann walked over from the welcome desk.

"No problem," I said, "Oran just noticed the mess of wires up there on the gantry, and we're trying to figure a way to make them less of an eye-sore. I think we have it now. It'll be fine."

He nodded, clearly weary with the perhaps unexpected effort it had all taken, and with nervous anticipation of what lay ahead. He looked somehow a little older than when I had arrived back in Howth.

"It looks fantastic," I said, looking around, and seeking perhaps to reassure him a little if I could. "You must be really pleased."

He nodded again, and allowed himself the merest of smiles.

"It is indeed a splendid setting," he said. "But there is so little time. And we have still to position, hang and light the pieces. Fifty of them. That will take time. Always more than one imagines."

"The workmen will be done tomorrow," I said, with more confidence than I felt, "and that leaves us a whole day to hang them. Even if it takes us all of tomorrow night, sure we'll get there."

He nodded, but with little conviction.

The Gallery door opened behind us, and I looked around to see Hélène, flanked by two other girls whom I did not know. She walked over and kissed both of my cheeks in Gallic greeting, then Lochlann's.

"Hello," she said, looking around the Gallery. "Wow, this place looks amazing. It all seems to have happened so quickly."

She gestured to her companions.

"This is Eimear, she is Gerry's sister, and this is her friend Nuala," she said, then introduced us to them. "This is Lochlann and Aengus, that I told you about."

She turned to Lochlann amid the flurry of hand-shakes and greetings.

"We were thinking about the music you asked us to play, and we would like to talk to you about it. Do you have some time, now?"

"Yes, yes of course," he said, ever the gallant despite the pressure he felt with the approach of opening night.

"Well," Hélène began her well-rehearsed words to the nodded support of her two accomplices, "you suggested some violin concertos – Vivaldi, Mendelssohn, perhaps – and we agree they would be very beautiful. But we thought that perhaps some traditional Irish airs would be more appropriate, given the theme of your show? With perhaps a female vocal from time to time? Gerry cannot make it, unfortunately, but maybe it is better – three women playing Irish music? It is in a way what your show is all about, no?" She looked at the others, standing nervously almost behind her, and they nodded again their mute agreement. Then her honesty got the better of her. "We also thought that, well, we would really need to practise, to prepare the others, they are quite challenging. But the Irish airs we know well and it would be easier. Eimear and I will play violin, and Nuala plays flute."

He was quiet for a moment, then he began to nod slowly.

"You make a very good point, Hélène," he said, and I could sense that it was more than mere chivalry, he was convinced, and impressed at the thought they had given it. "The right Irish melodies would make a fitting accompaniment. What do you think, Aengus?"

"I think it's a great idea," I nodded, and my eyes widened to make clear my approval. "I don't know why we didn't think of it before. And maybe we could pick tunes to go with each of the four sections of the show? I wouldn't overdo the vocals – I think it's important that the music accompanies, doesn't dominate – but one or two, particularly towards the end of the evening, would be nice. And I think slow, haunting airs would really create an atmosphere – especially with the flute."

Lochlann nodded slowly like a teacher assessing a child's answer, and the three girls drew a collective sigh of relief.

"Thanks for understanding," Nuala said to Lochlann, "we won't let you down. We promise."

"I have no doubt," Lochlann said. "Now, if you will excuse me…"

With his customary faint bow, he turned and left.

Hélène and her two friends excused themselves and hurried away, amid excited whispers and waving arms, to prepare their repertoire.

The people we are "under pressure" are strangers to our everyday selves. We probably wouldn't recognise them in the street, nor recognise their description from the mouths of friends. We might have met these alter egos, in fraught moments, but until we do, we can never know whom to expect. We might be ashamed of them, like the rogue cousin never mentioned at family gatherings. Or proud of their noble strength in the face of what we could never resolve nor retrieve.

We go through so much of our lives without needing them, with neither drama nor crisis from which to be rescued. So we have invented our own mean, pointless pressures to satisfy some need to overcome. In our world, pressure in that guise has become a way of life. We don't make life and death choices, but we make their banal equivalents every day. And we clutch and barge and grasp and hoard and snatch because we're afraid not to, afraid of losing, no matter if others have a keener need or a greater right. The artificial stress of our everyday and the pressure of normal life have conditioned us not to think or to consider or to judge, but to act lest somebody else acts first. We have grown mean under a siege of our own making and our everyday selves are poorer for it, unworthy versions of the people we would like to be.

Our under pressure selves are the selves we would have been in the Somme's fetid trenches or on Titanic's icy decks. With decorum and social propriety stripped away, they are our selves when instinct takes over. We either shield our comrade on the muddy charge or linger in his lee. We either help him into the lifeboat or push him out of the way.

Oran's under pressure self, I have no doubt, would raise the drawbridge and defend the innocent and fight side-by-side with the virtuous. Quietly, without ostentation, he would simply get the job done.

And that is the Oran that strode around the Gallery the following morning. Oran's everyday self had no truck with the self-inflicted stresses of modern Dublin. He had neither patience nor sympathy for those who fretted over decisions that would change nothing at all save an imagined reality that he would gruffly dismiss. But when faced with a threat to something he held dear, his under pressure self would bid him step aside and calmly take over.

I don't think it was the art that had sparked his determination, though he saw its value, had come to feel its energy. No. I think it was the realisation of a good man's dream and his right to tell a story that deserved to be heard. Lochlann wanted to stoke a passion and give the world some beauty, and Oran wasn't going to let incompetence or laziness or apathy derail that ambition.

O'Leary knew all too well, and had suffered at the hands of, every day Oran. He knew what to expect and had built his defences. But as his judgment day drew near, the colder alter ego that stalked the Gallery unnerved him, and he oscillated between moodily shuffling and nervously scuttling around. In truth, and perhaps no thanks to O'Leary, the Gallery was as good as done. Oran's bad tempered badgering and berating had done its work and what had been an empty shell when I arrived in Howth was now a temple worthy of art and debate. Oran's consistent and persistent belittling of O'Leary, and of the workmen's craftsmanship, had perhaps achieved its end, but in truth the beleaguered exhibition manager had delivered a beautiful home for Lochlann's work. And given a moment to reflect, I think O'Leary might well have been proud of his own work.

Such a moment still denied him, he laboured under Oran's whip until, early in the afternoon, there was nothing outstanding, no obvious faults or failures, no last minute corrections or repairs. A weary and beaten O'Leary emerged from behind the curtains and walked reluctantly over to Oran.

"The fusebox is ok now," he said, having addressed the latest of Oran's interminable complaints. "It was the hoover – the hoover, can you believe it?"

"Good," said Oran.

"Can I let the lads go, so?" O'Leary asked.

Oran looked around. His vision was, to all intents and purposes, complete. He might have kept them there to handle any unforeseen problems, but instead he nodded.

"Yeah," he said. "Is there someone on call?"

"I have their numbers," O'Leary answered, "just call me if you need anything."

"OK," Oran nodded.

O'Leary nodded back and turned to discharge the troops.

"Stephen," Oran called after him.

O'Leary stopped and turned in weary anticipation of another tirade.

"Oran?"

"Tell the lads. Good job. This place is a credit to them." He looked down and scratched the floor with his toe. "And to you. Thanks, man."

O'Leary stopped and looked hard at Oran. He grew a little taller in front of my eyes, and a smile gently broke his features. Not the dishonest, sycophantic simper that had so irked me, but a thin, crooked smile of genuine, exhausted relief and no little pride.

"I will, Oran," he said, "See you tomorrow."

"Good luck, Stephen," Oran said.

All that had gone before was past and so the deal was done.

CHAPTER 32

"We'd better make a start hanging the paintings," I said to Oran, "Lochlann reckons it'll take ages, we don't want leave it too late."

"You're probably right," he said.

He went over to the folder that he carried everywhere with him and pulled out a sheet of paper.

"This is the list of paintings, by section," he said.

"How many?" I asked.

"Fifty-two."

"Do you have the order within the sections?"

He shook his head.

"No, don't think so. We'll have to check with himself."

"Where are they?"

He nodded towards a small store room at the end of the Gallery.

"All wrapped in cellophane and stacked in there. They're numbered, I think. Best to start by putting them in the right room, I suppose."

And so we started the painstaking process of taking the paintings from the storeroom, one at a time, checking them against Oran's list, unwrapping them and putting them in the appropriate chamber. When we had finished, I gathered up the piles of torn and crumpled cellophane and I took them to the skip outside while Oran went to the house to find Lochlann. Back inside, I stood at the centre of the Gallery, darkness nearly complete outside. There was no sound, and although I couldn't see them, I could feel the accusing eyes of a hundred or more of Lochlann's Irish women burning into me from within the four hushed chambers. Determined eyes, lost eyes, resigned eyes, ambitious eyes – women with little in common except a fruitless search for their place and for peace. I shivered a little under the weight of their wordless angry stares.

I heard the voices approach with a pang of relief, and Oran and Lochlann walked into the Gallery. Oran waved yet another list at me from the door.

"Our instructions," he called out to me.

He walked over and put the list on the lectern, and the three of us pored over it. The blueprint for the completion of everything that Oran and Lochlann had worked so hard to deliver. Lochlann had, of course, given great thought to the sequencing of the paintings within the rooms, and had carefully and precisely listed the order, the spacing between them and the respective heights at which we should hang neighbouring pieces. Each piece would have to be hung on two specially designed hooks, and then its individual spotlight, all of which had been already wired, had to be centred and fixed to the wall four inches above it. No more. No less.

Oran nodded approvingly. A doer not a thinker, his world was built on clear instruction and logical, mechanical process.

"Right so," he said, "I think it goes like this. Aengus, you put in the hooks and hang the painting, I'll follow you round and put up the lights." He looked at his watch. "If we get cracking, we can have this done tonight."

"That is a little ambitious," Lochlann said.

"Sure we've hours," Oran quipped. "You go on back to what you were doing, Lochlann. Come on, Aengus, let's make a start. If we hurry, we'll be in McGrath's for last orders."

Last orders were long over and the closing bell had long been rung as we set to work on the last of the fifty-two paintings in the fourth chamber. It was almost five o'clock in the morning and, fuelled by regular coffees and sandwiches cobbled together on raids of Pauline's fridge, we fought the tiredness and the cold of pre-dawn to hang the final frame. We had dared not leave anything until the following day – the day of the opening night – lest any last minute disaster should derail our best-laid plans. And so we had persevered, getting undoubtedly slower as the night progressed. And now Oran was fixing the last light. We stood back and looked around the chamber, bold images of young women challenging us with defiant eyes.

"Not bad," Oran said, almost to himself. "Not fuckin' bad."

He looked at me.

"Good job, man," he nodded.

"Not bad yourself," I grinned. I shook my head. "You know, I'm never letting anyone take these down. Ever."

"I know what you mean," he said. "It's just beautiful, isn't it? Magical."

"Jesus, you're not going to get all soft on me now, are you?" I joked.

"Feck off," he said, with a grin, throwing a rolled up ball of rogue cellophane at my head. "You don't have a monopoly on culture, you know?"

We put away our tools and the left-over hooks and screws and bulbs, and locked up the Gallery. Oran set the newly installed alarm system, and we walked to his car. The sun showed the first faint signs of rising over the distant Wales, and the first birds had started to sing. Oran started his car and pulled away towards the village and like Gray's ploughman, I made my weary, plodding way to the house and to bed.

Lochlann's calm demeanour usually betrayed little of what was happening under the surface. As a boy, I never knew when he was excited or disappointed, lonely or angry or scared. He greeted my successes and failures with the same moment of consideration, the same look of faint disapproval or the same formulaic words of encouragement or congratulation.

But the next morning, the nervous energy breached the dam and seeped out of him. Not that he became animated or gave any outward evidence of stress – but to those who knew him well, his nervousness was infectious. Except to Oran. The barely subdued explosive temper of the weeks before had given way to controlled activity, and he walked quietly through the Gallery tightening a screw here and buffing a rail there, a picture of barely recognisable serenity. O'Leary too seemed calmer and somehow, in this his moment of triumph, perversely less determined to impress and inveigle.

Lochlann walked over to where I was helplessly surveying the last minute preparations, even his movement a fraction faster as though the very cadence of his being had been turned up a notch.

"Aengus, we should hang your work," he said, simply.

In the bustling urgency of the days gone by, I had, if not forgotten, then at least lost sight of the fact that my portrait would hang here. Having watched the Gallery's evolution from empty shed to this quiet sanctuary of tribute to the ages of our women, that I was a part of this, that Hélène was a part of this, as she deserved to be, had been swamped in the crowd of activity and progress. Now our work of the weeks gone by would reach its final resting place.

I went into the studio and gingerly took the painting down from its easel where I had diligently resisted tampering with it while it dried. The canvas board remained frameless, simple, and even a little stark. It asked a question.

I carried it back out to the Gallery, where O'Leary was putting in place a two-metre high hardwood stand draped in dark satin. It stood on the carpeted trail that led from the fourth chamber to the meeting area at the centre of the Gallery.

Once he was happy that it was secure and stable, we attached the hanging wire to the board and two hooks to the stand.

Lochlann picked up the board and handed it to me, and nodded with no word. The culmination of a profoundly personal labour, the realisation of a long-held ambition is not always accompanied by the fanfare nor set on the dramatic stage of our vain and wistful imaginings. More often, it emerges from the flow of the everyday. But when it does, it stops the flow for just a moment and becalms us. When we look up from the ordinary, we find that we have arrived without warning at the place of which we have dreamed for so long. And the suddenness of the arrival and the wonder of the place finds us unprepared, like a child at his surprise party. The feeling, though fleeting, is sometimes deeper and stronger than any we could have conjured in our minds.

I hung the board against the darkened stand, fussily straightened and centred it and lit the spotlight. I stood back, and just for a moment Caitríona's eyes looked out from the frame with kindness and love and pride. This piece would be the show's post-script, would perhaps snag in the memory of visitors still thinking about what they had seen, not prepared for the final question.

"You must of course decide on a title for the piece," Lochlann said, "but I wonder if, for the purposes of the exhibition, we might call it 'What will be...'. It is a statement that positions the piece as looking to the future, and yet asking a question that underlines the uncertainty that she feels, that you can see in her eyes."

I nodded.

"That's fine," I whispered, then coughed hard to shake myself from the self-indulgence. "I mean, it works really well, it's exactly what we talked about."

And so he fixed a small plate that he had already prepared to the stand below the painting, and Hélène's soulful eyes peered out among the hundred eyes of Lochlann's mothers and workers and quiet revolutionaries. And she belonged.

Hélène, Nuala and Eimear arrived with their instruments and began to prepare for the sound-check. While the others adjusted microphones and fine-tuned a violin, and positioned and repositioned the high stools on which they would be perched, Hélène walked slowly over to where I stood, still staring at her image.

"I never expected that it would make me want to cry," she said with a quiet smile. "But I do."

I nodded without looking at her, still staring.

"I know." It seemed irreverent to speak and so I echoed her hushed tone. "I know. I can't quite make myself believe that it's real, that we did this. It sounds so vain, so boastful. I don't claim that it's a wonder, it's just a wonder that we created it." I smiled at the unintended pun, and shook my head. "You know what I mean," I said.

She smiled and nodded.

"I should go and get ready," she said, touching my arm. "See you later."

I nodded and she floated away.

As the Autumn sun lost its fight against sleep like a pyjama-clad child peering through the banisters at his parents' party, the invitees began to arrive, the besuited cognoscenti of the Irish art world – dealers and professors and critics and artists. I stood, trying to fade into the background in an ill-fitting suit borrowed from Oran, while my father greeted his guests at the reception desk with a recovered, almost dispassionate, calmness that belied what I knew continued to churn below the surface. The catering staff hovered unobtrusively with trays of champagne and canapés, and from the sound system came the slow, unmistakably Celtic strains of the flute-accompanied violins.

Slowly and deliberately, they moved toward the first chamber, lingering with glasses of wine and champagne in front of the wizened old woman clad head-to-toe in sombre black, mending nets on the upturned *currach*. Or the young girl carrying water from the well, her young dog beside her, looking up at her with rapt attention. Her pretty lips suggesting that she was perhaps talking to him or singing some absent-minded tune.

Then they carried on to the second chamber, and stood in front of my mother. She was pruning a rose bush, and she was captured turning around as though someone had called out to her. Her face was bright, an almost-smile playing on her lips, and her eyes shone with a compassionate calmness, with a hint of concern lurking beneath as though she was nagged by a perpetual, constant worry. Or they considered the woman gazing out to sea from some west coast cliff, her back to the viewer and her skirt billowing in the breeze. Gazing out to where her sons had gone to seek, if not a fortune, then at least a future in Boston or New York or Chicago. From where their own sons now trickled home to a new Ireland. Or the young girl wheeling her baby in a decrepit old pram, with fearful eyes that searched for a lost life that had promised so much but had been so rudely taken away.

Then to the third chamber, and the smart young woman with a briefcase hanging from her shoulder, speaking intently into a mobile phone and glancing at her watch while hurrying toward an office building. She looked a little nervous, out of place like an interloper, but determined to belong. Or the portrait of the President borrowed for the occasion of the exhibition – not just a woman in Áras an Uachtaráin, but a woman from the North? A million Irish fathers spun simultaneously in their graves, while proud and powerful Irish women stood determined to make a difference and leave a mark.

And finally to the fourth, with its images of placard-wielding protestors with shaved heads. And of the young woman sitting behind her band, beating her drums in eyes-closed reverie, lost in the rhythm of their music. And the pierced and tattooed beauty of the girl, basking in the sunshine in St. Stephen's Green. Anarchic images become normal, everyday.

And then to Hélène. And to the questions she asked.

"Well, *gosso'n*, what a triumph, eh?" said a beaming Master, appearing at my side. He was almost beside himself with excitement, grabbing my hand and shaking it vigorously. "What a remarkable triumph. I don't think I've ever seen the like of it. And he's a proud man today. He was so worried that he might fail, but sure there was never any chance of that. A triumph, and no mistake."

He sipped from a glass of champagne, and prodded me with a stubby finger.

"And a triumph in which you play no small part, do you hear me? Your painting nearly took my breath away. And he's put it in a great place." He grinned in satisfied vindication. "'What will be...', eh? As much a reference to you as to the girl, there's no doubt."

"Thanks, Master," I said. I drew a breath to argue, but let it lie. Because in truth, I felt a genuine part – albeit a small part – of the show, and that I had earned the right to be there. And whenever my confidence ebbed and uncertainty raised its head, I looked to Hélène's haunting eyes peering out from the painting and it reset my self-belief.

"I'll see you later, *gosso'n*."

The Master squeezed my shoulder and winked at me, then hailed a friend across the room and marched away to talk with him.

I had spent so much time and energy in the search for meaning and for purpose. It is the curse of my generation, or at least of my Irish generation. We have never known peril, or hardship, or pain – not really, not in the context of what our forefathers suffered or what people in cursed, stricken lands still suffer every day. Without that focus on survival, we have grown terrified by aimlessness, by the drift through life with no destination and no measure of success. And so in the comfortable safety of our privilege, we have looked for our own context and for the new definitions of achievement and accomplishment.

Why then, given the unprecedented opportunity to set our own path without risk of ruin or wreckage, have we set our sights so low? Why have we compromised on the accumulation of meaningless, self-indulgent fripperies as the new definition of our lives? Our culture places the greatest value on celebrity, and not on how that celebrity is earned. And because it is not founded on merit, it has to be publicised by ostentation.

Is it naïve to think that success can only be defined by the value we add, however that value is denominated? Is it too innocent to think that the good we do is measured in lives enriched? Whatever we think we achieve, surely it counts as nothing if it fails to add something to the world's pot, no matter how small or how apparently insignificant. If all we achieve is the reallocation of wealth or value to ourselves, then there is no glory.

Oh, it's not about selfless sacrifice on some mass scale, nor hair-shirted self-denial, nor even about giving up the chance to build a better life. That would be truly naïve. But the rewards in the endless search for material self-betterment are hollow and short-lived. The pride and sense of achievement that goes with the even greater accumulation of chattels lasts only until the next target appears on the horizon, then are forgotten, like so many of Santa's discarded presents on St. Stephen's Day.

I watched the guests meander slowly through the Gallery, watched them stand in front a piece for ten or fifteen minutes, a finger to their lips in quiet contemplation. I watched them in intense conversation and vexed debate, stabbing a certain finger at a canvas then throwing up their arms in despairing resignation, or smiling in nodded epiphanous agreement.

Lochlann was enriching the life of every person there. Some might not have enjoyed his work, might have argued that it was an anachronism or a too-subjective version of the truth, but everybody there considered its aesthetics or its message or both and left richer for the experience.

And Lochlann was richer for it too, not materially, but emotionally and spiritually and personally. Because to strive for a better place filled with better people is not to ignore or subdue your own need to succeed and thrive. The satisfaction and pride that he felt, that he had earned, would be a lasting legacy that lived on beyond the life of any material gain.

What enriches the world enriches us. And yet we can't see it for the mounting heaps of meaningless trinkets that clutter and swamp our lives. Maybe we can never see it in a world where profit is the motivation. The corporate masters to whom we dedicate so much of our time have misplaced and left behind the often pure ideals on which their own dreams were founded. They have become blinkered by the eternal and overpowering quest for gain. The virtue of what they had set out to do and the good it spawns is clouded, superseded even, by the cracking whip of greed and the pursuit of success exclusively for its own sake.

And at some point we stop, take a step back and survey our world from above. And we can see clearly for perhaps the first time that the end is no nirvana. That success just perpetuates the pursuit of success. And that failure is not tolerated. But the wheel is spinning and there is no way off. There is nothing else and no way to find it. Is that why we have children? To provide meaning where there is none? To provide a distraction from the monotony? How ironic then that we bring them into a world of our own creation and where they will, in all likelihood, make all our mistakes all over again.

I tore myself away from the vantage point from where I could stand and stare at what Lochlann had titled 'What will be...'. I took a glass of wine from a tray, and made my way to the little stage where Hélène and her friends were playing. I nodded and smiled stupidly at those whose eyes met mine, and they looked back blankly at the lone, shabby, out-of-place figure whom they didn't recognise, but about whom there was something familiar...

The gathering point was still quiet, the majority of the guests still making their way through the chambers. Hélène was perched on a high chair close to the lectern, on the platform below the gantry. Her eyes were closed as she swayed gently to the bewitching rhythm of *Carrickfergus*. Beside her, Eimear was equally lost in the moment, while Nuala's flute punctuated the violins' languid tones. They were all dressed much as Hélène had been in our painting, demure and shyly fading into the background.

Niamh broke the spell their music cast on me, gently touching my arm and kissing me on both cheeks. She looked a little ill-at-ease, perhaps feeling, too, like one who didn't really belong in this company. I was glad to have found an ally, or grateful that an ally had found me.

"She is beautiful, isn't she?" Niamh said, nodding towards Hélène and taking a sip from her glass of champagne.

I nodded.

"She's a very beautiful girl."

"You've done her proud. In the painting, I mean," she said. "God, Aengus, you're some dark horse. I had no idea you had that in you. You must be really delighted with it?"

I smiled and nodded again.

"To be honest, Niamh, I didn't know myself. But yes, I am delighted with it. And I'm very grateful to Lochlann for giving me the chance."

"So who is she anyway?" Niamh asked, carelessly.

I smiled.

"That, Niamh," I said, for the last time, "is a very long story." I looked at her, and she was again the Niamh that I had

365

known for so long, as though we were still seventeen and none of the rest had happened. "But I'll tell you soon."

I could see her mind working, trying to solve the cryptic riddle, then giving up.

"You'll find it hard to go back to an office job after this?" she said, and I was grateful that she didn't persist.

The prospect of going back to my old life left me achingly cold. I shook my head.

"I don't know that I can, Niamh," I said. "I don't think I can."

"I can see you now," she grinned, "flogging your paintings on Merrion Square on a Sunday morning!"

"Or doing caricatures on Grafton Street maybe?" I smiled. "There's good money in caricatures, you know!"

"Your father would be very proud!" She sipped the champagne again and I sipped my wine.

"So what are you going to do?" she asked. "Any ideas?"

I exhaled through pursed lips and shook my head again.

"None whatsoever. And do you know what? It's not a bad feeling."

"Will you stay?"

"I have nowhere else to go. And this place has..." – I searched for the words – "has, I don't know, it's looked after me, it's cossetted me somehow. Lochlann and Oran and the Master and Pauline – and you, Niamh – it's like you've all given me a clip round the ear and told me to get a grip on things. Everybody's got stuff to deal with, but they're not sitting in a London pub having a good mope. I didn't know I was leaving it behind, and now I don't want to go back to it."

She looked down at her glass. "And Hélène? You'll stay for her too?"

I looked over at Hélène.

"In a way yes. But not in the way you're thinking."

The music had stopped, and I looked over to where they sat. The gathering area had filled slowly and was now full of

366

guests discussing and considering and no doubt criticising what they had seen. The lull in the music caught their attention, and the din of conversation faded as they looked to the stage. Hélène had put down her violin, and was standing at her microphone. To the strains of Eimear's single violin, and with her eyes closed, her angel's voice rose softly on the lilting words of *Raglan Road*.

The remaining voices in the room went quiet as, to a person, they stared at the young woman on stage. The power of a female vocal taking on such a masculine song disabled the crowd and there was no other sound. The hopeless regret of the ballad was made achingly poignant by the vulnerability in her voice. In the second verse, Nuala's flute joined suddenly and the melancholy was complete.

The crowd was rapt and for a brief moment after the final words and notes had faded away, there was silence. Then a cheer and loud applause of unfettered appreciation for the pure beauty they had been given. Eimear and Nuala stood and they, all three, took a bow and, smiling nervously at each other, they left the platform.

Lochlann greeted Hélène with a gentle embrace as they left the stage, nodding and smiling in his own uniquely paternal way. It was, for Lochlann, a display of unadulterated emotion. Then he took to the platform himself and stood behind the lectern. The crowd applauded again then hushed.

"I chose, unwisely as it turns out, to speak directly after the musical finale. I fear I cannot hope to follow that."

The guests laughed kindly and applauded again, then allowed him to continue. He thanked them for coming and hoped they would leave fulfilled. Thanked those who had made it all possible, and hoped he had been worthy. Paid the necessary dues to his staff and hoped he had made clear his gratitude. The requisite, unavoidable banalities of the public occasion.

Then he paused, looked down at the assembled dignitaries, and took a deep breath.

"There have been dark moments when I doubted that I would present my work in a forum like this again. Dark moments when I feared that I had lost my eye and, with it, my way. You had your doubts also, I know that, and I understand your scruple. But I see now what has been hidden from me for so long – I see now that my capacity for recognising and capturing and expressing beauty is in the hands of the people and the place around me. It is born of agreeing to belong. Thank you."

The applause began softly, and slowly grew, and by the time his guests had deciphered his message and its humility, it had risen to its peak. The triumph the Master had predicted was complete.

Hélène, who had been standing by the side of the stage, joined in the applause and beamed her delight. As the guests returned to their conversations and their drinks, she and the two girls gathered up their instruments and various belongings and climbed down from the stage again, walking over to where Hélène had seen me.

I hugged her, and then held her by the shoulders at arms length, shaking my head and smiling.

"Jesus, Hélène, I don't know what to say. I love that song, but I've never heard it like that before. That was just beautiful..." I searched for the words that would do her performance justice and express the depth of the emotion it had conjured. But I couldn't find them, so I just embraced her again. "You've made a real impact tonight, Hélène. Well done."

I suddenly remembered Niamh, who was standing awkwardly to my side. I introduced Hélène and her colleagues and she congratulated them warmly. She took Hélène's hands in her own, and smiled with genuine affection for this girl she didn't know. She spoke to her as though she was the only person in the room, as though we weren't there.

"I really don't know how you can manage to get out a single note in front of a big crowd like that, never mind sing and play so beautifully. You made this evening even better than it might have been, you really did, Hélène. You should be delighted with what you've done tonight, it was very special."

Hélène flushed slightly, and squeezed Niamh's hands.

"Thank you so much," she said. She beamed again, and put her arms around the other two. "We did well!" she said to them, and they all laughed with relief and delight and giddy excitement.

"Let me get you girls some champagne," I said, waving to one of the waiting staff.

"No, Aengus, thank you," Hélène said. "We have a rehearsal early tomorrow, I really have to go. But I will come tomorrow and we can have a coffee or something?"

"OK, sure. I'll see you then."

I kissed each of them goodbye, and they marched out like proud children through the admiring crowd.

Oran, whom I hadn't seen all evening, appeared beside me, uneasy in a collar and tie. I hijacked a glass of champagne from a passing tray and handed it to him.

"If anyone deserves this," I said. "Cheers."

He smirked and took a mouthful as though drinking beer, then grimaced.

"Never could get the hang of this stuff," he spluttered, "no stout, I notice?"

"Later, man," I assured him. "We'll have a few later."

Niamh threw her arms around Oran and hugged him.

"Well done, Oran, this is fantastic. Fantastic. You've done him proud."

Oran nodded wearily.

"I thought we'd never get here," he admitted. "But thank Christ that's over." He raised his glass to me. "And thank you. Who'd have thought you'd turn out to be useful?!"

I grinned and toasted him back. "Stop it, or I might cry."

Niamh raised her eyes and punched my arm playfully.

"Honest to God, do you two ever say a civil word to each other?" she laughed, shaking her head. "You're still the same two bold children you were when we were in the school. Worse, probably."

"Oh, you mark my words, Niamh, it's definitely worse they're getting, not better," said the Master, coming over to join us and still grinning with the heady glee of Lochlann's success. "It's only a pity they're too big now for me to give them a *scelp*!"

"Too true, Críostóir," Niamh laughed, "too true."

"Actually, I was hoping to catch you two boys," the Master said, becoming suddenly more serious.

"This sounds serious – I'll leave you men alone," Niamh joked, ever tactful. "I should make sure Daddy hasn't had too much champagne!"

Niamh's father was a professor of Art at University College, Dublin and it was on his arm that she had come to the evening's event.

When she had left, the Master turned to Oran.

"Now, Oran," he said, all traces of flippant camaraderie suddenly gone and his tone serious and stern, "how did you get on with the solicitor?"

"It was a bit of a shock to the system to be honest," he said with a sigh and a weary shake of the head. "He gave it to me straight. I'm looking at a few months if the judge is the hard-arse he's supposed to be. He made it very clear. But he thinks he can help me."

He shrugged.

"So we wait and see, I suppose."

The Master nodded and was silent for a moment, his mind processing Oran's words beneath a furrowed brow.

"Hmmm," was all he said. "Did he suggest you do anything?"

"Not really," Oran shrugged, looking to me lest he was missing any important detail.

"No," I agreed. "He said that character references will count for a lot with the judge, from you, from Lochlann, from Oran's old boss at La Bella Cucina."

My frustration was clear, I think, in my face.

"The guards don't really want to pursue it," I said, raising my hands in despair, "old man McGrath doesn't want to pursue it – but Joyce has them all over a barrel. And then we get Tobin on the case. Pearse was clear that we're up against it, but he'll do what he can. I'm sure he'll be able to help."

The Master nodded.

"If he thinks there's anything I can do or Lochlann can do," he said, "anything at all, just make sure you let us know. And if he needs a good word put in with anybody else who might be able to help. Same thing."

"I will, Master," said Oran, humbly. "Thanks."

The buzzing noise that had been barely audible had grown louder and though, still faint, registered in Oran's still on-duty mind.

"That's the PA – I'll just go turn it off."

He left us and headed for the gantry.

The Master looked after him.

"He's putting a brave face on it," he said, "but it's not good, is it?"

I shook my head and my frown betrayed my fear.

"It's not, Master," I said, quietly. "If it was anyone other than this Tobin character, I'd say he'd maybe get away with a severe rap across the knuckles. But it seems like this one is always out to make a point. And this is cannon fodder for him."

The Master groaned silently and took a long and recuperative draft of red wine.

CHAPTER 33

The emptiness of loss is what takes you most by surprise, I think. Anyone we lose occupied a greater or lesser place in our lives, but a place nonetheless, and that place is suddenly and permanently empty.

Do you remember the old Indian man who had the grocery shop at the corner of our road? A kind, warm man but quick with a sharp rebuke and with a mournful narrative on social decline always at hand for a customer with time to listen. I would drop in every morning on the way to the Tube to buy the newspaper, and often on the way home to collect whatever we were short for the evening. If I was coming from the pub and he detected the waft of beer, he would frown and warn me about the perils of casual drinking. If I was late home from work, he would look at his watch and wag a finger of warning that "life will simply pass you by", his head bobbing sternly from side to side. He would ask about you and when we would have children, unable quite to understand that we would not, then putting it down to some medical flaw in our reproductive systems and squeezing my arm in knowing sympathy.

And then he wasn't there. Suddenly, abruptly, he was gone. It was three or four days before I asked the young man behind the counter, worried that perhaps he had a bad cold or flu or worse. His uncle, he told me simply, was dead. A heart attack.

I called in for my paper for the next few mornings as I always had, but then I stopped. And I never called in again on my way home from work, preferring instead to go to the cold convenience store beside the station. The old man meant nothing to me, I never even knew his name. But the space he filled was empty, and it disturbed the equilibrium of my world.

And I can still see in my mind's eye the image of my grandmother standing alone in the crowd by her husband's graveside at his burial. Tiny and frail and white, she stood wrapped in black against the chill graveyard wind. It was just after the priest had finished the service and the mourners had crossed themselves and the low murmur of conversation slowly and respectfully swelled and mothers finally dared to let their toddlers run loose and watched them carefully as they bent to pick up and carefully examine a shiny white pebble or a petal or a leaf.

I was standing nearest her, talking to some cousins or aunts, and I heard her softly start to sing, low and shrill and cracking. Nobody else heard, I'm sure. Just me. And the empty sadness of it almost overwhelmed me. It was his favourite, his party piece. It had been with her and filled their home for her whole adult life. And she would never, ever hear it again. The chair by the fire, his place at Mass, the very air around where he used to be, would be forever empty, a vacuum that would haunt her, always.

She finished, her old voice quivering with the pain of it, and she nodded a conspirator's nod to the grave. And I know she nodded to say that she would see him soon. Because there was nothing left here. Not a grief-stricken wail of wretched anguish, but the nodded acknowledgement of a simple truth.

I can never fill the empty place you left, the vast cavern will forever be a vacuum, sucking the very life out of me should I get too close. But maybe I can learn to survive. I can never, perhaps, go back to the corner shop, but I can take you with me to a new place, maybe? I can't go back there, love. You know that it only existed because you were there, was only a home when you were home. I don't belong there, and I can't be there without you.

So I might try somewhere else. I'm not leaving you, I promise. I will always take you with me because you are such a part of me, you complete me. But maybe we need to start again somewhere new. Somewhere old.

CHAPTER 34

The crowd had slowly dwindled and only the last coterie of six or seven guests was still engaged in recounting flowery stories or making their point in wine-fuelled animation. Lochlann was in their midst, sharing their good humour with appreciative laughter and faux-admonishment, while ushering them gently and imperceptibly to the door and out. Having bid them all goodnight, he made his way over to us with raised eyebrows and a guilty smile.

The Master reached out to clasp Lochlann's hand, to congratulate his friend and to share his own delight at the evening's success, the peppering excitement of earlier replaced by a deep and calm satisfaction. Reinforced, perhaps, by a strong sense of relief.

"You must be a happy man, Lochlann," he said, shaking his head at the almost impossibly successful realisation of his plans.

"I am, Críostóir," Lochlann replied, clearly weary and obviously content. "I am. It was a splendid evening, everything I had hoped for and indeed more." He paused and looked hard at the Master. "And thank you for your support, Críostóir. Not just this evening, but these past weeks, during which I was, no doubt, insufferable. Thank you."

The Master accepted his thanks with a gracious nod and a smile, and no words of protest. He had contributed greatly to the exhibition's genesis and its evolution and was proud to have done so.

"Well, I for one am positively shattered," he said. "So I'll be off to my *leaba* and I'll see you boys tomorrow." He turned for the door, and looked back just as he reached it.

"You two have a bit of talking to do, I suppose," he said, deliberately so that we could not misconstrue his meaning, "and tonight would be an excellent night to start. Goodnight now to you both." He saluted with no flourish and was gone.

We stood awkwardly looking after him, as though half-expecting – and half-hoping – that he would come back. But he didn't. And so we shuffled and looked around for a distraction to delay the inevitable.

I saw an open bottle of wine on a table, so I went over to pour two glasses and took one back to Lochlann.

"Thank you," he said, and raised the glass slightly. "Your good health."

I raised mine and we took a sip in silence.

"You know," he said eventually, choosing his words with obvious care, "I have had a number of comments this evening about your work, all of them very positive, very complimentary. It is a very fine piece, and not only in my opinion." He looked at the floor then back at me, and then sighed and seemed to lose an inch in height as his stance softened. He shook his head, then looked almost through me, stared into my eyes.

"I didn't know how to tell you that," he said. "I've been trying to think all evening how to tell you, but I couldn't." He shrugged as though perplexed by some great mystery. "Perhaps Críostóir is right."

And so the box was open.

I looked down and then back at him and then out through the window and into the murky after-dusk.

"How did we get here?" he asked me.

"We've always been here," I said, simply. There was nothing else to say.

After a moment, he nodded.

"I suppose we have," he said, to himself more than to me. "I suppose we have."

I poured another glass of wine, I felt that I was going to need it.

"Why do you suppose that is?" he asked, suddenly

"I suppose," I started uncertainly, "I suppose we have a history. We got off to a bad start, and it just didn't get any better."

And then, without warning, I couldn't hold back the feelings that a whole life had failed to express.

"You see, I have always felt that you blame me for her death – that you would have preferred to have lost a baby than to have lost your wife. The two of you could somehow have got through that, but I left you with nobody."

I drew a deep breath, there was no point in stopping now.

"And then I let you down over Aoife. That I was stupid enough to get myself in that position for a start, but more that I gave her up. It was in such sharp contrast to the sacrifice that Claire made for me."

He said nothing, didn't move, just stared at me.

"And then, I suppose, I took the filthy penny – I used whatever talent I had been given and whatever I had learned in university and took it across the water to work in the corporate world. You see me, I have always thought, as unreliable, weak even. I don't think it's fair, of course. But it's what I think."

I shrugged at the patent clarity of it.

"You can't help blaming me for Claire, I can see that. You're not wrong about Aoife, but maybe you don't understand the full story – not that it absolves me. And if I had ever believed I had the ability to dedicate my time to my art and to earn a living from it, then maybe I would have chosen that route. I have never let you down carelessly or with any pleasure. If I have failed you, then it was because I couldn't see a different way."

I sighed a deep sigh of… what? Of relief? Of resignation? Of defeat?

"So I understand how you feel," I said. "I'm past being angry and tired of being at loggerheads. I wish things could be different, but I can't change what's done."

It had started to rain outside and the gathering, buffeting breeze threw the drops against the windows of the Gallery like children throwing handfuls of pebbles. He was silent and motionless, only the glint of wetness in his eye gave the slightest clue that he had heard and had understood and had been moved. But moved by what? By disappointment or by remorse or by the cruel truth that I was never going to be what he had wanted me to be, what he and Claire had dreamed I would be? I cursed the wine or the occasion or the adrenaline that had freed my tongue. I cursed the Master. I cursed myself.

"You don't, Aengus," he said. "You don't understand how I feel."

He spoke so quietly that I could hardly make out the words.

"I am, and have always been, proud of the boy you were and of the man you have become. But you're right, I have not always been proud of the things you have done. Those are decisions you have had to make and with which you have had to live. I hope – I believe – that you made them for the right reasons, even if, privately, I wished you had chosen a different way. I had no right to presume nor did I expect that you would follow my path, but I hoped always that you would make your choices with the purest motives at heart. I might not have seen the good in everything you have done, but I can say that I have never seen the deliberately malign."

The wrong deeds but at least for the right reasons. The lesser treason, the faintest praise. And yet, when I looked back later on his words – and I did dissect them over and over and over again – I took comfort from the fact that at least he liked the melody even if he didn't agree with the words. It was my actions that had disappointed him, not the person I was. The reverse would have been far more difficult to remedy.

"But when I was a boy, before I had the chance or cause to make my own decisions, even as a child I could see that we were not like the other fathers and sons, that you kept a distance between us. I wanted you to be proud of me. I tried to be what I thought a father wanted a son to be, I wanted everyone to see that I was your son and that you loved me – but I don't think that's ever what they saw. It's not what I saw."

He sighed a deep sigh and rubbed his eyes, his head lowered. Then he looked up and at me again.

"When Claire died, Aengus, I could simply see no way to raise you as my son. I don't claim to understand the psychology of it and in those days Dublin was not awash with support groups and counsellors – not, I suppose, that I would have engaged them anyway. And so I undertook to provide for you, and to fend for you, and to protect you, and to give you every opportunity to grow and thrive. But I could not see you as my *son* because that was something I wanted so badly to share with Claire, and she was no longer here. I didn't blame you, but I could not be your father, only your guardian."

Lochlann was not the kind of man to make an apology just to fill the space, just to make the line scan and the metre complete. In his mind, he had done the right thing and all that he could and no expression of regret or remorse was necessary.

He raised his eyebrows, and let out a long breath that framed a mystery.

"But then you came back, quite out of nowhere, and it is as if the landscape has been altered. I cannot continue the painting as it was. I have to invent a new context, a new perspective. You have grown, Aengus, these past weeks, and you have made me proud. Your strength, your compassion, your work, have made me proud. I can never be a father to you and it would be disingenuous of me to try. But you have

379

changed the landscape. You have set out to find Aoife. You have shown kindness to Hélène. You have confronted a bitter past to help Oran. I see you with your friends – with Niamh and with Críostóir – and there is a kind, benign calmness in you that I have not seen before."

He paused, taking a sip of wine to camouflage the silence and the search for the right words. Then he nodded, slowly.

"You are a good man, Aengus, and the way you have behaved stands testament to that. I would be proud to call you my friend. I can offer no more. I truly hope that it is enough."

I nodded.

"As long as I don't have to call you Dad!" The words came out in a croaked whisper with a weak smile.

He smiled back, relieved perhaps that the tension was broken, but nothing else.

"I don't think that would work for either of us."

He looked at his watch.

"It's late and it's been a long day." He raised his eyebrows. "And quite some day, I think it's fair to say. I'll go to bed, I think."

"Yes, sure. You must be exhausted."

He nodded, and picked up his jacket from the back of a chair. He brushed some dust from the collar, paused a moment and then turned back to me.

"This has been festering inside both of us for far too long. I am very, very glad that we have had a chance to at least begin to put it right, Aengus. Very glad indeed."

"Me too."

And one more deal was closed.

When he had gone, I sat down heavily into a chair, let out a long, deep breath and closed my eyes. What a day. What an extraordinary day. It would, I supposed, take me some time to fully digest Lochlann's explanations of the past and to craft my own view of our future. But my immediate reaction was that it provided a flicker of light in that future and that the past was best left in the past. I had never, I now realised, had a father. I didn't really *need* one. And it was now too late and too futile to try creating some saccharine stage show that neither of us wanted and neither of us could pull off.

Oran came in through the Gallery door.

"Looked like you were having a heart-to-heart with the oul' fella," he said. "Thought I better leave you to it. How're you doin'?"

I stood up.

"I need a pint," I said, and we made for McGrath's.

"So what was that all about," Oran asked when I came back from the bar and set two pints on the table.

"The Master made us talk," I said, and shook my head. "You'd honestly think we were both nine years old and we'd had a fight in the playground."

"So you've kissed and made up?" he asked, frozen in wide-eyed mid-movement as he lifted his pint. "Jesus, I never thought I'd live to see that." He put his glass back on the table, the pint's creamy head still intact "That's fuckin' great, so it is."

"Well, there was no kissing. But I think we made up. You know, I'm not exactly sure what we did, to be honest. But it's not worse than it was, so there's a good chance it'll be better. After all this time, we can't expect too much more, I suppose."

"Well. I'm glad. It's about time someone cracked your two heads together, and no better man than Críostóir."

He reached again for his pint and drank deep.

"So does this mean you're staying on?"

"I don't know. I was talking to Niamh about this earlier. I have nowhere to go, I'm not in a hurry, and I don't think I'm going back."

"Really? To London, you mean?"

I nodded.

"I just can't see myself there anymore, you know? I don't belong. It's like Lochlann said when he spoke on stage earlier – he only made it back because of the people and the place. Because he belongs here. I don't know where I belong, but it's sure as hell not there. I wouldn't have done the things I've done these last few weeks if I was still in London. Partly because I wouldn't have been able. Partly because I wouldn't have cared enough to try. All that's there now is a big hole where Caitríona used to be. And I can't do anything worthwhile as long as I'm afraid of falling in."

"It's funny how your picture of the world changes, isn't it," he said. "When we got out of school, we'd have done anything to get the hell out of here. To try new things. To be in new places. Everything here just seemed like more of the same, I never thought I'd be in one place forever. Suddenly twenty years have shot by and I'm still here and you're back. And we're both looking at it and thinking, sure, maybe it's not too bad, it's nice to belong.

"But look at the trouble I've been in, Aengus, the trouble I'm still in. Just remember – when you fall into that very Irish trap of romanticising home and fond reminiscence about rebel song singalongs in the pub and Six Nations weekends and lazy Saturday afternoons on Grafton Street and seven creamy feckin' pints comin' out on a tray – just remember that this is the place that beat me up, and then kicked me again when I was down."

He pointed a warning finger at me.

"You might not like the way things happen in London, but don't fool yourself that they can't happen here."

"I know, Oran, I know. I'm not saying that it's Neverland. But how much worse would it be for you if you'd been somewhere else, not in Dublin? With no Master and no Lochlann, and no Guards that look out for you because you played football with them and no publican that wouldn't see you barred because you've been going there for years?"

He said nothing for a moment, then nodded.

"It'd be a cold fuckin' place, Aengus," he agreed, reluctantly. "I'm just saying that Dublin doesn't get very warm either."

"You two boys are looking very serious tonight!" Ella chirped, wiping our table and dropping fresh beer-mats. "Did someone tell you a joke you didn't understand? Go on, tell me and I'll explain it to you!"

Oran looked at me and said earnestly:

"Jaysus, Aengus, these feckin' immigrants are getting' fierce cheeky, aren't they? Time we sent them all home, if you ask me."

Ella grinned.

"No chance. There's no getting rid of me!"

"So you're here for the long haul?" I asked her.

"Hell, yeah," she said, with a broad smile. "My mates are here, my boyfriend is here, my job – why would I leave?"

Oran grinned at me.

"What's so funny?" Ella asked.

"Oh, nothing," I said. "Just… well, we were just talking about why it's good to belong, good to be at home."

"I suppose it is good to belong," she agreed, leaning on the table and looking to the ceiling for an answer to the riddle. "But you don't need to be at home to belong, you just have to be where you want to be."

Her youthful wisdom was unencumbered by the baggage of time and experience, and took her straight to the point without wondering or speculating.

"What about that bar in Queenstown?" I asked.

Her face lit up with a spontaneous smile and she nodded.

"Definitely some day, it's a good dream to have, I guess. But there's a lot to happen and a lot of places to see before then. So for now, I'll stick with Dublin." She looked at us and grinned. " Even if the men are a bit miserable!"

"Again," Oran said to me, "cheeky."

"Admit it, that's how you like us! Now, another pint?"

"If that's what it takes to make you go away," Oran smirked.

She grinned back and made her way to the bar.

"Any word from Pearse?" I asked Oran.

"Yeah, actually. He spoke to Paolo at the Bella Cucina. Apparently the old man will be happy to give me a character reference. According to Pearse, he was able to write it for him and he'll just sign it."

"That's good news," I said. "Pearse seems to think that references will count for a lot with Tobin."

"He does."

"How are you feeling, about the whole thing? Only a couple of days away now."

"I know. Seems to have come around fast." He drew a deep breath. "I don't know, Aengus. Pearse seems to know what he's doing, better than the other lad, for sure. But he's not very optimistic. I'm trying not to think about it, to be honest. I can't do anything more now, just let it happen. But thanks for bringing it up!" He smiled and raised his glass to me.

I smiled an apologetic smile.

"Sorry, Oran. I don't mean to keep banging on about it. I just don't know how you can be so calm . How you can just sit here and have a pint."

"I might not be having too many more for a while, better get them in now while I can!"

I shook my head, at the strength of his resolve I suppose, but perhaps also at the naïveté of his dispassion. I'm not sure.

We left after only a couple more. Two days before a court appearance was not the time for Oran to be seen revelling in the very pub where the offence took place. I spent the following day pottering around the Gallery, tidying away what needed no tidying in preparation for the evening's public opening, straightening what was already straight. I had missed a call from Hélène, and she had left a message to say that she was feeling tired after a hectic few days and, not to worry, but she was going to spend the afternoon chilling out by the fire with a pot of coffee and a book. Oran was busy attending to some small crisis and so I was, for perhaps the first time since I arrived in Howth, at a loose end. So I went to my room, pulled on my running shoes and made for the Head.

Away from people for the first time in what seemed like days, and alone on the trails in the breezy gathering gloom of the early evening, I pieced together the events of the days gone before and tried to put some context around what had been a passage of, it was now clear, great significance.

Equipping Oran for his imminent day of judgment, the exhibition's triumphant debut, the completion of Hélène's image – all important moments, landmarks almost. And somehow in their midst, I had managed to lose sight of what had been the most significant thing of all, the very reason for my being here. I was ashamed to admit that I had, just for a brief moment in time, forgotten about finding Aoife. Not forgotten – that is too absolute. But the search had slipped temporarily from its position of absolute prominence.

Now that all of those distractions were behind me, and with my emotions perhaps sharpened by my disquiet for Oran, my thoughts turned guiltily back to her, to where she was, and to when I might finally find her. The distractions had helped to pass the time until she came here. Its passage served only to question whether she ever would. The decision where to go and what to do could only really be made once I knew where the search for her would lead. I was no closer to the answer, but I had to find a way to make a choice.

CHAPTER 35

O ran and I met Pearse in Dublin, in a café by the river not far from the courthouse. The place was filled with an incongruous assortment of bespectacled, grey-haired and balding legal professionals in smart suits and gleaming brogues, and shaven-headed youths in cheap, ill-fitting suits and sports shoes. The outwardly respectable and those without respect. There were some parents there too, alternately berating the solicitor or the barrister and then the son who had brought shame on the family by getting into trouble. Or by getting caught. From time to time, a raised voice punctuated the sombre pessimism of the place. After a while you stopped looking up. Outside, the early morning was clear and crisp and cold, and Dubliners hurried about their business wrapped in coats and scarves and hats plucked from Summer hibernation. In contrast to their haste the murky river flowed quietly through the city, ambling obliviously past the cars that sat in daily gridlock along its quays, down to the port and out to sea.

Pearse arrived just as I ordered at the counter, right on time and looking unruffled and calm – almost bored. He must have briefed and instructed and calmed a defendant in this very place or in places just like it a thousand times, I thought. He nodded muted greetings to some of the others in his gang, each of them wearing the same look of diligent yet detached dispassion, and for a brief moment, I was deeply jealous of him. Of his confidence in this place. Of the fact that, whatever happened today, he would not lose. Not really. He must get jaded by the persistence of those who will hurt and steal, tired of their nonchalant indifference and disheartened by the impotence of the legal system to change them. But at least, and day's end, he can leave it behind.

He briefed Oran one more time, summarising his instructions from their previous meetings and making quite sure that he understood and would do as he was told. It was, I suppose, a lesson he had learned from previous encounters, but he need not have worried. We walked the short distance to the court building and Oran said not a word. Unlike some of Pearse's charges who, I'm sure, had been there, seen and done that many times before, this was a shocking new other-world for Oran that he didn't understand and had never expected to see. Like me, he had only ever considered the court system from the other side, taking for granted that it was there to serve and protect people just like us. The stark, cold reality of it – the ageing grubbiness of the waiting rooms, the hard carelessness of his fellow accused, the very meanness of it all – robbed him of his customary truculence. His antipathy to direction had been left behind, its place taken by an almost frightened meekness. For perhaps the first time in my memory, Oran needed and wanted to be told exactly what to do.

We sat in the ante-room for what seemed like hours, but there was a comfort in it that I didn't want to end, the frightened comfort of a hiding place. When we were called, we stood up and Pearse shook Oran by the hand. Oran turned to me and we nodded to one another and I hugged him roughly without a word. Pearse and Oran went into the courtroom. I took a moment to say a silent prayer to whomever might be listening, then joined Lochlann and the Master, who had taken their seats in the public gallery.

The courtroom was a desolate, sterile space, bereft of the dramatic atmosphere and the enthralled crowds conjured by so many television report sketches. The cracks in the tiled floor were filled with a packed grime, the once-white walls were stained a dirty brown. The whole place had the air of the tired old hospitals that I remembered from a time long past. I felt like I was in the maternity hospital again, the same sense of lost foreboding, the same sense that we didn't belong here, among these people.

The judge's corpulent figure and reddened face was at odds his reputation. I had built an image of a hawkish, mean-faced man with piercing eyes and a nasal, guttural voice, a straggled-haired Dickensian villain. Instead, he reminded me more of a supermarket Santa in December than a ruthless defender of public order.

That the appearance belied the man, however, was immediately apparent when he called the court impatiently to order and fixed Oran with a contemptuous stare. The guilty plea and the relatively minor nature of the offence meant that there was no jury, and the court's only concern was sentencing. It appeared from Tobin's demeanour that he wanted to be shot of the case and adjourn for lunch with the minimum fuss and delay.

The prosecutor was an enthusiastic young man, perhaps not long enough in the job to be disillusioned by its repetitive monotony. He recounted the series of events that would end here, apparently blind to the judge's impatient grimaces, and asked the court to act decisively to safeguard the rights of innocent people going about their daily lives... and so on, and so on, and so on. It was only when he gestured to Joyce, sitting near the front of the court, that I recognised Oran's tormentor. Far from the smug, self-satisfied countenance I had expected him to wear, he too seemed overcome by the place and the occasion, and sat quietly, almost squirming at the centre of attention.

Then Pearse was called. In contrast to his energetic young adversary, he appealed wearily to the judge with a jaded assessment of the sad state of a national conscience that could beat down a diligent, honest young man while gorging on the fruits of its new-found affluence. His performance was masterful. Never antagonising Tobin by defending Oran's actions, he villified the society that had driven him to it and, without ever mentioning his name, characterised Joyce as personification of that society's worst excesses.

He referred to Oran's spotless record and to the written references from Lochlann, the Master and the old Italian restaurateur as clear evidence of his client's integrity, of the affection in which he was held in his community and of the wholly uncharacteristic nature of his aberration. By the time he sat down again, Joyce's squirming had reached feverish proportions and he looked more like the man accused.

Tobin was silent. He donned his reading glasses and looked again through the sheaf of paper on his desk. Then he removed the glasses, sat back in his chair and carelessly tapped a tooth with the one arm of his spectacles. The tapping echoed around the room.

I stole a sideward glance at Oran, somehow afraid that to look at him might remind the judge that he was there, might get him in trouble. He sat absolutely straight and still, his face impassive. If Pearse's performance had given him some hope, as it had me, he showed none of it.

Tobin laid his glasses on the desk. When he spoke, he spoke to Oran directly and his voice was even and matter-of-fact.

"You know, you don't strike me as typical of the people I see here day after day. And I hope you never do. You made a mistake. And by all accounts, it was out of character and out of kilter with your behaviour in the past."

He picked up his glasses, and pointed them at Oran.

"But your mistake had a profound and terrifying impact on an innocent man and on his family. He has a right to go about his lawful business without fear of an attack like the one you visited on him. There is, quite frankly, too much of this kind of behaviour in Dublin, there is no excuse for it, and it cannot go unpunished. Two months custodial sentence."

Abruptly, he brought down his gavel with a crack that made me start.

"Court adjourned until 2pm this afternoon."

And so it was over.

I couldn't take it in. I couldn't fathom how something we had feared and dreaded and talked about and pondered for so long could be over so quickly. The judge could surely not understand the potentially devastating effect of his decision, and yet he had made that decision in no more than twenty minutes. He had made his decision in time for lunch. As I watched Oran being led away, without even a look back, I felt stunned and horrified and sick. I looked at Lochlann and the Master, speechless, and they too were lost for words.

The court emptied and we stood up from our seats and made our way blindly to the door. Pearse was standing outside, waiting for me.

He put his hand on my shoulder.

"Listen, Aengus," he said, softly, "I know this feels terrible, but if he behaves himself he'll be out in a month. Four weeks and then he'll be out and able to get on with his life without this hanging over him. I'm sorry we couldn't keep him out, but I hope you can understand that this is about the best we could have expected."

I nodded. Of course he was right, of course he was. But I couldn't even begin to explain that this was my friend, this was the man who had helped me to reassess my whole world in a few short weeks. I couldn't begin to explain how much better he deserved and how damning an indictment this was of the system of which he was a part. Couldn't explain that I was afraid of how he might react to jail and to the people he would find there. I couldn't and it would have been unfair to Pearse. And so I didn't.

"I know," I said, "and thanks, Pearse. I know you've done what you could, and we all really appreciate it. You know that."

He nodded.

"I do. And listen, let's get together soon, I mean it. It'd be good to talk in better circumstances."

I shook his hand, and he turned and left.

"I suppose we might as well get back home," the Master said, wearing the face of the bereaved.

I had always imagined that the Master would be the great stalwart in the face of crisis or trouble, that he would be quick to find the positives, and that his energy and resourcefulness would reveal an answer when all seemed lost. He would surely know someone, have an old friend with influence, call in the reinforcements with a boyish wink. But as we left the courthouse, I saw the dazed, small old man that he was. As ever, Lochlann's demeanour betrayed little of what he felt beneath the impassive surface. But his silence and the steely anger in his stare told the real story.

We hailed a cab outside the court and travelled back to Howth in silence. As we climbed out of the cab at the house, I turned to Lochlann.

"I'll check with O'Leary that everything is ok for the exhibition this evening."

"I don't think we'll open this evening," he said, wearily.

I shook my head.

"I think you're wrong," I said, flatly. "He's not dead. He put a lot of work into this show, a hell of a lot. We can't just close it up after a few days. You know what he'd say to that."

He just nodded, and I went to the Gallery to talk to the manager.

After a few nights, the show effectively ran itself, and the events crew had everything in hand. I said I would call back later to make sure everything was ok, and then went for a run to try to clear my head. Despite the afternoon sun, and the blooming heather and Goldsmith's furze "unprofitably gay", the Head seemed grey and flat, a dull monochrome version of itself. It wasn't that I would miss him or even that he would have a tough few weeks. Such trivialities were no more than an indulgence. What worried me was the Oran that would emerge, his anger at losing his livelihood exacerbated by a new anger at the harshness of his punishment. The thoughtful, kind, faithful persona which hid just below the rough hewn exterior might be driven deeper, might even disappear for a while. The scum with whom he would spend a month, or even two, might show him a path paved with cynicism and self-preservation. Oran was better than that, but bitter disillusionment can tarnish the brightest gold.

All at once and for no apparent reason, I realised that I had no grasp of the basic logistics of it all, and suddenly I had a thousand unanswered questions. I cursed myself for not asking Pearse where he would be taken, how would he get his things, would he need money, when could we visit? I spun around and headed back to the house. I would call Pearse before his day was over and his mobile phone shut down. Nature at last conceded that she couldn't lift my mood, and dark clouds drifted in from the sea and cloaked the sun. A chill air enveloped the Head and I shivered in spite of my thumping heart. Why is it that, in times of pain, we take a querulous satisfaction from gathering gloom, as though nobody else should be content as long as we are not?

CHAPTER 36

I got back to the house and ran upstairs. I showered quickly, and then from the bathroom I heard the persistent metallic ringtone of my mobile phone. I ran back to my room and grabbed it lest the caller give up or be diverted to the messaging service.

"Hello," I wheezed.

"Oh, hello," said a woman's voice. "Listen, I'm sorry to bother you. My name is Nurse O'Connell, at the hospital in Beaumont. I'm really sorry to do this, but we had a patient admitted yesterday and we're trying to sort out her personal details. We found this phone in her bag, and your number was the last number dialled. Again, look, I know this is hard – but do you recognise the number?"

I took the phone away from my ear to read the display. There are so many clichés that we use to express the effect of desperate shock, but I think my heart did, physically, miss one beat and I was, physically, paralysed for a brief moment. Clichés are only clichés because of our consistent experiences, because they are consistently true. The number was Hélène's.

"Hello? Are you still there?" I could hear the nurse's voice in the distance.

I brought the phone back to my ear.

"Yes," I said, "yes, I'm here."

"And do you know this number?" Her voice betrayed a faint but restrained impatience.

"Yes. Her name is Hélène. Is she ok? What's the matter with her?"

There was a pause at the other end of the line, and then the voice returned.

"And do you have a surname?"

I didn't. How could I have spent so much time with her, been so close to her, every day, and not even know her name? But it had never arisen, I had never needed it.

"Actually, no," I said. "Listen, what's wrong with her?"

"Hélène? You're sure?"

"Yes, I'm sure." Now it was me getting impatient.

"Can you describe her for me?"

I described Hélène in artist's detail, and asked again why she was there, why she could not have given them these details herself.

"Look, you're obviously not a family member," she said, her voice softening. "So I'm sorry, but I can't give out any information. I'm sorry. Listen, thanks for your help. I have a few more numbers on here, I'm sure we'll get to the bottom of it. Thanks for your help."

And she was gone.

I got dressed in frantic haste, and ran downstairs to Lochlann's study. I knocked on the door and opened it without waiting for an answer.

"Lochlann, I need your car," I blurted. "Hélène's been taken to Beaumont."

Lochlann stood instantly and pulled his keys from his pocket.

"Here, go." No pointless questions, no meaningless words.

I grabbed the keys and bolted from the house.

I used to know every road and street and short cut on the north side of Dublin, but time away and years of improvements and development had turned my home town into an entirely different place. After half an hour of angry wrong turns and u-turns, I finally emerged from the maze of residential streets that surrounded the hospital and found the entrance to the car park. I abandoned the car and ran to the front door.

The lady at the front desk looked up from her computer screen and smiled kindly at me.

"Can I help you?" she said.

"Yes, I'm looking for a girl called Hélène, she was admitted yesterday I think."

"And her surname?"

I shook my head in growing frustration, as though she should have known that I didn't know.

"I don't know her surname."

She looked at me with a puzzled frown, opened her mouth to speak but then thought better of asking the question. She must have seen a thousand people like me over the years, whose mental capacity had been temporarily suspended by shock and horror.

"Right so, let me see if I can find her for you. Hold on there," she said, and tapped the keyboard of her computer.

After a few moments of tapping and sighing and head-shaking, my impatience reached snapping point.

"What's happening?" I said, with the growing irrational certainty that I could do this much more quickly myself if she would just let me at the computer. "Have you found her?"

She looked up patiently.

"No," she said. "There's nobody called Hélène here at all, it's such an unusual name. Let me call..."

A nurse, who had been standing near me at the desk scribbling furiously in a journal, came over to me.

"Did I hear you're looking for someone called Hélène?" she asked.

"Yes, yes I am. Do you know where she is?" I turned to her and clutched at the slim straw of hope.

"I might. Look, wait here and I'll get the Administrator."

I breathed out my shoulder-sagging impatience, but there was nothing I could do, no way I could accelerate the trundling process.

After what seemed like an age, she returned with a flustered looking grey-haired man in a suit.

"Are you the man our nurse spoke to on the phone earlier?" he asked brusquely, with no introduction.

I nodded.

"Yes" I said, "I spoke to a nurse here this morning."

"Hmm. We admitted a young woman yesterday. When she was admitted, she was confused. We have given her sedatives to make her more comfortable, but we are unlikely to get to the bottom of this while she is under sedation.. She gave her name to our admissions team as Hélène, but didn't give them a surname. So they checked her bag for identification and found her driving licence, which had a different name altogether. Although the picture was clearly the young woman we had admitted. After our nurse spoke with you, we checked our records for a woman called Hélène on the basis that there probably wouldn't be too many, and it looks like she has been treated here as an out-patient for the past month or so. The only question that remains, therefore, is that of her actual identity. I'm hoping you can help us clear that up."

"What did her licence say?" I asked, sure that there must be some obvious explanation or that they had simply made a mistake.

"Let me see," he said, looking through his notes. "The name on her licence is O' Neill. Aoife O'Neill."

I just stared. Stood stock still and stared. At him, but not seeing him. Seeing only her face, and those lost, frightened eyes. After all this time, after all of the daydreams I had had of finding her and her anger or her joy or her apathy, never could I have conjured a scene like this. In Beaumont hospital on a dark afternoon, the cloud-covered sky outside growing ever more ominous with approaching evening. It was all so real and so normal, yet so surreal and fantastic.

For weeks, I had shared the studio with her. Every day. We had laughed, we had fallen out, we had talked endlessly, we had worked together so closely. She had touched me. She had kissed my face, squeezed my arm, hugged me. And she had known, of course. She had known and she had said nothing. Testing me? Perhaps. Trying to understand, trying to quench the anger she so clearly felt? Anger that she had thrown at me, but whose source I hadn't understood. I had been blind to what was suddenly so clear.

All the time, it was Aoife.

"Do you know the young woman, or not?" the administrator asked, plucking me impatiently from the mess of thoughts spinning in my head.

"I think she's my daughter," I said in quiet disbelief, as much to myself as to him.

I explained as best I could. I had no proof, of course. No certificates, no striking common physical features, no shared half locket that we could piece together amid the glow of an emerging sun and the radiant joy of smiling faces. But he believed me, the old administrator, he believed whatever he saw in my bewildered, staring eyes. And so I was taken to her room.

She looked small amid all of the beeping, buzzing machinery and trailing wires and tubes. Small and fragile, just as she had been that first morning on the front step in Malahide. My daughter. The daughter whom I had last seen in a room a bit like this, in a baby's cot. Sleeping peacefully, blissfully unaware of the twisting turns of her life that would take her here. I hope you can forgive me, were the last words Caitríona spoke to her. Forgive us for what, love? For leaving her? Or for ever making her suffer this wretched world in the first place.

I stood by the bed, not six inches from her. I itched to reach out and hold her hand, to squeeze it and whisper that everything would be ok. But I couldn't. If it had been Hélène lying there, I would have. I would have held her hand and stroked her hair because we were friends and friends have that right. But it was Aoife. And I gave up that right more than twenty years ago. The girl I thought I had grown to know so well, and I didn't know her at all.

But there was nobody there to hold her hand. No parents or siblings, no close friends who had shared her joys and pains since childhood, who could reminisce fondly about boys and the first crush, or about music or dancing or school... She was alone, and that had been my worst fear. When she had talked about Aoife, had she really been talking about herself? Was she really the one so uncertain of her place in the world? And so I reached over a took her hand. I held her hand.

"Aengus?"

Lochlann's voice came from behind me.

I turned round slowly and I felt a surge of relief that I didn't have to do this on my own.

"Lochlann," I whispered. "It's Aoife."

He looked at me for a moment, and then he just nodded. He came over and he hugged me, for the first time I could ever remember.

"Doctor Walsh is an old friend of mine," he said, quietly. "He told me what had happened." He stepped back from me, and was not embarrassed by the affection. "He said they're not sure what's wrong with her, that they've been treating her for some weeks and she has very suddenly become ill. He said that her white blood cell count is very high, that it may mean an infection of some sort. They have run some tests and they expect to know more in the morning."

Two nurses came in, and one of them smiled kindly and touched Lochlann's arm.

"Would you mind waiting outside a few minutes?" she said. "We're just going to settle her down for the night."

"Of course," he said. He turned to me. "Let's get some coffee," he said, gently but firmly.

We went down to the hospital café and he got us two coffees. The café was filled with a hospital's damning sense of futility. Families and friends reassuring patients, who no longer noticed the indignity of dressing gowns and slippers, that it would all be fine. And neither of them knowing whether or not to believe it. Or believing that if it was fine, it would only be a matter of time until it wasn't. It's always just a matter of time.

Lochlann swept biscuit crumbs from the seat of the chair with his newspaper and a wrinkled lip.

"Are you alright, Aengus?" he asked, looking hard into my eyes.

I shrugged because I felt nothing.

"I don't know, Lochlann," I said, with a shake of my head. "Christ, how could I not have seen it? It was so obvious." I buried my head in my hands and sighed hard and long.

He nodded, maybe he had been asking himself the same question.

"In the back of your mind, I suppose, you were not looking for a young French woman," he said. "You had no reason to question her story, and it was so plausible."

"Maybe. But I should have seen Caitríona. She's in her eyes Lochlann, she's right there – and I missed it. She never wanted me to look for Aoife, but it's as if she's relented and she was pointing her out to me, telling me where she was."

"Aengus, you will not want to hear this nor will you see the truth in it for at least a while. But you know that I will not seek to salve your pain with platitudes, and so know that I mean this sincerely. Whatever has gone before, you have nothing to regret in the way you have behaved and in what you have done since you arrived here. You have sought to do the right thing for Aoife. You tried to help and protect her when you thought she was Hélène. More than at any time in your life, you have the right to be proud, if not the circumstances. In time it will become clear. Until then, trust yourself to do the right thing. If it feels right, it almost certainly is. If you believe that Caitríona is helping you, then that is surely why."

I nodded, and smiled a brief ironic smile. I had always said, in my more acerbic moments, that it would take a confluence of disasters to bring Lochlann and me together. And so it had transpired. But it was a fleeting scepticism. I knew what it was like to need him and not to have him, I knew it well enough to know how much I needed him now.

"It's never enough, though, Lochlann," I said, "is it? Not for Oran, not for Aoife now, not for Aoife twenty years ago. You like to think that if you put everything you have into it, commit yourself fully and with every last stroke of your strength, that you can achieve anything. Isn't that what all those self-help books would have us believe? That we can do anything if we set our minds to it? But it's just bollocks, isn't it? Whether it's all predestined or it's a random game of chance or some divine power decides our worth and defines our fate – it's got fuck all to do with doing your best, hasn't it? Just look around you." I waved my arm around the café, drawing curious looks from those sitting quietly around us. "How many of these people will walk out of here because their families pray hard for them or because they really believe that if they fight this thing, they can win? And how many will walk out with some cancer still destroying them from the inside, knowing that it's not over yet, but it's not over? And how many will never walk out."

Lochlann looked at me and I swear he understood. He knew exactly what I meant. He had probably had the same rant at God a million times since the day I was born and Claire was taken away. And he nodded.

"I know, Aengus," he said. "I know it well. All you can do is try to make nobody's life any harder than it has to be. And then do what you can to deal with your own."

Once, on a winter weekend away in the Alps, Caitríona and I fell victim to wild weather – gale force winds and heavy snow – that closed in on the mountains and drove us to the village coffee shops, peering out wistfully over steaming mugs and urging the clouds to part and the sun to emerge over powdery slopes. They didn't and it didn't and so we moved from the café to the bar and settled in for the evening. I don't remember how, but we got talking to a young New Zealander who was spending the winter season bumming around the Alps in search of deep snow, steep slopes and beautiful girls. In stark contrast to the bar full of frustrated, griping Anglophones bemoaning the waste of their days in the mountains, he was calm and unruffled. And as the evening wore on and the beer opened our minds and our mouths, he shared his wisdom with us.

"Life," he said, "is just the sum of your experiences. Life without experiences is just an existence."

Life is just the sum of your experiences. It stayed with me, and as we rode the wave that was our life, we started to define that life by the experiences we had. He was right, life without experiences is just existence, the daily monotony of the suburbs. And experiences don't have to involve leaping into steep couloirs or jumping off a bridge suspended on an elastic rope. Experiences are whatever triggers the *frisson* of excitement in your gut and the spark of wonder in your soul, and we are all different. But a day without that surge of passion or a day that doesn't take you even a little closer to it, is a day wasted.

He was right, but in time it occurred to me that he had missed something. It only counts if you share it. An experience tasted alone is surely just an event? It only accentuates the loneliness of being alone. And it's not just about not being alone. Sharing it with someone who means nothing to you – who might be there but can never be *with* you – is sometimes even lonelier. The people that share your world define the experiences that in turn define your life. And when the wave crashes, and you emerge spluttering and coughing from under the water, it's only the people who really shared your world that will still be there to soothe your hurt.

It's how I define a friend. Someone who allows you to experience the passion and someone who is still there to pick you up when the passion deserts you and someone who helps you to find the passion again. Lochlann, as usual, undersold himself when he said that he just tried never to make anybody's life harder. Perhaps that was true of those people he didn't know. But if he called you a friend, then although he might not often stoke the flames of wonder, he would always be there to pick you up when they had been doused.

I never really had a family. Maybe that's why I struggled with the distinction between family and friend. Either someone was your friend, or they were not. The fact that they were your brother or your sister or your cousin was just nomenclature. Lochlann was never really my father, but I had craved his friendship. And now that we had gone some way to clearing the air, I found that I was happier to have found a friend than recovered a father. A brother is just someone you have been around your whole life, someone you have had a better chance to know and understand. Someone who shares some genetic componentry, whatever that means. It doesn't mean that he is your friend. It doesn't mean that he can turn an event into an experience. But if he is your friend, if he does share and stoke and intensify the passions in your life, if you will both be there when you have lost sight of the wonder and you know that you will both look for it again, then that is a bond stronger and more pure than mere blood can ever forge.

The café lights were turned out one-by-one, and I looked up to see that there were only a few people left. I looked at my watch.

"I think they will probably ask us to leave quite soon," Lochlann said. "Do you want to go back up for a few moments?"

I nodded.

"I will wait for you in the reception," he said.

I went back up to her room, and stood at the open door. A nurse was checking and adjusting, and noting every detail on the clipboard that hung at the end of the bed.

I stood and stared, wanting just to be allowed to look at her. This was the baby we had left behind in the cot in that musty old maternity hospital room. Had she woken up that day from some warm and cosy dream, and looked around for us? Had she listened for the voices she had come to know from the womb? Had a wide-eyed panic welled up inside her when she couldn't find them? Perhaps that lost, frightened look in her dark eyes had been etched there at that moment, when the days-old infant realised that we were gone? And perhaps it was made permanent by a life spent searching, not for us, but for something she could never quite explain? I might never be her father – I had no right and no idea – but I could try to be her friend. I had failed her once when the wonder disappeared. I would not fail her again.

The nurse turned from her work, and smiled at me gently.

"It's getting late and you know you shouldn't really be here," she said, softly. "Tell you what, I have to go and check on someone, I'll be back in a few minutes. You can say a quick goodnight."

She winked at me kindly and hurried off out the door, and I walked slowly over to the bed. Aoife lay still, her eyes closed, and her breath seemed worried and shallow. I took her hand again, small and soft and smooth, and stared at her. In the days before, Hélène had been passionate and vibrant – in the studio, at the concert in the Arena, at the exhibition. But today Aoife looked tiny and delicate, almost childlike. It wasn't just that she was ill, not just the shadow of this place, she just looked different. It was nothing I could have pointed to, it was simply that she was a different person now. The metamorphosis was complete, and the butterfly had emerged from the cocoon.

Her eyelids fluttered, like the butterfly's wings, and then opened slowly. She lay still, but turned her eyes to look at me. After so many hours behind the easel, I knew Hélène's eyes so well. But Aoife's eyes took my breath away. I squeezed her hand gently.

"I'm going to make it right, Aoife," I whispered. "I promise I'm going to make it right, and I won't ever let you down again."

Her eyes never left mine and she lay still. Then, her grip on my hand tightened just a fraction, and I thought I saw the shadow of a smile flicker across her lips, like the fleeting shapes you think you see in summer fields when the breeze plays with the long grass. She closed her eyes again, but still she held my hand.

I stood there, wanting just to be near her. After a few minutes, the nurse came back into the room. She laid a hand gently on my shoulder.

"You get yourself off home. I'll look after her, I promise."

I nodded and quietly promised the same.

CHAPTER 37

The wind from the sea is steady and cold, and from time to time it carries a thin spray of rain. The gulls are fighting and scrapping to make their way out to the water, giving up and taking shelter on the ground to regroup and try again. Dark clouds are trundling across the morning sky, and below them the sea rumbles and rolls, punctuated by the white caps that brave the angry water. I'm sitting on the Head and watching the sea and the birds and the waves as they go about their business. The tides still ebb and rise. The world continues to turn. The broken old bench has been rotted by years of salt on the wind. The Baily's light is flashing bright against the sullen sky.

I found her. After all this time, time spent wondering and dreaming and fantasising, I finally found her. Have you forgiven me? Do you understand? Are you quietly glad that I looked for her? And found her?

And I didn't see it. You must have shaken your head in frustration at my failure to see. Gullible and naïve, that's what you used to call me, right from those very first passionate days.

"Did you know there's no such word as gullible in the dictionary?" you said to me once, and then you howled at my fascinated surprise until I thought you might be sick.

Were you screaming at me, these last weeks? Gullible, blind eejit! I can hear you now, softly mocking me while you shake your head and smile and tell me you love me all the same. I saw you looking out at me from her portrait, but still didn't see. I felt the comfort of a past even though we shared none, but I still didn't see. I saw Lochlann take her to his heart from the day he first met her, but still I didn't see.

You know that I loved her even before she was Aoife. Of course you do. You would have loved her too. You know that I would have done anything for her, to protect her or to bring some light into those lost eyes. I was proud of her already, before she was Aoife, proud of her music and her angel's voice. Proud of her gentle kindness. She was to me everything that I had prayed Aoife would be. I was even pierced with the guilty fear that I might love this stranger more than my own daughter.

Our little girl grew and blossomed. From the seeds of the fairest flowers are the fairest flowers born.

And then our little girl passed away in the night.

Just slipped away peacefully, they said. But they always say that, don't they? How can it be peaceful? How the hell can it ever be peaceful? Wouldn't you always be fighting? Wouldn't you always be scared?

I feel like I've lost two people. I knew Hélène for only such a short time, but she was my friend. I think we were going to be close friends. She was so kind and gentle and calm, and I just wanted to look after her, to make her happy. And now I've lost her and I'm going to miss her. I'm going to miss spending every day with her in the studio. I'm going to miss chatting about her music and her gigs and where they're playing at the weekend. I'm going to miss listening to her talking fondly about Gerry in that achingly coy way she had, not even realising she was in love with him.

And I've lost the chance I had of meeting Aoife. Because I never did meet her, not really. I only ever met Hélène. And now I feel like I'll never meet my daughter. And I feel this raw guilt that it's Hélène I'm going to miss most, and not Aoife. How do I make sense of it? How do I make it right, when I can't even figure out what's wrong?

I should feel lost. I should feel desolate and beaten and hopeless. Just like I did before, just like I've felt almost every day since you went away. I've been flapping around in the dark like a bird trapped inside the house, and now I should feel like I'll never, ever find a way out. But I don't. It hurts, of course it does. The pain of losing Hélène, of losing my chance to know Aoife, of losing the chance to get a little piece of you back, it's like a knife turning over and over in my gut. The sadness in her eyes still haunts me, it will always haunt me, and it hurts to know that I wasn't there to make it go away, that I was never be able to make it go away.

But I can live with pain. The desolation of these past years sucked the life slowly out of me. But I can live with simple pain. And I've had enough. I'm angry with the past. It's just been playing with me, like a cat before it kills the mouse. It's been taunting and tormenting me. And now I've had enough. I don't want to go on living like this, I can't. It has to stop now. Yes, it hurts, but the pain can no longer be all there is. After every end we search out a new beginning. This time, I need to find mine.

Look at Niamh. And Oran. And Lochlann. They have all had to fight their own darkness, and they have found the strength to fight. When I saw Oran's dignity in the face of everything, it made me feel ashamed of my own weakness. I look at Niamh and the way she controls her own world, because she has to and she accepts that responsibility. I look at Lochlann and the way he's learned to live with the grief, and the way he's still able to care about other people and the way he still wants to help them.

They all make me ashamed, and they make me want to be strong. Because they are all what you would want me to be.

You have to let people help, they told me when I lost you. But they have to be the right people, that's what nobody told me. The people with you when you're riding on the great wave of your life aren't always the people you need around you when it crashes. And nobody tells you that. And you think they'll help you through it, but they can't. Or they won't. Or they don't know how. Or they don't even see that you need help. The people we had in our lives are not bad people. We just never owned enough of each other. So they were always on the outside, and I just couldn't let them in.

And it's not just about your friends and the people that share your life, it's about the place too, and everybody in it. Everywhere is different, that's why we want to explore. That's why we left Dublin, to break free and to taste something new. The differences were exciting and new and they made life fresh and interesting. We always had something to explore and somewhere new to go. But it's when your life takes a different path from the one you had planned, when it goes wrong, that the differences don't seem so exciting anymore. They seem threatening and mean and spiteful. And a place and a culture that will never be your own can suddenly alienate you. Remind you that you don't really belong.

I never thought I'd come back to Dublin, even in the days after you left. But now I'm not so sure. I always wanted to create something beautiful, but I never tried. I talked to you about it until you must have been tired of hearing it, but I was always afraid that if I tried to capture the dream, it might evaporate in my hand. Because I couldn't do it. Or because it wasn't what I thought it would be. And then I wouldn't have the dream anymore. Best never to try because then you always have the hope. But I tried and I still have the dream and I want to try again. Oh, I'll never be as good as Lochlann, never achieve his acclaim. But that's ok. If it lets me live my life then that will be enough. That will give me a purpose and a direction and I won't flap and flounder my way through the world anymore.

People I've known my whole life, whom I deserted and who have taken me back. The place we left behind, but where I somehow still belong, where I will always belong. And a new sense of purpose to give me a reason to go on. All this time I've been searching for the answer, and all this time it was right here.

"Aengus? Are you ok?"

Niamh's voice was even softer, even more gentle. I looked around and nodded.

"Yeah," I said, "I think I'm ok."

"Do you want some company? I can just leave you alone if you'd prefer?"

"No. Some company would be nice. I think I've had enough of being on my own."

I smiled at her weakly, and she smiled weakly back, relieved perhaps.

I shuffled along the broken bench and she sat down beside me.

"Lochlann told me," she said, wringing her hands. "Oh, Aengus…"

She put her arms around me and hugged me close. We stayed like that, motionless and quiet, forever. The only sound on the Head was the wind as it tiptoed self-consciously around us.

Eventually, she sat back and looked deep into my eyes.

"Are you going to be ok?" she said again.

I shrugged and raised my eyebrows against the great unknown.

"I have to be, Niamh, I just have to be. What else is there?"

She nodded.

"Come on," she said, "it's cold out here. You must be freezing."

She stood up and reached out for my hand. I took it, and we wandered slowly back up the trail. Around us the old landmarks quietly watched us walk away. The world carried on, but took a moment for my trouble. The Pigeonhouse stood silent sentry at the entrance to the port. The Baily's watchful beacon never missed a single beat.